God's Sacred Feast

God's Sacred Feast

Healing for the Wounded

Carol Gosa-Summerville

ISBN: 0692948732
ISBN: 13: 9780692948736

Acknowledgements

The decision to write *my* stories from my heart on *my* terms was liberating but sometimes ridden with anxiety. I thank God for the gift of observation and the ability to put what I see, hear and feel into words. I also thank Him for the survival of our ancestors; their strength in the face of tragedy and their faith in the face of despair.

I thank my husband, Wendell Summerville, for his love, support, and encouragement, and for never doubting that I could pull this off. I'm forever in love with you.

To my sisters, Mattie S., Helen, and Robbie, you're my rock and my strength, and you bless me every day of my life. And to my sister friend, Ruby, I thank God for sending you to Alabama State University the same year he sent me. No one ever had a better friend.

To my brothers, Richard, Pastor Terry, and Pastor Curtis, and cousin brother, Joe Nathan, I salute you. You're simply the best. God knew what he was doing when he put us together. Your love, faith and character inspire me to be a better servant and a better person.

For my brother-in-law, Randy, sisters-in-law, Phyllis, Carolyn, and Venessa: thank you for being kind and supportive.

It doesn't feel right not to acknowledge my siblings that're living happily in the Lord,

Laura, Frances, Robert, George Harold, and Walter Lee. You're always in my heart and the

memories of you motivate me to keep going. I love you still.

Finally, I thank the readers who encouraged me so much after my first novel, *The Burden of Sweetberry*. You validated her and me. I love you, and I'm forever grateful for your support.

Sincerely and always,
Carol Gosa-Summerville

Readers' Note from the Author

In the African-American culture, it is common for an individual to answer to more than one name. Sometimes the given name (the one on the birth certificate) isn't known until the person's funeral or some other important event. In this series, Deacon Branhope "Sugarfoot" Collins is such a person. Friends call him Sugarfoot. Church members call him Deacon Collins. And certain members of his family refer to him as Bray. Each name is significant to him and those in his circle. I considered using only one name for this character but decided against it because I wanted to stay true to the culture and the character.

Love
. . . He threshes you to make you naked.
He sifts you to free you from your husks.
He grinds you to whiteness.
He kneads you until you are pliant;
And then he assigns you to his sacred fire,
That you may become sacred bread for God's sacred feast.

Kahlil Gibran – The Prophet

Introduction

The Friday afternoon regulars at the Queen of Sheba Beauty Shop were enjoying their moments of leisure before going home to their mundane lives.

Clarice Vanderway was sitting under the dryer reading a magazine. Lucy Dash was in the stylist's chair demanding that Darlene make her hair look as perfect as the model's on the poster. Elvira Jones was waiting for Kizzy, the sarcastic shampoo girl, to figure out how to operate the new cash register so she could pay her bill. And several walk-ins were waiting for one of the stylists to start on their hair.

Mary Newlins, the gossiping church lady, was keeping up a lively conversation with master stylist, Annette Henderson. As Annette carefully pressed her edges, Mary mocked her fellow church member, Maxine Jefferson. She said, "Maxine made up a lie about having a heart attack in Detroit. But word got back that it wasn't true. And now that the cat is out of the bag, she's walking around mad at everybody."

Annette chuckled, always amused by the messiness of her favorite client.

Suddenly, Freddie Dee Varner burst through the door in a fit of rage. Her eyes blazed fire as she stormed over to Annette's station. She shouted, "Didn't I tell you to stop messing with Sugarfoot?"

Everything stopped and everybody went on alert. Lucy had just warned them that Freddie

Dee had been threatening to 'beat Annette down' for going to the picture show with Deacon "Sugarfoot" Collins.

Hot flames burst from Freddie Dee's eyes. She was a

solidly built woman with a pretty face. But her beauty was masked by unpredictable behavior. Annette, petite and quiet, wasn't known for public brawling. But she didn't back down. Placing the straightening comb back on the burner, she turned to Freddie Dee. "You don't tell me what to do. Sugarfoot ain't married to you."

She'd barely gotten the words out when the full force of Freddie Dee's fist punched her in the face. With a clatter, she crashed against the iron-framed styling station. Somebody screamed as Freddie Dee began battering Annette's head. Annette tried to fend her off but she was no match for the enraged Freddie Dee.

Darlene screamed, "Y'all stop that! Don't fight in my shop!"

Freddie Dee ignored her, grabbing Annette's hair and wrapping it around her hands as if she was trying to pull it out from the root. Annette's hands flailed crazily about trying to land blows anywhere on her body.

They tussled, knocking things over as one tried to get the better hold. Finally, they landed on the floor. Freddie Dee ended up on top. She pommeled relentlessly as Annette squirmed around trying to push her off.

The customers were so stunned they were paralyzed. Even Lucy Dash, a glutton for this kind of savagery, sat frozen in her chair.

Suddenly, Clarice sprang up, determined to do something. Darlene said, "Clarice, go to the telephone and call the police. This heifer ain't coming in here disrespecting my shop. I'm having her arrested."

Clarice sprinted for the back wall.

Kizzy rushed over and pulled Freddie Dee off Annette.

She said, "Stop this, Freddie Dee!

You're making a fool outta yo'self. Annette ain't forcing Sugarfoot to do nothing."

Freddie Dee stood up. Her hair was standing on her head and her clothes were torn. There were spots of Annette's blood on her shirt. She pointed a warning finger at Annette who lay battered on the floor. She said, "Sugarfoot is *my* man. Stay away from him!"

"Get outta here!" Darlene demanded. "You oughta be ashamed of yourself."

Kizzy and Elvira helped Annette to her feet. Marks of the fight were already showing on her face. Her left eye had puffed up and her lip was busted. There was also an ugly cut over her left eye.

Clarice said, "Darlene, I've got the operator. Do you want her to send the police?"

"No," insisted Annette. "I'm alright."

*****

The fight happened about a year ago shortly after Deacon Branhope "Sugarfoot" Collins led a Saturday night resistance against the Ku Klux Klan. He was the hero of the community, and women were clamoring for him.

Through it all, he'd tried to keep a level head.

But it'd come to the church's attention that he'd been playing fast and loose with the young women in town. This sloppiness had led to the knock-down-drag-out fight at the beauty shop. The deacon board raised a critical eye.

To make matters worse, now that his name was in the wind, women who'd admired him from a distance before were now boldly interested. On the outside, he was tall, dark-skinned, and very handsome. But those in the know said it was more than that and spoke of his hot-bloodied nature.

At the beauty shop that day, Elvira had put it crudely. She'd said, "Sugarfoot's got a reputation for putting it downtown. Freddie Dee done staked a claim on it and Annette is trying to move her out. That's what they're fighting about."

The women sat with their mouths opened. After Annette went into the restroom to nurse her wounds, they scolded Elvira. Then they asked for more details.

Part One

Chapter One

Sugarfoot was restless and didn't know what to do. It was Saturday night, and he would like to be doing something interesting, preferably with a female. But ever since the big fight between Freddie Dee and Annette, he'd been laying low.

He'd had to go before the deacon board and apologize for having his name mentioned in a public scandal. Then he'd had to listen to a lecture from perfect and upright Deacon Johnny Goines.

"If you gon be out in the world doing sexual things with these women, you need a wife," he'd reprimanded, not even *trying* to be civil. "The bible says he that finds a wife finds a good thing, and if you want to stay on this board, you need one."

He'd been adamant, and the other deacons had backed him up.

So here he was alone on a Saturday night, riding around in his brand new pickup truck, observing the behavior of the people.

He turned onto Cedar Road and saw his cousin, Manny Fulgham, hobbling toward the Quarter. He stopped and picked him up. "Where you headed?"

"I'm just out walking, but I'm going to Maw Shatling's later."

Sugarfoot frowned. "You go there?"

"Yeah! Everybody goes there. It's the most fun place to be on Saturday night."

Sugarfoot shook his head. "I don't go there. But I've

been thinking about going to the fish fry at Lucy's."

"Let's ride by there," Manny suggested.

He rounded the bend, and drove up the hill to Lucy Dash's bright yellow manufactured house. Sitting on the front porch wearing a light blue dress was Annette Henderson. Sugarfoot groaned and kept driving.

Manny laughed. "You must not wanna see her?"

"No, I don't," he admitted.

They left the Quarter and cruised around. As they passed Three Yards Lumber Company, someone darted behind a tree as if to hide. In the darkness, they weren't sure who it was, but Sugarfoot was pretty sure it was Batch Blaine.

"Whatever is Batch up to?"

"Ain't no telling." Manny snarled in disgust. "If I had a brick I'd throw it out there and knock him out."

Sugarfoot stared. "What's your beef with Batch?"

"He's a' a--hole and a Uncle Tom," Manny sneered. "He keeps up mess everywhere he goes, and he's always trying to steal somebody's woman."

Sugarfoot laughed. "Did he steal your woman?"

"He's trying to."

"Well, I'm sure you're keeping it together."

"I'm just trying, but you're the man around here. Everywhere I go women are trying to get me to put in a good word for them."

"Aw, come one," Sugarfoot downplayed the claim. "Who do *you* like?"

"I like Syretta," he answered frankly.

"Syretta?" he scoffed.

"Yeah. I know people talk about her, but she's got a good heart, and she goes to church. And if you give her two or three dollars, she'll give you some ----."

"Get outta here!" Sugarfoot howled. "What's the matter with you? I know you ain't paying no woman."

"Yes, I am. And I ain't the only one."

Sugarfoot shook his head. He and Manny had always gotten along well. Not only were they cousins, but they were also friends. Manny's mother was Sugarfoot's aunt and they'd been raised to look out for each other.

But life had dealt with them differently. Sugarfoot was strong, outgoing, and popular in the community. His independence gained him respect, and he was looked upon as head of the Carrie Mae Rudolph family.

Manny was loved, but little was expected of him. Light-skinned, clean shaven, with a bald head, he was a fine looking young man. But, as a child, he'd been stricken with polio, and he walked with a limp. This limited his physical activities and prevented him from working the kind of job he wanted.

"Got anything to drink?" He asked as they drove past the Homestead Housing Projects.

Sugarfoot nodded. He had a case of beer in the cooler in back of the truck.

Further down the road, he pulled onto the campus of the high school. Automatically, he whipped around to the gymnasium and parked.

He took four beers from the cooler. Getting back into the cab, he noticed Drucilla Kilgore's car easing down the road below. She was driving so slowly it looked suspicious. He watched until the car was out of sight.

"What a threesome." He shook his head. Drucilla was Mary Newlins's sister. She, her husband, and their dog liked nothing more than driving around at night spying on people.

Sugarfoot couldn't help but laugh. "I hope they find what they're looking for."

When he got back in the truck, Manny was fidgeting with the radio. He happily grabbed two beers then went on to brag about how much he could drink without getting drunk. Sugarfoot listened doubtfully knowing that the only time Manny got anything to drink was when somebody gave it to him.

Enjoying the buzz, Manny brought up the recent argument between their grandmother and Sugarfoot's sister. "I guess you heard about it," he said.

"I did," Sugarfoot studied the label on the beer bottle. "Did they settle it?"

"I don't think so. Daisy Ruth wants Aunt Alma to keep Boot and Bear while she goes to night school for her GED. Big Mama said no and said she shoulda got her high school diploma when she had the chance. Daisy Ruth said she woulda stayed in school if Big Mama hadn't been so mean. And it went on from there."

Sugarfoot sighed. "Big Mama can be hard to understand sometimes."

"All the time," Manny insisted. "But the problem is that she worships that house and she's scared them boys gon mess it up." He shook his head. "I don't see how you live there. Coming there on Sundays is about all I can take of Big Mama."

"She's getting old," Sugarfoot reminded him. "We have to be patient."

"It's just crazy. She still thinks the reason I got polio is because somebody hoodooed Rita Jo. She don't b'lieve what the doctors say."

Sugarfoot understood Manny's anger. He remembered how their grandmother had shamed Rita Jo when they were kids, calling her names and blaming her for Manny's condition. Feeling sorry for his cousin, Sugarfoot took a swig of beer.

Manny changed the subject. "Don't you wanna see what's going on at Maw Shatlings?"

"Not at all. Remember, I was in the army for ten years, and I spent eight of them overseas. I've seen everything I want to see. Trust me, there's nothing going on at Maw's that I haven't already seen."

"Well," Manny drawled, "I ain't been so lucky. I ain't never been out of Alabama, so all that stuff's exciting to me."

Sugarfoot grunted a laugh. He said, "Did you know Maw used to belong to First Macedonia?"

"Get outta here!"

"Yeah. Hattie Lou Curry says she was a good usher and a good member."

Manny growled. "I can't b'lieve Maw was ever good. How come she left?"

"Sugarfoot scratched his head. "I'm not sure. Apparently a problem came up that they couldn't resolve. Just think," he joked, "Maw Shatling could've been another Mary Newlins or Maxine Jefferson." He raised his can. "Let's drink to her soul." Manny laughed, taking a big gulp. "It's sad," he said. "But she runs the best hoe house in town, and I still wanna go down there. Once in a while I just like to go there, hang loose, and be myself."

Sugarfoot didn't try to talk him out of it. He steered the truck toward the Cove at Sixth Street.

Manny said, "Now, pay attention to who you see here. It ain't just the sinners that come here. It's also the ones you see sitting up in church on Sundays."

Maneuvering down the narrow street, Sugarfoot drove slowly to avoid the haphazardly parked cars. Immediately, he spotted Amos Rangle, a former deacon of First Macedonia. He was walking in the front door with a strange woman. Elvira Jones and Deacon Levi Warner were standing in the yard chatting with a group of men he didn't recognize. Other church members were coming and going.

He stopped the truck and Manny got out. "Don't do nothing I wouldn't do."

"Ha, ha," Manny chuckled. "I'm gon do as much as I can."

Returning to downtown Sipsey, little things caught Sugarfoot's eye; White men lurking in dark alleys; Strangers meeting in open spaces; married men parked in secret places. "Saturday night in Sipsey," he chuckled.

As he reached the entrance of the Quarter, Syretta Attaway appeared out of nowhere walking towards the housing projects. He started to offer her a ride but decided against it. Given her reputation, somebody might be picking her up for a rendezvous, and he didn't want to spoil it. Then, sure enough, before the thought left his mind, Batch Blaine came trotting behind her. "Poor Manny," he whispered.

He was bored and couldn't think of anything to do. He decided to go the Blue Goose Cafe, get something to eat, and call it a night. But as he passed the foot washing church, he noticed the lights were still on. "I think I'll go in and speak to Sweetberry."

"Jericho," he immediately corrected himself. Every

time he called her Sweetberry, he got a mental nudge that reminded him that she'd changed her name. But like many in Sipsey, he found it hard to call her anything but Sweetberry.

When he walked in, she was singing a hymn as she scrubbed down pews. The glow from the lanterns showed traces of a once beautiful woman.

"How you doing, Brother Collins," she spoke brightly. "You're just the man I want to

see."

"Oh," his brows went up.

"Yeah. I got a word for you. The Lord told me to tell you that he's done picked out a wife for you."

"A wife," he gasped. "The Lord told you that?"

"Yes, he did. He's got work for you to do, and you need a help meet. So, he's gon send the woman you need."

Sugarfoot couldn't imagine that the Lord had told her any such thing. He said, "The Lord knows how to get in touch with me. Why didn't he tell me that?"

"Because you don't believe."

"I believe in God," he maintained.

"You don't believe in the *power* of the Holy Ghost," she emphasized.

"I just don't see marriage," he shrugged earnestly. "I'm not financially able to get married."

"The Lord will provide your needs according to his riches in glory." And with a wicked glint," she smiled. "I'm gon make a prediction. By this time next year, you gon be a married man."

"Stop," he wailed. "It ain't gon happen."

"Come on, let's pray together," she insisted. "Let's ask the Lord to open your heart that you may receive whatever he has in store for you."

They held hands and she prayed:

"Lord, this is your child and my friend. He is smart in the ways of the world, and he wants to be a good servant. But his flesh is weak. Strengthen him in the flesh. Give him the faith to believe that all things are possible with you. He can't see the wonderful blessings you have for him. And he can't see how badly he is needed in your kingdom. So open his eyes, his heart, and his mind that he may see in himself what you see in him, what I see in him. This I ask in your son, Jesus's name, a-men."

There were so many questions he wanted to ask her about this wife. It wasn't that he didn't want to get married. He did. But it was complicated. He was living in the house with his grandmother and her sister. He'd spent his savings building that house. Now he was saving to buy a twenty-five acre tract of land south of the Quarter. It was his hope, his dream, to build decent, affordable housing for the Colored people of Sipsey. By his calculation, it'd be four or five years before he was on his feet.

"Have you ever thought about marriage?" Jericho asked.

"Yes," he responded. "I want to get married. To tell you the truth, I'm looking forward to it, someday. But right now, I don't have anything to offer a wife."

"You've got more to offer than you think," she declared. "A wife could be just the thing to straighten you out."

He brushed if off and asked how things were going at the church.

"The Lord is blessing First Primitive in the year of 1965," she said. "I got no complaints."

"What about the girls? How are they?"

"They're doing well. Janelle is overseas, in England. She was awarded what's called a Hippocrates grant to study at the University of Cambridge. She likes it over there. Her letters are full of places she's been and things she's seen. She says it's very different from the United States." She raised an eyebrow and smiled. "She's even been to see the Queen."

"Wow, that's stepping in high cotton."

"Yes, she's always been interested in things like that."

"What about Temeka?"

She winced. "Temeka's harder to figure out, but she's doing well too. She moved into

the dormitory this year. I wanted her to stay at Miss Fannie's, but she said she was giving up her

room to someone that needed it more. Temeka is more finicky than Janelle, so I hope this

dormitory thing works out."

"She'll be fine," he said comfortingly.

He helped clean the pews and swept the sanctuary before leaving. "Keep up the good work, and I'll be checking on you," he promised. Then, just to humor her, he said, "This woman that the Lord has for me, is she gon love me?"

"Oh yeah," she cried. "She's gon love you more than you'll know."

"Thanks. I'll be on the lookout."

Chapter Two

The March evening was crisp but pleasant. Sugarfoot suddenly felt recharged and wasn't ready to go home. And why should he? "I don't wanna go home," he said aloud. He turned his truck toward Lucy Dash's. "I want a fish plate, and I'm gonna get one. If Annette or Freddie is there, I'll just ignore them."

*****

A festive crowd had turned out to Lucy's beautifully landscaped backyard.

Lucy Dash knew how to throw a party. She mixed good food with good music and her own magnetic personality. But her secret ingredient was that she had no respecter of persons. She invited everybody, and everybody came.

Tonight's guests, whether talking, dancing, or eating, did so to the sound of sweet soul music. Lucy circulated, flattering everybody and thanking them for coming. She'd hired two women to cook and one to serve freshwater and store bought fish. Her menu also included baked beans, cole slaw, and the best hush puppies any of them had ever tasted. Guests could order their food and have something to drink while they waited. Sugarfoot ordered a fish plate and took a seat in the shadows away from everybody.

Zack Burns, the dancing king, had caught everybody's attention with his frenetic rendition of the "Shake." As the crowd cheered him on, his body went into convulsions as he moved his hands, feet and body to a rhythmic beat only he recognized. Then he hit a mindboggling split, sprang up and began the fast sophisticated footwork that'd made him a legend.

Sugarfoot shook his head, admiring the charisma Zack brought to a party.

Lucy came over and handed him a beer. He wanted to take it, but declined, asking for a soft drink instead. "Don't be cute. I know you drink beer."

He laughed. "But I try not to do it in public."

"Hypocrite," she snorted, and they both laughed.

She sat down beside him and caught him up on the latest gossip. "Darlene and Deacon Porter are still going strong. They think folks don't know, but we do."

Sugarfoot mumbled but didn't say anything. He'd learned a long time ago not to comment on anything Lucy said.

"Elvira and Deacon Warner broke up," she revealed. "Deacon Warner finally figured out she was using him. I don't know why she won't get a job like everybody else. She thinks she's too cute to work. But he swears he's through with her."

"Really?" he said, recalling that he'd just seen them together.

"Annd," Lucy paused. "Here's my gossip. I'm 'bout to quit Sherman."

He didn't respond, knowing she was going to give the reason.

She said, "He's just boring, Sugarfoot. He's thirty-two years old, but he acts like an old man. He even dips snuff. I don't want to spend the rest of my life with my daddy." She sighed. "And he's a mama's boy and thinks his mama can do no wrong. He believes everything she says, and she lies on me."

He was listening for a specific lie when loud cackling from a group of women diverted his attention. Clarice Vanderway and her Kappa Gamma Nu sisters were joking around with Buck Dobson. He was boasting that he could outrun any man in Sipsey. The sisters were calling on different men to challenge him. The men were gracious but chose not to make a fool of themselves by racing Buck.

The sorority sisters brought a different flavor to the party. They'd arrived shortly before Sugarfoot and were already in a merry mood having attended a wedding reception in Myrna earlier. They were smartly dressed (overly dressed for a fish fry), wearing various styles of cocktail dresses, glittering jewelry, and high heel shoes.

Unmistakably beautiful, they were the brown paper bag women, so named because their complexions were no darker than a brown paper bag. They ruled the Negro aristocracy and were the desired mates of successful Negro men.

At the moment, they'd grabbed the spotlight, and the men were captivated by them whether they'd admit it or not.

Regaining his position, Zack called for a dance line. Sugarfoot watched as couples paired off and strolled down the line showing off their finest dancing skills. Zack grabbed Clarice Vanderway's hand and they sauntered together, twisting and sliding, making an exciting if odd couple.

Lucy started meddling. "Clarice just dumped another one of her fiancés," she said. "I like her, but she is *not* a serious woman. A few months ago, she was all set to marry that cute guy from Virginia. Well, something happened, and she broke it off. According to reliable sources, she sent his ring back through the mail. Now you have to admit, that was cold. And that's the third guy she's dumped since she's been back. I don't think she wants anybody. She's spoiled, and she just wants to stay at home with Felix and Mary Ann and be their little girl."

Sugarfoot had no opinion.

Criticism of Clarice notwithstanding, Lucy called for the sisters to give them a taste of the K G Nu stride. They happily obliged, luring the crowd with their trademark stepping and strolling. Clarice let her hair down in ways she seldom did.

"See," Lucy snorted. "She don't even feel bad about it. I guess that's what having money can do for you. You can marry or not marry cause you have your own money. Most of us don't have that luxury. We have to marry, shack up, or prostitute."

He shot her a sour look, and she said, "It's a few snobs in that sorority, but if I'd have gone to college like Uncle Johnny wanted me to, I'd be a Kappa Gamma Nu."

Sugarfoot studied the young women from the finest families with a sigh. He had nothing against them, but they weren't his type.

He quietly sipped his drink and watched them complete their routine.

Suddenly, Lucy cried, "Get up, Sugarfoot and dance. Women came to party, and they wanna dance. *I* want to dance."

Reluctantly, he got up and danced with her. Afterwards, to be sociable, he danced with others, including some Kappa Gamma Nu sisters. To his surprise, they made a fuss, vying for his attention and begging to be the next one he danced with. In spite of himself, he was flattered. Later, as the sorority sisters prepared the leave, Clarice Vanderway gave Lucy a quick hug then threw him a peculiar look. He barely knew what to make of it and wondered if she was mocking him.

Around midnight, Lucy's boyfriend, Sherman Jacoby, arrived. Returning from his job at the tire factory in Lancaster, he brought the disturbing news that there'd been a big commotion downtown. "It's police cars all over the place," he said. "I don't know what it is, but something bad has happened in Sipsey."

A few minutes later, a police car drove up. Judd Burch and Ricky Lee Howser got out and approached the crowd in their customary formal manner. Lucy didn't trust the police and was immediately defensive. She yelled, "What y'all want?"

"We need to speak to the owner of the house," Judd said.

"You know doggone well this is my house," Lucy fumed.

"We need to speak to you."

"About what?" Lucy was beside herself. "Every time something happens, y'all come running to my house. I ain't no freaking criminal."

"How long has this party been going on?" Judd asked.

Lucy stared, refusing to speak.

"Answer the question, Lucy," Sugarfoot said softly.

She heaved a frustrated sigh. "My *party*," she snarled, "has been going on for a couple of hours."

"Thanks, Lucy. Has any strange person or persons been here?"

"No," she said in a calmer tone. "The only people that have been here are the people I know and invited."

"Have any strangers moved into the neighborhood in the last few weeks?"

"Not that I know of." Suddenly, she remembered one stranger. She said, "Well, the only person that's moved here recently is that West Indian man that works at the meat market. But he's been here for two or three months."

"Have you seen him tonight?"

Again Lucy was silent and Sugarfoot advised her to answer the officer.

"Yeah. He came here around nine o'clock. He got three fish sandwiches and left."

"Did anybody know him before he came here? Is he kin to anybody in Sipsey that you know of?"

"All I know is he was at the bus station and Lewis Standeffer brought him over here. He's been staying with Jack Bynum. I don't know if they're kin or not."

"What's his name?"

"I don't know," Lucy went cold again.

Zack said, "His name is-"

"Shut up, Zack," Lucy snapped. She stared at the policemen and said, "Don't nobody know his name."

Two young men had already slipped away and gone up the hill to warn the West Indian. Ricky Lee Howser said, "Jack Bynum's an ex con. Let's go."

The policemen left and the crowd stood staring at each other. "Wonder what that was about," said Sherman. "I bet it had something to do with all of them polices I saw coming home. I wonder what's done happened."

"I don't know," said Zack, "but it looks like the West Indian might be in trouble."

The party soon broke up. Sugarfoot stayed and helped Lucy and Sherman clean up the yard. With a thankful sigh, Sherman said, "I sho' am glad I ain't the one the poo-leece was looking for."

Lucy looked at Sugarfoot and rolled her eyes. "Punk," she mouthed.

Sugarfoot smiled. "I hope to see you at church in the morning."

"You will," she promised.

*****

Sugarfoot left Lucy's house feeling heady. He was still pumped up and didn't know why. He wasn't ready to go home. He wanted to do something, to be with someone, a woman. He envisioned a tryst with Annette or Freddie Dee. Just for tonight, he thought, he could slip one in. He banished the thought. Pleasure for the moment would only satisfy the moment, and then he'd have to live with the consequences.

Sweetberry's words returned. He wondered what a wife would look like, sound like. And where would he find her? He didn't see her being in Sipsey. The last time he'd found a woman interesting was in Paris when he was training with the French army. Those women were intelligent, free thinkers. They also knew how to please a man. He'd been to places with them he didn't think possible. Colette, a con artist, had been his favorite. Those days had been fleeting but the memories were sweet.

As he pulled into his yard, the headlights illuminated budding flowers on each side of the driveway. They were the handiwork of his grandmother and aunt. The early bloomers had the yard alight with beauty.

He hesitated to call it pride, but he was humbled every time he remembered how happy they'd been when he'd presented them with the four bedroom brick house.

"I just can't believe something this nice would be mine," Carrie Mae had shouted. She

looked desperately at her grandson. "You mean this is mine, Bray?"

"It's yours, Big Mama," he'd assured her. "I've been planning this house ever since I left home. Now I'm back, and it's done. And it's paid for."

Going into the house, he was surprised to see her sitting at the kitchen table. Her bible was laid open, and when he walked in, she looked up. "It's after twelve o'clock, Bray."

"I hope you weren't waiting up for me."

"I wasn't," she claimed, but he knew it wasn't true. "Freddie Dee came by looking for you. I told her I didn't know where you were."

"Thanks. You told her the truth."

"Umf, umf, umf," was her response.

As he headed for his room, she said, "Bebe came looking for you too."

He turned back. "What did she want?"

"She didn't say."

"She must not be working his weekend. Did she say where she was staying?"

She grunted. "She didn't say and I didn't ask. Y'all need to leave her alone, Bray. You're trying to make something out of yourself, and Daisy Ruth is trying to raise her boys to be decent. The best thing for her to do is to stay away from here and leave y'all alone."

He took a deep breath. "Big Mama, she's our mother. She doesn't come around that often, and she doesn't cause any trouble. It makes sense that she might want to see her children once in a while."

"Well, if she'd have listened to me, she wouldn't have to sneak around to see her children. She wouldn't have to be ashamed to show her face."

"I know," he said, suddenly tired and eager to go to bed. He wasn't in the mood to relive his mother's mistakes or his grandmother's resentment. "Good night, sleep tight, don't let the bed bugs bite.

He kissed her forehead and hurried to his room.

Chapter Three

He slept beautifully. When he awoke, he had no idea what he'd dreamed about. He just knew it'd been wonderful, sensuous, and filled with passion. "That's the life I want," he smiled as he got up to shower.

On his way to church, he stopped by to see his sister. She lived in a community of small, Cracker Jack style houses across the street from the city dump. Their aunt, Rita Joe, and her three children lived next door.

Seeing his truck, Manny came out on the porch. He said, "I guess you heard the news. Somebody broke into Prengle's Hardware and made off with a lot of money. The police done been all over the place questioning people. They came to Maw's asking if any strangers had been around. It's a mess, man. Stuff like that just don't happen in Sipsey."

"I know. It's crazy. Just when you think things are settling down, this happens. Do they know who did it?"

"I don't think so," he shrugged. "But they say Mr. Godfrey had a stroke when they told him about it." Manny shook his head. "It's a shame. I can't say this about all the Prengles, but Mr. Godfrey is a good man."

Suddenly, Manny's sister, Jeannie, raised a window and called to Sugarfoot.

"Good morning, Jeannie," he smiled at the snarky ten year old.

True to form, she spoke irritably. "Sugarfoot, will you tell Big Mama to stop being so mean to us? She hollers at us for nothing, and she don't even want us to walk in the house. We ain't gon tear that house up."

He could only smile. "I'll see what I can do."

Daisy Ruth burst through her front door and stepped off the porch, laughing at what Jeannie had said. Dumpy with the complexion of a pecan shell, she looked nothing like her handsome brother. But they were close, strengthened by a volatile childhood in which they felt that all they had was each other.

She said, "Hey, Sugar Brother," and stood on tippy toes to kiss his cheek. She stepped back and said, "Look at you. You look like a million dollars in that pretty blue suit. No wonder these women love you."

He could barely keep from blushing but was glad she noticed his new suit. He'd special ordered it from Keppler's in Lancaster and worried that it was a bit too fancy.

From next door, Jeannie said, "That suit do look good, Sugarfoot." And carefully looking him over, Manny agreed.

"Come on in and eat some breakfast with me," urged Daisy Ruth. "I got everything you like."

He followed her into the kitchen and watched as she set out a lavish breakfast. "Did you see Bebe yesterday?" he asked.

"I did. She looks good. I tried to get her to spend the night but she wouldn't."

"What did she say?" he asked curiously. "Did she tell you where she's living?"

"No, just that she lives with the people she's working for, somewhere in the county."

"Who are they?"

"All she'll say is they're nice and she likes working for them. She gave me some money and told me to buy me something pretty."

Tears formed in her eyes and he put his arm around her. "I love her," she confessed. "I don't care what Big Mama says, I love her."

"I know," he said, wiping her tears. He suddenly brightened and said, "I hear you're going back to school."

"I want to," she answered, pulling herself together. "But I need somebody to keep the kids. Big Mama won't keep them and she won't let Aunt Alma keep them. They ain't no trouble." She paused. "Well, Bear ain't no trouble, but Boot can be a handful."

Sugarfoot made a snap decision. "Don't worry, Aunt Alma will keep them."

"You sure?"

"I'm sure."

They sat at the table and were soon joined by her sons, eleven year old Kenneth, known as "Bear" and nine year old Joseph whom they called "Boot." Bear was slender and quiet while Boot was burly and loud. "Where's Youngblood?" Sugarfoot asked, inquiring of Daisy Ruth's husband.

"He's in his room where he always is," answered Boot. "Daddy don't bother nobody and don't nobody bother him."

Sugarfoot laughed. "That's a fair compromise."

He ate a few bites of eggs and toast and drank a glass of orange juice. Daisy Ruth

prodded him to eat more, but he shook his head, "Gotta go. I don't like to go to church on a full stomach." He gave her a playful pinch as he got up to leave.

Beaming, she said, "Alright, Sugar Brother, when I see Bebe again, I'll tell her you want to see her. Now go on over to First Macedonia and straighten them hypocrites out."

In a playful manner, he punched Boot on the shoulder.

"Y'all have good service in the country, and I'll see you at Big Mama's for dinner."

As he left, he heard Boot grumbling about wanting to join First Macedonia. Sugarfoot sympathized. He'd never liked going to the church in the country and was glad that he made the decision to leave. But at Carrie Mae's request, most of her family still attended her childhood church south of town.

He headed to First Macedonia with a feeling of anticipation. It was his Sunday to lead devotion, and he still hadn't decided which hymn to lead. It was the duty of every deacon to learn how to pitch hymns to the congregation in a way that stirred emotions and ushered in the spirit of worship. He had a few favorites, but the one that came to mind was, *I Love the Lord, He Heard My Cry, and Pitied Every Groan.*

In the Deacon's Hall, he ran into Deacon Johnny Goines. The senior deacon was in unusually high spirits. "It's a beautiful day," he said brightly. "The Lord made it and we will rejoice and be glad in it."

"A-men."

Sugarfoot had no idea why Johnny Goines was in such a good mood. Ever since his friend, Josiah Hess, had died, he'd been brooding over the loss. Several times, while teaching his Sunday school class, he'd had to stop and wipe back tears. Today's change was sudden and very welcomed.

"I trust you're well this morning, deacon?"

"Very well," Sugarfoot answered pleasantly. He tried to think of something spiritual to say, but all he could think of was, "I can't complain, deacon."

Johnny Goines chuckled. "There's honor in not complaining. Would that we'd all live our lives without complaints. Would that we would just fear God and keep his commandments."

"Mighty right, sir; mighty right."

Johnny Goines started off but turned around and asked, "Deacon, did you go to the fish fry last night?"

"Ah, ah, ah . . ." he stuttered, "yeah, ah, I went for a little while."

"Good. It's good for young people to socialize and have fun with one another."

Johnny Goines continued down the hall. Sugarfoot stared after him. "That's a switch," he mumbled. "Wonder what's come over him?"

As he started towards the sanctuary, he noticed two young boys standing outside the pastor's study. One was Lucy Dash's son, Theodore, and the other was Elvira's son, Jimmy.

"Good morning, boys. How's everything going?"

"Good morning," the boys spoke politely then informed him that they were waiting to see the pastor. "We got something important to tell him," said Jimmy.

"Well, here I am," Pastor Brough said, coming around the corner. He nodded at Deacon Collins and said the young boys were becoming regulars to his study on Sunday mornings.

"They're Marcus's classmates," he said, referring to Marcus Mixon, the child prodigy who'd been called to preach at eight years of age. "I think they're proud of their classmate and are happy that he's doing such a good job."

"That's very generous of them," Sugarfoot said approvingly.

Smiling patiently, Pastor Brough led the boys inside his

office. "Have a seat, young men and tell me what's on your minds this morning."

They sat across from his desk and started talking. Sugarfoot could hear their conversation and chuckled as they complained to the pastor.

"Marcus been bad," Jimmy said.

"Un huh," agreed Theodore.

"And what has he done?" the pastor asked.

Jimmy said, "He always be doing bad stuff at school. Like, he all the time be cheating when we play ball. And at recess, he be standing under the sliding board, and when the girls go up the steps, he be looking under their dresses."

Pastor Brough asked "Are we sure he's looking under their dresses and not just waiting his turn?"

"He be looking under their dresses," Theodore insisted. "He be trying to see what color panties they got on."

"Did he say that was what he was doing?" the pastor asked.

"Naw," Jimmy answered, "but that's what he be doing. We started to tell the teacher, but we decided to come and tell you."

I'm glad you came to me," Pastor Brough said cleverly. "These things need to be handled in person with the proper persons present. And I'm sure that neither one of you has ever done anything like that?"

Jimmy hesitated then held up a finger. "I did one time, but I didn't do it no more."

Pastor Brough nodded. "I'm glad you've seen the error of your ways."

Theodore popped his fingers one at a time and wouldn't admit to doing anything wrong. As they waited for him to come clean, he said, "E'rybody do something bad sometime."

Pastor Brough heaved a sigh. "Well, let's pray that we'll all do better."

The boys bowed their heads and the pastor prayed? *"Dear God, I thank you for these very brave and observant young men. We pray that all the boys and girls at school will follow the golden rule and be respectful of each other. Bless them for looking out for their classmate and your servant, Marcus. And thank you for making them good citizens at school, at home, and at church. In your son's name, a-men."*

"A-men," the boys responded earnestly. Pastor Brough shook their hands and told them to continue being well behaved pupils at school. Then he handed them lollipops, and they left happy.

******

Worship service was filled with songs, scriptures, and prayers. Deacon Collins's version of the metered hymn was well received. The older saints found it impressive that the young deacon had poured his heart into the cherished hymn.

During altar call, Elvira Jones brought the house down with a rousing rendition of *Give Me a Clean Heart*. But there was no shortage of women mocking her as they held in their memories vivid images of her smoking cigarettes, drinking beer, and most notorious of all, sneaking around with Deacon Warner.

A more earnest plea came during announcements when Viola Kane solicited prayers for her foster daughter, Irene Roman. "She's competing for the intermediate championship in the Potoama County Spelling Bee," she said. "And we're asking for your prayers."

By the time Pastor Brough came with the message, his audience was ready to receive it. But after reading the scripture and giving his text, he had a change of heart. He said, "Forgive me church, but I have to stop and speak what's on my heart. There *is* a word from the Lord, but I need to say something else first."

He paused and let out a groan. "Brothers and sisters, it is true that we are our brothers' keepers." Knowing something serious was coming, the church sat on full alert. He continued, "When a brother stumbles, we are duty bound to lift him up with prayers and supplication."

"A-men," echoed throughout the church.

He said, "To the gossipers of this great church, let me remind you that we're required to keep our tongues when we don't know what we're talking about. And we're to ask God to guide us when we put words to tongue. Having said that, my brethren, I have some troubling news to deliver." He sighed before saying, "Last night, Prengle's Hardware was broken into, vandalized, and a large sum of money was taken."

At the shocked gasp, he took a deep breath. He said, "It is with profound regret that I announce that Brother Batch Blaine has been taken into custody and charged with breaking and entering and first degree robbery. He is being held in the Potoama County Jail without bail. The Lord have mercy on his soul."

Nervous excitement produced guttural noises. Worshippers turned to their neighbors and asked if they'd heard the rumor. Few had, and there was tremendous interest in learning more about the crime.

Pastor Brough said, "I know that Mr. Blaine isn't a favorite brother among many of you. I've heard your charges and accusations against him. Some of them may be justified and some not. But please, consider his mother. And do me this favor, temper your tongues and hold your opinions until we have the facts." He pushed his glasses upon his nose. "Many of us have the tendency to talk a thing to death," he said. "But I beg you not to do that in this case. A man's life is at stake. Let's wait until we've got some details. And let's pray that justice will be served."

By now, worldly curiosity had overtaken spiritual hunger. Hardly anybody wanted the sermon. Curiosity over what had happened and why Batch was accused was uppermost in the minds of most. Realizing this, Pastor Brough kept it short and dismissed them without taking up the obligatory second collection.

His parting words were, "Brethren, and especially sisters, this next week is going to be a challenge for some of you. Please remember Ephesians 4:25. Frankly put, don't spread lies and rumors about your neighbors; for that is exactly what Satan, our enemy, wants you to do. Tell the truth to the best of your ability. And don't rejoice in the downfall of others, for we are all part of the family of God."

"A-men," came their pious response.

Still, after dismissal, the robbery was all anybody could talk about. It seemed everybody had an I-can't-stand-Batch story to tell. In his forty-something years, Batch Blaine had managed to piss off just about every Negro in Sipsey.

The group of women that met in the powder room after church could hardly contain their glee. One said she'd never despised anybody as much as she did Batch. "Years ago, he tried to court me and I turned him down. He went and lied on me and said I was going with my sister's husband. She didn't speak to me for three years."

"He's a scoundrel, alright," Maxine Jefferson stated emphatically. "Once I bought a little space heater from Prengle's. One of them younger Prengles waited on me and he didn't me all of my change. I told him he owed me some more money, but he said I was wrong. They were gon give me my money," she sniffed. "So I went to Mr. Dave, and I told him I wanted the rest of my money. Sneaky Batch was standing behind him looking at me out of his little beady eyes. And I heard him whisper to Mr. Dave, "She can't count. Don't give her nothing.""

A collective cry went up from the women.

Mary Newlins, said, "I sho ain't got nothing good to say about him. He came to my house late one night trying to get me to go out with some White man. I told him to get out of my house and never set foot in it again."

"I told him the same thing," a voice from a stall declared.

Sister Hattie Lou Curry shook her head in despair. She said, "It's a shame when nobody can speak a decent word over you."

Chapter Four

The robbery of Prengle's brought out the worst in everybody. Negroes remembered and repeated every dirty, sneaky, lowdown thing they could think of that Batch had done, and they rejoiced in his downfall.

It didn't matter whether he was guilty or not.

The local television station interviewed an "eye witness" who claimed to have seen Batch running away from the hardware store around nine o'clock Saturday evening. His story was compelling. He said, "I saw the Nigger run through the back alley of Prengle's. Then he went down First Avenue and turned left toward the river. I tried to follow him but he was running so fast I couldn't catch him."

"But you're sure this was a Negro?" The reporter asked.

"Yeah, it was a Nigger."

The man, identified as Bobby Doyle Hatfield of Sipsey, added, "He was wearing khaki pants and a red and white checkered shirt, and it was a Nigger."

Everybody knew that was Batch's trademark outfit.

"The law oughta throw gasoline on him and set him afire for what he done to that fine family," the man opined.

Sugarfoot was one of the few Negroes that didn't weigh in on the case. But he had bad memories of Batch too. As a young boy, he'd worked in construction with his cousin, Abner Nichols. Abner often sent him to Prengle's to buy supplies. He hated running into Batch. He'd yell at him and call him a Nigga in front of the White people. Once when he was collecting nails and screws, Batch rushed over and accused him of stealing. "Put them thangs down and gwon way from here, you little thief," he'd said.

Sugarfoot was so humiliated he started crying. He left the store and went back and told Abner what'd happened. Abner stopped what he was doing and came to the store. James Prengle listened to the complaint and said he'd take care of it. From then on, Batch wasn't allowed to say anything to Sugarfoot when he came into the store.

It was also known that it'd been Batch that'd alerted the Ku Klux Klan to where the resistance group had gathered on the night of the brawl. But Sugarfoot didn't hold that against him. The Klan had been on a rampage and one way or another would've found their way to the Blue Goose Cafe.

Still, Batch's most serious offense was cloaking Colored women for White men. And that sin was unforgivable.

Now that he was locked up, people laughed at his stupidity.

Sugarfoot was surprised that Batch had been charged with the robbery. Judging from what he knew of him, there was nothing in Batch's character or demeanor that said he had the nerve to rob any White establishment, let alone the Prengles. Yet he didn't dispute it.

But when the janitor from the jailhouse showed up on his job to tell him that Batch wanted to see him, Sugarfoot was confounded.

One afternoon, as he and Revish Kane painted the sanctuary at First Primitive, he mentioned it. "I got word that Batch wants to see me. I'm thinking it over, but I find it strange. I've never had a real conversation with him, so I can't imagine why he wants to see me."

"You going?" Revish asked.

"I don't think so. What's the point? There's nothing I

can do, and I don't want to get

involved." There was a tinge of frustration to his voice. He said, "For the life of me I can't figure out why he'd do something like that?"

"Has it been proven that he did it?" Revish asked rhetorically. Revish had had a few brushes with the law and distrusted what he called 'The White man's justice system.' And he questioned everything about it.

"You doubt he did it?" Sugarfoot asked.

"I don't know. But there's one thing I do know; nobody loves Mr. Dave Prengle more than Batch. And it's hard for me to believe he'd rob him."

"So you think I should go?"

He hunched his shoulders and dipped his brush into the paint. "It wouldn't hurt to go down there and see what he wants."

Sugarfoot didn't have a reason not to go. Still he was vexed by the notion that a Negro would rob a local business. It was stupid, even for Batch. Mumbling absently, he said, "He's gon spend the rest of his life in prison."

"And that's the reason for you to go and see what he wants."

It was that simple for Revish. Now that Batch was in trouble, he seemed to feel some sympathy for him. But the issue wasn't settled with Sugarfoot, and he wanted to discuss it further. But they were suddenly interrupted by Clarice Vanderway who'd breezed into the sanctuary with Irene Roman.

Holding the young girl's hand, she cried, "Make way for the Potoama County Spelling Bee Champion!"

The highborn lilt of her voice was startling and drew

everyone's attention. The missionary women, working on senior care boxes, stopped what they were doing to digest the news. Revish grinned and Sugarfoot halted his painting to stare at the delighted educator and the beaming little girl.

Clarice was refreshingly stylish in a full-skirted floral print dress accented by pearl stud earrings and a double strand of pearls necklace. She wore classic black pumps with a matching leather purse.

"Irene won the spelling bee!" she exclaimed. "Oh my! She was something to see,

standing there spelling those fifth and sixth grade words like a pro. She's done Sipsey proud and she deserves a round of applause."

The ladies clapped with delight.

"What did you spell?" someone asked.

Irene stood tall and held her back straight. Her two thick plaits stood awry, and her sweet oval face shone with pride. She said, "I spelled a lot of hard words. But I won when I spelled the word that nobody else could spell. I spelled enthusiasm, e-n-t-h-u-s-i-a-s-m."

"Yaay! That's a winner!" Clarice cried, shaking her fists in the air.

Clarice was supervisor of the county's Colored teachers. She functioned in all the Colored schools, assisting with curriculum and staff development. She was also responsible for evaluating teachers and hiring new employees.

Her office was located at the board of education in Creek where the spelling bee was held. Viola had asked her to bring Irene to Revish after the contest.

It was a moment not to be overlooked. Irene and her sister, Shirley, were orphaned a few years ago when their parents died within months of each other. Viola and their mother had been friends, and she knew the children well. But Alabama laws concerning custody favored blood relatives over concerned friends. Their mother's cousin, Pauline Roman, had been granted custody. But neighbors and school officials immediately began complaining that the girls were being neglected. Viola decided to do something about it. Armed with advice from a lawyer, she took Pauline to court. After a review by the Department of Children's Services, the judge reversed his ruling and awarded custody to Viola and Revish.

Now, in her sweetly casual voice, Clarice said to Revish, "Your wife says she'll be here

around six. She and Irene went for ice cream after the spelling bee so she was a little late getting back to work."

"Thank you, Miss Clarice, for dropping off my little girl." Revish made a puckish face and bowed to her. It was awkward tomfoolery and both Clarice and Irene snickered. He said, "Be forewarned, Miss Irene, Mama Viola will try to take credit for your winning."

The child meekly deferred. "It's alright. I'm just glad I won."

"Spoken like a champ," Revish complimented.

He and Sugarfoot went back to painting and didn't discuss Batch any further. It was a striking decision. Had it been a popular member of the community, the reaction to his imprisonment would've been treated quite differently.

But because it was Batch, it was forgotten.

Clarice chatted with the missionary ladies and watched as they put the boxes together.

"This is so thoughtful," she said, examining the boxes

packed with fruits, vegetables, and other goodies.

"You'd be surprised how much they help," one of the ladies said. "There's so much need in this county."

"In this world," said another.

"Yes it is," Clarice said. "And we all have to do what we can to help." She took some

bills from her wallet and handed them to one of the ladies. "Use this to help with your ministry," she said.

The woman's eyes bulged in surprise at the amount of money she'd given.

It was no wonder. A young woman putting down that kind of money on the spur of the moment was unheard of. But Clarice had the money and thought nothing of it. With ease, she turned her attention to the wrapping paper. "I love the design of the paper and you're doing such a good job tying the ribbons," she said. "First Primitive is on the move. You're doing wonderful work in this community."

The setting was charming. The men were busy painting the walls as the women fussed over the care boxes. Their leader, Sister Jericho, was in the kitchen taking inventory of the pantry.

She called into the sanctuary. "Revish, you need to pick up some bread and sugar and milk for the feeding on Friday. We're having more and more people coming to eat since the grist mill closed. Last week, we had a couple of White men to come. Thank God we're here for anybody needing a good meal."

One of the ladies said, "The White men offered to pay, but we don't take no pay."

"But we do take donations," Revish quickly added.

Clarice smiled sweetly and said, "I'm enjoying the company, but I've got to go. I have an errand to run before it gets dark."

She said good-bye and headed for the door. Sister Jericho said, "Clarice, let me speak to you for a minute."

Clarice went into the kitchen and they embraced. She gave details of the spelling bee, bragging about how beautifully Irene had performed. But as they talked, her voice changed from light chatter to urgent whispers, and her face began to show varying degrees of stress. From the vantage point that they were working, the men could see into the kitchen.

"That must be some conversation," Revish remarked.

As it became more intense, Clarice began frowning and sniffling and suddenly broke down in tears. Jericho took her in her arms and patted her back.

As is often the case with men, they kept silent. But both wondered why "the girl with everything" was crying her eyes out in the kitchen of a foot washing church.

"Keep your head up," Jericho advised. "It's gon be alright. The Lord will send you the right man at the right time."

Clarice came back into the sanctuary, her smile returned. The men had finished painting the long wall and it stood out. They'd used an off-white flat paint to create an atmosphere of calm and peaceful tranquility.

Inspecting it, Clarice cocked her head and said, "Gentlemen, you've done an outstanding job. I love the color. It brings out the character of the room."

In his most gracious voice, Revish said, "Thank you, ma'am. We like it when the ladies are pleased."

But Sugarfoot pretended not to hear and didn't look up.

Clarice said good-bye and started for the door. Irene ran

to her and grabbed her around the waist. "I love you, Miss Vanderway," she said, looking up with adoring eyes. "And thanks for bringing me to my daddy."

Clarice held her chin in her hand. "I love you too, and keep on being the hard working student that you are."

"Bye, bye, Miss Vanderway," Revish called with naughty affection. "Have a wonderful evening."

She crooned a pleasant goodbye.

As she disappeared outside the door, Revish sighed. "I just don't know what to say for the men in this town. They don't have a lick of sense."

"Why do you say that?" Sugarfoot asked in alarm.

"Not you, my brother," he said carefully, "but the other men. They're a bunch of cowards. They let a beautiful, educated woman like Clarice Vanderway walk around here sad and crying and they don't even offer her a shoulder to cry on. Now before you know it, some man from some other city or municipality will have her in his arms, and she'll be gone. If I was a single man, I wouldn't let that happen. I'd let her cry on my shoulders."

Sugarfoot was stumped. He said, "I never heard tell, but was she ever involved with a man in Sipsey?"

Revish chuckled knowingly. "That's not the question. The question is, has any man in Sipsey ever asked for any of her time? It's not for her to go after them. It's for them to go after her."

Sugarfoot shook his head. "According to rumor, she's been engaged a few times. She's apparently hard to deal with."

"She wouldn't be with the right man. Probably with the right man, she'd be kind and sweet and easy to deal with."

Sugarfoot didn't respond but grabbed his paint bucket and began painting the next wall.

The missionary ladies also had thoughts about Clarice's love life. But they held their tongues until they heard the church door close behind her and her car tires screech away.

Then they started talking:

"She's so pretty; I wonder why she has so much trouble with men. One minute she's engaged, the next minute she's not. What's the problem?"

"I don't know, but it seems like she could make it work with somebody."

"Well, I'm just glad she ain't married and gone off and left us. She's a lot of help to our school children. Anyway, she's got everything she needs."

"Well, not *everything.*"

They laughed and sneaked a peak at the men. But they were discussing whether the kitchen needed a little touch up paint and didn't catch the suggestion.

"Marriage ain't for everybody."

"A-men," said Sister Jericho. She was standing in the doorway listening to their conversation.

Clearly disapproving, she didn't scold but gently lectured. "Ladies, it's never appropriate to talk about other people's business. It leads to hard feelings and confusion. How would you feel if you donated to a good cause and the minute you walked away, people started talking about you? Most of us wouldn't like it. So let's set the example. Concentrate on fixing the boxes, they gon actually help somebody."

Chapter Five

Clarice drove across town, basking in the warmth of the afternoon sun. She was headed to the Goines's farm to take cloth and a pattern to Liddy for a bridesmaid dress she was making for her. Stephanie Murray, formerly of Sipsey now living in New York City, was coming home to get married. She was planning a big wedding, and she'd asked several friends, including Clarice, to be bridesmaids.

"Always the bridesmaid, never the bride," she recited the adage as she crossed U.S. Highway 82.

"Who wants to be a bride anyway," was her flippant retort.

She exhaled as the memory of her failed engagements muddled her mind. They were unwelcomed reminders of how difficult it'd been for her to find a husband. Her last fiancé, Paul DeLorean, had been the perfect match, on paper. Yet, when he was exposed for the greedy gut he was, she promptly ended the engagement.

Her two other prospects hadn't turned out any better.

She cruised for half a mile down Memorial Hills Cut Off before turning onto Mount Bethel Road. Suddenly, she was in the land of Johnny Goines. And impressive it was! On each side of the road, as far as the eye could see, was a display of nature at her finest. Acres and acres of cotton fields were being groomed for summer picking. As they ploughed the unearthed soil, men in overalls and flannel shirts wore straw hats to shield themselves from the parching sun.

Women wearing long dresses, their heads wrapped in knotted scarves, followed behind them dropping seeds. Further down the road, the fields morphed into low growing crops. Cabbages, collards, field peas, and pole beans had begun a rapid growth spurt. And far off on a grassy knoll was the grazing of Jersey cattle.

One couldn't help but be in awe of Johnny Goines's skills as a farmer. People came from far and near to buy directly from him, and regional marketers carried his produce from summer til winter. She bet that if his farm was the only source of food in the county, they'd be living with plenty for years to come.

"I love this farm," she said as she surveyed its vastness.

It was a second home. As a child, she'd come to visit whenever Felix had business to conduct with Deacon Goines. She'd been friends with Gina and Ivan Goines. In fact, when she was in the fourth grade and Ivan in the second, they'd been girlfriend and boyfriend. But Ivan had been so bossy and such a know-it-all that she'd had to quit him. She laughed thinking of how superior he'd acted even though she was older.

She made a left turn off the road and headed up the long driveway to the colonial style farmhouse. It was a white wooden structure with double windows bordered by blue paneled shutters. The porch wrapped around the house and divided into three separate spaces, ideal for a large family's convenience.

She was surprised to see Sherri Lynn Goines-Pratt, middle daughter of the Goines's, sitting on the front porch. Sherri Lynn lived in Jefferson County but was a frequent visitor to her parents' home.

"Good afternoon," Clarice called to her.

Suddenly the Goines's dog, black Labrador Retriever

mix trotted up to her. "Hi, Trapp, how're you doing, boy?" she cooed sweetly. He yapped and yelped and bounded upon the porch beside her. Then he curled up under the swing.

Clarice and Sherri Lynn greeted each other with a hug. A serious woman in her mid- forties, Sherri Lynn was midway between short and tall with a stunningly curvaceous figure. Now, as rays of sunlight beamed over her face, her reddish-brown skin, a flawless blend of her parents' complexions, glowed.

Smiling, Sherri Lynn said, "Clarice, you look so fresh, it's hard to believe you've worked all day."

"Well I have, but I'll take the compliment. And this is a surprise; I wasn't expecting to see you."

"I'm here for a few days. Landon's out of town this week. Normally, I'd be with him, but Johnny Jr.'s coming home for the weekend." She sighed. "He says it's looking more and more like we're headed to war with Vietnam. He's passing through on his way out West before going overseas."

"Brave Johnny Jr.," Clarice exclaimed.

He was the oldest of the Goines's children. As a high ranking officer in the United States Army, he'd earned his stripes. And he wore his successes well. On the occasions that he visited First Macedonia, his uniform was adorned with rows of stripes, medals, and ribbons. He'd done so well in his military career that his achievements were a bragging point for their father and a source of envy to his male siblings.

Now, hearing that war was in the air, Clarice cried in alarm, "He wouldn't actually be *fighting, would he?"*

"I hope not," Sherri Lynn said glumly. "But knowing him, he'll volunteer for it. Aside from family, being a soldier is the most important thing in Johnny Jr.'s life."

"I don't think men count the cost of war," Clarice spoke as she sat next to Sherri Lynn on the swing. "The other day I heard a group of men talking about it as if it was some great adventure. But from what I can see, it's the family left behind that suffers. What is this war about anyway?"

"Only God knows for sure, but let's be real. Men fight for power, to show off new weapons, ego, anything." She cast a forlorn look toward the horizon. "And no, they don't count the cost."

Then more cheerfully, she said, "So, what're you up to this fine day?

Clarice pointed to the bag in her hand. "Aunt Liddy is making my dress for Stephanie's wedding." She showed Sherri Lynn the pattern and the fabric.

"Wow! It's gonna be a beautiful dress!"

"Lucky for me I've got the best in the county to make it."

"So you do."

Sherri Lynn expressed regret that she hadn't learned how to sew as a teenager. "Madea wanted to teach me but I didn't have time to learn," she confessed. "But I'm fine wearing store bought clothes."

They sat in quiet appreciation as nature carried out her ancient duties. The sun began its trek toward the west as budding flowers wilted then tightened their blooms.

There was a level of comfort with each other borne of time and familiarity. The sweet smell of honeysuckle drifting through the breeze reminded them of days gone by. Clarice studied the landscape and observed, "This farm is as interesting now as it was when I played here as a kid, and the yard is just as beautiful."

"I agree, and you know Ivan did a lot of it."

"I remember," Clarice recollected. "I can just see him now with his little shovel and pail, digging and watering."

Sherri Lynn nodded. "He had some kind of project going on all the time. Pointing a finger, she said, "He planted those boxwoods and water lilies. And he also planted Madea's rose garden on side of the house."

"My busy playmate," Clarice reminisced. "Every time I think about the things he's doing now, I realize it was all there when we were kids."

"Yes," Sherri Lynn reflected, "I suppose it was."

"So how is he?" Sherri Lynn wiggled her nose.

"I'm not sure. Sometimes he seems happy, and then again, you just don't know. But he definitely hates living in Atlanta."

"So did I. It's growing too fast. Several Fortune 500 companies have located there and that's brought in all kinds of people. But Ivan's holding his own. In *Educators Today Magazine*, his "Unlocking Mathematics" is a Critic's Pick and recommended as a tutorial guide for struggling college freshmen."

"He's doing well professionally," Sherri Lynn acknowledged. "But," she paused, toying with the ruffles on her blouse, "I don't know about his personal life. Madea's worried about him and so am I."

"Why? What's going on?"

"We don't think he's happy. For one thing, we don't know anything about his wife.

They jumped up and married so fast that Calvin and Earl didn't even make the wedding. It's all a mystery."

As a family friend, Clarice felt it her duty to share what she knew. She said, "The word on Deanna is that she's pushy and ambitious and not altogether honest. It seems she's enamored with the Atlanta social scene, but people don't like her." She frowned. "If somebody had told me Ivan would marry somebody like her I'd have said they were crazy."

"I know," Sherri Lynn seconded. "We're dumbfounded. I've tried to get to know her by calling her on the telephone and inviting them to come for the weekend. But they won't even come for an afternoon. Madea says the one time he brought her to Sipsey, Deanna was so bored that she was relieved when they left."

Clarice didn't want to reveal the more troubling things she'd heard about Ivan's wife. So she let the conversation hang.

A squirrel peeking from behind some bushes suddenly caught their attention. His eyes scanned the landscape before scampering across the yard. Clarice laughed and cried, "Run, run, fast as you can, or you'll end

up like the gingerbread man."

At that moment, a stray cat appeared out of nowhere, dead on his heels. The squirrel scurried up the tree, rapidly vaulting his body. The determined cat was right behind him. "Hurry up, Mr. Squirrel," Sherri Lynn shouted.

The squirrel zipped further up the tree and just in time, disappeared inside a hole. The cat yowled angrily and hovered over it. The women laughed as the cat assessed whether he could squeeze into the opening.

"Scat," Sherri Lynn clapped her hands loudly. "You might as well leave 'cause there's no way that squirrel is coming out."

But with the prospect of a tasty meal inside, the cat didn't heed her advice. Yet later, when it became clear that the squirrel wasn't coming out, he gave a piercing yowl then grouchily crawled back down. Clarice waved him off. "Better luck next time, Mr. Cat." She said, "I used to enjoy coming here and watching the animals interact with each other."

"As I recall, you'd prop yourself up on that back fence and stay there all afternoon. Then you'd come back with the wildest stories, claiming the animals were talking to each other. You had such a vivid imagination."

Clarice fondly recalled it. "I was lonely, and they were my playmates. You know, if I ever get married, I'm gonna have more than one child. I missed not having siblings."

"Are we close to marriage?"

"No," she shook her head, not trying to hide her regret. "Not at all. I'm beginning to wonder if I'll ever find the right man."

"Take your time," she advised. "Let him find you."

"That's what everybody says, but so far he hasn't found me and I haven't found him."

Flippantly, Sherri Lynn said, "Pray about it."

Clarice laughed. "You sound like Sister Hattie Lou. Every time something comes up, she says, 'let's pray about it.' Does it work with love too?"

"Absolutely," Sherri Lynn's tone was decisive. "Once when I was listing the many qualities I wanted in a husband, Poppa said, 'Sherri Lynn, when you get ready for a husband, ask God to bless you with a man that you can love and be a wife to and a man that can love you and be a husband to you."

"Well, that simplifies it."

"It does. After all is said and done, that's what you want."

Clarice brightened, "So no regrets with Landon?"

"No regrets. You'll recall that I broke off a high profile engagement before I married him."

"Yes, John David Unger from Birmingham. Everybody was shocked when you ended the engagement. If you don't mind my asking, what happened?"

Sherri Lynn shrugged. "The love wasn't there. And being the son of a wealthy banker didn't make up for it. When I met Landon, he was struggling to get through undergraduate school. He was working in the cafeteria during the week and in the library on weekends."

"How did you get together?" Clarice wondered.

"One Sunday afternoon, I went to the library to study, but I ended up fooling around with my friends. Clearly, I wasn't serious," she laughed. "But I left my Literature book in the library. My dorm was on the other side of campus. It was pouring down raining when I realized I'd left it. I dreaded going back, but I needed the book. But just as I mustered the courage to go back and get it, the dorm mother called me to the lobby. Landon had walked over there in the pouring rain to bring the book. He said, 'You left this in the library and I thought you might need it.' He was a lanky, geeky, soaking wet country bumpkin. But I saw his heart, and I fell in love."

Clarice seemed confused. "Forgive me, Sherri Lynn," she said, "but Landon doesn't strike me as a country bumpkin. He's intelligent; sophisticated; classy."

"He is *now*," Sherri Lynn said pointedly, "but he wasn't back then. Everybody was shocked when I started dating him."

"Why?"

"Well, he's not from an educated family, not even a land holding family like mine. His father was a janitor at Milan's Department Store, and his mother took in laundry and sold turnips and collard greens on side of the road in Hamilton. Landon has done well in his law career," she

acknowledged, "but class hasn't factored into our marriage."

"How romantic," Clarice held her heart. "It gives me hope."

"Be patient. As sweet and lovely as you are, he'll find you."

"Thanks," Clarice blushed.

Liddy Goines suddenly appeared at the screen door. "Clarice, I thought I heard you out here."

"Yes, ma'am, it's me."

"You got your pattern and cloth and everything?"

"Yes, ma'am."

"Well bring it here and let me look at it."

She and Sherri Lynn went into Liddy's bright yellow sewing room. As Liddy studied the pattern," Sherri Lynn said, "Madea, I've been telling Clarice about Ivan. I told her how worried you are about him."

Liddy looked up and sighed. "I can't help it," she said. "I don't feel right about that marriage. I've thought about it, and I've prayed about it. I know my child, and something ain't right. It just ain't."

Sherri Lynn shrugged. "When Madea says something ain't right, it ain't right."

Chapter Six

Clarice visited with the Goineses until the sun went down, enjoying the witty conversation of Sherri Lynn, and the comforting presence of her mother.

Johnny Goines joined them later, and as usual, took over the conversation.

They'd gathered into the spacious den and listened as he brought them up to date on the goings on with the rooster Hemlock. He said, "He sits on his perch and crows like a king while Frieda keeps a mess going in the chicken yard."

Clarice and Liddy found his frustration funny, but Sherri Lynn offered an opinion. She said, "I guess males of all species are afflicted with that particular malady."

"It's Freida," his voice rose in aggravation. "Hemlock is the boss, but because he won't take charge, Frieda takes over. And it's the younger hens that she picks on. That youngest hen don't respect the pecking order so Miss Frieda bullies her. And every time I go out there they're clucking and clacking at each other."

"And Frieda alone is responsible?" Sherri Lynn's voice was doubtful. "She must be the laying queen."

"She ain't the only one that's laying eggs," he recountered.

"But she's laying the most," argued Liddy. "She'll give you her fair share every time. You can set the clock by Frieda."

Clarice found the discussion of squabbling hens interesting. "I always knew animals had ways of communicating with each other," she said.

"Sure they do," Johnny Goines confirmed. He leaned back in his worn recliner and pulled on his pipe. "God, in all of his wisdom, provided every creature a system of communing with his own kind."

He went on to reference the bible, telling how God gave mankind dominion over the Universe and all creation. "He controls the land, the air, the sea, and all the animals," he declared. "That's why they live in our yards and not us living in theirs."

Sherri Lynn conceded the idea but steered the conversation back to the present," She said, "Do y'all remember how Clarice used to make up stories about the animals talking to each other?"

Johnny and Liddy laughed. Clarice said, "But Deacon Goines just proved that what I said was true. Animals do communicate with each other."

To prevent her husband from overwhelming them with more talk of the bible, Liddy interrupted to inquire about Stephanie Murray's wedding. She said, "How big of a wedding will this be?"

"Pretty big and showy," Clarice answered.

Sherri Lynn grunted. "I don't mean to sound messy, but it sounds like she's coming back to Sipsey just to prove a point."

"It's been said," Clarice winked.

"Ummm," Sherri Lynn moaned. She was about to say more about the mysterious wedding when her mother gave her the look that said leave it alone.

Clarice asked about the Goines children wanting to know the latest news. She was given an update on everybody, including Karen, twin to their second oldest son, Calvin. She'd struggled for years to get pregnant. Now, Liddy happily announced that at the age of forty-six, Karen had given birth to twin boys. "They're beside themselves," she glowed. "Her husband was so excited that he took two weeks off from his job."

"Well," said Sherri Lynn, "I guess being a daddy is more important than being president of a college."

Clarice felt a pang of jealousy. Karen had everything, a beautiful home, a successful husband, and the babies she'd always wanted. Then she felt ashamed. Karen was one of the sweetest people she knew and deserved happiness. She smiled. "Give Karen my best. I can't wait to see the babies."

As darkness loomed, she prepared to leave. Deacon Goines stood and said, "Don't be a stranger, Miss Clarice. We still like good company."

She embraced them and promised to come back soon. They walked out on the front porch and waved good-bye. Trapp trotted from the back of the house to escort her to her car.

****

As she drove down Mt. Bethel Road, a remnant of sunlight peeked out from a crimson sky. It was the warning that only a few minutes of daylight remained.

She pressed the accelerator. Country roads were eerie, especially the parts closest to the cemetery.

Like Liddy, Clarice had questions about Stephanie's wedding. She also wondered about the man she was marrying? She hadn't said much about him just that he was handsome, well-educated, and successful.

"He must be pretty tough to take her on," Clarice thought.

In the fading light, the thought of finding love was still prevalent.

She imagined a knight in shining armor galloping upon a horse and sweeping her off her

feet. She thrilled to the thought. "Who doesn't want to be swept off her feet?" Maybe not technically swept off," she acknowledged. But as far as she was concerned, every woman wanted to be raptured in love and ecstasy, to feel the excitement of her man's arms, and to anticipate the moment when he declared his love for her.

Returning to the city limits, street lights had begun to flicker on. Children's voices happily echoed as they made their way home. A pang of sadness hit her reminding her of how lonely she was for a family of her own.

She drove past Ellington Square and entered her family's enclave called Vanderway Circle. It was a broad cul-de-sac of stately homes including the sprawling Georgian estate she lived with her mother and father.

The house was a three story, twenty-two room mansion; a showcase. Thanks to the original owners, there was a guesthouse in back. When she'd moved back from Atlanta, Felix had suggested she move into it for privacy. It was good for entertaining and hosting out-of -town friends. But she preferred staying in the main house with her parents.

Bess, their housekeeper, greeted her as she came into the foyer. She said, "Miss Clarice, Telma wants to know if you want dinner in your room?"

Telma was their temperamental cook. Clarice never knew the kind of mood she'd be in, so she preferred dealing with Bess. "Yes," she answered. "I'll take a light tray but I'll come and get it."

"No, you've had a long day. Go on to your room and relax. I'll bring it to you."

"Thanks, Bess, you're a gem."

She climbed the winding staircase to her room and changed clothes. Immediately refreshed, she turned on the television to catch the evening news. By the time Bess arrived, she'd dozed off.

Bess set the tray on the bombe chest and said, "Sweet dreams, Miss Clarice."

She stirred but didn't sit up. The television provided background noise as she recapped the day's events. Her visit to First Primitive had been pleasant even though she'd had a brief lapse of sadness. But being in the company of Sister Jericho had been comforting. And before she knew it, she'd given way to tears. With no pretense of modesty, she shared the misery of her failed engagements.

"I've had the worst luck with men," she'd said. "You'd be surprised at some of the things I've been through."

Jericho had listened with compassion. Then, in her self-deprecating manner, she'd said, "Remember, I used to be Sweetberry, and Sweetberry was the b- word I can't use in church. If it could be done, Sweetberry did it. And all of it came out in court with the whole county listening. So you can't shock me. But know this; there's no law against good character and decency. You're a prize," she'd said, embracing her, "and you're gonna be a blessing to the man God sends you."

Clarice admired Jericho. She'd been accused of doing terrible things and she'd suffered at the hands of Sipsey gossips. But she'd owned up to her mistakes and turned her life around. She was now living life on her own terms, in her own truth. People still gossiped about her, but their gossip didn't hinder her. She'd tell all who'd listen, "the devil is busy. But ain't nothing gon stop me from preaching the word and ministering to my congregation."

Clarice wanted to live in her own truth too; she just didn't know what it was.

Putting her troubles aside, her visit with the Goineses worried her. She loved them and felt guilty for not telling them everything she'd heard about Ivan's wife. "What if it's not true?" She challenged herself. "If the gossip isn't true and I repeat it, then I'm guilty of spreading lies." She flinched. "I don't want people pointing the finger at me and saying I caused trouble between Ivan and his wife."

What was known was that Deanna Goines had recently resigned from her job at Sheffield College, Clarice's alma mater. Reasons for her resignation abounded. But the college had handled it quietly, issuing a press release that said, 'Dr. Deanna Goines has submitted a letter of resignation, ending her short tenure at the college. Dr. Goines is a strong voice for civil and women's rights. She's been an inspiration to our students and an asset to the college. We're grateful for her service and wish her the best in her future endeavors.

It had sounded professional, and it was believable. But there was a different report circulating among alumni. It said Deanna Goines had been fired from the college for salacious and fraudulent reasons.

"And it's not the first time she's been fired from a college," said Clarice's great aunt who sat on the Board of Trustees of the college. She revealed that Deanna had been fired from a religious college in Kentucky for doing 'terrible things.' I just couldn't believe that a young Colored girl would do something like that," she'd said. "She's a wheeler dealer and a fraud but a very clever young woman."

To snitch or not to snitch was the question. If true, the things being said about Deanna would be an embarrassment not only to Ivan but to the entire Goines family. All of the Goines children were upstanding and successful. If Ivan was the one to bring shame on the family, it'd be devastating. "I wonder if he knows," she said. "If he doesn't, somebody needs to tell him."

She thought of Deacon Collins. He and Ivan were friends. "I should ask him what to do," she said.

It was only then that she realized that Deacon Collins hadn't spoken to her this evening. Each time she'd spoken, he'd turned his back to her. "I wonder why?" She asked, but quickly shook it off. "It must've been an oversight," she reasoned.

Chapter Seven

A light drizzle had begun as everybody left First Primitive. Sugarfoot offered to drive Jericho home, but she declined. "I thank you, my brother, but I'm gon stay here and tarry with the Lord a while longer."

She pointed to the newly built rectangular attachment on side of the church. She said, "Ever since you and Revish built that little dwelling, I don't feel like I have to rush home every evening." Her mind wandered, and she muttered, "This place is my shelter and my refuge; my shield from the fiery furnace of hell."

"Okay," Sugarfoot replied, realizing she was in one of her moments. He wished her a good evening and said, "I'll see you later."

As he drove off, she went through the sanctuary turning off lights until she reached her residence. In the sitting room of the cozy little apartment, she turned on the lamps and settled on the sofa. As her mind focused, she reached for the bible. It was on her heart to preach Sunday's sermon from the book of Job. He was known for his courage in remaining steadfast in the face of tragedy. It was the perfect example of faith, something she wanted to instill into her congregation.

She read the first three chapters to formulate the subject. The exchange between God and Satan was revealing and took her by surprise. "I never realized this," she exclaimed. "God *allowed* Satan to test Job!"

The discovery moved her. She got up and walked around the room, unable to contain her joy.

She said, "Job's faith pleased God, but Satan doubted

it. So God removed his hand from Job and allowed Satan to test him."

Her mind raced. She said, "Satan started a streak of evil that wiped out everything Job had. But he held fast to his faith."

She recited the scripture in song:
Job said, in all my appointed time,
I'm gonna wait til my change comes.
Job said, in all my appointed time,
I'm gonna wait til my change comes.
Job said, the Lord giveth, and the Lord taketh,
Blessed, oh, be the name of the Lord.

The devil came running to Job,
He said, all your children are dead,
The devil came running to Job,
He said, all your children are dead.
Job said, the Lord giveth, and the Lord taketh,
Bless, oh, be the name of the Lord.

Job's wife came running to him,
She said curse your God and die.
Job's wife came running to him,
She said curse your God and die.
Job said the Lord giveth, and the Lord taketh,
Blessed, oh, be the name of the Lord.

Thoughts ran through her head so fast she couldn't keep up with them. Satan wouldn't give up and Job wouldn't give in. Satan's final curse was to touch Job's body, piercing it with sores from his head to his feet.

Looking at her own beautiful skin, Jericho flinched. "What would it feel like to have sores all over your body?"

She couldn't imagine it. "I have to preach this," she declared and considered whether to begin with God's challenge to Satan or Satan's challenge to Job?

As the sermon began to take shape, there was a light tapping at the door. She sighed, knowing it was the neighborhood kids wanting candy. Tonight, she didn't want to be disturbed. She shouted, "Y'all children go home and get outta this rain."

She went back to the scriptures, reflecting on the conversation of Job's three friends. "They thought Job had sinned and urged him to repent. But they didn't know that Satan had set the whole thing off."

The tapping became loud knocks. She was about to yell again when the melodious sound of a familiar voice said, "Mama."

She ran to the door and snatched it open. By now, the rain was pouring and the wind swept it inside the foyer. Yet the vision before her brought happiness to her heart. "Janelle!" She cried and grabbed her drenched daughter.

"I'm so glad to see you," Janelle cried happily.

She'd been gone for over a year, and in that time, Jericho had received only a few letters from her. She set her tongue to scold her but was distracted by a movement behind her. Two men were trying to push their way into the room. One was a one-legged Negro on crutches, and the other was a golden haired White man.

Cautiously, she threw her arms against the door frame and blocked their entrance.

Casting a warning look, she said, "Where *y'all* going?"

Janelle rushed to explain. "Mama, I brought you some company."

"I can see that," she said, refusing to invite them inside.

The one-legged Negro hopped up in her face and said, "Who the hell are you?"

"Who the hell are *you*?" She shot back.

"This is my father," Janelle said calmly.

The shock was so great that Jericho couldn't speak. Memories of the man she'd known long ago flooded her mind. He was a slick con artist willing to do anything to get what he wanted. She was the foolish young girl that fell in love with him. She traced the tragedy that her life became back to him.

Finally, she spoke, and it was in an angry voice. She said, "So, Eddie Simpson is a one-legged old man now?"

It was a surreal moment, a weird reunion between two people with a history so deep that it'd ended with the death of a man and the birth of Janelle.

"He's not old," Janelle maintained. "He's just tired."

Jericho was alarmed by the fact that she'd rushed to his defense. She could only conclude that Eddie had worked his trickery on her. "I'm sure he's got her thinking he cares about her," she thought. "But the only person he really cares about is himself." She sniffed. "I just wonder what he did to worm his way into her life."

As if reading her mind, he said, "I know you ain't gon b'lieve it, but I ain't the man I used to be, Candy. I've learned some lessons. Prison is the best teacher in the world."

She grunted and wondered if it was true.

As the rain pelted against the roof, she studied him. There were traces of the Eddie she once knew. His dark skin was still smooth. His teeth were in good shape. And his face; broad nose, full lips, and playful eyes, was still handsome.

If she'd thought about it, she would've expected him to be a bitter and broken old man. In fact, except for the missing leg, he looked pretty good.

It wasn't fair. He'd been as much a crook as she'd been. A sudden urge to expose their ugly past struck her, and the only thing that kept her from doing it was the presence of the White man.

Which raised another question! Who he was he and what was he doing here? She looked to him for an explanation. But before he could speak, Janelle butted in, "Mama, this is Jeremy Mulligan, my fiancé."

Her stare was one of horror. She wanted to scream, "Girl, have you lost your mind?"

Instead, she beheld her daughter. She'd matured in a good way. Her flawless skin was complimented by loosely hanging dark hair. And her smile reminded her that Janelle was her sweet child.

"That's the problem," she thought. Janelle's beauty and kindness are magnets for such vultures as the ones she's showed up with tonight. Eddie Simpson was a known predator; she could only guess about the White man.

"Good evening, Miss Armstrong," the young man held out his hand. "It's good to meet you."

He spoke politely and in a foreign accent.

She had no idea what to say to a White man standing in her home on a rainy evening calling himself her daughter's fiancé. What she wanted to say would've been rude, so she tried to think of something appropriate. A small voice murmured, "Just say hello?"

It was all she could manage. Eventually, she found her voice. "Where're y'all staying?" she asked the men.

Janelle's embarrassment was evident. But being the optimist that she was, she smiled and said, "We're staying with you, Mama. I thought you'd be glad to have us."

"I'm glad to have *you*," she stated frankly. "And it's ill-mannered of you to bring strangers into my home."

"I'm sorry, Mama," she said. "I know I should've written, but I've been moving around so much. . ." she shrugged.

Jericho grunted.

Janelle gently apologized to her companions. "She's surprised. Mama's very cautious and doesn't handle surprises well."

Jericho shook her head at the unlikely trio. Mocking Janelle, she said, "You always were good at taking up with stragglers, weren't you? And one wasn't enough, you had to bring two?"

Janelle sighed as if she'd had no choice.

Jericho turned her wrath on Eddie. Whistling naughtily at his missing leg she said, "Did a 'hoe chop it off?"

"Mama!" Janelle cried. "Was that necessary?"

"Well, did she?" Jericho disregarded her.

"Naw," he said, unfazed by the question. "Diabetes got me. I wasn't eating right . . .

wasn't taking care of myself and gangrene set it. The doctors said if they didn't amputate, it'd kill me."

Her grunt sounded like laughter. "So you decided to drag it out?"

"Naw, I decided to live."

"Well, well, well. After all the hell you've raised, you're still trying to live."

He was expressionless.

She frowned. "Look at you, a one-legged old pimp with nowhere to go. I ain't heard from you in years and you show up out of the clear blue sky on my doorstep. I guess all your money's gone, all your women are gone, and you're down here with a child you don't know nothing about. Where's your family? Don't tell me they ran out on you?"

"You might say that," he answered honestly. "My wife died, but, of course, we hadn't been together for a long time. And my other children," he shrugged. "They don't have much to do with me."

"So you ain't *got* nobody?"

"Janelle's the only child I've got that cares anything about me."

"Janelle is *my* child," she corrected, "and she cares about everybody. I raised her that way."

"*You* raised her?" He looked as if he couldn't imagine it."

"Yes, I did, and I did a doggone good job. Look at her. She's beautiful, educated, and decent. Too decent for you," she snorted. "Tell me this, Mr. Big Stuff; what're *your* children doing with their lives?"

He grunted sourly and said, "Not much. One of my sons is strung out on drugs. Another one is hustling from Jersey to New York. And my daughter, she got married and moved to the Carolinas."

"So sad, so, so sad," she responded hatefully.

"Well," was all he'd say. Then, changing the subject, he said, "I heard you left New York after I was convicted."

"I got out of town as fast as I could, and it was the smartest thing I ever did. I came back here with not a cent to my name. I had to beg and borrow just to get by. But this was the best place in the world for me to raise my baby. And thank God you weren't around to ruin her

life like you did your other children."

"Mama, could we do this later?" Janelle pled softly, picking up her suitcase. "We're tired, and we'd like to get some rest. Could we please come in?"

They'd been standing in the foyer all that time. Jericho had done nothing to make them feel welcomed. Furthermore, she didn't immediately respond to Janelle's request.

But after an awkward pause, she stepped aside and showed them into the sitting room.

Chapter Eight

When Sugarfoot left First Primitive, he went to Deacon Goines's house. The deacon's barn had been damaged by a late February storm and he wanted to discuss repairs. Visiting the Goines's was always a treat for him. He and Ivan Goines had been friends since elementary school, and he was no stranger to the farm.

Trapp ran to greet him.

"How you doing, boy?" Sugarfoot rubbed his damp coat and cooed to him. Trapp panted and barked in the way he did when he was glad to see someone.

As the rain came down in a steady flow, he and Trapp played tag. "Come on, Trapp, come on, boy." Trapp ran and jumped good-naturedly, making playful squeaks and yelps.

The rain was refreshing and the dog's play relaxing.

But Trapp had his limits. When he started making low growling sounds, Sugarfoot knew he'd had enough. "You're getting lazy," he kidded and walked the dog back to his house. Then he sprinted to the front door and knocked.

He was delighted to see Sherri Lynn. "Haven't seen you in a while," he said. "How's life treating you?"

"I can't complain." And noticing his appearance, she said, "Ohh, you're wet!"

"I've been playing with Trapp," he confessed. He noticed a few gray hairs flirting around the edges of her hair and found it charming. In his opinion, Sherri Lynn was the ideal woman and the only one that could make him blush.

She informed him that her father was in his study and would be out shortly. They sat in the cozy plaid and pleather den and caught up on family news. Liddy busied herself putting dinner on the table.

"And what's Ivan up to these days?" he asked.

Sherri Lynn shrugged. "Ivan's written a text book for college freshmen, and it's selling well. I'm happy to report that our little brother is on his way to becoming a distinguished man of letters."

"Good for my boy," he smiled delightfully. "Ivan always had a far reach."

"I just wish he'd come home sometime," Liddy Goines looked out from the open-faced kitchen.

"She misses her baby," Sherri Lynn said softly. "We all do. I might as well tell you, we're concerned about him."

"What's going on?"

"We don't know. He's only been home once since he got married."

"Really? That doesn't sound like Ivan."

"I know," Sherri Lynn fretted. "Much as he loves this place, it's hard to believe he's stayed away so long. He writes and calls, but he doesn't come."

"Maybe that's what being happily married looks like?" he suggested.

"You could be right; if so, God bless him."

Sugarfoot didn't know what to make of her suspicions, but it was hard to believe that Ivan's character had changed. Not wanting to say the wrong thing, he said, "When you talk to him again, tell him to come home sometime. It'd be good to see him."

"We'll do that, deacon," Liddy Goines promised.

Deacon Goines came into the kitchen with ledger in hand. Sugarfoot joined them at the table, anticipating the meal. Once Liddy set a glass of lemon water beside his plate, Deacon Goines blessed the food and helped himself to a reasonable portion of pot roast, green beans, and cornbread.

He took a large gulp of water and shared a shocker. "Deacon," he said, "this world is changing right before my eyes. I saw something in downtown Sipsey the other day that I wouldn't have believed if I hadn't seen it with my own eyes."

"And what was that, deacon?"

He replied, "I saw a Black boy draw a line on the sidewalk in front of the drugstore and dare a White boy to cross it. And you know what, that White boy didn't cross that line." He laughed. "That's a new thing, and it bears watching."

New thing aside, the shocker for Sugarfoot was that the boy had been referred to as "Black" and not Colored or Negro. That, he wagered, was the new thing.

As the meal went on, Deacon Goines talked of other things, including tips on how Sugarfoot should perform his duties as the newly elected Sunday school superintendent.

He said, "Get to church on time. Make sure the teachers have the books and bibles and things they need. Visit the classrooms and tell the women what a good job they're doing. If you don't brag on them women, they'll talk about you. And the last thing you must do," he advised, "is to make sure Sunday school ends at ten-thirty sharp so Pastor Brough can start eleven o'clock worship on time."

He sipped water and continued, "Later on, other things will come to you, but this'll give you a good start."

Sugarfoot thanked him for his insight as he, by turns, dipped black-eyed peas, sweet corn, and fried cabbage onto his plate.

Johnny Goines ate slowly to get in more talking. He made cynical remarks about the behavior of certain towns-folk. But he also reflected on what he called, "the realities of life," things that could make or break a man.

After dinner, he picked up the ledger, and he and Sugar-foot headed to the barn. It was still raining so they stood on the back porch. Deacon Goines, who wasn't a great reader, showed the barn's damage from drawings he'd made in the ledger.

"Deacon," he said, "I'd be much obliged if you'd get started on this as soon as possible. Here lately, we've been hearing strange sounds like, you know, a wolf or maybe a panther. I don't want nothing laying into my cows and pigs."

Sugarfoot promised to begin within the week.

As they talked, they heard a low growl and two snappy barks.

"Good night, Trapp," Johnny Goines said affectionately.

"Night, Trapp," Sugarfoot called.

They went back into the house. Johnny and Liddy went into the den to watch television. Sugarfoot stayed in the kitchen with Sherri Lynn. He leaned against the bar while she sat on a stool and began talking about civil rights.

She said, "You know, the Klan killed another freedom worker in Mississippi a few days ago."

Sugarfoot frowned in surprise. "Really?"

"Yes, he'd been trying to register a group of Colored people to vote. They'd warned him to get out of town, but he stayed. Then late one night on a country road, he was ambushed by a robed mob. Landon says Mississippi is the worst state in the country for Negroes trying to register to vote. They kill as many as they can and penalize the rest with ridiculous tests or poll taxes too high for most of us to pay."

"I've experienced that," he admitted.

"So have I. And speaking of our ongoing nuisance, have you had any more trouble out of the Klan since the big fight at the Blue Goose?"

"No," he answered. "We took a group from First Macedonia down to Creek to register. We were prepared to tangle with them, but they didn't show up."

"It's amazing," she glowered. "In some places, county officials do everything they can to keep us from voting, including killing us. In other places, they pretend to accept the change and then figure out other ways to stop it."

"That's our battle," he accepted. "When I was in the military, like Johnny Jr., I served willingly. I wanted to be on the front lines, to be a good soldier. I thought I was fighting for my country. It took a Frenchman to make me see the situation for what it was."

"And what did he reveal?"

He sighed, "He made me see that, although I was fighting for my country, my country was actually fighting against me. I mean, what're these lynchings and killings about except them fighting us?"

"You sound like Landon."

He groaned. "Unfortunately, any Black man from coast to coast could tell the same story with the same outcome."

"So true," she declared. "But cheer up. With men like you and Landon on the case, we shall overcome."

He laughed, thankful that she'd prevented the conversation from becoming a whine fest. "I'm glad you have faith."

"I do." She picked up an apple from the fruit bowl and tossed it into the air. It bounced off her hand and hit the floor.

She picked it up and started juggling other pieces of fruit.

"Look out!" She yelled, tossing an orange. With rapid speed, apples, oranges and pears came flying across the room. He had to move quickly to catch them.

"There's that old Sugarfoot magic," she laughed and threw faster.

It got so crazy, he said, "Hey, hey. Stop!"

She obeyed, but the tone of his voice was so firm that it startled her. She started laughing.

"What's so funny?" he asked.

"You," she said.

He looked puzzled.

"You're too serious."

He frowned. "How's that?"

"Look at what you just did. You corrected me as if I was a child even though I'm much older than you."

"I wasn't trying to correct you. I just didn't think that was the best use of the fruit. And you're not that much older than me."

"I'm a lot older than you, but we won't tell."

He shook his head. "All because I didn't want you to ruin the fruit?"

"Maybe you're just a bit too conservative."

"I never thought of myself as conservative," he said. "Enlighten me. Tell me why you think so."

Her brows furrowed as she weighed whether or not to continue. His curiosity was stoked by her hesitation. He said, "Surely it's not that deep."

"Not deep," she said. "It's just that I've been wondering for some time, why aren't you married? You're such a catch."

This caught him off guard. "I'm not ready," he answered frankly.

"That's no answer. Nobody's ever ready. You just fall in love and do it."

He cocked his head and smiled. "Easier said than done."

"No, you're just over thinking it."

He was uncomfortable with the conversation. He didn't want to tell her that he couldn't afford to get married. He also didn't want to tell her that he didn't have enough relationship with anybody to consider marriage. So he changed the subject. He said, "When we were in school, I actually envied Ivan."

"Really? Why?"

He didn't think he had to explain. Everybody knew Ivan Goines was the golden boy; born with a silver spoon in his mouth? And surely everybody knew why he, a bastard kid, born out of wedlock and brought up in poverty, would be envious.

He was so slow in answering that she thought she'd overstepped. She said, "I didn't mean to pry."

"Oh, no." He didn't like talking about his childhood, because it brought back unhappy memories. But standing there in the comfort of Deacon Johnny Goines's kitchen talking to his very nice daughter made it less difficult.

He said, "You're not prying. I envied Ivan because he lived in this really nice house with a real family. He wore nice clothes and knew how to talk to girls. On top of that, he was smart, and the teachers liked him."

"And your life?" she inquired. "You've turned out pretty well. You must've had a pretty good upbringing here in Sipsey."

He wondered how she'd arrived at that. "We were poor and I had to grow up fast. When I was nine years old, I had to go to work. Abner Nichols is Big Mama's cousin and he wanted to help out, so he hired me."

"So young?"

"Yeah, I worked after school and on weekends. During the summer, I worked all day. My

job was to hand them things; hammers, nails, lumber, and I carried the water jug. I also had to go back and forth to Prengle's to buy stuff. At first, that was all I did. But as I got older, Abner saw I could do more and he let me do it. And he paid pretty good money considering I was only a kid."

"I'll say," Sherri Lynn was impressed with his story. But the pleasant mood was suddenly interrupted by the ringing of the telephone. Liddy got up and went to the back hall to answer it. From the shrill rise of her voice they knew something was wrong. She yelled, "Come here, Mr. Goines!"

Deacon Goines moved quickly to get the phone. "It's Mr. Herbert," she said.

Herbert Edmund was the White farmer down the road. They'd been neighbors for years and had a gentleman's agreement to look out for each other's farm.

Johnny Goines listened and said, "And when was this? Well, did it kill anything? Aw, naaw. I sho' hope they'll be okay. And you say it was just a little while ago that this happened. Alright, I'm gon go out there and check mine. It might still be roaming around. Alright, Mr. Herbert, thank you."

He hung up the phone looking grim. He said, "Deacon, I was just telling you I was afraid of a night creature coming upon my livestock. Mr. Herbert said something got in his pen and attacked a couple of his pigs."

"What?" Sherri Lynn cried.

"He heard the pigs squealing. At first, he didn't think much about it. But they kept on, so he knew something was wrong. He went out and saw a strange looking four-legged animal in the pen. He took a shot at it and it ran off. He don't know whether he hit it or not, but it buggered up several of his piglets."

"My word!" Liddy Goines exclaimed.

Sherri Lynn stared in horror.

"Let's go," Sugarfoot ordered.

Johnny Goines grabbed his rifle from the gun rack, and loaded it. Sugarfoot dashed to his truck and got his .357 Magnum. Prepared to shoot to kill, they went out to the barn and checked on the animals. There was no sign of the predator. They searched all over the farm but saw nothing suspicious.

Sugarfoot asked, "Is it normal for panthers to come this far south attacking livestock?"

"Not normally," he said. "But once in a while, one will turn up.

They drove down the road to the pasture and checked on the cattle. Then they went to his handyman, Joe Alan Martin's, cabin and asked if he'd heard anything.

The gruff talking handyman said, "I heard something further down the road a while ago. I went out to our pasture to check it out but I didn't see nothing. But I'll go back and make sure everything is fastened up real tight, Mist' Johnny, and I'll keep an ear out."

"Much obliged," Deacon Goines said.

They returned to the house and Sugarfoot went inside to say good night. Sherri Lynn was visibly shaken by the news. She said, "I hope that . . . whatever it was kept moving."

"Just stay alert," he advised. "If you hear anything unusual, don't hesitate to let your Poppa know."

Liddy Goines shouted a cheerful parting. "Come back and have dinner with us like you used to do, Deacon Collins."

"Will do," he promised.

Chapter Nine

Rain was pouring down when he left the farm. The recently paved road was a welcomed improvement to the mud and potholes nightmare that rain usually brought. As the wipers swished back and forth, his thoughts returned to Ivan. Sherri Lynn's concern for him had been real.

"Maybe he's got the big-head." He reflected on the idea, wondering if it was possible. "Could becoming Dr. Goines and writing a book have gone to his head?" It was a fleeting thought that he quickly dismissed. "I owe him the benefit of the doubt."

Ivan Goines. The name commanded respect. Coming from different worlds, they could easily have become enemies. But luck had been on his side. Where he'd been the friend in need, Ivan had been the friend indeed.

As a first grader, when he'd been hungry, Ivan had shared his food. When Big Mama didn't have money for school supplies, Ivan always had extras. As a sixth grader, when he was too embarrassed to wear old clothes, Ivan offered his brother Earl's hand-me-downs. Whatever the problem, Ivan had the answer.

As they grew older, they talked about their hopes and dreams. Sugarfoot was certain about what he wanted from life. He wanted to build his grandmother and aunt a decent house to live in and to make the Sipsey community a place for Colored people to prosper.

Ivan was more vague, conflicted. He liked school and learning. He was a whiz at math; but he could also recite the Periodic Table of Elements backwards. He was excited about birthing calves; but he also liked tending a garden, eating fruit off trees in the summertime, and going to the cotton gin with his Poppa.

Ivan was so gifted that it was hard to know what he'd end up doing. Still, Sugarfoot was surprised to learn that he'd married some socialite from Chicago and was living it up in Atlanta.

"I hope it worked out for you, my man," he muttered thoughtfully. "I hope you're happy."

He turned on the radio and drove at a very slow speed. Not a soul was stirring. He was suddenly overwhelmed by a feeling of calm. It was nights like this that he liked his hometown best. He knew every street, every corner, every building, every house, and everybody that lived in every house.

"Sipsey is a nice town," he remarked.

As he approached the railroad station, he saw a diminutive speck moving along the road. At first, he thought it was a drifter headed for who knew where. But as he got closer, he recognized the figure. "What is she doing out in this weather?" he mumbled.

He drove even with her and stopped. Reaching across the seat, he opened the door. "Get in, I'll take you home."

Clumsily, she climbed into the truck. Her clothes were wet and her face was streaming with water. He tried not to stare but couldn't tell whether it was rainwater or tears.

He said, "Aunt Ginny, it's pouring down raining out here. Where in the world are you going?"

The humble face of Aunt Ginny Blaine looked dolefully at him. She said in her trembling voice, "I'm going home, sir."

"Going home? Where're you coming from?"

"I'm coming from Creek, sir. You know my son, Batch, is locked up down there."

"How did you get to Creek?"

"I walked, sir."

He frowned, his voice frantic with concern. "That's thirty miles!"

"Yes, sir," she responded.

Sugarfoot felt sorry for her. Batch was a scoundrel that nobody liked, but Aunt Ginny was beloved. They were such an odd pair that it was easy to forget that they were mother and son. "Do you go down there every day?" he wanted to know.

"Yes, sir," she answered meekly. "I go every day. I gen'ly walk over to Blue Stone Lake near the Bruin Highway. Most days a White woman picks me up and lets me ride with her. She comes from Chauncey. She works at the water plant in Bruin, and she lets me ride back in the evenings too."

It didn't seem right, an old lady hitching rides along the highway, especially after dark.

At a loss for words, he scratched his head. Aunt Ginny was one of the "old folks." They were the ones who'd come through the hardships of the second slavery. Their meek and submissive manners towards everyone, including other Negroes, made them sympathetic and cherished members of the community.

Sugarfoot moaned in frustration. Aunt Ginny needed someone looking out for her. Anything could happen. A driver not expecting to see a little old lady walking in the darkness might accidentally hit her. A stray dog or that roaring panther could come along and tear her apart.

"This is a shame," he mumbled and silently cursed Batch

for being an idiot.

She and Batch lived in a shed in a ravine across from the railroad tracks. When they reached the house, it was so dark that he got out and walked her to the door. She invited him inside, and out of politeness, he went in.

A rancid order hit him, making him nauseous. She fumbled around on the table and found a match to light a lamp. Suddenly, a small portion of the room brightened.

He surveyed the gloomy little house. It was barely habitable. There was no electricity or sheetrock on the walls, just dry wood and exposed beams. The floor was packed with dirt and covered with cardboard and rags. Rain made loud pelts against the tin-covered roof. And pots and pans were spread about to catch the rainwater.

The fact that she was living here alone in this dingy hut seemed all the more sad.

On the wood burning stove was a pot of something simmering. He was sure that whatever was in the pot was stinking up the shack.

"What you got cooked?" he asked.

"It's 'possum," she said.

"And where did you get 'possum?"

"Mr. Peter Emory went hunting the other day, and he give it to me. Won't you have some?"

"No, thanks," he said. He'd tasted 'possum before and didn't like it.

"Have a seat, sir," she gestured toward a rickety chair at the table. With a sad sigh, he sat down. One part of him wanted to run away, and another part wanted to shield this old woman from her sad life.

The scene reminded him of their old house. His mind

began roaming. What could he do to improve it? He asked, "Aunt Ginny, do you own this house?"

"No, sir," she said, taking a seat at the table. "We rent it from Mr. Peter."

Sighing, he asked, "When is Batch's trial coming up?"

"They ain't said."

He felt a restless energy and a strong indignation at the wrongness of life. He knew God was all knowing and all powerful, and he'd been taught not to question him. But he still wondered why people had to live like this?

"I'm sorry about what happened to Batch," he said sincerely. "I'm sorry he did that."

He shook his head, unaware that he'd convicted her son.

Aunt Ginny, however, didn't take offense. And speaking with the conviction of a mother certain of her child's innocence, she said, "He didn't do it, sir. He didn't rob that store."

****

When Sugarfoot arrived home, Big Mama was sitting in her recliner in the den. "I been waiting on you," she said the minute he walked in the door. She adjusted her full-figured body and said, "Freddie Dee came by here again. She stayed for the longest waiting on you to come home."

Sugarfoot swore under his breath. Freddie Dee had become a problem. He sighed. "Wonder what she wanted? Did she say?"

"She want you," Carrie Mae said in her characteristically blunt manner. Her gold teeth sparkled as she stared at him. "You need to tell her something."

"I *have* told her, Big Mama," he said impatiently. "It's

not like we were that tight to start with. I don't know what she's trying to make out of it."

She eyed him suspiciously. "You ain't got her big, is you?"

"What! Pregnant? The question was shocking. He, the most careful of men, wouldn't

leave something so important to chance or to a woman. "No!" He stated emphatically. "Absolutely *not!*"

He stared absurdly.

She said, "Well, that can happen when you start doing these things with women, laying up with them and things. She thinks you're her man. If you're through with her, make it plain so she'll stop running behind you."

"I don't think I can make it any plainer," he said in vexation.

He started for his room. "Here," she called him back. "You got mail." She handed him two envelopes. Pointing to the one with an air mail border, she said, "This came for you today." Then, handing him the other, she said, "and Freddie Dee left this."

He took the envelopes and went to his room. Flopping down on the bed, he looked at the air mail envelope. "Good grief," he groaned, "these women!"

"You need a wife," the voice of Johnny Goines haunted him.

"A wife, a wife, a wife!" It was out of the question.

The air mail letter had a return address. He looked at it with a sinking feeling. "What a fool I was getting involved with her," he cried. "My God, my God!"

Responding to the letter couldn't wait. He took out notebook and pen and wrote back to her. First thing in the morning, he'd drop it in the mailbox.

The letter from Freddie Dee had an evil feel to it and his first thought was to throw it in

the trash. But curiosity got the better of him and he took the folded letter out of the envelope. As he began unfolding it, pictures fell out.

He gasped, not believing his eyes!

The pictures weren't of good quality, but they were clear enough for him to see the raw sensuality of Freddie Dee Varner.

She was slouched on a fur wrap in several erotic poses including one with her legs suspended in the air. And she was butt naked!

It was mindboggling, but he couldn't take his eyes off her. She was beautiful and vulgar all at once. Transfixed, he couldn't move as thoughts of the times they'd spent together raced through his head. He knew he should throw the pictures away. Instead, he cursed her and tucked them under the mattress.

Chapter Ten

Around nine o'clock in the evening, Ivan Goines drove along Interstate 20 towards his home in Decatur, Georgia. He was exhausted and very much out of sorts. It'd been a helluva day, starting with him flooding his antique car in an effort to get to work on time. Then he'd had to wait fifteen minutes for the thing to flush out and crank.

Arriving at his office, he was immediately reminded never to expect anything to be done in a timely manner in the Thaddeus P. McClury Math and Science Building. Their clerk, though cute with a tempting butt, didn't know that records should be filed in alphabetical order by last name. He'd had to sift through a drawer of folders to find the publisher of a textbook he was using next semester. Then, Dr. Thornton, Department Head, had failed to notify him of a called meeting to discuss curriculum changes.

He'd left the meeting with a chip on his shoulder. Dr. Salem had wangled his way out of teaching Calculus I next semester, and it'd been dumped on him. Not that Dr. Salem needed to be teaching Calculus I. Ivan didn't think he knew enough about the subject to teach math to kindergarteners, let alone college freshmen. The man was clueless; an imbecile with the haughty manners of an uppity Negro. But he'd been there since the first brick, and uprooting him would take very heavy lifting.

If he followed his heart, he'd never go back there again. The stress of dealing with an incompetent administration plus immature men and women not much younger than himself was exasperating.

He grunted, "I have to teach them, grade them, and practically diaper them through these classes."

The very idea! A young man's mother had called him today about her son's poor grade. And she'd actually thought he was gonna discuss it with her. "Ma'am, you need to talk to your son," he'd said, ever so politely. She hadn't appreciated his tact and started berating his character and his teaching style. At that point, he realized he was wasting both their time and hung up on her.

After work, he'd stopped by the Pink Panty Strip Club on Spring Street. It was a dirty hole in the wall but a good place to relax. He'd eaten a burger and downed three beers. His thirst had called for more but he decided not to indulge.

One of the girls had tried to buy him a drink and give him her telephone number. Eyeing his towering statue, she complimented his bushy hair and said, "You're a yummy glass of lust. We could have some fun together."

He was tempted, but declined. There was already too much drama in his life. Adding another shady woman wouldn't help at all.

He gave in at the last minute and had half a beer for the road. As if it would help, he mixed it with cola. Outside, he did his own sobriety test, making sure he could walk without staggering. Getting drunk wasn't an option. The last time he'd gotten wasted, it'd been with his coworker Alonzo Franklin. He'd dropped Alonzo off at home and was traveling through Snapfinger Woods when he'd hit a deer. The glassy eyed creature was literally staring in the headlights when he'd seen it. His brakes failed and he rammed into it. The deer bounced off the fender and went flying into the woods.

The car was totaled, and he'd had to buy the old Chevy he was driving now.

Passing the Wesley Chapel exit, he regretted the anxiety he felt going home every night. Sometimes it was so intense that his mind urged him to keep on driving until he reached South Carolina. But then what?

Miles later, he left the interstate and turned onto Panola Road. The thought of stopping at the service station to pick up a six pack was tempting, but he decided against it.

Turning onto Pine Lane Court, his anxiety became more acute as his heart raced nervously. What intrigue awaited him when he walked through the door?

He parked on the car porch, got out of the car, and instinctively grabbed his hair. Taking a deep breath, he put the key in the lock. To his regret, his wife was in the kitchen lounging beside the refrigerator. His antennae went up. He wondered what game of chicken she was playing tonight. He held onto the doorknob, taking in the beauty of her. Her slender, well-made body was the bait and her beautifully slanted eyes the switch that disguised her treachery.

She faked a grin and said, "Guess what? We're moving!"

"You don't say," he said cautiously. "Moving to where?"

"Wentworth," she replied. "The real estate agent called and said this magnificent house had just come on the market. It's a short sale, and it's fabulous!" Her voice rose excitedly. "I went to look at it right away, and he was right. It's a two story Tudor with everything; a nursery, a wine cellar, and a guesthouse. It belongs to a millionaire. He's fallen on hard times and wants to sell as quick as possible. It was too good of a deal to pass up, so I made a down payment."

"Did you now?" He said coldly.

"Just wait til you see it."

He sneered. "My dear wife, you've been keeping secrets. Apparently, your rich uncle has dropped a pile of money on you." When she didn't respond, he said, "Huh?"

"Well, sorta," she came back evenly. Her dark eyes swept the room. "Ivan," she motioned with her hands. "This house is old. It's tacky, and it's too little. If we're going to have kids, we need a bigger place to raise them."

Unmoved by her argument," he said, "How much was this down payment, and where did you get the money?"

Her mouth curled into a pout.

"Are you suddenly hard of hearing?"

Deanna pondered whether getting the house outweighed the method she'd used to do it. After a pause, she said, "What's the difference? We aren't planning to live here forever. Since we've got the money to buy a nicer place, we might as well do it now."

Hearing her decree, his lanky body stiffened. He rubbed his face and groaned. Suddenly, he felt older than his twenty-nine years. This, he fretted, was the reason he hated to come home. Whatever demons drove her thinking never rested.

"With the down payment," she was saying, "the monthly payments won't be bad. And it's worth it. I think you'll agree when you see it."

Impending doom sounds a warning, and he heard it loud and clear. Fighting the rising rage in his gut, he kept his lips clamped together.

She said, "Actually, I think I made a good choice."

Forcing himself into calmness, he stared at her. He said, "Deanna, I've had a long day. I've got to start working on a

Calculus syllabus for next semester. This conversation needs consideration and time. Let's not have it tonight."

He sighed and started to walk away.

The rebuff infuriated her.

"When do you want to have it, Ivan?" Her voice broke shrilly. "You never have time to talk things through. You come home drunk or high, every night, and you go in that room and don't come out until I'm in the bed asleep. So when . . . when do you want to have this conversation?"

"Never," he shot back. "I don't ever want to have this conversation with you!" He made a growling noise and again headed for his study.

There'd been a menacing aspect to his tone that she refused to acknowledge. Frowning in frustration, she said, "We might as well have it now, because I've put the money down on the house, and I've already started packing for us to leave."

He swung around, his eyes flaming. "Now tell me again, where did you get this down payment?"

"I used the royalty check," she retorted.

"No, you didn't." The calmness in his voice hid the rage that he felt. For a moment, he couldn't say anything else. So many emotions were running through his body that he was sure a metamorphosis was taking place.

"Deanna," he asked the question in the form of a statement, "tell me that you did *not* spend money that *I* made to buy a house that *I* don't want to live in without talking to *me* about it? Please tell me that."

"I did," she admitted. "That house is a steal and it won't be on the market long. Somebody from Michigan called while I was there. They wanted to buy it sight unseen. So I went ahead and made an offer, and the seller accepted it. I had to put up some honest money. So I gave her the check. Now all we have to do is go to the bank and close." When he didn't respond, she said, "I took a chance that you would see this for the opportunity it is. There're only a few Black families in Wentworth. It's the most elite neighborhood in Atlanta. Don't you understand that?"

Furious, with a sense of desperation, he leapt the few feet between them and grabbed her by the shoulders. Haven't I told you about going behind my back and doing things, Deanna? I had…I *have* plans for that money. And I thought we agreed that we wouldn't spend any of it until all of these bills you've made have been paid."

"Turn me a loose," she shouted, snatching away from him. "You're stingy and you're mean. You don't want to spend the money at all, not even to buy yourself a decent car. You're still trying to do things like you did in the country? We live in suburban Atlanta, not the cotton fields of Alabama."

Her criticism of his country upbringing always angered him. Until now, he'd let it go. But tonight, he was taking her on.

He said, "You have no idea what you're talking about, Miss City Slicker. You could learn a thing or two from country people. For one thing, they live within their means. That means paying for what they get with money they have. Charging everything may be a city value, but it's not a smart strategy." "Yes, I'm a city girl and proud of it," she spat angrily. "I don't understand the ways of the country and I don't want to. Atlanta is not Chicago, but it's growing. Black people are the future doers of this place, and I want to be a part of that crowd."

"Well, I don't," he shouted.

"That's because you're stuck in the country," she yelled. "You can't give up the fantasy of living a perfect life on a farm. You forget about the terrible things that still happen to Black people in those little towns. They still lynch you down there, and I don't understand why you want to go back."

"Because it's my home!" he screamed. "I grew up in that little town. My Poppa and Mama live there. I've got friends there. And if it's good enough for them, it's good enough for me."

"Well, it's not good enough for me," she countered. "I don't want to live on some stupid farm in Alabama. I don't want to feed chickens and slop hogs. I want to live in Wentworth and enjoy the finer things of life."

"You go right ahead," he recommended. "But you won't do it with my money."

He stared at the woman he once thought so beautiful and oh so savvy. Now, knowing her for the crook she was made him cringe.

She said, "I really want this house, Ivan."

"Why?" he asked.

She shrugged. "We deserve it, and it's the place to be."

"No," he shook his head. "It's not the place to be. I don't know anybody in Wentworth, and you don't either. Why would you even want to live in a place like that?"

"I just do," she yelled.

He said, "You want to live there because you have delusions of grandeur. You want to be important, to be greater than you really are. You haven't learned anything from your mistakes. And no matter what material things you acquire, it won't be enough. Whatever is wrong with you can't be fixed with money and things."

Ignoring this indictment, she said, "I'll admit it, I want a better life than the one I was brought up in. I like having money. I like being in society, wearing nice clothes and going to nice places. And I want to live in a big, fancy house. That's living, and it's the life I've always dreamed about."

"Right. The life *you've* always dreamed about. I don't want that life. It sounds more like a nightmare to me. And tomorrow, you're going to that real estate woman and get my money back."

Her body tightened as her mouth set in a stubborn scowl. She said, "I will not!"

"Oh yes you will," he declared.

Suddenly, a staring contest between them began. They were both disgusted, but for different reasons. Ivan was disgusted with himself. He looked at his wife and saw nothing of his mother's character. That he would marry a woman that bore no resemblance to the only woman on the planet he thought was perfect, puzzled him. His thought now was, "What on earth was I thinking."

Deanna's disgust was with him. He hadn't lived up to her expectations or bolstered her dream of who they could be as a couple. Ivan Goines was her knight in shining armour. He was handsome, charming, and brilliant, with the potential of making a lot of money. Just as importantly, the Negro aristocracy was enamored with him. A historian that had studied ancient dynasties had recently remarked that in another lifetime, he was probably the son of a king. With her guts and savvy, they could be the toast of any town. If only he'd cooperate. Her frustration was that he just wouldn't cooperate.

Studying her, he said, "What was I thinking marrying you?"

She sneered, "When I met you, I thought you were going places. You were fun and had big ideas. But ever since we've been down south, you've been going backwards. I had a bad feeling when you kept turning down those good jobs. We could be living in Los Angeles, Boston, or Chicago for that matter. But no, you wanted to come back to the south to work these starvation level jobs. Honestly!" She cried in exasperation. "I didn't realize I was marrying a loser!"

"Just get my money back," he warned and walked away. As an afterthought, he said, "I guess you've forgotten about the deal we made. You haven't been to the psychologist, and as far as I can see, you've made no effort to turn your life around."

"There's nothing wrong with me," she shouted. "I might be a little more creative in the way I operate, but I'm fine."

"No, you're not," he disputed. "You're not fine, and you don't understand me." His voice turned sad. "I never said I wanted to live in high society, Deanna. I told you what I wanted before we got married, and *nothing* has changed."

"Well I've changed!" She spoke, pompously. "The world is changing and you need to change too. With the money you're gonna make selling books and patenting those gadgets you like to play with, we'll be rich."

"I want my money back," he said firmly.

"No!" She cried. "I won't do it."

For him, the end was here. It'd been coming for a long time. There was some relief in knowing that it was finally over. He breathed out tiresomely. And rather than antagonize her further, he blew her a kiss and left the room.

Chapter Eleven

The clock above his desk showed a few minutes after ten. He'd been home a little over an hour, but it seemed like days. He'd taken refuge in his study to work on the syllabus. But his mind had been so unsettled that he'd turned on the radio to drown out his thoughts. All he could think about was his parents, and that brought tears to his eyes. They'd raised him right and had expected him to go out into the world and represent them.

And what had he done? He'd dishonored them by rejecting their teachings. He'd forgotten everything they'd taught him about honor, decency, and self-respect. As a result, his life had become a joke and he an embarrassment.

His soul was in pain and he wanted to go home. Broken and disgraced as he was, he craved the nurturing of his parents' love. Every night, before he went to sleep, he closed his eyes and conjured up images of the farm. Life at home had been so simple. It was where he found happiness and peace.

But he didn't dare go. If he did, Madea would know something was wrong and he'd be forced to explain himself.

He heard Deanna moving around in the kitchen and raged stirred within him. She was his nightmare; proof of the fool he'd played. He hadn't used an ounce of judgment in choosing a wife, and now he was paying the price.

Forgetting all else, he realized that Deanna was trying to trap him into staying with her by binding him to a mortgage. Well, she'd played the wrong hand.

"Oh, my God," he cried aloud, "it would've worked a few months ago!" In fact, it probably would've worked a few weeks ago when he was still in denial about who she was. But today, after receiving the call from Hancock State, he had to face facts. She wasn't serious about changing and he couldn't save her.

He went back into the kitchen. She was sitting at the table with a book and paper. He said, "What scam are you working on now?"

"I'm studying for class," she retorted.

"What class? You know you don't go to class. Why go to class when you can fake your way through?" He picked up the book and pretended to read the title. He read, "How to Scam Your Way to the Top."

She snatched the book away from him. "I'm not scamming. I'm serious about getting my degree," she said.

"No, you're not. Wanna know how I know?" He poked his face into hers, taunting her. He said, "I received a call from Hancock State today. The personnel director was trying to get in touch with Dr. Deanna Goines. When I inquired as to why she wanted to get in touch with you, she said she wanted to set up an appointment for an interview. She said it was for a position you'd applied for. I asked what position and she said it was associate math professor. I asked if she was sure about the name and she said yes. Then I told her that there was a mistake. The Deanna Goines I know is not a doctor and has no credentials as a college professor. The only degree she has, I told Miss Gilbreath, is a B.S. in bullshit."

She showed no reaction but said, "I didn't apply for a job at Hancock State. I don't know what you're talking about."

"Yes, you do," he jeered. "You're up to your old tricks and you'll never change. So let me make myself clear. I'm not paying out another dime on your scams. You clearly think you're smarter than everybody else. Only time will tell if you're right. But the next time you steal somebody's identity, forge a check, or engage in illegal behavior of any kind, it'll be between you and the po-leece."

"Are you ready to talk about the house?" She asked, ignoring his warning.

"As a matter of fact, no," he stated. "There's not going to be any house, anywhere."

The courage it'd taken him to say that had come from a place he didn't know existed. Having taken the first step, he sat across from her and spoke earnestly. He said, "Deanna, the time has come for us to resolve this once and for all."

"Resolve what?"

"Us," he returned. "We've tried and failed."

"What're you saying? You said we would start over!"

"We can't. We're not in the same place."

"Because you won't let bygones be bygones," she sobbed. "You won't let me live anything down. You're paranoid and suspicious of everything I do. You see a boogie man around every corner."

"Maybe, I do," he said calmly. "But it's because I'm scared that if I turn that corner the boogie man will indeed be there."

"You don't trust me at all," she accused.

"Experience has taught me not to."

"Well what do you want me to do?"

The penetrating gaze he gave her indicated that he wanted her to draw the conclusion.

He said, "What do you think is the best course for us right now?"

She bristled, casting a cutting look at him. "If you're thinking about a divorce, you can forget it. We're married and we're going to stay married."

The finality of her voice didn't dissuade him. As a matter of fact, if anything about Deanna was easy, he wouldn't trust it. He said, "This marriage isn't working, and I can't think of a thing I could do to make it work."

"All because of a check?"

"It wasn't just a check. It was *my* check, and it was not to be used as down payment on a house in Wentworth. The fact that you could do it so easily and underhandedly tells me that, as always, you're only thinking of yourself. Sadly, that will always be the case." "So, deceitful Deanna, I want my money back."

"Well, you won't get it. And it was our check."

Her eyes shot daggers at him, but he kept his cool. In a firm voice, he said, "I hope you understand what I'm saying to you. My name, and only my name, is on that check, and I advise you to get it back before it's deposited."

"You heard what I said," she said stubbornly.

"Well, hear this," he decreed. "If that check isn't in my hand by this time tomorrow, I'm reporting it stolen."

He stood up to leave. She jumped up too. Her eyes bulged and a blazing fire discharged from them. "Are you threatening me?" she screamed furiously. "Are you saying you're gonna put the police on me, Ivan?"

"Get that check," he ordered.

"I will not," she argued.

He was done and turned to go back to his study. Her breath came rapidly as she experienced a systems overload. Ivan Goines was her lifeline. Their marriage was all she had, and she couldn't let him walk out on her. "Don't walk away from me, Ivan," she said desperately. "We need to finish this."

"I have nothing else to say."

"There's nothing wrong with me," she said frantically.

"I beg to differ, but I won't belabor the point. Get that check," he repeated as if he was talking to a stranger.

For a brief moment, she considered terms of surrender. She would agree to stop spending and pay off her credit card debts. She would promise to bring back their old relationship, become that girl he thought she was and wanted her to be. She would promise to stop being creative in her approach to doing things.

But she'd read between the lines and knew none of it would matter. He didn't want her. For some time, she'd suspected he had another woman but didn't dare ask him for fear of what he'd say.

His face was stern as granite and showed no sign of changing. This was an Ivan she didn't know, and she had no idea how to reach him. His anger needed time to subside. Then she could reason with him.

Apparently, he read her thoughts and fired the death blow to their marriage. He said, "Don't plan anymore schemes for me, Deanna. I'm cutting my losses and moving on. I don't want you for my wife, and I certainly don't want you to be the mother of my children. Now get my money."

Just like that, it was over.

She was stunned but wasn't gonna take it lying down. Her mind raced, searching for the thing that would stun him, confound him, and stop him in his tracks.

But it was hard to think through her anger.

And then it came to her as clear as day. It was the trump card, a never failing strategy designed to hurt, and she knew it would.

Her eyes squinted as a cold chill came over her. She, Deanna deAugustin Goines, knew what she was about to do. It was one of the great taboos of her race. She knew the special bond that existed between Black mothers and their sons. And tampering with it was always dangerous. She also knew that Ivan Goines honored his mother more than anybody she knew. If she'd had time to plan another strategy, she might've done something different. But she had no time. So she went for what she knew.

They were squashed between the refrigerator and the table. He was glaring at her with contempt that was rising from his soul. Words weren't necessary. She knew that he'd seen the blackness of her heart and found it repulsive.

She had no choice but to fight back. Clenching her teeth and looking at him with sheer hatred, she said, "You're nothing but a loser, a mama's p----. Go back to Alabama, country boy, and suck on your Mama's tit. Maybe she can wean you into a man."

The words struck like a two by four causing blood to rush to his head. His mind snapped, and he backhanded her with a ferocity that threw her off balance. She stumbled and fell against the sink. Knowing what was coming next, she girded up. He knocked her backwards and started for her throat. With quickening speed, she grabbed a knife from the wooden block and came at him. He tried to grab her hand but wasn't quick enough. A look of rage, or was it panic, glazed her eyes?

The outcome was predictable, and he saw rather than felt

the point of the knife go into his chest. Then a sizzling pain, one like he'd never felt before, seared through his body.

After that, everything went black.

*****

Sirens from the ambulance of the DeKalb County Emergency Services shattered the night. It went screaming towards the address in Pine Lane Court. Arriving, the scene was wholly horrific.

Deanna Goines stood over her husband's bleeding body, her face wild with shock.

"He was choking me!" She screamed to the paramedics. "I thought he was gonna kill me!"

The floor was streaked with blood. The young victim lay unconscious, not breathing, the very picture of an ended life.

"Is he dead?" she screamed.

Two men, who identified themselves as Bill and John, knelt beside Ivan and immediately went to work. "Clear the airway, Bill," said John.

Bill, the redhead, moved quickly, inserting a tube into his mouth as John, a heavy set blond, checked his breathing. He began administering CPR. Deanna called out questions of concern, but they didn't answer. Rather, John asked, "What name does he answer to?"

"Ivan," she said.

"Ivan," he called loudly. "Ivan, can you hear me?"

Nothing.

Bill pumped air into him.

A pressure bandage was placed at the stab site but the knife wasn't removed. It stuck like a woodsman's axe in the trunk of a tree. Bill kept pressing his wrist.

After a few grueling minutes, John said, "He's not re-sponsive. We've got to get him to Georgia Medical."

Quicker than a wink, they hoisted him and slipped his body onto a backboard. It made a

popping sound when they raised it up. They started out the door. Bill looked back at her. Showing no emotions, he said, "The police will be here shortly." Her eyes widened in askance. "This'll have to be investigated whether it was self-defense or not," he said. They carried the body to the waiting ambulance. Deanna stood there hugging herself, trying to process what she'd done. The ambulance went screaming off into the night with the injured body of Ivan Goines as its cargo.

Chapter Twelve

The Goineses stayed up later than usual on Wednesdays to watch the Matthew Ferison Show. It was an hour long variety show featuring singing, dancing, and silly stunts by aging comics. It was also their chance to see the performance of their favorite cast member. She was a young Colored girl who exuded talent and beauty.

This evening Johnny Goines had puffed on his pipe as she sang. His face held the same pride it would if she was one of his own daughters. "Colored people are coming up," he said proudly.

She sang, *Somewhere over the Rainbow,* in a sweet, melodious voice. When she finished, the studio audience clapped with approval. The host embraced her and bragged that only the original artist could sing the song as well as Jacqueline.

Deacon Goines agreed. He said, "Now that's how you sing a song. You notice she didn't do no hollering. And she didn't say the same thing over and over again. She just flat foot sung that song. I like that."

They went to bed about nine o'clock. Their intention was to get a good night's rest and rise early to begin a new day.

The knock on the front door at three o'clock in the morning was so unusual that the three of them jolted out of bed and reached the front door at the same time.

"Johnny," the voice of the Sipsey Valley Police Chief rang from the other side. "Johnny Goines, it's Police Chief, Hank Givins. I need to talk to you."

Their hearts dropped at different rates. There was no question that something was wrong. The question was what?

Sherri Lynn thought the panther had returned and attacked someone nearby, and the chief was calling to let them know. Johnny Goines didn't wonder. It was a bad sign for the police chief to be at his house at three o'clock in the morning for any reason.

But it was Liddy who looked terrified. She began preparing herself, for her heart had alerted her to the fact that something had happened to one of her children.

"Come on, Jesus," she prayed.

The chief took off his hat and his ashen face looked sad. He said, "Johnny, I'm sorry to tell you this, but I just got a call from the DeKalb County Police Department in Georgia. Your son, Ivan, done been stabbed." He sighed. "He's at Georgia Medical Center in Atlanta. They didn't say if he made it or not."

"Oh God! No! No!" Sherri Lynn bent to her knees screaming. "Lord, please, let him be alright."

Deacon Goines stood there, calmly absorbing what the policeman had said. At Sherri Lynn's outburst, he said, "Gone back in the house, Sherri Lynn."

"Poppa, please, let me stand here," she begged. "I'll pull myself together. Then

composing herself, she asked, "Who did it?"

The chief shrugged. "From what I understand, it was a domestic dispute. I b'lieve his wife done it."

"I knew it," Sherri Lynn cried. "I've always known something was wrong. But I didn't say anything. Why didn't I say something?"

Though he was shaking like a leaf, Deacon Goines spoke

soberly. He said, "Thank you,

Chief Givins. I 'preciate you for letting me know about my boy." His body drooped dejectedly. "I'll get ready and go to him now."

But once they were back in the house, he seemed unsettled and confused. He mumbled as he absently walked in and out of rooms without purpose. Eventually, he ambled into his study where he stayed.

In fact, Deacon Johnny Goines was praying. He was the man who'd raised his seven children to be respectful of all men; honorable in their dealings with all people; and diligent in all manners of life. He'd built a powerful agricultural industry from the ground up. He'd loved and been faithful to his wife, Liddy, for the fifty-one years they'd been married. He loved God and mankind. And he was proud of his children.

But now, his youngest child was in trouble.

Ivan. The thought of him brought tears to the deacon's eyes. Ivan. The son who'd followed him around the farm asking what he could do to help when he could barely walk. Ivan. The son who thought his Poppa was the greatest man in the world. Ivan. The son who'd taught him to read; had forgiven him when he couldn't defend him when a White man in downtown Sipsey had called him a "Nigger." Ivan. The son that would never have left home if the deacon hadn't made him.

That son was possibly lying dead in a morgue in Atlanta, Georgia. In his study, the deacon could only talk to the Lord.

He prayed:

Almighty and eternal, God. My Lord, and my God, it's me. You know why I'm here. But before I get to that, I want to thank you for what you've already done for me. I want to thank you for being the good and gracious God that created this Universe. I want to thank you for the sun that shines on the just as well as the unjust, and I thank you for letting it shine on me. I want to thank you for the air I breathe, without which I wouldn't be able to take another step. I want to thank you for food, clothing and shelter. And then Lord, I want to thank you for my family, especially my wife. She's kind, obedient, and faithful. Thank you for giving her to me when I was nobody and didn't even know my name when I seen it. I thank you for my children, all normal, healthy, and well-learned. They have brought me more pride and joy than I ever thought a man could have. I thank you for looking over this Universe, seeing all manner of men, but choosing me to be their earthly father. You couldn't have granted me a greater honor.

And now, Lord, you know the condition of my boy, Ivan. You know all about him even down to the number of hairs on his head and the number of days he's allotted on this earth. If his days are up, and it's nothing that can be done, I ask you to help me, my wife, and my children to accept it. But Lord, if there's any possible way that his life can be spared, I ask you to move now, and save him. Give him another chance. He's only twenty-nine years old, and he's been faithful all his life. If it be your will, I beg in Jesus's name that he be restored to good health. But it's your will, and whatever happens, I give you the glory. Thank you, and a-men."

*****

Sugarfoot was in a deep and riveting sleep. Something big was happening. Even in his state of inertia, he felt the excitement of the event.

The dream bounced, and he was upstairs in the educational wing of First Macedonia. There he saw the back of her. It was the profile of the most beautiful woman in the world. She was promenading down the hall in a pleated pink dress and beige high heeled shoes. Her dark hair hung below her shoulders, and her gait was poised and swift. As she sashayed down the hall, she smiled a greeting to those she met.

The scene changed and he was in the sanctuary, packed with family and well-wishers.

Beautiful bouquets of flowers with wide ribbons adorned the church. It could've been a funeral, but it wasn't. It was a happy day. He could tell by the smiling faces of the congregants and their busy, joyful chatter.

He sensed rather than saw his family, including Bebe. And suddenly he knew this important thing was happening to him.

He saw himself all dressed up in an elegantly styled suit. He was standing at the altar under an ornamented arch. The spirit of goodness surrounded him. Suddenly, the music stopped. The congregation stood and looked back anxiously towards the doubled doors. The organist began playing a sweet, enchanting piece of music. It was soon joined by the stirring sounds of violins and flutes.

The music played for an uninterrupted period of time as the audience waited in anticipation. Then the wide doors opened and she stood there, captivating in a glittering white dress. A lace veil covered her face, and there was a radiant smile on her lips.

It was their wedding day! And he waited with the eagerness of a groom excited to see his beloved's face.

And then it got confusing. The scene changed and he didn't know where he was. He felt himself floating into an empty space where something bizarre was going on. Loud voices were calling him. He tried to answer but was paralyzed. It was the witch's curse; alive, awake, but unable to respond.

"Sugarfoot, Sugarfoot!" Loud banging on the door was followed by hysterical cries. And

still he couldn't move. "Sugarfoot! Sombody was screaming and banging from far away. Sugarfoot!"

From dreamland to nightmare, his mind betrayed him. He tried to hurl himself back

into the fairytale, to the beautiful bride coming to meet him. But the witch was insistent, determined to crush his dream.

Abruptly, his eyes flew open. Big Mama was standing over his bed, still in her night clothes, shaking him awake. "Wake up, Bray," she urged. "Sherri Lynn's out there and she's done brought some bad news. Get up!"

He jumped up, but his mind wasn't clear. "What is it, Big Mama? What's wrong? What time is it?"

"It's 'bout four o'clock in the morning," she answered. "You got to get up and go over to

the Goines's house. Sherri Lynn's done brought some bad news. Something's done happened to

Ivan. Get up. They need you."

Putting on his pants and a shirt, he rushed to the door. Sherri Lynn was standing in the backyard in a raincoat, crying. "Sugarfoot, Ivan's been stabbed."

He pulled her into the room. "Have a seat," he gestured toward the bench at the foot of his bed.

She was so distraught she could barely speak. She said, "We just got word. Ivan's been stabbed and we don't know if he's dead or alive. The police chief told us and says he's at Georgia Medical Center in Atlanta."

"Who stabbed him?" Sugarfoot said sharply.

"That woman. That. . . that woman he married."

"And you don't know how bad it is?"

She shook her head. "The police chief wasn't able to say. He just said Ivan had been stabbed and that it was a domestic dispute."

"How're your parents?"

"Not good," she answered. "We've got to go to him. Poppa wants to drive, but he's in no condition and neither am I."

"I'm on it," he said quickly. "Just let me get dressed." Looking at her pitiful face, he said, "Try to calm down, Sherri Lynn. It may not be as bad as it sounds."

It was preposterous, he thought. Why would somebody stab easy going Ivan Goines? Earlier, he'd thought Sherri Lynn was overreacting, maybe exaggerating the trouble in his marriage. Clearly, she wasn't. And what kind of socialite stabs her husband? Sherri Lynn's face was etched in grief. He could only wonder at the state of her parents. He said, "Don't assume the worst, Sherri Lynn."

"We're just praying," she sobbed. "I already feel guilty. I knew things weren't right with them and I should've said something to Ivan. At the time, I thought it was best to stay out of it. Now, I wish I'd said something."

He disappeared into the bathroom where he showered and dressed. He returned and said to Sherri Lynn, "You don't seem to be in any shape to drive. Ride with me and we can come back later for your car."

"I can drive home," she insisted. "That's the least I can do."

"Well, pull yourself together. This is no time to fall apart."

Chapter Thirteen

Chuck Okafor, the African doctor attending Ivan Goines, stood over his knife riddled body and shook his head in sadness. Hooked up to a breathing tube and an intravenous device, he saw a young man slowly losing his life.

As far as he was concerned, this man could be from his own village, the victim of intertribal conflict that'd plagued his country for hundreds of years. America, he quickly discovered, wasn't devoid of the madness. On any given weekend, three or four of these incidents occurred. He was still trying to understand the interpersonal relations between African descended Americans.

Presently unresponsive, they could obtain no firsthand knowledge of events leading up to the stabbing. X-rays showed the extent of damage, and it was considerable. The knife, deeply lodged in his chest, painted its own grim picture.

Initial tests revealed a penetrating chest wound, internal and external bleeding, and trauma to soft tissue. There were punctures to the chest wall. An accumulation of air in the pleural space was preventing the flow of blood back to the heart. Pressure from the air had caused his right lung to collapse.

Added to these complications was the threat of infection.

Immediate surgery was required.

First, the knife had to be removed. Dr. Okafor stared at the wooden handled weapon before firmly grabbing hold of it. Then carefully, with self-taught expertise, he eased it out of his chest. The wound began hemorrhaging and Ailene

Thompson, the lead nurse, pressed the sides to stem the flow. Then she gave him a shot to clot the blood and control the bleeding.

Minutes later, she demonstrated how to rinse the wound to the young nurses. She said, "After rinsing, we have to examine it to make sure there're no foreign objects. The weapon could've had food or rust or some other substance on it, so you always want to make sure the wound is cleaned and disinfected.

The doctor ordered more tests to check for other injuries. Then he studied the patient. He believed that the manner in which the body processes trauma is very important. It gives clues as to whether the patient has the will to live. Presently, he saw no sign that Ivan Goines was going to fight for his life.

In due course, the medication took effect and the bleeding subsided. Ailene applied an antibiotic ointment as well as adding one to the intravenous device. Suddenly, his heart rate quickened as his blood pressure began to drop. They administered beta blockers to restore normal heart rhythm and reduce blood pressure.

Then they waited some more.

What had to be done took shape in his mind and he made a quick outline. Due to the tremendous loss of blood, he'd need a transfusion. The dead tissue would have to be removed and the damaged tissue disinfected and repaired. He'd also have to insert a small catheter in his chest. This would remove the air pressure between the lungs and allow him to inflate the collapsed lung.

It would be a five hour process at minimum, provided the patient lasted that long.

The doctor's mind wandered back and forth. He'd been at Georgia Medical Center only two years and had seen many of these violent cases. "How marvelous," he mumbled. "Medical science has ways of treating injuries and disease, but healing the spirit," he sighed feebly. "It's a much harder job."

For the doctor, Ivan's case was baffling. Even in his unconscious state, he seemed different than most of the victims that came to Georgia Medical. He was clean shaven and professionally dressed. The lines of his face showed a concentration of thought that indicated he was a man of distinction.

Still, tests showed alcohol and illegal substances in his bloodstream. Furthermore, he was dehydrated and nutritionally deprived. Dr. Okafor surmised that his nonresponsive state was due to these factors plus the overall shock to his system.

He looked from the tests to the lifeless body. Probably the worst part of being a doctor is *not* saving a life. He said, "It'll be hard facing your family if you don't make it. I have no strategy for easing their pain and telling them that the hopes and dreams they had for you are gone forever. And what about you? You'll enter eternity having lived less than half of your life's expectancy.

The nursing team noted Ivan's blood pressure and other vital signs. The only organs functioning normally were his kidneys. His arterial blood pressure was just below 54mmHG and the systolic pressure was 62. Those numbers would have to be raised before he could begin surgery.

In the intermission, he meditated.

*****

An operating room is a cold and impersonal space, and luckily for the patients, they're asleep. This operating room was different from most in that Ailene Thompson was one of its attendants. Presently, she stood over Ivan and prayed, reminding the omniscient God that time was of the essence and that they could use some help in the healing of this young man.

Back to the task, she checked his airways to make sure there were no obstructions.

Satisfied, she tested his breathing and circulation structures. Several minutes passed before all systems were acceptable. She nodded and said, "Pressure rising, heart rate stable. We're ready, doctor."

Anesthesia was administered to make sure he didn't awake during surgery. His vitals were checked again and they were ready to go.

But shortly after the operation began, machines began screaming. "Blood pressure dropping, heart rate rising," Ailene warned. She spoke to Ivan, saying, "Stay with me, young man. Your whole life is ahead of you. I don't know you, but you look like a fine young man. You didn't deserve this. And God's not ready for you."

It was times like this that she wished she'd gone to medical school. She'd wanted to be a doctor; a surgeon. But coming from a poor South Georgia family, she hadn't the educational background or the finances to go to college. Instead, she'd come up to Atlanta and gotten work as a custodian in a department store.

But she yearned for a better life. Education was the way to get ahead, she'd always been told. Atlanta had many schools of higher learning. So, after four years at the store, she decided to enroll in the technical school near her home. It had a highly respected practical nurse's program, and she was accepted right away.

Upon graduation she went to work at a nursing home near Decatur. But she continued working towards her nurse's certification. When she received it a year later, she applied to several hospitals. Some were third rate facilities that were desperate for any nurse they could get. But one foot inside Georgia Medical and her heart began throbbing with excitement.

She knew she'd found her home.

Dr. Okafor liked having her here. She was a caring nurse that believed in medical science but also in the power of a healing God. Her faith was a work in action as she petitioned God to intervene on behalf of her patients. This motivated Okafor. To him, Ailene wasn't just a coworker but a partner in the fight to save lives.

****

For two hours, Dr. Okafor had worked to repair Ivan's body and now stopped to assess the progress. He still had a way to go.

"It's turning out to be a long night," Ailene sighed.

In her heart, she felt Ivan Goines was so badly injured that he wouldn't make it through the surgery. Still, Chuck Okafor was the man you wanted to give you your last shot.

Now, he called upon everything he knew about repairing ruptured tissues and organs to aid him. The steady hands for which he was known were his chief assistants. And he worked deliberately, not rushing but allotting the time required.

He was grateful to be working in a facility that had so many advantages for patients. Easy transport to hospital, diagnostic equipment, an array of antibiotics, and other life-saving medications were just some of the benefits. One day, he hoped doctors in his own country would have access to these lifesaving devices.

He felt a sudden pang of homesickness at the thought that he might never see his homeland again. It was still a sore subject. He'd been a top ranked surgeon, enjoying many social and political advantages. But civil war had loomed. Concerned about threats against his tribe, he'd secretly consulted with the opposition government, giving financial aid, and as a former military officer, tactical advice. And he'd made every effort to operate with the greatest discretion.

But one of his own tribesmen had exposed him. A search team had been assembled with a warrant for his arrest. He'd gone on the run, barely making it to the American Embassy to appeal for political asylum before soldiers overtook him. If the Americans had turned him away, he'd have been executed without trial.

In America, he'd kept up with the progress of the revolution, but returning home was out of the question. So he dedicated himself to saving lives in this country.

He wondered what'd happened to Ivan Goines. Who was he? What kind of work had he done? Under what circumstance had someone become so agitated as to lodge a weapon into his chest? Professionalism dictated that he not dwell on the personal but treat the condition. But he was human. Again, he wondered what human condition destroyed this young man's life?

The nurses watched the monitoring machines as the doctor worked. The indicator lines on the wall monitor went up and down and then started flat lining.

"He's hemorrhaging. We're losing him," Ailene Thompson cried. "Oxygen! Pressure! Come on, ya'll, help us out!" she cried to the assistants.

The pulmonary specialist said, "Dr. Okafor, breathing uneven."

"Keep supplying," the doctor responded.

Dr. Okafor slowed the process, giving Ivan's traumatized body time to adjust. His blood pressure fell so low that the machine began screaming again. The young members of the surgical team sighed and shook their heads in defeat.

But Ailene Thompson screamed, "Oxygen. Come on, young man, breathe. Pull up on your strength. You can do this. Breathe!"

His blood pressure rose, and Dr. Okafor began again. The pressure went down again. He became frustrated. He was only half way through the surgery and every second counted. If he waited too long, he ran the risk of infection setting in. Willing the young man to hang on, he began again but the machines warned that his system was shutting down.

Now was the time for Chuck Okafor to talk to the patient. "Come on, man, fight!" he implored in his heavy accent. "Fight for your life. Think of your mother and your father. Think how they're gonna feel when we tell them you're dead? Do you have children? What about them? No father to raise them? No father to teach them right from wrong? Your family needs you. Fight man, fight for your life."

Ailene Thompson was watching the monitors as he talked. She'd been through this too many times, seen too many young Black men in emergency situations. Most were the result of Friday and Saturday night brawls between friends who'd had too much to drink and with maybe too much stress in their lives. So they sought relief by turning on each other. Occasionally it was a disputing husband or wife who got angry and lost control.

"With things going on the way they are these days, it could be anything," she mourned. "But my heart goes out to his family, especially his parents. I'm sure they love him. But it's on him. If he wants to live, he's gon have to fight for it."

She suddenly felt that something else needed to be said. She cried, "Keep talking Chuck. The least we can do is talk to him."

The doctor kept talking, switching to the melodious language of his homeland in a quiet and calming manner. Only he knew what he was saying. But it sounded like he was praying and singing all in one sound. He worked diligently, still talking to him.

Ailene's hope sank further. "He's going," she whispered. "His heart rate is barely registering and I can't get a pulse."

Dr. Okafor worked faster, disregarding what was happening. His motto was to continue working on a patient as long as there was a glimmer of hope. The human body was an independent and complex machine. Sometimes all it took was for the machine to reset itself.

So he kept working, realizing that, but for a miracle, he'd soon be facing a bereaved family.

"He's not gonna make it is he?" one of the nurses whispered.

The other nurse sighed and shook her head.

Chapter Fourteen

Ivan Goines's life was over and he'd done few of the things he wanted to do. He hadn't been to the Grand Canyon or stepped foot outside the United States. He hadn't loved a woman the way she should be loved; fathered children; taught his sons how to make a sling shot, or bragged to his daughters how beautiful they were. He'd never told his Poppa how much he admired him; never told Johnny Goines that it took courage for him to press on and build the life he had in the face of persecution and terror.

Had he even told Johnny Goines that he loved him?

Yet he had no regrets. He was looking forward to a new life. Where it'd be or what it'd be like, he didn't know. He just knew it'd be perfect, and the anticipation of it made him feel freer than he'd ever felt before.

Now, he saw it clearly. It was the bountiful field of forever, with the most beautiful of flowers, the bluest of lakes, and the greenest of pastures. The sun shone so brightly that he couldn't see the sky. And he was surrounded by love and peace and encompassed with the eternal spirit of God.

Suddenly, a light far off in the distance surrounded him. It shrouded him with bliss, and he delighted in it. It was as old as the Ancient of Days, and it glowed with a radiance that gleamed from everlasting to everlasting.

Beyond it, he envisioned things too marvelous to comprehend.

Suddenly, he saw faces, images and spirits that he knew. He'd known them forever, and now it was time to go join them.

They called to him and he became as an innocent child skipping happily towards his destiny. The visions became bigger and even more astounding. He saw a fierce creature with knowledge beaming from her forehead and knew it was Liddy's mother, a grandmother he'd never seen before. She smiled, and it filled his heart with joy.

He ran faster.

"Ivan, he heard her calling to him. "Ivan. Ivan."

"I'm coming," he shouted, running and laughing with joy.

But the road got longer and stretched farther and farther away. "I'm coming," he called as she began to disappear out of sight.

Suddenly, he heard another voice, stronger and firmer, yelling, "Go back! Go back! You're at the beginning, not the end. Turn around and go back!"

He watched as his life rewound before him. He saw himself, the baby Ivan, in the crib crying and reaching out his arms to be picked up. He saw himself pedaling his bicycle with training wheels. Then he heard his brother Earl mocking him because he was afraid to pedal without the wheels.

He beheld his older self. He was sitting at the dining room table with his sisters and brothers. They listened as their father taught them the scriptures and urged them to repeat what they'd learned. Then he lectured them on the "realities of life."

In another vision, he saw himself playing in the yard with his foxhound, Roper. He was a good dog and the only creature on the farm that Ivan could boss around. He saw the day that both of them squealed with delight when his father drove up in his pickup truck with a bed stacked with watermelons.

Then in a panoramic series of memories, he saw himself kneeling beside his bed, saying his prayers, waving good-bye to Madea, and boarding the bus for school.

It was an enigma, things he'd forgotten in the natural, but with his third eye, remembered clearly.

Suddenly, flecks of color revealed warts on his soul. Joy and peace were heartbreaking blues. Patience and kindness had crumbled like rust; goodness and love became petrified mulch; and trust and faithfulness cried tears shot with blood.

And this was Dr. Johnny Ivan Goines.

No judgment was pronounced upon him. What he saw was the man he should've been, the life he should've lived, and the impact he should've made on the world.

He acknowledged his transgressions and repented.

Then, fate brought him to the scene of his demise. In the kitchen of his home, he didn't recognize himself. He was as a stranger, far removed from his true-self, and he grieved for the man he'd become. The evil that'd destroyed him entered his home the day he entered it. And it'd been his constant companion.

His time was up. The light was now in reach and summoned him with an allure he couldn't resist. Liddy's mother was now joined by Johnny's mother, a petite, fair-skinned woman with silky hair. They stood side by side on a cumulus cloud that wavered underneath their weight. Adorned with hearts full of wisdom, they spoke to him, telling him of things he understood but couldn't speak. He rushed towards them with outstretched arms and called, "I'm coming, grandmothers. I'm coming home."

****

Deacon and Liddy Goines were dressed and ready to go when Sugarfoot and Sherri Lynn returned to the farm. Sherri Lynn had to rush to get ready. "Now, you ain't got time to be curling hair and putting on makeup," Liddy Goines warned in an anxious voice. "Put on some clothes so we can make haste."

When Sugarfoot asked if they'd heard anything else about Ivan's condition, Johnny

Goines sighed wearily. We been sitting by the telephone ever since Sherri Lynn left. Ain't nobody called and told us nothing else. So we gon have to be patient and get the news when we get there."

"It'll be in order for us to say a word of prayer before we get on the road," Liddy said. "We can do it while we wait for Sherri Lynn. Mr. Goines, would you pray?"

"Let me do it," Sugarfoot volunteered.

They held hands and Sugarfoot prayed:

Eternal, God, thank you for being faithful through all generations. Thank you for the very breath we breathe and for all creation. Lord, you know what's going on tonight, and you know our hearts are heavy. We don't know what we're gonna find when we get to Atlanta. But we do know that it's in your hands. Strengthen this family, this mother, this father, this sister, and me, this friend. Let ours be the hands that pull him back from the jaws of death. Don't let this be the end for him, Lord. We don't know why this came about. We don't know why this evil was visited upon him. But we do know that with your help, he can overcome it and be a better man. We ask you to step in and give him that chance. Guide the doctors' hands that they may bring the medical healing that you have put in the earth for our benefit. Finally, give us traveling graces that we may reach our destination safe-ly. These blessing we humbly ask in your son, Jesus's name, a-men."

Sugarfoot felt the tears of the family. Sherri Lynn said, "This is the worst thing that's ever happened to our family. We're so thankful that you're here. I don't know what we would've done without you tonight."

Liddy's agreement came as a pained mumble.

"I'm honored to be here," he said. "Ivan is my friend, and I want to learn first-hand what the situation is."

Deacon Goines carefully locked up his house and had the presence of mind to make sure

Trapp had food and water. He called Herbert Edmund and told him what'd happened. He promised to check on the farm. Then they packed into Deacon Goines's prized Pontiac and headed for the east bound interstate highway. Hoping for a miracle, they prayed all the way to Georgia Medical Center.

Part Two

Chapter Fifteen

During morning meditation, Jericho extolled the magnificence of God and thanked him for his tender mercies. Then she petitioned him for strength. Only God could keep her from going off on Janelle for bringing Eddie Simpson and a White man she knew nothing about into her home.

It was a scandal, the kind of thing she talked about with her best friend, Bobbie Sue Carter. But Bobbie Sue had gone to Cincinnati to be with her baby sister, Cindy. She was having her first baby, and since their mother was dead, Bobbie Sue felt it her duty to go and support her.

The day after her visitors arrived, Jericho had moved back into her house in Hillside. Eddie and Jeremy were assigned to Janelle and Temeka's bedroom, and Janelle slept with her, which vexed Jericho.

She hated that her privacy was gone. She couldn't walk through the house with no clothes on, talking to the Lord, shouting his praises, and glorifying his name. She couldn't drop to her knees and repent of her sins, seen and unseen. The only time she felt free was when she was in her study at the church, cleaning up Dr. Nielsen's office, or taking inventory at the Holiday Inn.

It'd been two weeks and they'd made themselves at home. But for Jericho, the atmosphere was charged. Getting up every morning and tiptoeing around strangers put her at odds with the day. So she walked around grumbling under her breath and swallowing back questions. The main answer she wanted was, "When are y'all leaving?"

But Janelle was on cloud nine. She flounced around

laughing and talking as if having two strange men in the house was the most natural thing in the world. And she worshipped Eddie. Everything was "daddy this and daddy that."

Jericho felt like telling her a few things about "daddy." But seeing Janelle so happy, she didn't have the heart to do it.

She thought, "Eddie Simpson is playing me for a fool, again. He knows he ain't got no business in my house. When we were together, he treated me like dirt. If he had any decency, he'd be ashamed to show his face."

She wrung her hands but felt helpless. The more helpless she felt, the madder she got. "He's taking advantage of my child," she thought.

Recognizing this, she decided to be as nasty to him as she could be in hopes he'd see that he wasn't welcome and leave.

But Eddie knew he was on a slippery slope. Every chance he got, he apologized for his clumsiness and thanked her for tolerating him.

"I really 'preciate you letting me stay here, Candy," he said after she'd insulted him a number of times. "I was scared you were gon throw me out that first night. I realize things didn't turn out good between me and you, but I'm a changed man."

"You can't help but be changed with only one leg," she snapped.

He tried to help out with household chores, but he didn't know how to do anything. He'd broken several dishes and burnt up so much food that she'd banned him from the kitchen.

"You need a peg leg or a wheelchair so you ain't in the

way all the time," she said one day after almost knocking him down. She expected him to comeback with a smart remark. But in his humbled state, all he said was, "I'm sorry. I have an artificial leg, but it's being readjusted. It should come in the mail any day."

So Eddie Simpson was one story; Jeremy Mulligan was another. Jericho didn't know how to talk to him. He was a visitor and a stranger. He was also somebody's child and a guest in her home. So she tried to treat him like she'd want a stranger to treat her child.

"What do you think of America?" She asked one morning at breakfast.

Janelle butted in before he could answer. She said, "He thinks America is great. He's wanted to come here for a long time. He used to dream about it. And now that he's here, he's just taking everything in."

Jericho smirked and said, "I hope he didn't lose his tongue along the way."

"I'm sorry," Janelle apologized. "It's just that his take on America is entirely different than mine."

"I wonder why?" Jericho snorted.

Not catching the hint, Janelle said, "England's small and there's a shared culture among the people. Everybody's nice and polite; hardly anybody is rude. America is big and diverse with all kinds of cultures and it seems that everybody's rude. But," she sneered, "they're at least ten years behind us in just about everything."

Jericho looked from Jeremy to Janelle, still wondering why she wouldn't let him speak for himself. Observing her, Jeremy smiled and said, "She's right. I'm blown away by the size and the diversity of people in this country."

Jericho liked him. He had an ease and innocence about him that she found refreshing. Were it not for his blond hair and blue eyes, she'd have forgotten he was White and looked upon him as simply a nice person.

But he *was* White and this *was* Sipsey. There was no denying that his living in her house was taboo. Likewise, she was tired of pretending that his relationship with Janelle was anything but that, or that she approved of it. And now she wondered how long he planned to stay and whether or not he needed to get back to a job.

Yet nothing seemed to be bothering them. He and Eddie had established a morning routine. They got up early and went out on the back porch to drink coffee and talk. To her surprise, Jeremy made himself useful. He took out the garbage and cleaned the yard of trash every day. After she went to bed, he mopped the floors. When she mentioned that her shrubs needed pruning, he got up early one morning and pruned them.

"You're pretty good at that," Jericho remarked.

"Thanks. *Me Mom* taught me yard work," he said. "She'd love the flowers."

He seemed comfortable in the neighborhood, but his presence didn't go unnoticed. Neighbors passing by stared rudely and grumbled under their breaths. "Who is that White man at Sweetberry's house?" they asked.

One day, as he tended the shrubs, he tried to engage a group of young women in conversation. They rolled their eyes and kept on walking.

Jericho was peeping out the window and witnessed the scene. "That's just a taste of what you gon get married to her," she scoffed.

She had some questions for Janelle. For one, she wanted to know how long she planned to lug Eddie Simpson around. Surely she knew he was baggage she didn't need. He was old, sick, and probably broke. And though she understood Janelle feeling sorry for him, he hadn't earned the right to be considered her family. And he certainly wasn't Jericho's. So what made him think it was alright to intrude into their lives?

And while she was at it, why hadn't she mentioned anything about a boyfriend let alone a fiancé in her letters? How long had she even known Jeremy? She felt Janelle was moving too fast but didn't know how to put it into words.

As for Jeremy, if he wanted to marry her daughter, why he hadn't come to her and properly asked for her hand. Wasn't that how it was done? "I guess my opinion don't matter," she sniffed.

Chapter Sixteen

April arrived with rain showers and thunderstorms. The men were forced inside. In the cramped space, Eddie's handicap became more pronounced. He kept knocking things over and breaking them. After downing a shelf of bric-a-bracs, Jericho lost her temper. "You need to get somewhere and sit down! It's too *tight* in here!"

The men retreated to the bedroom and designated it their rainy day hangout. Janelle stayed out of the way as well, writing in her journal or typing letters at the kitchen table.

One rainy afternoon, as Jericho prepared dinner, she watched as Janelle's fingers darted along the keyword.

"What you doing? It looks important."

Janelle stopped typing and looked at Jericho. "I'm writing to charity organizations for donations for the clinic. "Mama," she explained, "I've learned so much in my travels. It's hard for us to believe, but there're a lot of wealthy people in this country. And many of them are looking for worthy causes to give money to."

It occurred to Jericho to warn her not to mention those wealthy people to Eddie. He'd find a way to get their money into his hands. She wasn't at all convinced that he'd changed and thought him quite capable of running a scam.

But she kept it positive. She said, "Yours is a worthy cause, and it's mighty brave of you to ask them for money."

"Oh, I have no problem asking for it," she admitted. "Matter of fact I'm good at it. You should hear me. I had a room full of people crying when I told how Miss Lizzie Lee suffered from breast cancer and didn't get any treatment. I also talked about how my Great-Grandma Beulah died of kidney poisoning. It's something that could be cured with antibiotics today." She shrugged. "I can tell it and not even have to lie."

Jericho laughed, imagining the serious looking Janelle shaking sympathetic rich people down for money by telling the truth.

This was her favorite side of Janelle, the one that cared about others and tried to do something about it. It was the other Janelle that disturbed her; the one that brought strangers home and treated them like family and expected her to do so too.

She coped with the disruption at home by going to work early and staying late. She

suspected that they were relieved to have a break from her too. Nevertheless, when she got

home in the evenings, the house was clean, the men were out of the way, and Janelle had started

dinner.

One evening, Jeremy praised her cooking then gently inquired about the history of the area. "I don't mean to be intrusive," he said, "but I'd like to know what has been handed down to you from your slave *uncestors.*"

Jericho found the question remarkable. Her ancestors had been slaves in three counties in Alabama and one in Mississippi. All her life, she'd traveled between the states. Yet, no White person had ever asked her about anything handed down from her slave ancestors. It took this White man, a foreigner from thousands of miles away, to even acknowledge that the slaves existed.

She began talking, pointing out local settlements that had been plantations. "When I was a girl, there were people in town that'd lived on those plantations," she said. "They used to tell awful stories about things that happened to them."

With a look of awe, Jeremy grabbed his journal. He said, "If you don't mind, I'd like to write down what you say."

The readiness with which he flipped through pages surprised Jericho. "What exactly do you want to know?" she asked.

His face beamed with curiosity. He said, "I've heard a lot about the songs they sang and their meanings. I'm interested in knowing how they related to the hardships they were going through."

"You heard right," she nodded. "They couldn't speak freely, so they had to figure out ways to communicate with each other without rousing suspicion. The songs were a way of passing on messages about meetings, runaways, or if somebody was being sold away. The songs were their newspapers."

"I think I get it," he said eagerly, "but can you give me an example?"

Jericho had to think about it. She'd never thought about the spirituals as being something to study. For her, they were songs from that dreadful period of time when her people were in bondage. When she was in school they sang them during "Negro History Week." It was a tribute to their struggle and their strength.

"I have some favorites," she acknowledged. "*Over My Head*," is one of them. It's a song that speaks of faith." She looked thoughtful. "I always imagine them working in those hot cotton fields, tired and discouraged. I think they envisioned God looking down on them and seeing their struggle. Music was their way of connecting with him and letting him know that they had faith that he would deliver them."

She sang:

Over my head, I hear music in the air;
Over my head, I hear music in the air;
Over my head, I hear music in the air;
There must be a God somewhere.

She explained, "They added verses to describe the moment. They might say *I see Jesus in the air,* or if the overseer wasn't around, they'd say, *I feel freedom in the air.'* But something was always going on in the air,"

"Incredible!" he declared. "So 'music in the air' was their representation of God?" He shook his head. "It speaks to a deep, sort of, unique intelligence. It was as if the experience was a musical, although a tragic one."

"I've never thought of it that way but I guess you're right," Jericho acknowledged.

"I *con't* wrap my mind around the horror of it, but I admire their fortitude and incredible creativity."

Janelle jumped in. "I know about the spirituals and the hardships they represent. Sometimes when I get discouraged and think about giving up, I think about them. I

say to myself, if they could make it through what they went through, I can get through this. They let me know I have to keep trying."

Eddie had sat as a silent spectator. Finally, he said, "I grew up hearing stories about the rice and indigo workers.

They were some of the first slaves that were brought to this continent.

I'm kin to the Geechee people that live off the Sea Islands of South Carolina," he revealed. "They came from the tribe of the Mendes people in West Africa. They still speak in that language. I used to love to hear my Uncle Isaac tell Bruh' Rabbit and Shine stories."

"Really, daddy?" Janelle's ears perked up.

Eddie nodded. "They made up stories about everything; ghosts, hants, talking animals, even talking trees." He laughed. "Anansi was a spider and he was always up to something. He was funny and smart."

His eyes watered. He said, "The used to tell how the slaves got together on Saturday nights. They say they'd sing, tell jokes, and sometimes they'd have a buck dance contest." He sighed sadly.

"It seems like they had some good times, even in bondage," said Janelle.

Yes," he replied. "All they had was each other, but they made the best of that very bad situation."

"And they were gifted," Janelle maintained. "My college roommate did a study of American folktales. She learned that many of the stories we think Europeans created actually come out of the African storytelling tradition. Bruh Rabbit, Aesop, and Uncle Remus stories originated in Africa."

"They brought other things to this country too," Eddie said. "The Geechee women still weave the sweet grass baskets. They were taught that knowledge back in Africa and

they didn't forget it. They still teach it to the young girls coming up."

"They weave them in the public square?" asked Jeremy.

"Yes. Any day of the week, you can go to the City Market in Charleston and see them sitting together weaving their baskets."

Suddenly, Eddie became quiet. He said, "I couldn't wait to get away from there. I thought it was the worst place on earth. I wanted to live in the city, be a star." He sighed sadly. "Now I realize what a wonderful place it was."

After a pause, he said, "I wanna sing one of my favorite songs. The slaves sang it when

somebody was being sold away. There would be sadness all around because they knew they might never see each other again. So they put their feelings into a song."

He sang:

Fare the well, (fare the well),
Fare the well, (fare the well),
If I never, never you see anymore,
Fare the well, (fare the well),
Fare the well.....
I'll meet you on the other shore.

He said, "The worst time was when families were being broken up.The ones that weren't being sold knew their time could come any day. So they stood in a circle and laid hands on each other. And they sang:"

Live the life (live the life,
Live the life (live the life),
If I never, never see you anymore,
Live the life (live the life),
Live the life......
I'll meet you on the other shore.

As he sang, Jericho wiped back tears. She recalled hearing the song at church when she was a child. It was one of the songs that stirred up powerful emotions. Men would sit on their pews with their face in their hands and rock back and forth. Their bodies would shake with grief. The women would scream and shout and call on the Lord. Sometimes the singing and crying would go on for so long that she feared the service would never end. And even as they left the church, they'd still be crying.

"I had no idea what that song meant," she said.

When Eddie finished, he was still sniffling. Jericho handed him some tissues. Jeremy was

red-faced with embarrassment. He said, "That was *fontastic*! I think I started something, and I

didn't mean to . . ."

But Janelle had jumped up and rushed across the room. She grabbed Eddie in a hug and said, "Daddy," I didn't know you could sing like that!"

Jericho was also overcome with emotion. She said, "That was beautiful, Eddie!"

It was the first time since he'd been there that she'd felt anything but contempt for him.

"Well," she said, "I guess it's true that the Lord works in mysterious ways his wonders to perform. Who would've thought you could bring the Holy Ghost down like that? Maybe the Lord can find some use for you after all."

Chapter Seventeen

On the day that Eddie's leg arrived, Janelle and Jeremy drove to Lancaster. Being left alone with him was Jericho's biggest concern. Eddie had a way of bringing up the past when she least expected it. It upset her and left her feeling as if nothing meaningful had happened in her life since she last saw him.

Today, she had no intention of reliving her past. She didn't want to talk about who she was before, with, or after him. Her life was her business. So she kept as much distance between them as she could.

But he didn't cooperate. No sooner had she gone to the sink to wash dishes than he began hobbling around the sitting room. She wondered why he didn't put his leg on. But she didn't ask for fear he'd start a conversation.

The next thing she knew, he'd hopped into the kitchen. He went to the refrigerator and got his insulin then hopped back into the sitting room. As he injected himself, he gave a deep grunt. Minutes later, he was bringing the insulin back to the refrigerator.

By now, he was out of breath. "Now I got to go to the bedroom to get my blood pressure medicine," he spoke to himself. "Janelle wrote me a new prescription."

Jericho wasn't aware that Janelle had written him a new prescription, and she wondered

why. As he hobbled back to the sitting room, he muttered, "Thank you Lord for your grace and mercy."

She grunted, trying to blot out the effort it had taken just to get his medicine. And she was glad when he got situated and sat down.

Since they were alone, it occurred to her that Eddie could answer some questions about Janelle. She'd like to know when Janelle started driving and where she'd got the money to buy a car. She also wanted to know what the sleeping arrangements were between her and Jeremy in New York City. But she didn't dare ask. She didn't want him to think that the two of them had anything in common.

Janelle and Jeremy came back in the late afternoon with a wheel chair and a television set. Jericho objected, thinking the television set was an unnecessary extravagance. She said, "How much did that television cost?"

"It was on sale," she hastily replied.

Without scorning Jericho for being backwards, Janelle said "Mama, it's time you came into the Twentieth Century. Everybody has a television set. And you like watching television. Remember how we used to go next door and watch television on Friday nights? Remember how Temeka used to cry when we had to leave?"

Jericho did remember and didn't say any more about it.

******

Knowing the nature of town gossip, she'd been wondering how long it'd be before tongues started wagging about Janelle. Walking the streets, she realized the time had come. The swords were drawn and they were ready for battle.

A nasty word surfaced from Maggie Fowler, a longtime enemy of Jericho's. According to

rumor, she'd said, "White man, blue man, green man, gold man, what's the difference? And

what do y'all expect of Janelle? She's Sweetberry's

daughter, ain't she? Is anybody ever

surprised at what Sweetberry do? The apple don't fall far from the tree."

It bothered Jericho that people were talking about her child, and she waited for the right time to bring it up. Talking sense into her wasn't going to be easy. Janelle's head was in the clouds and she either ignored the gossip or thought it didn't matter. She only seemed concerned about opening the clinic and getting married.

"She's so beautiful," Jericho studied her as she hung clothes on the line one breezy afternoon. Her brown skin glowed as her dark hair blew in the wind. There wasn't a blemish on her body or character. "Her life would be perfect if she wasn't hauling those freeloading men around," Jericho fumed.

Later in the week, she got up early to fix breakfast before going to work. She was still wondering what to say when Janelle bounced into the kitchen smiling as if she hadn't a care in the world. Jericho had had enough of her careless attitude and decided that this was the right time to have the talk.

But before she could say anything, Janelle said, "Mama, I want to talk to you about something."

"Good morning, daughter," Jericho spoke coolly, "I wanna talk to you too."

"Well," Janelle tittered, pouring herself a cup of coffee. "I'll go first. Jeremy and I want to get married in November. I'll need your help with the planning, so put it on your agenda. Also," she added, "we're going to Washington in two weeks to meet with the Department of Health and Medical Services. They say I can begin setting up the clinic as soon as my residency is over."

She sat down at the table and blew across the hot coffee. "I'm so excited about this clinic. It's going to make all the difference in the treatment of disease in this county, especially diabetes and heart disease. These are problems that we Colored people suffer from in much higher numbers than Whites. With proper preventative measures, they can be reduced or eliminated altogether."

"That's all good," Jericho said warmly. "We do need a clinic. And it sounds like you know what you're talking about."

"I believe I do, but," she happily chatted. "I've got so much to do. Finishing my residency, opening the clinic, getting married, then setting up a house . . . it's gonna be crazy!" she said gleefully.

"Where are you and Jeremy gon stay once you're married?" Jericho inquired.

"Oh, that's what I wanted to tell you," she said eagerly. "We went to see Tameka when we were in Lancaster. She says we can rent Josiah's house. We checked it out yesterday. It's dusty and musty from being shut up so long, but it's a very nice house. All it needs is a good

cleaning and a little paint."

Jericho was taking a carton of eggs out of the refrigerator. Hearing this, she almost

dropped the carton. Heat began forming in her gut and spread throughout her body. For a minute she couldn't speak, and when she did, it was with foam and venom.

She said, "Janelle, I've been trying to be patient with you. Ever since you got here, I've prayed that you would come to your senses. But I see now you don't have any. So,

I'm done tiptoeing around you."

"Mama, what're you talking about?" she cried.

"I'm talking about you and these foolish notions you have. You ain't moving into Josiah's house with that White man."

Janelle bristled. "But Tameka said we could, and it's her house."

"I don't care *whose* house it is," Jericho snapped back. "You ain't moving in it with no White man."

"Mama, I can't believe you said that," her voice broke in anguish. "My fiancé's name is Jeremy, and I hoped you'd understand."

"Understand *what*? Her voice rose higher. "What do you want me to understand?"

Janelle flinched. "I knew you would have a problem with Jeremy. But I thought after you got to know him you'd see what a nice person he is."

"He *is* nice. But this ain't got nothing to do with him being nice. It's plenty nice White folks right here in Sispey. But so what? Nice White folks don't count for nothing where Colored folks are concerned. They ain't never stopped a White mob from taking a Colored man out, beating him, and leaving him for dead. Where're your senses?" she yelled. "And what do you know about this man? Where'd he come from?"

"I met him in England."

"England? And you brought him back here to Sipsey? In other words, you're responsible

for him, is that what you're saying?"

"Not technically. He's here on a visitor's visa."

"But he's visiting you," she argued. "Who else do he

know in the United States."

"He's here with me, but we're gonna get married, and he'll become a citizen."

"So you went overseas and found a White man to take care of?"

"No, Mama," she said calmly. "I went overseas to study, and to learn, and to experience

other people and their cultures. I met Jeremy and we fell in love. He's not looking for me

to take care of him. He'll get a job."

"Doing what?" She shouted. "What kind of job is he gon get?"

"Writing songs. He's a lyricist."

"A what?"

"A lyricist. He writes words to music. He told you before he's interested in American Negro music."

Jericho laughed. "Janelle, do you know how stupid that sounds?"

"Why, Mama? American Negro Music is highly celebrated. It's one of the most recognized forms of music in the world."

"But it's for Negroes!" she cried. "Not him! I'm sure you're the only Negro he knows. Just tell me this; how in the hell is he gon write songs about people that he don't know nothing about?"

"Mama, that's so narrow-minded. I've never thought you were intolerant or bigoted, and neither is Jeremy. He doesn't see color. The British are very civilized people, and they don't look down on you because of your skin color. They're very accepting."

"So you're counting on him not being able to see your

skin color?"

"That's not what I mean. I mean it doesn't matter."

"Do you really believe that?"

"I want to believe it," she said desperately.

Many thoughts went through Jericho's head. On days like this, she wished she'd stayed crazy. That way, she wouldn't have to deal with a delusional daughter who refused to see things for what they were.

She considered grabbing a belt and whipping her but knew the thought was absurd. Her

daughter was innocent; had always looked on the brighter side of life and given everybody the benefit of the doubt. She believed in fairy tales and happy endings and thought she could wish the world into a happy place.

And it was Jericho's fault. She'd neglected to present the world as it really was. In her eagerness to push her daughters towards success, she'd taught them that they could be anything, do anything they wanted. It was that kind of teaching that had convinced Janelle that she could live happily ever after with a White man in Potoama County.

She yielded her position. "Janelle, you're a grown woman now. You've done well in your schooling, and you've carried yourself well. I've done what I could for you, and I want you to be happy. If you think you can be happy with this man, go ahead and marry him. But you can't do it here."

"Why?" she exclaimed. "This is my home. I want to be married here among my family and friends. I'm getting married at First Macedonia," she said stubbornly.

Jericho shook her head disbelievingly. She said, "Janelle, maybe you should've gone to

law school instead of medical school. I'm surprised you

don't know this, but it's against the law for Colored and White to marry in Alabama."

"What?" she screamed, strangling on her coffee. She coughed so violently that it took a minute for her throat to clear. She said, "Interracial marriage isn't legal in Alabama? Mama, are you serious?"

"Very serious. I doubt they'd even give you a license at the courthouse. And if you go down this road, you gon find that a lot of things you thought were legal ain't. You're about to make your life so much harder than it has to be."

Janelle was bewildered. "I don't understand. People are people. What difference does it

make what color you are?"

"It's make a lot a difference to the ones that care about it." Then, seeing how hurt she was, Jericho quietly repented. "I'm sorry, Janelle."

"For what? It's not your fault."

"I'm sorry for not educating you to the facts of life. I never explained segregation and the Jim Crow Laws of the south to you because I didn't think I had to. Most Negroes figure it out on their own." She looked thoughtful. "I don't want to paint a dark picture of the world, but it's not always a fair place. There're roadblocks for Colored people that'll stop you from doing a lot of the things that you want to do."

"But things are changing, Mama. Colored people are doing all kinds of marvelous things. You taught me and Temeka that we were a strong race of people and that God had blessed us with strength, faith and gifts that other people don't have. I believe that. We're also very competitive. Nobody can hold us back."

Jericho was thankful that she remembered her teachings,

and she spoke in a way that showed she grasped the gravity of the problem. But she still didn't seem to realize that Negroes hadn't overcome yet.

"Things might be changing but not that much," Jericho maintained. "And it's gon be quite some time before the change you want to see comes to Sipsey."

Janelle was disheartened by Jericho's acceptance of injustice. This wasn't the feisty Sweetberry of her childhood. She wanted to see that mother, the tough, dogged Sweetberry;

the one that believed all things were possible. She wanted the mother that would go to bat for her and stand up to any bully that tried to hold her back.

"Mama, I just wish you understood."

"What is it that you want me to understand?" she asked.

"I want you to understand," her voice trailed off tearfully.

Jericho said, "What I understand is that you've fallen in love with the wrong man. I did that too one time. I fell in love with the man you're calling daddy. It was the worst mistake of my life, and I have the scars to prove it."

"Mama, please, have a little faith."

"I'm speaking from experience. It's what living in the world has taught me. True enough things are better now than they were for the generations that came before you. But Colored and White people are not equal in this country. We never have been. From the very beginning, there's been a dividing line between us and it's still there. And marrying one?" She blew out loudly. "I've never been married, but I think it's hard enough being married to your own kind let alone somebody from another race. And when this kind of stuff hits the fan, it's the Colored person that suffers the most."

"But, Mama, I need your support," she pled tearfully.

"This ain't my fight," Jericho said sternly. "And I don't think it's worthy of *you*. I raised you and Temeka to believe that you're as good as anybody. And I'd fight anybody that said you weren't. But it wasn't for this, and I'd spit on my own grave before I fought for your right to marry a White man."

Janelle's dejected expression showed that she understood that if she pursued this path, she was on her own.

Jericho said, "I'll respect whatever decision you make. Go on and marry your White man, but do it where it's legal."

Jericho suddenly felt hollow and made the decision not to cook breakfast after all. She said, "I've got to get ready for work. If y'all want to eat, you can cook yourselves." She started out of the kitchen then turned back around. "Make sure you get all of Eddie's stuff when you leave. Take him away from here and don't bring him back."

Janelle nodded absently.

"And one other thing," she said, "don't say nothing else to Temeka about moving into Josiah's house. I've put her through enough, and I don't want her involved in another scandal. Besides, it ain't her job to provide you and your man with somewhere to stay."

Chapter Eighteen

After breakfast, Janelle went to the back porch and announced that she was going downtown. Eddie was entertaining Jeremy with tales of growing up in South Carolina.

"We used to go swimming butt naked in them muddy creeks," he laughed. "God was with us 'cause nobody ever got snake bit and it was snakes all over them woods."

Then he talked about gorging on his granddaddy's low country boil. "Ain't nothing like a spread of shrimp and crab legs with new potatoes and corn-on-the-cob dipped in butter with a little garlic salt." He smacked his lips. "That's good eating."

Janelle stood in the doorway and listened, delighting in the sound of his voice. She said, "I'm gonna walk downtown. I. . . I'll be back in a few minutes."

The hesitation in her voice suggested she wanted to go alone.

Her words drifted around the house to Jericho who was eavesdropping from her bedroom window. She finished buttoning her uniform and rushed to the back porch.

"Janelle," she commanded. "Take your boyfriend with you."

Janelle looked impatient. She said, "He was gonna stay here with daddy."

"Nope, take him with you. Take him downtown and introduce him to your friend, Tom Jenks. Tell him y'all gon get married."

Janelle's lips quivered as they always did when she was anxious. She breathed unevenly and Jericho saw the pleading look in her eyes. She needed this time alone to think without distraction. Jericho saw her desperation but refused to let her off the hook. "Take him with you," she insisted.

Janelle pasted on a quick smile. "Let's go, Jeremy."

He said good day to Eddie and followed her.

When they were gone, Jericho started back in the house. Eddie said, "Candy, can you sit here and talk with me for a minute?"

"I'm late for work," she said urgently, but sat down opposite him.

"I'll be quick," he promised.

She eyed him suspiciously. Observing her, he realized that, in spite of everything she was doing to disguise it, Jericho was still a beautiful woman. He smiled and said, "Janelle is a marvelous young lady?"

"Yes, she is." She'd finally accepted that Eddie and Janelle had formed a special bond. She didn't like it but knew it wouldn't be wise to challenge it.

He confessed. "I don't deserve a daughter like her." He paused. "I don't think you know this, but she went out of her way to find me. When she came to the home where I was living and told me she was my daughter, I didn't believe her. I thought she was a hustler running a scam. I asked her what she wanted from me and she said she didn't want nothing; said she was studying to be a doctor and was doing her internship at a hospital in the South Bronx."

Jericho took issue with the narrative. "Why didn't you believe her?" she asked. He shrugged remorsefully. "You have to remember the kind of life I'd lived. I'd hustled and conned my way from the time I was a teenager. I didn't trust anybody. To tell you the truth, I didn't want to believe her. Or maybe I was scared to believe her. I just wanted to sit there like a coward and lick my wounds. I told the staff not to admit her anymore."

"What changed your mind?"

"She wouldn't give up," he answered. "One day she brought her birth certificate. It had your name on it and that convinced me that she was really my daughter."

"How did she find you?"

"She went through one of them lost families' agencies. I guess you told her enough about me that they were able to find me. I thank you for that," he said. "She's been my life-line. I was sick and all alone in the world, and she nursed me back to life. Right from the beginning, she treated me like family. And she told me something that broke my heart. She said all her life she'd prayed that I'd come and find y'all. She said, 'you're my daddy, and I'm gon take care of you.' That tore me up inside," he pointed to his chest. "To hear your child that you ain't never done nothing for, not even thought about that much, come to you with so much love in her heart; that did something to me."

"And naturally you took advantage of it."

Eddie heaved a sarcastic grunt but stayed on point. "No-body would've known that I'd never laid eyes on her be-fore." He looked earnestly at her and said, "She is as decent a human being as I've ever seen. You done a good job with her."

He didn't wait for her to thank him but proceeded to give his opinion concerning Janelle and Jeremy. He said, "You oughta cut them some slack. They're young. They don't see the world like we do. They think they can make a marriage work."

"Well they gon find out different," Jericho stated firmly. "They gon find out that everything they thought was hard before is gon get ten times harder. And you should be ashamed of yourself indulging them in this. You know a marriage between them ain't gon work. It's hard enough being in a mixed marriage in a place like New York City where everything goes. But she wants to live with him here. Do you realize how much trouble that would cause? And it wouldn't only be trouble for them; it'd be trouble for me and my other daughter too. If Colored and White could live together so easily, we wouldn't have half the problems in this world that we have."

Eddie grimaced. "You're probably right, but I don't talk against it. If they think they can make it work, it's not for me or you to tell them it can't."

She shot him a hateful look. It occurred to her to inform him that he didn't have a right to an opinion. But she restrained herself. "For your information," she spat, "I haven't told them it can or can't work. I raised her to believe she could do anything she wanted to do. She's good, and she believes in the goodness of people. But I don't!"

"You *are* bitter, aren't you?"

"You could call it that, but I call it life. Janelle is young. Her whole life is ahead of her. There're all kinds of bumps in the road, but the ones you hit the hardest are the ones you put there yourself. I have not and will not tell her how to live her life. But I have every right to tell her how I feel about it."

With that, she got up and went back into the house.

******

Janelle had left Sipsey with the good will of the people and an excellent reputation. She was remembered as a peacemaker by her classmates and studious and kind by her teachers. As for the elders at First Macedonia, they called her an angel; said she was obedient and willing to do whatever they asked of her.

But since she'd been back, her name was being dragged through the mud. The wrath of the wounded came against her and Negroes began calling her a 'sellout.'

"Who do she think she is?" asked Mary Newlins, "bringing a White man to this town like she's Miss Godrock. 'Just done got besides herself."

So now, instead of being a modern woman with a mind of her own, she was a pariah, the scorned recipient of her community's anger.

And it was personal. The Negroes' abhorrence for interracial relations began with stories of sexual abuse of slave women by White men over a hundred years ago. The stories were validated by the relentless lightening of skin tones in their race. In their minds, mixing with a White man was the lowest thing a Colored woman could do.

Janelle knowledge of their dark history was vague, and she didn't comprehend the depth of it. In her mind, it happened so long ago that it shouldn't factor into their present day decisions. So she entered downtown Sipsey on top of the world. She was radiant in a sleeveless black blouse and checkered pedal pushers. Her hair was twisted into a thick braid and tucked under in the back, and her face glowed with happiness.

Main Street was bustling with people. Smiles and greetings rang throughout. It was this feeling of warmth and friendliness that she wanted Jeremy to experience. And she wanted people to meet her handsome fiancé and hear his charming accent. She'd never met anyone like him and neither had they.

Their first stop was Jenks Department Store. She'd always liked Tom Jenks and visited the store whenever she came home. Other Negroes couldn't stand him. Their complaint was that he was prejudiced and only cared for Negroes that played the fool.

He was talking to Manny Fulgham and noticed their reflection when they walked through the door. Tom Jenks had probably heard about the couple just as everybody else in town had. And he seemed ready to let them know just how he felt about them.

He refused to greet them as incoming customers. Instead, he turned his back and talked to Manny who was repairing the broken door of the soft drink machine.

Janelle cleared her throat to get his attention. He heard but ignored her, making a big deal out of helping Manny. When Manny finished, he nodded politely towards the couple and limped away.

Tom Jenks still wouldn't turn around.

They waited as he opened and closed the door over and over again as if testing Manny's work. "This is my favorite store," Janelle said enthusiastically. "When I was a kid, I came here every day after school to buy candy."

This tidbit was shared to get Tom Jenks's to turn around and acknowledge them. She chattered on, saying nice things about him and the store, but his back was a stiff board with a cool breeze oozing from it.

He finished inspecting the door. But instead of greeting

them, he turned his attention to the cigarette case. Moving packs around, he started humming some offbeat tune.

The casual Negro could've interpreted his actions. It was the rage of a White man seeing his greatest fear come true; a Negro woman breezing into his store with her White boyfriend acting as if it was the most natural thing in the world. And the boyfriend standing idly by behaving as if she was right.

"Hi, Mr. Jenks, how are you today?" Janelle spoke sweetly.

He waited before turning around. When he did, he looked past her and stared at Jeremy.

"Can I help you?" His cold tone was meant as chastisement to Jeremy for betraying his race.

Jeremy shrugged and gestured towards Janelle. Tom Jenks still wouldn't look at her but continued glaring at him. The uneasy moment was so obvious that Janelle shifted her weight and began shaking. Her heart sank and her eyes blinked with hurt. Yet she waited, hoping that the merchant she'd known since childhood would recognize her as an old friend and begin chatting with her like he used to do.

Like wax figured caricatures of themselves, they looked past each other. Memories of him suddenly came back to her. She knew him when his hair, now peppered with gray, was jet black, and she remembered his pudgy stomach being flat.

She also recalled rushing into the store after school and heading for the glassed in candy case. Joyfully, she'd choose what bubble gum and penny candy she wanted. Sometimes she'd only have pennies, and he'd stand there and watch her count out the correct amount. In her merry voice, she'd declare her love for banana taffy and chocolate kisses. Sometimes he'd give her two for one. To her, he was a friend, and she treated him with the same respect she did the saints at First Macedonia.

It was only now that she realized Tom Jenks was a short, mean, little man.

The voice in her head whispered that this was the man Negroes, including her mother, had always known.

She stood there stubbornly waiting for him to ask if he could help her. Her heart pleaded, begged him to look at her. He refused, as determined not to acknowledge her as she was for him to do so.

The standoff ended when the door swung open and a Colored woman burst inside. Tom Jenks looked relieved to finally be rescued from the impudent Negro girl expecting him to dignify her.

"Howdy, Mabel," he said to the stout woman.

Ignoring the interracial couple, Mabel Higgins came towards the merchant baring teeth and flashing a buoyant smile. "Morning, Mr. Tom," she replied.

"What can I do for you?"

She was a pleasant, genteel woman, housemaid to the President of the First National Bank. She was also Mary Newlins' half-sister. She was known for her extravagant taste in clothes and her beautifully decorated house. She and Mary didn't get along well because Mary said she cared too much about material things.

Mabel cried, "Mr. Tom, I wanna put one of them chenille bedspreads you got in the front window on layaway. I want the pink one with the curtains to match."

"Well, we can do that," he smiled, escorting her to the back of the store. They chatted about practically nothing, but their voices filled the room.

"Here we go," he said, taking the spread down from a high shelf.

Janelle heaved in anguish, knowing that any other time Mabel Higgins would've walked herself to the back of the store, gotten the spread, and brought it to the counter to be written up.

Tom Jenks notwithstanding, it upset her that Mabel Higgins was part of his charade.

With her pride hurting, they left the store. This hadn't gone as she'd expected. She was ashamed of the merchant and embarrassed for her fiancé to see her so disrespected in her hometown. Recovering her posture, she pointed to etchings in the sidewalk. "We used to play hopscotch in these squares," she said and did 1,1, 2, hops in the squares.

Jeremy grabbed her hand as if to say it was alright, but she pulled away, refusing to acknowledge what'd happened. "Sipsey is a great place to live," she said airily, not wanting him

to think poorly of it. "It just takes time for people to accept things they're not used to. It'll be alright."

But they quickly discovered that Tom Jenks's reaction to them wasn't the exception. The stares of Sipsey shoppers became sneers as they tried to put up a good front. A large White man followed them, deriding them with insults. "What you doing walking down the street with that Nigger?" he barked to Jeremy. "We don't do that around here."

Jeremy ignored him but asked about the literacy level in the county.

Hoping for a better outcome, they headed for Brane's Department Store.

Inside, they were met with the bitter stares of Dora Street and Lettie Cleveland, Miss Emma Brane's Colored employees. Lettie was a coward who knew how to wiggle out of a tricky situation. Speaking politely, she rushed past them. Then she looked back, winked at Dora, and made a mad dash for the storage room.

Dora, known for being rude, made no effort to avoid them. She stood in a middle aisle with her hands propped up on a broom. A toothpick stuck out of the corner of her mouth. Her sneering nose was a sign of how she felt.

Janelle smiled and waved at her. She twisted the toothpick and stared at Janelle as if she didn't know who she was. "Hi, Miss Dora," Janelle spoke sweetly. Dora's cold eyes looked her up and down before stingily nodding her head.

Emma Brane had felt a quickening heartbeat at the sight of the couple. She knew Janelle and had always liked her. She also knew her customers were watching to see how she'd handle the situation.

Panic gripped her. Several Negroes were in there and they were tricky. They pretended not to notice things, but they saw everything. What if she made a misstep and they started

gossiping? Her name would be mud on every Black tongue in the county.

The couple was heading towards her. There was just enough time to sneak to the restroom and leave the mess to her perky young clerk. Then nobody could say she'd been too nice or too nasty to them.

Immediately, she felt a jolt of conscience and knew she couldn't retreat. She was, after all, an astute businesswoman. For years, she'd been the top earning merchant in Potoama

County. This distinction had been earned by extending credit to Negroes, hiring them to work in the store, and treating them with kindness. As a result, they came from all over the county to trade with her. And they were loyal to a fault. Thus, they were the backbone of her business.

She made the snap decision to do the opposite of what Tom Jenks had done. Ignoring the White stranger, she directed all of her attention to Janelle. She asked about medical school, her travels abroad, even about her mother. She said, "Your Mama is so proud of you. Every time she comes in here she's talking about where you are and what you're doing."

"Ohh," Janelle beamed happily, giving the perfectly coiffed brunette a summary of her doings. "I did my internship in New York City, and I'm finishing up my residency there too. It's so big," she gushed, "and everybody's in a hurry."

"I know," Emma Brane smiled generously. "Rayford and I honeymooned in the city many years ago. He loves baseball; we went to three Mets games back to back." She rolled her eyes. "Not very romantic, is it?"

Janelle exclaimed, "Anywhere you go on your honeymoon is romantic. But Miss Emma," she said, "I've also been to Europe. I've seen Paris and the Eiffel Tower, and I spent six months in London."

"How lovely," Emma Brane said sweetly.

They chatted on pleasantly. But when Janelle tried to introduce Jeremy, Emma Brane suddenly called to Dora to put the 'Out to Lunch' sign on the door.

She said, "Does Reed's serve catfish on Wednesdays?"

"No'm," Dora answered, throwing Janelle a dirty look.

"They got meatloaf and smothered chicken today."

"Umm, they both sound good."

The two women got busy chatting about the diner down the street.

Janelle was again flushed with embarrassment. She realized Emma Brane's stunt was a dodge. She no more approved of them than Tom Jenks; she was just smarter about it.

She wished everybody a goody day. As she and Jeremy headed for the door, Dora

stood in front of them like an angry toad. Again, Janelle smiled. Dora opened the door for them to exit and slammed it shut behind them.

Outside, Janelle gave a relieved sigh. But disappointment showed on her face. Never before had she left downtown Sipsey feeling so miserable.

Jeremy didn't say anything until they were on the sidewalk walking home. Then, in his proper British accent, he said, "So this is the wonderful Sipsey?"

Chapter Nineteen

The Potoama County jail wasn't fit for human habitation. It was dank, filthy, and made no made no concession to the dignity of its occupants.

Batch Blaine had been there for six week and his brain still hadn't adjusted to its horror. His 6x8 cell contained an old sink with cold water that dripped so slowly he'd practically given up on washing himself. The toilet was a mere hole in the floor. It was hard to navigate, and smelled so abominably that he was constantly threatening to throw up.

His mother was his only visitor. Dutifully, she made the trip every day. And every day he mourned the same words, "Mama, I didn't do it. You learned me better than that. I wouldn't rob nobody, least of all Mr. Dave Prengle."

Aunt Ginny tenderly held his hand and replied, "I know you didn't, son. The Lord's gon work it out. Just trust him."

But he had no trust. So all he could do was cry.

On Friday and Saturday nights, he could count on companionship from the ranks of rowdy drunks and young Negroes that got into weekend brawls. They didn't have real names but were called by handles such as Punt, Dabble, Sleaze, and Butter Bean.

They crowded the cells, janking, teasing and turning the place into a shameless free-for-all where nothing was too outrageous to be said. On these occasions, Batch folded himself into a knot and pretended he wasn't there.

But they were only there for the weekend, jailed for such small offenses as fighting and disturbing the peace. Some were caged for illegal gambling, and one was there for choking his girlfriend's mama.

They made merry during their stay and after two or three days were bailed out.

Alone again, Batch cried; and cried; and cried. That he, who'd lived his life so carefully, would end up in this predicament was heart breaking. "I tried to do what was right," he moaned, crying himself to sleep each night. "I'm sorry, Mama. I didn't do it. I didn't do it."

He didn't know who to blame. The Prengles were too decent to lie on him. And he was too loyal to blame them for making a mistake. So, with no one else to blame, he blamed himself. And he mourned his sad predicament.

But in the company of the young Negroes, self-pity wasn't allowed. Once, in the middle of the night, he awoke with the pathetic, "I didn't do it, Mama." Butter Bean yelled, "Shut up, Nigga, you know you broke in that sto'."

Other times they mimicked him. "I didn't do it, Mama. I didn't do it."

Sometimes they came as a group. Other times they came in twos or with other hooligans. But he could count on at least one of the originals coming to jail every weekend.

If he'd have allowed himself, Batch might've been amused by them. They weren't disheartened by their deeds. Oddly, they scoffed at them, bragging and making merry over what they'd done as if it was funny.

"Man, I was messing with this married woman and her husband came home and almost caught me in the bed with her," Punt boasted. "I didn't even have time to get my drawls, I heard him come through the front door and I broke for the window. To this day, I don't know how I got

out of that little bitty window. But I squeezed through

and took off. I ran about a mile and a half through a muddy pasture. And I was butt naked."

The jailhouse rocked with laughter.

To top him, Sleaze said he'd picked up a fine looking 'oman down near C'lumbus. "She was sitting at a table at a club smoking a cigarette. She looked pretty good, but I kept thinking something wasn't right. But she was talking trash. And I was liking what I was hearing. Folks kept looking at us and laughing and I didn't pay them no attention."

"This is taking too long," said Dabble. "Gon and tell what happened.

He said, "A woman came over and whispered something in his ear. 'If you change your mind, you can talk to me.' Then she switched over to another table and started talking to her girlfriends. But I kept talking to my girl. Her name was. I think she said her name was Amy. After awhile, I asked her if she wanted to dance. She said sure. So I stood up and looked around but I didn't see her. I was standing there looking like a fool. I felt like I'd been played. I kept looking but I didn't see her. Then a dude standing by the jukebox pointed down. Man, I looked down and there she was. She was a midget!"

The jailhouse rocked with laughter.

"Oh man," Punt shouted. "Did you dance with her?"

"Yeah," he said. "I thought it took grit for her to be out in the open hustling like that. I enjoyed her company and even went back down there to see her. But she had another Nigga, and he musta been in love with her 'cause he pulled a knife on me."

Laughter exploded. Even Batch cracked a smile.

They boasted of more scandalous capers with women.

Batch listened in awe, wondering how these young Negroes could be so happy, speak so

freely, and own so much of themselves. The terror of living life as a Negro man had been with him every day of his forty-four years. He'd never not felt the tightened noose of fear around his nervous neck.

His stay became long days listening to outside noises as well as the ones inside his head. In the cramped space, he was stagnant. It was harsh punishment for a man used to working long hours six days a week.

A quite unexpected character appeared on the scene. About once a month, Reverend Eugene Pugh came to jail. The first time he came, he flitted into the cell block as if he was Michael the Archangel sent to deliver a message from the Lord.

Waving his arms theatrically, he said, "Hello Brothers, how wonderful to see you. This is the day which the Lord has made; we will rejoice and be glad in it."

Reverend Eugene had a flamboyance that made him charming. He was pleasant looking; short and dark-skinned with hair permed straight with lye. He sported a black suit with a clerical collar, and under his arm, he carried a bible.

The cells were filled with Negroes, and he knew them all. "Hello, Brother Punt, Brother Dabble, Brother Quick, Brother Biggum, Brother Sleaze," he spoke warmly. "It's a blessing to behold your faces once again in the land of the living."

They returned the greeting with devious smiles.

Batch was sitting on his cot when Reverend Eugene entered his cell, and he stood up. The

preacher smiled and posed the question, "Are you saved,

brother?"

Shifting his weight, Batch scratched his head. For a moment, he drew a blank. Being questioned about his stewardship in jail was the last thing he expected. He groped for something to say. Recalling nothing, he admitted that he'd quit going to church and didn't know whether he
was saved or not.

"Well, I'm here to tell you that Jesus loves you. He gave his life on the cross that your sins would be forgiven. And he wants you to experience the beauty of his salvation." Batch looked befuddled. Reverend Eugene said, "It's freely given, brother. If you confess with your mouth the Lord Jesus, and believe in your heart that God raised him from the dead, you shall be saved."

He reached out to shake Batch's hand. As he gripped it, Punt said, "They done busted you again, ain't they, Gene? Don't b'lieve nothing he says," he told Batch. "He ain't no real preacher, and he ain't got the Holy Ghost."

The young thugs laughed. Sleaze said, "He don't even go to church. He be at his girlfriend's house drunk on Sundays."

"Or selling moonshine and home brew in his brother's woodshed," said Sleaze. "He ain't nothing but a fake."

"Quack, quack, quack," they sang.

Batch pulled his hand back and stared at the preacher.

With a confident smile, Reverend Eugene threw his head back, revealing a mouth full of gold teeth. He said, "Brothers, I'm a witness to the Gospel of Jesus Christ. His Word will save you, and it'll set you free."

Batch sat back down. He was confused as he listened to the young inmates tease Reverend Eugene.

Reverend Eugene sat on the cot opposite Batch's. He crossed his legs as if he was there to give counsel. He said, "Brothers, I'd like to render a few verses of the hymn, *Jesus Savior Pilot Me*. It's a song of submission, and it's the one I sing in times of trouble."

He sang in a rich, baritone voice:
Jesus Savior pilot me,
Over life's tempestuous sea:
Unknown waves before me roll,
Hiding rocks and treacherous shoal;
Chart and compass come from Thee-
Jesus Savior pilot me!

Then he read some scriptures and proceeded to preach a sermon on the beauty of salvation. To Batch's surprise, the young men stopped teasing and listened.

The preacher's voice was convincing as he declared salvation as the key to a fruitful life on Earth and the ticket to paradise after death.

"Every man is entitled to salvation," he declared. "It's a free gift from God. He wants us to have it so we can be one with him. To be one with the Lord is my hope for every man, woman, and child."

After the message, the young men began a serious discussion.

Butter Bean asked, "If God is for everybody, how come we have such a hard time and the White folks have it so easy?"

Reverend Eugene answered, "Whom the Lord loves, he chastises. We've suffered for a higher purpose. Couldn't it be that the Lord has used us to demonstrate his power in the earth? Can we not declare that God saw our people, the slaves, through a most barbaric situation? And are we not here today to tell about it?"

The blank look on their faces indicated that they knew nothing about their history.

Startled by their ignorance, the preacher smiled gently. "Finally, my brethren," he said,

"we're not here to have it easy. The last chapter of the book of Ecclesiastes says, "The whole

duty of man is to fear God and keep his commandments. And whatsoever rewards we're due, God will settle up with us when we meet him face to face."

Butter Bean looked perplexed. He said, "Gene, you do some good talk. But if you b'lieve that, why don't you live it? You talk God but you live in the gutter."

Reverend Eugene cocked his head unrepentantly. "My Brother," he spoke in a refined tongue, "I'm the perfect example of why Jesus went on the cross."

Butter Bean laughed. "That's what I like about you, Gene. You ain't no hypocrite like them other Christians. You don't fake being good."

Reverend Eugene was bailed out and didn't show up for several weeks. Batch began to think that maybe he'd been redeemed and had straightened up his life. But about a month after his first visit, Reverend Eugene was arrested again.

He pranced into the cell declaring, "My brother, we've all sinned and fallen short of the glory of God. How're you doing this evening, Brother Batch?"

This arrest was on shocking charges. Reverend Eugene had rammed his car into a café in Bruin and injured several people. His bail was set so high that it took his brothers several days to come up with the money. He talked bible and salvation day and night. He presented such a picture of goodness that it was hard for Batch to believe he'd done what he was accused of.

To be sure, Reverend Eugene was a man of unspecified virtues. But what wasn't in question was his appetite. Where Batch was repulsed by jailhouse food, the reverend ate everything put before him. One evening, having eaten Batch's breakfast and lunch, Reverend Eugene eyed his dinner. Batch had eaten a small piece of bread, drunk his milk, and pushed the rest aside.

Deciding not to beg for the food, Reverend Euguene said, "If I may be so bold, brother, what chain of events brings you to this renowned facility?"

Batch shrank as if the preacher had poked him. He hadn't talked about the robbery with anybody but Aunt Ginny. It was as if it wasn't real if he didn't speak about it. He responded, "It's a mistaken reason that I'm here. I'm ashamed to admit that I was charged with a crime that I didn't commit."

Reverend Eugene groaned sympathetically. After a respectable moment, he said, "Many of us find ourselves in your situation, brother. I must confess I've been the victim of mistaken identity and other unfortunate claims myself. But we must soldier on and live with the assurance that the Lords sees all and forgives all."

The last part of the statement troubled Batch. The Lord hadn't come through for him, and he knew why. He didn't know the last time he'd been to church. Neither had he sent any tithes or offerings. He hadn't done anything for the Lord and was afraid to call on him now for fear he'd remind him of this.

Sensing his anxiety, Reverend Eugene said, "I understand that a robbery took place at a hardware store in the town of Sipsey. The Colored man that worked in the store was charged with the crime. It's said that the man was a faithful and loyal employee to that particular concern. But the proprietors believed that this faithful and loyal employee betrayed them by breaking in and robbing them."

Batch started crying. "I didn't do it. I didn't do it, Mama."

Reverend Eugene felt sorry for him and began reading from 2 Corinthians: 12:10. 'Therefore I take pleasure in infirmities, in reproaches, in necessities, in persecutions, in distresses for Christ's sake: for when I am weak, then am I strong.'"

Batch's body shook with sorrow.

Reverend Eugene said, "Brother, God's grace is sufficient. His strength is made perfect in weakness. You're in the perfect position for the Lord to do a wondrous thing in your life."

Batch wasn't comforted. He folded his arms and rocked back and forth. "My Mama learned me better than to rob and steal. I didn't do it."

As Batch agonized over his plight, Reverend Eugene tried harder. He said, "Brother, I challenge you to try God and see if he'll make good on his promises. If you didn't rob the store, stop crying about it and stand in your truth! The Lord knows you didn't rob it. And the good part is, he knows who did. Give it to him."

The words had a familiar ring. He thought of his Mama, and started crying again. But the cold stare of Reverend Eugene jarred him. Batch said, "I been weak all my life, reverend. I know God can save me, and I will give it to him."

"Brother Batch," Reverend Eugene said sternly. "The Lord will save your *soul*, but you need a *man* to get you out of the mess you're in. Come on; let's pray to God to look over his vast Universe and send the man you need."

They clasped hands and Reverend Eugene prayed:

"Dear Heavenly Father, I come to you to intercede on behalf of Brother Batch. Demonstrate to him your ability to forgive us our sins and supply our needs according to your riches in glory. Renew in him a right spirit of fellowship and trust. Leave him to know that you are a problem solver with a hedge around him that his enemies can't move. Give him faith to believe in himself and you. And be his help in this time of troubles. I personally thank you for being an on time God. In the name of Jesus, a-men."

Batch wiped his eyes and thanked the preacher.

Reverend Eugene graciously accepted his thanks. Then he asked, "Brother, will you be eating the remainder of your meal?"

Batch pushed the leftovers towards him.

Reverend Eugene went to the dingy sink and washed his hands. Then he put the paper napkin under his chin as if he was about to dine on a gourmet meal. He said grace and then finished Batch's dinner. Afterwards, he sang:

If it had not been for the Lord on my side,
Tell me where would I be, (where would I be)
You kept my enemies away,
You let the sun shine through a cloudy day,
You wrapped me in the cradle of your arms,
When you knew I'd be battered and scarred.
So if it had not been for the Lord on my side,
Tell me where would I be, (where would I be).

Part Three

Chapter Twenty

The tragedy of Ivan Goines was the talk of Sipsey. Members of First Macedonia were devastated. That something so dreadful could happen to one of Johnny Goines's children was shocking. The church went into prayer. Sugarfoot could barely process it and went back and forth to Atlanta several times a week. Some days he drove to Georgia Medical, exchanged a few words with the family, and drove back to Sipsey.

******

The announcement made in church was that Ivan had been critically injured. Though rumors flew and the nosy speculated, details of the incident hadn't been revealed. He'd been in a coma at Georgia Medical Center for weeks. But at his family's request, he'd recently been transferred to Piedmont Hospital in Lancaster.

Last Sunday, Lucy Dash went to the altar to pray for Ivan. She got so emotional that she started hollering and crying and the ushers had to help her back to her seat. But after service, she composed herself enough to rebuke the women in the powder room. She said, "Don't start spreading lies about Ivan if you don't know what you're talking about. Y'all best mind your business and keep your mouths shut."

Somebody had hinted that he wasn't expected to live and the family wanted him closer to home when the worst happened.

*****

Clarice Vanderway and Sister Maxine Jefferson travelled along Highway 82 towards Lancaster in Sister Jefferson's 1958 Ford Fairlane. They were headed to the seventieth birthday celebration of Miss Fannie Agnew.

It was a beautiful Saturday afternoon and Clarice felt better than she'd felt in months. She looked young and fresh in an emerald green sundress with a square neck and an A-line silhouette.

She sat quietly thinking about Ivan as Sister Jefferson bragged about what a good driver she was. She said, "I drive forty miles an hour, don't care what. And if somebody runs up behind me and starts riding my bumper, I slow down to 35.

Sister Jefferson was trying to live down a rumor. It'd been spread all over town that she'd fallen with a heart attack while visiting her sister in Detroit. Because of this, her visit had lasted longer than expected. The congregation had been worried about her and was relieved when she returned home in restored health.

But ever so quietly, Sipsey gossips had got word from Lump Jackson, a former member of First Macedonia, now living in Detroit, that Sister Jefferson hadn't had a heart attack at all. "She got drunk at a card party and fell out," reported Lump.

Mary Newlins and Elvira Jones got wind of the rumor and put it on the grapevine.

Today, Clarice wasn't thinking of the rumor but of Ivan Goines. As Sister Jefferson crept along at snail's pace, she said, "I've been so worried about Ivan."

Maxine sighed. "I have too. I'm glad they transferred him to Piedmont. Staying up there in Atlanta was just about to wear Johnny and Liddy out. I don't think they've left his side since this happened."

"They're such a close family."

"Branhope's been hanging in there too," said Maxine. "Him and Ivan been friends since they were boys. Liddy says she don't know what they would've done without him."

Clarice mumbled her agreement.

Maxine said, "I heard about the big fight at the beauty shop. Were you there?"

"I was, and it was awful."

"Has anybody seen or heard anything of Freddie Dee?"

Clarice smirked. "I've seen her a few times at the post office. I guess she's had time to think about what she did. Hopefully, she knows it was a mistake."

"Naw, she don't," sniffed Maxine. "She'll try it again. Women like that don't ever learn. She thinks she can hold onto him by scaring off other women. Let her keep it up. She'll meet her match."

Clarice was listening but only slightly. She was annoyed with herself for being bullied into riding with Maxine Jefferson. She drove too slowly and she didn't drive after dark. Clarice had wanted to drive her own car. After the party, she wanted to visit with Ivan and then catch the big charity sale at the mall. But Maxine had insisted there was no reason for them to drive two cars to the same event. And being convinced she was the better driver, she'd talked Clarice into riding with her.

Clarice said, "Sister Jefferson, you think we'll have time to visit with Ivan after the party?"

She let out an impatient grunt. "Yes, but it'll just be for a few minutes. You know I don't drive after dark."

Clarice sighed. "Yes ma'am. I know that."

****

The battle for the soul of Ivan Goines was being hotly contested. Both the forces of darkness and the angels of light had a strong hold of it, and neither would let go. Anchoring the light with torches of righteousness were his glorified ancestors. They stood ready to lead him across the chilly waters of death.

He yearned to go, to experience their promise of peace and everlasting happiness.

Yet the path of perdition was powerfully appealing. The same passions, charms and temptations that'd trapped him in life were calling to him now. And they were enhanced with grander more extravagant indulgences. He wavered, wanting both, but lacked the strength to choose between them. So his life continued to hang in the balance.

As he agonized, his spirit floated above his body, hovering as if contemplating its loss.

He felt the presence of death. It was raw flesh baking in the broiling sun; a sinister world empty of moon and stars; and a murky nothingness as hollow as the Universe before the Creator stepped into space with a plan.

His grandmothers' light shone ever more brightly. He saw through the pearly gates and beheld the streets of gold. Suddenly, the gates swung open, and he viewed the stairway to heaven.

He started towards them. But he was suddenly pricked by the Prince of Darkness, and he turned back, headed for eternal damnation. He couldn't help it. Hell had chosen him, and it'd been too constant a companion for him to leave now.

Hastening headlong, he suddenly felt himself being hurled into the pit.

And then it happened. Somewhere in the vastness of this experience, he heard the guttural sobbing of his father. It was a pitiful plea born of love and fear, as pathetic as a lone cry in the wilderness.

Johnny Goines was indeed begging for his son's life. He prayed, *"Lord, if you just bring him back to me, I'll take better care of him, and every minute of the rest of my life will be spent thanking you."*

From the mouth of this servant, the plea soared into heaven, threw itself on the mercy

seat, and touched the heart of God.

Suddenly, he was grabbed and pitched into the abyss. The mortal, formerly known as

Ivan Goines, was no more. His soul was caught up in the whirlwind and went soaring through

the sandy banks of time.

His only recognition was of God as the Universal *I AM.*

His body was cleansed, sanctified and brought into a new covenant. He was shown things too marvelous to comprehend, understood the divine oracles of God, and revealed of things yet to come.

✶✶✶✶✶

His eyes opened. The atmosphere spun as if he was still in the whirlwind. Ringing in his ear was the woeful sound of his mother's voice, and he knew she'd followed him into eternity. He heard voices speaking in quiet somber tones. Still, his mother's voice reigned above all others, and she was calling him back to herself.

"Madea," he said softly.

His eyes were opened but he couldn't focus them. He wasn't sure whether he was in heaven or hell. He called again, "Madea."

A familiar voice called, "Quick, go get Madea. He's awake."

Fast moving feet dashed away, and in a second, his mother was standing beside him. With a pounding heart, she looked with thankful but disbelieving eyes at her suddenly alert youngest child.

"Son," she mouthed silently as tears of joy streamed down her cheeks.

"Madea," he whispered, "did I die?"

Liddy Goines took a deep breath. She looked up to the heavens and back at him. She said, "No, son. You didn't die. You tried several times, but the Lord heard our cry and had mercy on us. He brought you back."

He was overwhelmed and wanted to talk to her about what he'd experienced; the light, the darkness, the decision he'd had to make, the grandmothers and the mystifying whirlwind. He wanted to describe her mother so she'd know he'd seen her. And he wanted to thank his father for not letting him go down into the pit.

"The devil almost got me," he said, but she couldn't hear him.

His vision cleared, and he was surprised to see that he was surrounded by family. All of his siblings were there except Johnny Jr. It was so like his oldest brother to be off doing something and not know what was going on with the family.

Johnny Jr. was an honorable, courageous man, he acknowledged. And it was the first thing he'd tell him when he saw him again.

He wanted to call them by name but was too weak. So he just stared at them.

His brother, Dr. Calvin Goines, and Calvin's twin, Karen, stood at the foot of the bed. Their youngest sister, Gina, stood slightly behind them. Sherri Lynn stood on one side of the bed, and Earl stood on the other. His mother was at his head, holding his hand.

"Where's Poppa?" He whispered.

"He's in the chapel praying," Liddy said, rubbing his forehead. "His nerves won't let him stay in here. He's in and out; in and out."

Sherri Lynn shook her head. "This is the most upset I've ever seen him."

"We've all been upset," said misty-eyed Karen. "We didn't know how this thing would turn out."

To this they all agreed.

Calvin left to get their father. A nurse came in and said, "So you finally decided to wake

up? We wondered how long you were gon sleep."

Ivan groaned. "I would've awakened sooner if I could've."

The nurse took his vital signs and said they were good. She adjusted his pillows to make him more comfortable and said the doctor would be in shortly.

The family stood there and marveled at his recovery. Flaunting his brand of humor, Earl said, "Ivan, were you trying to scare us or was this done by accident?"

Ivan tried to laugh. It came as no surprise that Earl would make light of the delicate situation. "Believe me, I didn't plan it," Ivan assured him.

"Do you remember what happened?" asked Gina.

"*Don't!*" scolded Karen. "Later, when he's stronger."

Ivan had no problem with the question. Suddenly feeling stronger, he said. "I remember exactly what happened. In the kitchen of my house in Decatur, Georgia, my wife, Deanna, jabbed a knife in my chest."

After a prolonged silence, Earl said, "Well, she's outside waiting to take you home. You want me to get her?"

"That's not funny, Earl," cried Sherri Lynn.

Earl said, "Well, it's almost true. After she got out of jail, she was coming to the hospital every day. She said, 'I'm his wife, I have a right to see my husband,' he mimicked Deanna. "She put the police on us because we wouldn't let her see you. When that didn't work, she got a lawyer. Landon had to end up getting a restraining order against her. She thought because she was 'the wife' she had the final say. But, it turns out that if you try to kill your spouse, the court can suspend your rights."

Sherri Lynn said, "We thought it was best to have you transferred. You're in Piedmont General."

"How long have I been here?" he asked.

"About a week," they said.

Gina was furious. "That woman should still be in jail. She tried to kill you."

"No," Ivan hastily corrected," she did kill me. I'm back from the dead."

"And she's out on bail," Sherri Lynn said, overlooking his gruesome charge. "And I agree, she should be in jail. But she's claiming self-defense."

The idea was unimaginable.

"She's out of her mind," said Gina. "Ivan's not a fighter. I picked on him all the time when we were kids, and he never fought back. Madea had to insist that he stand up to me. So, this woman is just saying something to save her own skin."

Earl scratched his head. "He didn't like to fight, but I remember him having a fit because I took the training wheels off his little bicycle. He tackled me. You remember that, Pope?" he said to Calvin.

Calvin looked doubtful. "I remember, but I wouldn't call him a fighter."

Sherri Lynn said, "Ivan, Deanna told the police that you attacked her and started choking her. She claimed she panicked and grabbed the knife." Sherri Lynn's face was unreadable. She said, "Deanna had scratches and bruises on her neck and arms. Landon says the police are always inclined to believe a woman when she says she's been abused."

"Well, I don't believe her," said Gina, "I never liked her, never trusted her, and never understood what Ivan saw in her. The one time she came to Sipsey, she walked around with her nose in the air. She didn't want to be there, and she hasn't been back. And I know I wasn't the only one that noticed it. Madea dared us to say anything, so everybody kept their mouth shut. But I knew she was bad news for the beginning. And I hope and pray that this is the end of the marriage."

Earl laughed lightly. "Well, Gina, we didn't want you to hide your feelings. We wanted you to tell us what you thought."

They were talking as if Ivan wasn't there. When they'd finished, he cleared his throat and said, "She's telling the truth. We were fighting. And I did attack her. And if she hadn't killed me, I would've killed her."

Nobody knew how to respond.

"She wants to see to you," said Karen. "Do you want to see her?"

"Yes, I do" Ivan replied to everybody's surprise. "I definitely want to see my wife."

Chapter Twenty-One

Deacon Collins and Deacon Porter were cleaning out the baptism pool when Pastor Brough came to the back of the church with the good news.

He said, "Deacons, I just got word from the hospital. Brother Ivan has come out of his comma, and he's in his right mind. The doctor expects him to make a full recovery."

"Wooo!" Sugarfoot groaned, beside himself with relief. Laughing heartily, he threw the hose pipe down and shouted, "Yes! Yes! Thank you, pastor. I've been waiting on this news for weeks. I knew he would come through."

Deacon Porter's face exuded joy as well. "Lately, I've been thinking about that boy and his Poppa a lot. Ivan is good fellow and a smart one. And he really loves his Poppa. When he was a boy, every time you saw Johnny, you saw him. And he'd be talking, 'What you think about this, Poppa? Did you see that, Poppa?' And he was always doing something, making something. He taught Johnny how to read," he said in astonishment. "And he didn't want to leave Sipsey. They had a time getting him away from here."

"Really?" Sugarfoot's brows furrowed in surprise.

"Yes, Johnny wanted his children to get their education and go build their lives somewhere else. He didn't want them to stay in the south."

"Why?"

"'Cause he didn't want them to have to put up with the kind of treatment we get here. You know what a proud man Johnny Goines is. He figures this life is alright for him, but he wanted better for his children. He thought living up north or out west offered better opportunities for them to live decent lives. And they've all done well," he said proudly. "But most of them have stayed here in the south."

"Yes, they have," acknowledged Deacon Collins. "They're college educated, independent and successful. Apparently, they don't see life the way he does. And it's a good thing 'cause we got to stop running some time. A Black man ought to be able to build a decent life in the south just as well as a White man."

Deacon Porter agreed. "A lot of my daddy's people went up to Michigan. But my daddy said he weren't running away. Our foreparents were slaves down here. They worked for hundreds of years and never got a dime of pay. It was hard on them. The least we can do is stay here and try to accumulate something. It's gon be a better day. And I plan to be here when it comes."

"Me too," said Deacon Collins.

When Deacon Collins left the church, he headed home to clean up his truck.

At home, he parked outside the detached garage and swept the inside cab. Then he got cleaning supplies from the shed and washed the outside. As rhythm and blues music played, he hummed along. Besides sports, music was his passion and relaxation. It was one of the reasons he'd been determined to buy a new vehicle. He wanted a functional radio that played both AM and FM stations.

After washing the truck, he carefully waxed it, taking care to remove any noticeable streaks. When he was finished, he looked it over with pride.

From the back door, Big Mama called, "Bray, Abner came by. He said he'll be off Monday and he wants you to lead the crew. And you got another letter from that woman. She sent it by air mail again. It's got *six* stamps on it."

"Leave it on the dresser in my room."

He swore and scolded himself for having played the fool as a young man. But there was no way around it, he had to answer her letter and settle this mess once and for all. He'd misplaced the last letter but would definitely get this one in the mail.

"You heard about Ivan?"

"I did. I'm going to the hospital as soon as I get finished here. He shook his head. "That boy gave everybody a scare."

"Yes, he did," she agreed. She made a weary sound. "Freddie Dee stopped by again. She said she wasn't looking for you, but she stayed a good while. I don't know what you gon do 'bout her."

"I'm gon leave her alone, Big Mama," He sighed. Freddie Dee was one of those women you wished you'd never got involved with.

Immediately, his conscience whipped him because he was being a hypocrite. Those naked pictures she'd left still tempted him. Every time he tried to throw them away, something inside him wouldn't let him do it. "I'll lock them up in a strong box," he compromised.

He parked the truck in the garage and headed for the back door. Manny came around the house, smiling. "Sugarafoot, I need to see you," he said.

"What's up?"

"Can you let me have a few dollars?"

"For what, to go to Maw Shatlings?"

"Naw, I'm trying to take Syretta to the picture show in Bruin."

"You got a date?"

"I asked her to go and she said yes," he smiled proudly.

"So how you gon get there? Surely you don't expect the woman to walk to Bruin."

"Naw, I'm gon ride with Peter Ben and Millie."

"Double dating." Sugarfoot was a little surprised that Manny had pulled it off.

He reached into his wallet and took out two five dollar bills. Handing them to Manny, he good-naturedly slapped him on the back. "Have fun," he said, "but don't do nothing I wouldn't do."

Manny gratefully took the money. "Thank you, cuz. I been trying to get up the nerve to ask Syretta out for 'bout a year. I was scared she'd say no. But she acted like she was glad I asked." He looked at the money. "Don't tell Big Mama. She don't like Syretta."

"Your secret is safe with me."

As they started inside the house, Manny asked, "So where you going tonight?"

Sugarfoot shrugged. "I'm going to the hospital to see Ivan, and I'm coming back home. I don't feel like running the road."

"So you ain't got hooked up with nobody yet?"

"Nope, and I don't plan to."

"Well, we'll see about that."

Sugarfoot envied Manny. His life was simple. He'd found somebody he liked, and all he wanted was for her to like him back. Sometimes he felt like he was too picky, or even more frightening, that there was no one out there for him.

Later, as he headed for Piedmont Hospital, Manny

came to mind. He sympathized with his plight. Manny was good-hearted and hardworking. All he wanted was a chance to be a man.

People felt sorry for him because of his limp not realizing that there was nothing wrong with his brain. Yet, he didn't complain. What money he made piddling around downtown, he gave to his mother to help with his two younger sisters. But when he wanted something for himself, he came to Sugarfoot.

He let out a deep breath. "I wish I could do more for you, cuz."

He turned on the radio and a tune from the Detroit Sound was playing. The lead singer's heart was throbbing over the woman he was madly in love with.

"I'll climb the highest mountain, swim the widest ocean, and walk around the world for

just a chance to be with you," he sang.

Sugarfoot turned the radio off but immediately turned it back on. The song reminded him to his predicament. He was lonely and jealous of any man that had a woman so special he'd do those things for her.

He was a contradiction and knew it. One minute he wanted to wait until he was established before getting serious in a relationship, the next minute he was pining for a loving companion.

Complicated me," he laughed.

Chapter Twenty-Two

It was a little after three-thirty when Clarice and Sister Jefferson left Fannie Agnew's party. It'd been held at the Presidential Ballroom at DuBois College, and Miss Fannie's Thursday Club had gone overboard, lavishly decorating the room with fresh flowers, hanging streamers, and elaborate table arrangements.

There was so much food that the buffet table had sagged under its weight. Enticing entrees made the mouth water. Vegetable dishes too numerous to name. And the desserts were made by some of the best cooks in the district.

Toward the end of the evening, Miss Fannie favored her guests with two musical selections, *God Is My All and All,* a song that brought avid and ardent cheers; and her emotional version of, *If I Can Help Somebody…Then My Living Shall Not Be in Vain,* drew more than a few tears.

Per her guests, the party had been a resounding success.

And it must've been. As they left, Clarice waited for Sister Jefferson to point out all the things that had gone wrong. But Maxine shocked her. She didn't say one negative word about the party. What she said was, "Fannie must be doing something right for that many people to turn out for her birthday party."

"I couldn't agree more," Clarice responded.

At the hospital, as they waited for the elevator, Maxine announced that she was taking a quick detour to visit an old friend on the second floor, a Miss Caroline Moses. "She used to live in Sipsey," she explained, "but she moved to Lancaster some years ago. She had a stroke last week and I wanna see how she's getting along."

Clarice actually remembered Miss Caroline. She was a frail looking woman with thin lips and a soft voice. She wore a head wrap and tiny hoop earrings all the time.

"Should I come along and speak to Miss Caroline?"

"No," Maxine demanded. "Go on and check on Ivan."

The elevator arrived and Deacon Porter stepped off. He was beaming with excitement. He said, "I guess y'all heard the good news. Ivan's done woke up and he's doing fine."

"Hallelujah!" Both women cried at once. Maxine was momentarily confused about where to go. "I need to go see Miss Caroline," she said, "but I wanna see Ivan."

"You can do both," Clarice maintained, trying to put her mind at ease. "Miss Caroline is an old friend, so she's expecting you to visit. And Ivan's not going anywhere. He'll be there when you get there."

"She's got a point, Maxine," agreed Deacon Porter. He swelled with pride as he noted that First Macedonia had really turned out in support of Ivan. "He's had many visitors today," he announced. "And Johnny says they're getting cards and flowers all the time. It means a lot to the family to have folks lift them up like that."

They talked a while longer before he bid them a good evening. The women stepped onto the elevator still rejoicing over Ivan's recovery.

On the second floor, Maxine said, "Tell Liddy I'm visiting with Miss Caroline and I'll be up there in a minute."

Clarice waved her off and continued to the fourth floor. As soon as she stepped off the elevator, she could hear male voices coming from room 412. Reaching the door, she tapped lightly. Deacon Collins opened it, and she entered smiling.

Ivan's brothers, Calvin and Earl, were in the room as was Deacon Milton Whitehead.

When she was young, she'd had a hard time telling the brothers apart. Johnny Jr. was shorter than they, so she recognized him. But Calvin and Earl had a similar look. Earl was light complexioned with curly hair, and Calvin was brown-skinned with coarse hair. Still, the resemblance was strong and both men were handsome.

She spoke pleasantly then went and stood beside the bed. "I'm so happy you've come back to us, my friend," she said. "The town of Sipsey's been on a round the clock prayer vigil for you."

Ivan smiled. "I know, and I thank everybody for their prayers."

Deacon Collins offered her his chair then stepped outside. He soon came back with one for himself.

As the only female present, protocol dictated that she not stay long. She planned to

exchange a few words and leave. However, she didn't want to rush or appear to be hurrying off. So she relaxed and said, "It's so good to see everybody."

"Likewise," said Earl in his spirited manner.

After a studied pause, she said, "I thought I might catch your sisters. I know they're in town. Where are they?"

"Why?" Earl barked, pretending to be offended. "We're not good enough company for you?"

She laughed, but didn't take the bait. "I just wondered where they were, Earl."

"I shouldn't tell you," he sulked, "but they've gone to the cafeteria to get something to eat. And in case you were wondering about Poppa, he just left for Sipsey. Now that

Ivan decided to wake up, he's back on his saintly duties at First Macedonia."

The men found this amusing.

"Now, Earl," she lightly scolded. "Your Poppa is a dedicated man. He keeps things running smoothly at the church; he's the backbone of it."

"That he is," attested Deacon Whitehead.

It was an open secret that the Goines children fondly joked about their father's devotion to the church. And since Deacon Josiah Hess's death, Deacon Goines had doubled his efforts as overseer.

"He's consistent if anything," contended Ivan. "I can only hope to duplicate that quality someday." Ivan was propped up in bed. His eyes looked weak, but he seemed to be enjoying their company. Breaking a smile at Clarice, he said, "All dressed up in green and gold. Where've you been?"

She said, "I'm coming from Miss Fannie Agnew's seventieth birthday party. Do you know, Miss Fannie?"

"No, but I've heard of her."

She gave highlights of the party and went on to hail Miss Fannie's amazing humanitarian work. "She opens her home to girls that want to go to college but can't afford the room and board. It's a ministry for her. Several girls from Sipsey have boarded with her, including Temeka Armstrong. She offers them a lovely home away from home. She's a good cook and a wonderful person."

"Good God!" shrieked Deacon Whitehead. "I know Fannie, but I didn't know she was all that. I need to give her a call."

The men thought he was joking and started laughing.

His wife of fifty-three years had died two years ago after a lengthy illness. Lately, he'd been asking women at the church to go to the picture show. So far nobody had taken him up on it. Even so, he wanted the men to know he was serious.

He said, "Y'all can laugh if you want to, but I ain't playing."

They laughed even more.

Clarice grew comfortable enough to drop the news that the Potoama County Board of Education had been put on notice that they had to integrate their schools in the coming year. The superintendent received a letter from the Department of Education informing him that we have to enroll Colored children in all of the White schools in the county." She looked concerned. "I imagine it'll be a mess, but the change is coming."

"You don't mean!" cried Deacon Whitehead. "I never thought I'd see the day." He was about seventy-five years old and this news was a shock to his system. He twisted uncomfortably. "Ain't nobody ready for this. What will we do?"

"We don't have a choice," Clarice said. "It's federal law."

Calvin jeered impatiently. "It's been the law for ten years. Potoama County has moved with the deliberate haste that the court suggested which means they've put it off as long as they could. Several systems across the south have already integrated."

"Yes," said Earl. "My daughters attend integrated schools in Nashville. But my sons aren't ready for it. We've got to do compliance training before they're ready."

Calvin's face twisted into a frown. "My wife doesn't

trust the Charlotte Public Schools, System, so my children go to private school, Catholic school. She's convinced that anything that says private means superior." He smirked, "and she *loves* superior."

Earl poo poohed the idea. "I'm not paying for private school. Public school was good enough for me, and it's good enough for my children. If they go to private school, they'll pay for it themselves."

Calvin groaned. "Tell that to my wife."

At that moment, a nurse came into the room and the conversation quickly ended. She was all smiles and full of cheer and wanted to know if Ivan needed anything.

"No," he said kindly. "Thank you very much."

When she left, Earl turned the conversation to Clarice. He said, "Let's talk about you, Queen Bee. What's the matter with you? You're giving the hometown a bad name. The bourgeois from Nashville to Philadelphia are talking about you." He pulled on his ear lobe. "I'm surprised your ears aren't burning."

Clarice's upbringing was that of a well-bred lady. When in doubt, the best response was to smile and keep cool. And that's what she did. In a high-pitched but humorous voice, she said, "What're they saying about me, Earl?"

Earl Goines laughed. He liked teasing Clarice because she handled it with such grace. He said, "They're saying things too awful to repeat."

"Such as?"

"Well," he hesitated. "They're saying you're selfish and spoiled, that your standards for men are too high." His eyes shifted. "Some are saying you're a cold, heartless woman with no concern for a man's feelings."

"All of that?" Her voice sang with laughter. "Well, well, well."

The men were surprised by the ease with which she handled the criticism.

But Earl persisted. He said, "It's just a shame the way you do things. You had Paul DeLorean thinking you were gon marry him and you ran out on him at the last minute. Women had bought dresses and shoes and pocketbooks; folks had made plans to come to Sipsey to witness the big event. But you pulled the plug." He looked her over reprovingly. "You have to know that he hasn't gotten over it."

"He will," she waved confidently. "They always do."

"What! You practically left the man at the altar and all you've got to say is that he'll get over it? Shame on you."

For a split second, Clarice was tempted to tell him why she'd called off the wedding.

But, thinking better of it, she said, "Looks can be deceiving, Earl. He's not as serious a person as you might think."

"But that's the third man you've let down," he recounted. He looked at Calvin and said, "Pope, didn't she dump our frat brother?"

Dr. Calvin Goines, called Pope by family and friends, was a fraternity brother to both Earl and Ivan. But it was Earl that reveled in mischief. And though Calvin was more reserved, when they teamed up, their teasing could be vicious.

Calvin said, "Mitchell Savoy is a nice guy, and he was crazy about you too. He had big plans, bragging about what he was gonna do once you were married. Then, all of a sudden, he's in my garage crying in his beer. He didn't know what happened. The guy was in tears for months. I didn't think he'd ever get over it."

"But he did, didn't he?" Clarice shot back. "Like I said, they always get over it."

Deacon Whitehead was totally baffled. He'd known Clarice all her life and was very fond of her. Hearing her being described in such a ruthless way troubled him. Frowning, he said, "Clarice, looks like everybody wants you but you don't want nobody."

"That's not the case, Deacon Whitehead," she quickly responded. She was also fond of him. And she wanted him to know the woman Earl had described wasn't her. Speaking earnestly, she said, "I want the right man. I will marry the *right* man."

He nodded approvingly. "Ain't nothing wrong with that."

But Earl objected. "Don't believe it, deacon. She's gon keep playing games with these brothers 'cause she thinks it's cute. She thinks it's funny."

In defense of her, Deacon Whitehead said, "Ain't no harm in waiting on the right man."

"Yes, it is," he said quickly. "She'd better get somebody before it's too late. She won't be a pretty young thing forever."

Ivan had been listening closely to Earl's upbraiding. Now, rubbing his face, he said, "Clarice, take your time. Don't let anybody rush you into marriage. Take my situation as a warning, if you don't want to marry, don't marry."

"That's right," said Deacon Whitehead. "Take your time."

Calvin laughed, realizing that they'd taken Earl literally.

Before Earl could start on something else, his sisters burst into the room. Sherri Lynn, Karen, and Gina greeted

Clarice. By way of explanation, Gina reported that their mother was in the lobby talking to Maxine Jefferson.

The sisters were excited about something that'd happened in the cafeteria. Gina said, "Two women were going at it. They were screaming so loud at each other that I thought they were gonna fight right there in the hospital."

"What was the commotion about," asked Deacon Whitehead.

Gina cleared her throat. "It appears that the woman's husband has a girlfriend, and the girlfriend showed up at the hospital to see his Mama while the wife was there. Not smart," she declared.

"Were they Colored?" This seemed of particular concern to Deacon Whitehead.

"Yes, they were," Karen sighed. "And it was embarrassing."

"But," Gina held up a finger. "It was also telling. If you're the girlfriend, you don't visit the man's Mama at the hospital. That's the wife's place. Somebody ought to write a book on wife and girlfriend etiquette."

"Messy women," Calvin muttered.

Chapter Twenty-Three

The close knit Goines family was breathing easier. Ivan's ordeal had had them on edge, holding their breaths. It'd been the most challenging thing they'd ever faced, but they'd faced it together.

The night of the stabbing, the entire family had rushed to Georgia Medical. And they stayed by his bedside; sisters during the day and brothers at night.

When Colonel Johnny Goines Jr. arrived in Sipsey, Herbert Edmund informed him of what'd happened. He'd turned his car around and headed to Atlanta, breaking all speed limits along the way.

Johnny Jr. was the mystery of the family. With honey-colored skin and dark wavy hair, he bore the strongest resemblance to their father. But their relationship was the most complicated. Perhaps because he was first born and felt the weight of expectation, he didn't enjoy the easy relationship with him that his brothers had. Or maybe it was because he hadn't married and settled down.

This had caused a quiet misunderstanding between them. Johnny Goines believed that every man should get married and raise a family. Johnny Jr. explained that as a career soldier, he never knew where he'd be stationed. Therefore he didn't want to put a wife and family through the uncertainty. But that reasoning didn't appease his father, and their relationship remained cool.

Seeing him at the hospital, instead of greeting him with a hug as his brothers had done, Johnny Jr. greeted his father with a salute and a handshake.

"Poppa, I'd hoped to see you at home," he said light-heartedly. "I was looking forward to some of Madea's peas and cornbread and blueberry cobbler."

Johnny Goines sighed helplessly. "This come up all of a sudden." He shook his head and didn't seem able to say anymore. Johnny Jr. followed him out of the waiting room and into the chapel. "I know it looks bad, Poppa, but Ivan is young and strong. He has a lot to live for, and he knows it."

They stayed in the chapel all night praying.

Seeing the seriousness of the situation, Johnny Jr. took emergency leave and stayed with his family for two weeks. He wanted to stay longer, but the United States Army couldn't be put on hold. The mission he was on was important. His family understood. So he journeyed on to Texas but stayed informed of Ivan's condition.

Others took up the slack. Dr. Calvin Goines, a celebrated cardiologist in Charlotte, North Carolina, took leave from his practice. So did Earl, owner of a printing and advertising agency in Nashville, Tennessee. Gina, a high school counselor, fashion designer, and part owner of a boutique, also lived in Nashville and took emergency leave.

The other sisters, Karen and Sherri Lynn, were married to prominent men and were able to stay with the family unhindered. Karen lived near the Georgia line and had gone back and forth daily. Liddy had scolded her. "You got them young babies," she'd said. "You need to stay at home and take care of them."

Karen had responded, "They're well cared for, Madea. Andre's mother is there. Helping care for the babies is therapy for her since Mr. Alfred died. She's at the house bright and early every morning. Also, we have a reliable babysitter, so my babies are fine."

******

This morning, after Ivan opened his eyes, the family prayed and Liddy pronounced things back to normal. She said, "Y'all have made me very proud. You left your families and jobs and came here to look after your brother. Now it's time for you to go back to your homes and get on with your lives. Me and Mr. Goines can handle it from here. If we need you, we'll call you."

"So just like that you're throwing us out ?" said Earl.

"Yes," she replied. "I'm throwing you out."

******

Nevertheless, everybody was still there. The sisters were happy to see Clarice. After chatting with the men, Karen said, "Baby brother, we can barely stand to leave. But we'll be back tomorrow."

Sherri Lynn and Gina threw him kisses.

Ivan smiled and waved them off.

Gina suddenly had a bright idea. She said, "Girls, let's go to the mall. Clarice, you can come with us and help me choose some summer outfits."

Clarice frowned in disappointment. "I'd love to, but I can't. I'm riding with Sister Jefferson, and we'll be leaving soon. She doesn't drive at night."

Gina sneered. "That doesn't make sense even for Maxine Jefferson. I'm going to ask if she'll wait til we get back."

"Good luck," Clarice called.

Gina went outside and came back with Sister Jefferson.

Maxine Jefferson stepped into the room as if she'd been

summoned by the king. Her eyes swept the environment. "Good afternoon, everybody," she spoke civilly. Then she winked at Ivan and said, "My, my, you're a sight for sore eye."

With a hint of mischief, Earl said, "You're looking sharp in that purple outfit, Sister Jefferson. You must be looking for a husband."

She purred and thanked him for the compliment. But when Deacon Whitehead spoke, she refused to speak back. They had a strained relationship due to their differences of opinion on how the church's Fellowship Hall should be managed. She'd been mad at him ever since his late wife's repast. His second cousin, Slick Jackson, a thief and felon, had showed up to eat. Disgusted that he'd had the nerve to come, Maxine had refused to serve him.

Hearing this, Deacon Whitehead got up from the table, went into the kitchen, and fixed Slick a plate. Maxine got mad and ordered him out of the kitchen. He turned to her and shouted, "Maxine Jefferson, you ain't the boss of this food!"

Now, having forgotten the incident, Deacon Whitehead yelled, "Hey, Jeff, what you got for me?"

She turned to him with narrowed eyes. "Not even the time of day," she said in a spiteful voice. And she turned her back to him.

It was an awkward moment that quickly passed when she grabbed Ivan's foot and said, "Ivan, I've just been wondering, out of all the women in the world, why the devil did you marry one that wanted to kill you?"

The room went to sudden pause. Deacon Collins looked as if he'd swallowed a goat.

Until now, no one had known how to speak of Ivan's

tragedy. It'd seemed too awkward. But Maxine Jefferson stood there waiting for him to respond. It was so tactless and the shock of it so great that Clarice felt guilty for even riding to town with her. Sighing in exasperation, she stared at Ivan.

But Ivan wasn't offended. Showing remarkable tolerance, he shook his head and said, "Sister Jefferson, I must say, you're a woman of wisdom and insight. I've been asking myself the same thing."

He laughed, and put everybody at ease.

Gina, who didn't think the comment was funny, said, "Sister Jefferson, we want Clarice to go to the mall with us. Can you stay here 'til we get back?"

"I sho' can't," she retorted. "If I stay here that long, it'll be dark when we get on the road, and I don't drive in the dark."

"Oh, Sister Jefferson," Gina bellowed. "The car has lights."

"I don't care if it do, I don't drive at night."

"Oh dear," mused Karen.

Gina was about to fling a nasty rebuff when Sherri Lynn said, "Clarice, why don't you ride back with Deacon Collins? You drive at night, don't you, Sugarfoot?"

He was caught off guard. Recovering quickly, he said, "Yes, I do."

Clarice glanced quickly at him. She hated the thought, but she was beginning to think that he didn't like her. The whole time she'd been there, he hadn't said a word. And this wasn't the first time he'd shut down when she came around. She racked her brain trying to think of some insult she may have shown him but couldn't think of any. Another reason came to mind and she winced. He was from the Quarter and she from the other side of town. The rivalry that existed between the two neighborhoods had often caused conflicts. To her it was silly. But she didn't know how he felt about it. Interestingly, he didn't volunteer to offer her a ride and she took that as another sign that he didn't want her to ride with him.

She said, "I'll just ride back with Sister Jefferson."

"But you didn't ask Sugarfoot," Sherri Lynn exclaimed.

The room went silent as if everybody was waiting for her to ask.

Clarice resented Sherri Lynn for pressing the issue. What if he said no? She'd feel like a fool.

Sugarfoot didn't offer because he didn't think a classy woman like Clarice Vanderway would want to ride in a truck. All the fancy women in Sipsey rode in cars, and they liked them big and shiny. Clarice was the fanciest woman of all, and she drove an expensive sports car that put everybody's vehicle to shame.

He was also mindful of the rivalry. It had existed for as long as he could remember. Occasionally, tradition was defied and friendships were made. To him it was childish, founded on pride and ignorance.

But the feelings ran deep, and those that felt strongly about it didn't budge. Not knowing how she felt, he didn't want to be embarrassed. By keeping quiet, his face was saved, and she was given a way out.

But Clarice really wanted to go shopping with the sisters. They were like family and there was so much to talk about. With the Goines sisters, she could gossip about Maxine's fake heart attack.

"Ask Sugarfoot, Clarice," Sherri Lynn insisted.

"Ask Sugarfoot," Earl repeated.

She felt cornered but didn't let it show. Why did the Goineses have to be so meddlesome? And why did it seem like everybody was looking at her? She didn't want to come across as a snob or a chicken. So she swallowed her pride and said, "Deacon Collins, may I ride back to Sipsey with you?"

"Sure," he said pleasantly.

She felt relieved as if a weight had been lifted off her. She was going to the mall after all. And she was rid of Maxine Jefferson. Her heart did a quick dance. She said, "Thanks, Deacon Collins." To Maxine, she said, "I'm gonna ride back with the deacon. I'll see you at church tomorrow."

"Alright," Maxine scowled as if she'd been robbed of something special. Moments later, she said, "Okay everybody, I'll be on my way now." And she threw her pocketbook over her shoulder and said good night.

When she was gone, Gina said, "That is the most irritating woman I know. Clarice, how do you abide her?"

"With much patience," she smiled.

With her ride back to Sipsey secure, Clarice forgot about Maxine Jefferson. She was the first one out of the room. She intended to have a good time visiting with the sisters and bargain hunting at her favorite stores.

As they discussed what stores they planned to hit, the brothers warned them not to break the bank.

Earl said, "Remember, tomorrow is Sunday. Don't spend the Lord's money."

The women laughed, said good-bye, and happily headed for Druid City Mall.

Chapter Twenty-Four

With the women gone, the men went back to talking about what they'd been talking about before they came; sports, politics, war, religion, and women.

A deep discussion ensued between Sugarfoot and Calvin Goines as to whether Wilt Chamberlain was a better basketball player than Bill Russell. Earl, a fan of both players, was caught in the middle and left trying to defend both.

Sugarfoot said, "Wilt will go down in history as the greatest player that ever played the game. He dominates. Nobody else can shoot a hundred points a game. He practically wins the game by himself. And it's not just scoring. He passes for more assists and grabs more rebounds than anybody." He paused. "Russell is good, no question about it, but Russell is a team player, and he plays on a better team than Chamberlain. If he gets hurt, there're three or four players that can fill in. But it's not the same as going out there and winning the game in spite of everybody else."

"Chamberlain is good for sure," Calvin agreed. "But his game is offense. Russell is the best defensive player in basketball; the only one that can stop Chamberlain. Besides, he gains my respect for having the courage to live and play in a bigoted town like Boston."

"Here, here," said Ivan. "Normally, I like Chamberlain, but Russell is a great player, and he does deserve something for playing in Boston."

Deacon Whitehead quipped, "I'm a baseball man myself. And it was Jackie Robinson that broke down the race thing in sports. Them White boys thought they were playing real ball. But when Jackie got in the game, he showed them how it was supposed to be played."

Sugarfoot considered, "If professional basketball was truly open to Black guys, they would dominate the league. White guys can't play the same level of basketball; they're not fast enough or quick enough. They'd be out of the game."

"On that, my brother, we agree," said Calvin.

"Good," sighed Earl. "We all agree on something."

Ivan pushed himself up in bed. His concern went deeper than sports. He said, "It's hard to measure, but if American society was open to us, we'd be more competitive in everything. We don't know the full extent that segregation has held us back. I don't know if the civil rights bill they just passed is gonna change anything, but God knows we need change."

Deacon Whitehead wasn't hopeful. "They say change is coming," he said. "You heard Clarice say they gon integrate the schools in Potoama County. I'll b'lieve that when I see it. But it got off with me when I heard that Sweetberry's daughter, Janelle's, done come back here with a White man. They say she's gon marry him."

"Sweetberry's daughter!" cried Calvin. "Are you kidding? Where, pray tell, did she meet a White man to marry?"

"She met him overseas, in England," Sugarfoot answered. "She's about to graduate from medical school and Sweetberry says she's gonna set up a clinic in Potoama County."

Earl whistled. "How did I miss this?"

Ordinarily, Sugarfoot wouldn't talk about anything to do with Sweetberry. But the Goines were his friends, and their motives harmless. He explained, "Janelle doesn't spend much time in Sipsey. After she graduated from high school, she went off to college, and she's been gone ever since. But Sweetberry is worried about her. She says her head is in the clouds."

Calvin said, "I agree with Sweetberry. If she thinks she's gon live in Sipsey with a White man, her head *is* in the clouds." He paused in bewilderment and shook his head. "That's crazy on so many levels, and it'll present a number of problems. For one thing, it's against the law of Jim Crow."

"And that law works for me," Earl spoke emphatically. "We Colored people fare better when we stick together and build up our own communities."

"Here, here," said Calvin.

But Ivan begged to differ. He said, "I agree. We should absolutely stick together and build up our own communities. But the archaic laws that govern this country are unjust and stupid. They hold everybody back. You can't call yourself a free country and then restrict what people can do."

"But marrying a White man?" complained Deacon Whitehead. "Why in the world would she want to do that?"

"Why shouldn't she marry a White man if she wants to?" asked Ivan. "White men have been messing with Colored women since the first slave ship."

"Not marrying them," cried Deacon Whitehead. "They've been sneaking around in the dark with them. But they don't think she's good enough to marry. So it'll kill them to see a White man married to one out in the open."

"More like it'll kill her," Calvin said irascibly. "She's definitely the one at risk. I grew up hearing about White men killing Colored men over White women *and* Colored omen. Nobody fares well in those situations. But the Colored person always ends up paying the most. So, if she

marries him, she'll pay a price for it."

"Yeah, like Batch," Deacon Whitehead interjected. "He worked at Prengle's Hardware store for all them years. Now he's sitting in the county jail waiting on a trial that'll most likely put him behind bars for the rest of his life."

"Batch, in jail!" This came as a shock to Calvin. "For what?"

"They say he robbed the hardware store," Deacon Whitehead replied. "A White man claims he seen him running away from the store late that Saturday night. And if the White man said it, we know the law believes it. They won't even let Batch out on bail, not that anybody tried to bail him out. But you can see his little Mama walking back and forth to Creek every day. It's kinda sad,"

"It sounds sad," said Calvin. "I used to see him downtown all the time. He's one of the people in Sipsey that I felt sorry for?"

"Why?" Sugarfoot asked in surprise.

He shrugged. "He always had that scared, downtrodden look about him. It was like he was always looking over his shoulders, waiting for something to happen. Poppa used to send me to Prengle's to pick up hardware and gardening supplies. Batch would load the wagon. I'd sit there and watch him. As he stepped and fetched, those White men would make fun of him. But he never reacted. *'Yassir, naw sir, can I help you, sir?'* He was pathetic."

Clearly stunned by this news, Calvin paused. "Wow! Batch locked up for robbing Prengle's?" He shook his head. "I kind of doubt it. Do people *believe* that?"

Sugarfoot was ashamed that he hadn't thought anymore

about Batch since the night he drove Aunt Ginny home. He said, "Folks don't like Batch. I'm not sure anybody's thought about it one way or the other."

"Batch is just so messy," grumbled Deacon Whitehead. "He'll look you in the face and stab you in the back."

Calvin shook his head. "It's a shame. We've bought into White people's hatred of us. We either turn it inward on ourselves or outward on each other."

Sugarfoot was surprised by Calvin's concern for Batch. It was the first time he'd heard anybody explain it that way. He wondered why he didn't feel sorry for Batch? Where was his compassion?

******

Around eight, the women returned with their hands full of shopping bags. They were thrilled over the great bargains they'd found.

"We caught the annual hospital charity sale," said Sherri Lynn. "And it was fabulous. I can't believe the stuff I got."

"And we're all spent out," puffed Gina.

"But it was for a good cause," Clarice beamed.

The men congratulated them on their finds and gently ushered them out of the room. For Ivan, it'd been a long day and he needed his rest. The nurse was there to take his vitals, give him his medicine, and settle him in for the night.

"Thanks for coming everybody," he called as they sauntered out. "I look forward to your next visit."

******

Clarice was happy as a lark as she and Deacon Collins went down the hall. She chatted nonstop about her "bargains," boasting that she'd have had to pay full price for them if she'd gone to the stores the day before.

"I'm glad you were able to make it," he said graciously.

"She said, "It makes you wonder how much markup they do on the merchandise. They're still making a profit, even with the sales."

"You better believe they are," he agreed.

While struggling to keep a grip on her packages, she talked nonstop. Sugarfoot said, "Here, let me help." He took some of the bags and walked ahead to press for the elevator. When it arrived, an elderly White couple was inside. The gentleman held the door as they stepped on. They exchanged greetings as the elevator began its descent.

Clarice was still chatting about her purchases. "I think I overdid it," she said. "But the sales were so good."

He smiled indulgently. "I'm sure they were."

The woman, a petite blond, was well dressed and nice looking. She kept staring at them as if she wanted to say something. Finally, speaking to Clarice, she said, "You're very pretty. Then, looking over at Sugarfoot, she smiled. "I can see you love her very much."

Neither reacted but was shocked by the notion. Clarice tried to think of something quick and clever to say. She ended up saying, "Oh yes, he's full of love, and he's being very helpful tonight."

"So much shopping?" The lady said. "You must've made the charity sale. I went earlier in the day and I got some good deals."

"So did I," Clarice exclaimed.

The elevator reached the lobby, and the couple went towards the gift shop. Suddenly, the woman looked back and said, "Have a wonderful evening."

"Likewise," Clarice smiled.

Outside, she followed Deacon Collins to the parking lot. The evening had grown chilly and a mist of rain had begun. Surprised by the drop in temperature, she shivered, "Brrrr. It's gotten cold out here."

He set the bags down took off his jacket and handed it to her.

Gratefully, she put it on. She said, "Deacon, I feel bad taking your jacket."

He smiled. "You didn't take it, I gave it to you. I don't want you to be cold," he said thoughtfully.

When they reached her side of the truck, he opened the door, and she climbed inside. He handed her the bags and closed the door.

As he eased the truck out of the parking lot, Clarice began chatting. She said, "Ivan really gave us a scare. He's the last person you'd expect something like that to happen to. Have you met his wife?"

No," he answered. "I haven't had the pleasure."

She sighed. "It's a cautionary tale; a warning against marrying somebody you don't know."

His response was a cryptic grunt.

She couldn't read him. She wanted to say more about Ivan's situation. But seeing that he didn't want to talk about his friend, she changed the subject. She said, "I guess you've heard. There's another mess brewing in the Fellowship Hall?"

"No, what's going on?"

"This time it's Maxine and Darlene. And it's really unfair. Darlene is a businesswoman, and she tries to get along with everybody. But Sister Jefferson is so hard to get along with. Darlene says she was helping serve at the Annual Officers Conference when Sister Jefferson ordered her out of the kitchen. She's known for that. The deacons should remove her."

"That's not our job."

"Yes, it is. We both know that the deacons run First Macedonia. And Maxine thinks the kitchen is her personal domain. The church belongs to all of us."

"Well, the church should vote her out."

"It's not that simple."

He grunted a laugh.

She laughed too, realizing that trying to remove Maxine Jefferson from the Fellowship Hall wouldn't be easy. She also knew she shouldn't be talking about a fellow church member. But the inside of the truck was warm and cozy and he was easy to talk to, so she indulged herself.

Suddenly, a wave of happiness came over her. It was a perfect evening: the stars twinkled against an overcast sky; her friend was nicely recovering from a near tragedy; and her shopping spree had been a great success. All was right in her world.

As they neared the river, the lights on the drawbridge started blinking. Then the thunderous boom of the foghorn sent the warning that a boat was approaching. The cars in front of them slowed to a stop.

"Oh," Clarice leaned forward. "The bridge is going up."

They waited, and suddenly the drawbridge began its climb, broke into halves, and rose skyward, high enough for the approaching boat to pass underneath.

Not a word was said inside the truck. She sat captivated

as the boat inched its way across the channel. She never tired of watching this drama unfold on the Black Warrior River.

"Isn't it something."

"A marvelous feat of engineering," he acknowledged.

The boat took its time. But eventually it cleared the bridge and continued down the river. With lights twinkling, it blew its horn, signaling a successful crossing. The two halves began their descent back to the base and clasped themselves in place. The red lights turned

yellow and then green. Traffic across the river resumed.

Riding with Deacon Collins was revealing in that she didn't feel the restraint she normally did. Felix had very strict rules about her not gossiping about the good people of Sipsey.' But she felt it safe to share her thoughts with him.

When she took time to catch her breath, he asked, "Would you like to listen to music?"

"Yes, I would," she said eagerly.

He punched the radio's knob, and suddenly the tantalizing voice of Louie the Lover came at them. Louie said, "This is WTUV, 97.8 on your dial. You're cordially invited to the rhapsody we call Silky Sounds, the South's finest music for chocolate lovers. So if you love somebody, used to love somebody, or hope to love somebody someday, we've got a song for you."

Love ballads filled the cab. Both turned inward, deep in thought. Unexpectedly, rain came down in gushes as a singer crooned about a rainy night in Georgia. Against the swishing of the windshield wipers, Clarice asked, "Deacon, do you mind if I turn the sound up?"

"Help yourself."

She did and sang along, losing herself in the lyrics.

"So you like that?"

"I do," she cuddled herself. "It's one of my favorite songs."

He took quiet notice.

For Clarice, the ride from Lancaster had never been so eventful. Normally, she wouldn't pay any attention to the landscape. But tonight, as the music played, she was suddenly aware of everything. Billboards with flashing neon lights dotted the roadside. The two lanes leading out of the city had suddenly become four. Outside of town, a new service station had opened on the left. And how long had the apartment complex on the right been there?

Why, she was suddenly aware of everything!

Back in Potoama County, the rain had stopped. As they reached County Road 10, she said, "That's Sister Domaine's turn. Could we stop by her place for a minute?"

He obliged, making the left turn down the country road. It was very dark. And the countryside seemed frighteningly eerie.

She said, "I love coming to visit her, but I hate coming down this road."

"Why?"

"Because it's dark and spooky. Even in the daytime it's scary. But at night, it's terrifying."

"Do you visit often?"

"I come about once a month. When she comes to Saturday dinners at the church, I usually bring her home. But I'd come more often if I wasn't scared."

He said, "I'm her unit leader. I help her with her chores but, to be honest, she does as much work as I do." He laughed. "She's something."

"She's certainly independent," Clarice affirmed. "And she loves company. I just wish I could spend more time with her."

"Let me know when you want to come, I'll bring you."

"Thanks," she said, "I will."

She'd brought Sister Domaine's favorite treats, a bag of chocolate drop candies and boiled peanuts.

Delilah Domaine suffered from chronic arthritis and sometimes had trouble getting around. But she was stout with a strong constitution.

Her appearance was striking and distinguished looking. Of a deep brown complexion, she had high cheekbones. She wore her hair in a long braid wrapped around her head. But tonight it was undone and hung so far down her back that she could sit on it. This made it easy to believe she was mixed with Indian blood as folks said she was.

She said, "I was just sitting here hoping somebody would stop by. I'm so glad to see y'all."

Clarice greeted her with a hug. She said, "We won't stay long. Deacon Collins and I are just coming from the hospital visiting Ivan. I'm happy to tell you that he's come out of the coma and he's doing fine."

"Praise be to God," she said.

They stayed a little longer than Clarice expected because Sister Domaine started talking about the panther she'd been hearing howling at night. She said, "Sometimes it sounds like he's right outside my window. It's a terrible sound."

Sugarfoot said, "Deacon Goines has been hearing it too. Not long ago, something got into his neighbor's pigpen. Be careful, especially at night."

"I am," she said. "I got my shotgun, and I know how to

use it."

"Okay," he smiled.

As they left, she hugged them and asked them to come back to see her.

Heading home, Clarice said, "Sister Domaine is a strong woman. She's also wise and has a wonderful spirit. But she still grieves for her son. She keeps that picture of Willie Paul on the front wall so everybody can see it. I guess that's how she keeps his spirit alive."

"Maybe so," he said. "Doesn't she have a daughter?"

"No, she has a niece that comes to stay with her sometimes. Willie Paul was her only child. I understand he took very good care of her. So you can understand why she's taking it so hard, especially being killed by the Klan the way he was."

"Yeah," he mumbled, quietly grieving for the old woman.

Clarice was still doing most of the talking. As they neared the city limits, he said, "Is there anywhere else you need to go?"

She smiled. "If it's not too much trouble, I'd like to go to Nebb's to get Mother some barbecue."

"Really?" He raised an eyebrow. "Mrs. Mary Ann Vanderway eats barbecue?"

She looked at him in surprise. "Of course Mother eats barbecue. Doesn't everybody? When I'm out on Saturday night, I always bring her barbecue with extra sauce," she giggled. "Mother loves barbecue."

"Ookaay. Nebb's it is."

Chapter Twenty-Five

Ivan Goines counted his blessings. The memory of his soul hanging between two worlds was something he'd never forget. He hadn't spoken about it in the short time he'd been awake, but he remembered how close he'd come to death.

Calvin and Earl were spending the night despite the fact that, except for a little weakness, he was back to himself. His heart quickened with love as he recalled his family's reaction when he awoke. His Poppa had been so moved that he couldn't stand it. He'd simply said, "The Lord has answered my prayers." And he left.

Calvin and Earl made themselves at home. Earl sat in a straight back chair near the door, and Calvin sat in a recliner in a corner.

Ivan had tried to send them home. "Y'all can go now. I'm a big boy. I can stay by myself. Besides, Madea told you to go home."

But Earl shoo shooed him. "We'll stay one more night in case you decide to dose off again. Tomorrow morning we'll decide what to do."

It was settled. For the rest of the evening, they entertained themselves, teasing as they'd done as children about which one had done the most work on the farm. Earl had brought a transistor radio, and they listened to a National League baseball game. But around midnight, they were exhausted and fell asleep.

****

It didn't take long for Ivan to drift into a slumber. It was reminiscent of his childhood days when he was fast asleep as soon as his head hit the pillow. It was so peaceful that he wasn't even dreaming. It was the kind of sleep that carried you all the way to daylight and you awoke the next morning knowing that you'd had a good night's rest.

The night nurse peeped into the room, surprised that there were three of them. But thankfully, they were sound asleep. The last thing she wanted was to engage in conversation with anybody. She'd had a long day and wanted to get the job over and get home.

The room was dark; the only light was a dim lamp in a far corner. "Not that he needs it," she thought. He'd been in a coma since he'd been there. She knew the details of his case but dismissed them as unimportant.

She crept to the head of the bed to check his intravenous device. It was half full and wouldn't need changing for a while. She was surprised that they'd taken away his oxygen machine and he was breathing on his own. "Oh well, good for you," she whispered. One of the men stirred, and covering the patient, she said, "Sleep well."

******

Though it appeared that he was healing nicely, it wasn't so. Again, Ivan Goines's life was hanging in the balance.

Ridiculously, the darkness wasn't finished with him. All of a sudden, he was back in a struggle for his life. This time, the hand of evil had snuck upon him. His grandmothers reappeared, waving him back to his earthly mission.

Blackness engulfed him. Even in his deep sleep, he was confused. How often would he have to fight this fight? And this stupor was so different from the other. He wasn't sure how it was different, he just knew it was.

And he was suffocating!

Suddenly conscious, he opened his mouth but no sound came out. He struggled, trying to open his eyes, but his lids were clamped shut. Pressure plus the darkness prevented him from responding.

His arms were weak and pinned with a weight impossible to comprehend. He tried to roll his body. The battle intensified, and he knew that whatever was happening was crazy. As he gasped for breath, he felt his life slipping away.

Fight or flight; he had to do one or the other. He couldn't fly, not even run, so fight was all he had. With no other help, he evoked the battle cry of his father, "God is my refuge and strength, a present help in trouble."

He was in trouble, and he prayed, *"Oh Lord, help me. The devil is back again, killing me. I can't fight him by myself. Help me! Help me!"*

A sudden surge of strength allowed his lower body to move, and he began kicking, twisting, and jerking about.

"Be still," the desperate voice said, and he recognized it. He jerked his body harder, twisted it while kicking his legs.

Suddenly, Earl's voice boomed, "What the hell is going on?"

Ivan felt rather than heard his giant strides make a huge racket as he rushed to the bed. At once, he felt the pressure being lifted and Earl's furious voice screamed, "What're you doing? Are you trying to *kill* him?"

Gasping for breath, Ivan's eyes flew open and he recognized his assailant. He breathed heavily, knowing what'd happened.

In a panic, the nurse tried to leave the room, but Earl

grabbed her. She put up a fight, struggling and tussling with him. Then realizing she couldn't get away, she begged him to let her go. He relaxed his grip, and she broke for the door. He jumped in front of her, blocking her passage. She tried to push him out of the way. He grabbed her wrists in a vise grip. "What do you think you're doing?" He yelled.

She glared angrily but offered no explanation.

Suddenly Calvin awoke and looked frantically from Earl to Ivan to the nurse in curious, interlocking stare.

"What's going on?" he demanded.

Earl felt foolish. He'd tackled a woman and didn't quite know why. He said, "I woke up and she was standing over Ivan. It looked like she was smothering him."

Calvin laughed nervously. "But everything's cool now, right?" He looked at Ivan. "*Is* everything cool?"

It was all Ivan could do not to expose her, but he kept calm. He said, "It's my fault, bruh. I must've been having a nightmare. I thought I was in a black hole, struggling for my life. The nurse came in and I thought she was the devil in the hole, so I started fighting and kicking, and Earl woke up. Everything's cool."

Everybody looked at Earl. Not normally suspicious, his antennae were still up; what he'd witnessed had been star-tling.

He shook his head. "Well," he shrugged uncertainly. "Maybe I misread the situation. I was coming out of a deep sleep, and. . ." his voice trailed off.

Still, he didn't seem convinced that he was mistaken. He looked at Ivan, studying him for signs of distress. Ivan saw his concern and laughed it off. The nurse was standing there looking surrounded and trapped.

Ivan knew this episode wouldn't come to an end with his brothers in the room. Earl was looking at the nurse with such a frightful expression that he feared he might tackle her again. He had to get them out of there.

He said, "Brothers, excuse me, but I gotta go."

Calvin started outside but Earl refused to leave. He said, "Go ahead, Ivan. I've seen you use the bathroom before."

"Come on, Earl, I need my privacy."

As Earl walked towards the door, Ivan looked at the nurse and said, "Nurse, can you please help me?"

When they were alone, he looked at her through anguished eyes. He said, "Why are you here?"

"I'm your wife. I have a right to be here," she said arrogantly. They moved you from Georgia Medical to get you away from me."

He marveled that Deanna even looked good in a nurse's uniform. Oh so lovely and yet so cunning.

He sighed with regret.

Misreading his observation, she said, "I've set up an appointment for us to go to counselling to start working on our problems."

Ivan laughed. "I don't need no counselling. You do."

"Ivan," she pled, "I lost my temper that night. I didn't mean to stab you, and if you hadn't choked me, I wouldn't have done it. I'm sorry about it. I'm also sorry for trying to force you to do something you didn't want to do. I should've waited until you were ready to buy a house. And I shouldn't have used the royalty check to make the down payment."

He smirked. "That doesn't explain you coming here and trying to smother me."

"I wasn't trying to smother you!" she cried. "I was covering you up." She started towards him as if she meant to embrace him. He frowned and recoiled at the gesture.

She said, "Please, Ivan, give me another chance."

He ignored the plea. "You know, it would've worked out better if we'd just had an affair and left it at that. We never had a chance as a couple because we never dealt in truth. I don't know the real you," he said. "I don't know where you're from, and I don't trust you."

"I'll tell you everything you want to know. But, please, let's start over."

He sighed. "Deanna, you killed the man that would've considered anything you're saying right now. So, let me be clear; I'm not living with you again."

"You hate me that much?"

"No, I really don't. I appreciate your ingenuity. You're good, and one day, you'll either do something great, or you'll end up with life in prison or the death penalty. It's going to be interesting, but I don't want any part of it."

"I'm not *that* bad," she said.

"Yes, you are. He smiled ironically. "When I met you, I was impressed with the woman I thought you were. You were living on the rich side of town, driving a fancy car, flashing money, and teaching at a Big Ten College. I couldn't get over you. I said to myself, this is a fascinating woman. It never occurred to me that you'd stolen all of that stuff. That apartment and car belonged to a White woman your mother had worked for that you swindled while she was sick. Her family had to take you to court to get you out of that apartment. And you'd stolen the college credentials of a woman who'd been admitted to a mental institution." He gave a long, sad sigh. Sometimes I just wonder where you get the nerve."

"You don't know the whole story."

"And I don't want to. I've watched you destroy every decent thing that you've come into contact with. And it's crazy. You have everything you need to be legitimate. But you'd rather con your way. So, I've made some non-negotiable decisions. I'm moving back to Sipsey and starting my life over."

"Sipsey?"

"Yep, and all I want from you is a peace treaty."

He reached into the nightstand drawer and took out paper and pen.

He wrote: To my wife, Deanna Goines, I give all of the material possessions we acquired during our marriage, including the advance royalty check for my recent book and all royalties for the next year. Whatever money we have in South DeKalb Bank is hers. What I ask in return is a divorce on the grounds of mental and physical cruelty and that the marriage was a mistake from the beginning.

He wrote a note that he required her to sign. It said: I, Deanna Goines, agree to divorce Ivan Goines on the grounds of mental and physical cruelty and that the marriage was a mistake from the beginning.

He said, "This is all you get. Take it or leave it."

Before she could say anything, he'd called his brothers back into the room.

She said, "I'm not divorcing you."

"Thanks, nurse," he said as his brothers walked in.

When she was gone, Earl said, "That was the strangest thing I've ever witnessed."

Calvin said, "In all my years of working in a hospital,

I've never seen a nurse try to kill a patient. It's all in your mind."

Earl shook his head. "For a crazy minute, I wondered if your wife had showed up here.

Wait 'til I tell Madea."

"Earl, don't," Ivan said quickly. "You know Madea will take it seriously and I'll be stuck with you until I'm dismissed."

Earl blinked. "You're right, but it sure did look funny."

They went back to their respective sleep stations.

******

Ivan didn't close his eyes. His mind rewound to the summer he met Deanna. She'd

been in the library at the university claiming to be doing research on an article she was about to publish. She introduced herself as an associate professor at a nearby college.

"I'm up for tenure," she'd said, so I've got to up my publishing game."

She was charming and beautiful, and he was soon smitten.

When he finished graduate school and was ready to leave town, she asked him to marry her. "What we have is too precious to let go," she'd said. "Together, we could build sandcastles on in the sky or on Mars."

He said yes. It was a foolish notion. They'd only known each other a few months. But he was young and optimistic. He felt empowered to do whatever he wanted.

He quickly discovered the price of being married to Deanna. She was always up to something and the police was always on her heels. No sooner did one investigation of her end than another began. Most disappointing was that everything she'd told him about herself was a lie. And it was expensive. Six months after they married, he'd had to pay a lawyer five thousand dollars to keep her from going to jail for stealing the college transcript.

But sometimes money wasn't enough. The family of her mother's employer insisted that she get jail time. She was sentenced to three years confinement. But her conviction was overturned on appeal.

She didn't change at all. She went right on and forged records to get the job at Sheffield College in Atlanta. And the night she'd stabbed him, he'd learned that she'd committed another forgery to get a job at Hancock State. That was the move that made him realize he didn't have the luxury of dragging their marriage out.

He'd lost respect for himself and was so embarrassed by what his life had become that he'd quit going home. Her stabbing him was almost a blessing. It gave him grounds for divorce without exposing his family to the embarrassment his life had become.

It suddenly hit him that Calvin and Earl hadn't recognized her because they hadn't seen her before. They hadn't attended his wedding. And the one time he'd brought her to Sipsey, only Sherri Lynn and Gina had seen her. Neither one had liked her, but Gina's dislike had been loud and clear.

He wished he'd listened to her. It would've saved him a lot of heartache and money. Every day he'd been married to Deanna had cost him something.

Part Four

Chapter Twenty-Six

On the same day that Batch Blaine was rushed to Potoama County Hospital, reported to have attempted suicide, Janelle got a letter from the United States Department of Health and Medical Services informing her that her application to open a medical facility in Potoama County had been denied.

Reasons stated ranged from her inexperience as a doctor to lack of legislative support and compliance to state guidelines, 'requirements needed to establish a highly functioning facility.'

It further stated: *The Alabama Department of Public Health is presently surveying the need for expanded medical services throughout the state. West central Alabama is a targeted region. We applaud your commitment to the pursuit of primary health care for the citizens of Potoama County. Please be assured that every effort is being made by state and local governments as well as the U.S. Department of Health and Medical Services to accomplish this goal.*

Inasmuch as the State of Alabama has established guidelines in the effective management of hospitals and medical centers, and is much better equipped to meet the needs of its citizens than an individual doctor, your request is hereby denied.

The letter ended by saying:

We encourage your active participation in conferences, discussions, and forums designed

to research, assess, and ultimately provide quality health care to all Americans.

As if to further avert her dream, the packet contained a checklist of added requirements. Among them: a more detailed financial feasibility analysis, authorization from the Governor of Alabama designating the location as medically underserved, written commitment from a sponsoring hospital, and coordination with Potoama County Health Department.

All of the above must be met in a resubmitted application.

Janelle was inconsolable. The letter had come in the early afternoon as Jericho was getting ready for work. Janelle came into her room screaming and hollering so loudly that Jericho thought something terrible had happened in the house. Upon reading the letter, she tried to calm Janelle, but it didn't work. Janelle went into a crying fit so intense that her body began shaking with convulsions.

"I can't leave you like this," Jericho mumbled and went next door to use the telephone to call the hotel. She explained to the desk clerk that she was in the midst of a family crisis and wouldn't be able to come.

"I tried so hard," Janelle mourned. Her voice was hoarse, and her body was still shaking. "I thought I had everything in order. The clinic in Creek is just a band-aid station and doesn't serve anybody well. This is bureaucracy; cheap, stupid, bureaucracy."

Tears and mucus ran together as she angrily passed judgment on the bureaucrats. Jericho got a box of tissues and wiped away the slime. All she could think to say was, "Janelle, these things happen."

"But they assured me in Washington that my chances of being approved were excellent.

So many people thought it was a good idea, even the Assistant to the Secretary of Health and Medical Services. He was a nice man. He personally looked over my application and said it was one of the best he'd seen. I don't know what happened!"

Jericho bit her tongue. She wanted to say, 'I could've told you so,' but knew it would do no good in the moment.

They sat on the bed. Jericho cradled her in her arms and dried her tears. She wondered, how do you tell your child that her reach was too far? How do you express to her that getting through medical school and becoming a doctor was beyond what was expected? And how did you make her see that just making the effort was worthwhile?

Janelle told neither Jeremy nor Eddie about the letter. She left it to Jericho to break the news. As they absorbed the shock, Janelle stayed in Jericho's room and mourned the death of her dream.

At a point, Jericho knew she had to say something to Janelle. She said, "Baby, this is life. Things don't always work out like we want them to, but we don't give up. This ain't the end. You had this dream, and it was a good one. I'm just happy you've got a caring heart and want to do. something to improve the lives of the people of this county. But," she shrugged, "this might not be the right time to open a clinic. God might have something better for you."

"Better?" Janelle's voice rose in defiance. "What could be better than providing basic health care to people that can't afford it? Mama, I care about these people. And there are things they can do. They can live better and longer lives. But they need to be told about these things. Nobody's doing that. Nobody cares."

"But you do," Jericho said. "And in the Kingdom of God, that counts. This didn't work out, but something else will. Don't give up. You don't need no clinic to tell folks what they can do to help themselves. You can do that at church. Make an announcement and tell folks

to stop eating so much pork and cooking with so much salt. Don't lose hope. And next time, ask God to lead and guide you."

Janelle had no faith in the 'God is the answer to everything' argument. For her, there was no excuse for what'd happened. She wasn't asking for the moon or the stars. She was simply asking for the opportunity to help a deserving population towards better health and a better quality of life.

She stood up and kissed Jericho on the cheek. She knew her mother was only trying to help. But the responsibility shouldn't be on her to explain the unfairness of the system. And sweltering inside of her was the beginning of a deep anger at that system, so rich, yet unwilling to take seriously the needs of vulnerable people.

As the finality of it dawned on her, she said, "We've gotta get packed and get back to New York. I've got to figure out what to do. I've got to get a job; all of my plans have fallen apart."

Jericho said, "Take your time. You don't have to figure everything out today."

Suddenly, Janelle yelled, "I've got to figure out what to do about daddy! I thought the clinic would be approved and I'd get grant money and we'd rent a house. But now, without the clinic, I won't be eligible for the money. I promised daddy I wouldn't take him back to the home." In a fit of helplessness, she threw up her hands. "What am I gonna do?"

Sobbing pitifully, she fell back onto the bed. Her misery was hard to bear. It touched Jericho so deeply that she wondered what she could to do to help. And idea came about what to do with Eddie, and it was so repulsive that she quickly pushed it out of her mind.

Other thoughts surfaced; maybe Janelle should contact his children. Surely one of them cared enough about him to take him in. If they wouldn't take him, then maybe his family in South Carolina would. Southern folks believed in looking after their own. She remembered Eddie mentioning a sister and some brothers when they were together. Maybe one of them would take pity on him and offer him a home. Finally, she thought a better nursing home in New York might be the answer.

Mentally, she practiced the best words to use to convince Janelle. But before she could say anything, Janelle said, "I'll take care of my daddy myself. I don't trust anybody else, and I'm not gon risk losing him."

Well, so much with what to do with Eddie.

Janelle added, "I'm the only child he's got that cares about him, and I'm not gonna let him down."

Any remark Jericho could've made about him never doing anything for her was bitten back. Her heart ached for this wonderful daughter whose shoulders sagged under the weight of disappointment.

Jericho inhaled and exhaled several times. She knew she had to go with her first mind. But it took every bit of decency she had to do it. She hesitated, doubting herself. Finally, she put selfishness aside and said, "Don't worry about Eddie. Leave him here. I'll take care of him 'til you get settled."

"Will you, Mama?" Janelle's voice burst with relief.

"This is the best thing you could do for me. I know you don't want to do it, but I love you for it."

"Don't worry, we'll make it work."

She could feel Janelle's body relaxing.

******

Jeremy Mulligan was stumped by the rejection. He tried to come up with alternative scenarios in which the health council might reconsider her request. "Solicit a meeting with the President of the United States and ask if he'll intervene on your behalf," he said.

Jericho looked at him like he was crazy. "That is not something that's gon happen in our lifetime."

"This is the United States of America," he informed her. "There's got to be something that can be done."

"Well, when you come up with it, let us know," Jericho quipped sarcastically.

After supper, they went into the sitting room to watch the evening news. Janelle sat forlornly in a corner as the anchorman reported on world events. The sight of her was heart-breaking. The chatty and cheerful optimist had suddenly become somber and withdrawn. Eddie kept glancing at her, sighing like he wanted to say something. But when the conversation was paused for his input, he held back.

Jeremy kept trying to say something comforting. They appreciated his efforts, but his words fell flat. Now, realizing he should offer some words of comfort, Eddie gave a frank read of the situation.

He said, "Janelle, I'm gonna be perfectly honest with you. Your mama has been trying to tell you something that I haven't had the guts to say. But it's real. It's two things that should've warned us that this might happen. Number one, you're a Colored girl, and it would take a lot of people helping you for you to pull this off. And by a lot of people, I mean a lot of White people. Well," he shrugged, "they weren't willing to do it. On top of that, they're giving you the runaround, claiming they're gonna do something about the problem."

"But they won't," she cried. "It's all talk. "Potoama County won't do anything to help its citizens and they won't let anybody else help. It's just a shame. There's been no improvement in health services of this county since I was a kid. This isn't hard to figure out," she sniffed. "We need a clinic to offer basic health care for our people."

"It makes perfectly good sense," said Jeremy.

Ignoring him, Jericho said, "What was the other reason, Eddie? You said there were two warning signs. What was the other one?"

"Number two," he replied, "you took Jeremy with you when you went to talk to the people at the health department. That was a mistake. You young people don't get it, but race mixing is a very big deal in this country. Next to being a Negro, taking your White boyfriend down there was the worst thing you could've done. I can tell you what probably happened. As soon as you left the clinic, they got on the telephone, called down to Montgomery and nixed the idea. Montgomery called Washington and they wrote the letter. The thing was dead before you left town. That's how these things work."

"And that's about the size of it," Jericho echoed.

"But that's so bigoted, so wrong," declared Jeremy.

"But so real," cried Jericho.

Eddie looked at Janelle with tenderness and said, "Hold your head up, baby. This ain't the end of the world. There's a saying that says, 'it's not the number of times you get knocked down in life, it's the number of times you get back up that makes the difference. Get back up," he admonished.

Chapter Twenty-Seven

With her dream deferred and a heavy heart, Janelle and Jeremy left Sipsey the next week.

Eddie thanked her for all she'd done for him. As he embraced her, he muttered, "You brought me back to life, daughter, and I thank you for it. I'm gon make you proud."

He pulled up his pant leg and showed off his prosthetic leg. He beamed. "I'm really enjoying this leg. I can get around good on it, and I can do a lot of things that I couldn't do before." He laughed. "This leg is gon be the comeback of Eddie Simpson. Look out, world, I'm coming back."

Janelle smiled, looking proud that she'd had a hand in getting the leg. "I'm sorry I can't take you with me, but I'll come back and get you as soon as I can."

"Don't worry 'bout me," he winked. "Me and Candy will make it alright."

Jericho rolled her eyes. She would've railed against the thought if Janelle hadn't been standing there looking so sad.

"Y'all got the Green Book?" Eddie asked.

"No," Janelle said quickly.

Jeremy asked, "What's the Green Book?"

Eddie explained, "It a handbook that lets us Colored people know the places we can go and eat, use the restroom, spend the night; things you need to know when you travel. It's still against the law for us to go to the same places as White folks."

"Extraordinary," Jeremy whispered, processing the news. "It seems every day I'm learning something new about this country."

Janelle said, "I don't think we'll need it, daddy. The laws have changed. Colored people can travel freely in the United States now. We can eat, sleep and use the bathroom wherever we want."

Eddie didn't trust it. He said, "I don't go nowhere without the Green Book."

Jericho busily loaded the car with grits, sorghum syrup, homemade sweet pickles, ribbon cane, pear preserves, and other things of the south Janelle said she had trouble finding in the stores up north.

Before they drove off, she issued a word of prayer:

Heavenly Father, we thank you for this family and this fellowship. I thank you for my daughter, Janelle, the first pride of my life. Her heart is heavy and her spirit broken. But I ask you to comfort her. But also help her understand that this is life. It's not what did or didn't happen, it's what's in her heart that matters most. And bless Jeremy. He's a fine young man and a good friend. Give them traveling graces as they take to the highway. Cover them with your love and your protection. And give me the patience to deal with Eddie Simpson. In your name I pray, a-men."

Jericho stuck her head inside the car and kissed Janelle. She said, "Be of good cheer. The Lord is gon work it out."

*****

When Jericho and Eddie went back into the house, Eddie came into the sitting room and plopped down on the couch as if he was at home. He said, "Candy, if we gon live together, we gon have to get some things for our onvenience. We need a telephone and a car."

"A car!" Jericho's scream was earsplitting. "Where in

the devil is we gon get the money to get a car *or* a telephone? I ain't got no money to buy no car and I can't drive no way. You talk like a crazy man."

By now, Eddie had learned that when Jericho was in one of her rants to let her rant. And she did, saying quite a bit; warning him not to tell her what she needed or what to do. She ended by reminding him that he was down here on her and should be grateful for the sacrifice she was making.

When she'd said all she wanted to say, he said, "I can drive, and I got the money to buy the car."

"Where did *you* get money to buy a car?" She asked. "Don't tell me you shook Janelle and Jeremy down for what little money they had."

He laughed. "No, I don't shake anybody down for anything anymore. When I went to prison, I had good money. I guess you don't remember, but I used to write songs for rival groups. A couple of them became hits. While I was in prison, I left the money alone and it grew interest. Plus, every time one of my songs plays anywhere in the world, I get paid. I ain't no broke man. So, like I said, we need to get a car and a telephone. That way, we can stay in touch with Janelle, and we can drive up to see her sometime."

Jericho was astounded. And this was Eddie Simpson, still pulling rabbits out of hats.

Chapter Twenty-Eight

When word got out that Batch had attempted suicide, people thought he'd slit his wrists or tried to hang himself. It never occurred to anybody that Batch was starving himself to death. But it was soon cleared up. The revised report stated that he'd barely eaten anything the whole time he'd been in jail. And after a while, his body rebelled and shut down. By the time the ambulance picked him up, he was unresponsive.

The diagnosis was that his body was dehydrated, famished, and in shock.

The hospital in Creek hadn't been able to revive him. They rushed him to Piedmont Hospital in Lancaster where he was placed in intensive care.

The event was reported in the news media. The television showed an image of the ambulance speeding down Highway 82 towards Lancaster.

This brought out the eyewitness to the robbery, Mr. Bobby Doyle Hatfield.

It was the lead story on the news segment, *Focus on Sipsey*. The television reporter, Shane Houston, treated Mr. Hatfield as a celebrity. With a full news crew, Shane told his viewers, "We're here at the home of Bobby Doyle Hatfield, eyewitness to the suspect, Batch Blaine, fleeing Prengle's Department Store on the night of the robbery. In light of the news that Batch Blaine's hunger strike has led to his collapse, Mr. Hatfield has graciously consented to our interview.

Bobby Doyle stood smiling from the den of his home beside an impressive collection of long and short guns. The stuffed head of a buck, an eight pointer he claimed to have killed a few seasons ago, looked frightfully forward from a high wall.

On the mantle were photos of Bobby Doyle, barbecuing a pig, throwing horse shoes at the county fair, and cutting a jig at a hoedown. "Get some pictures," Shane commanded, The cameraman moved in closer, snapping several shots of Bobby Doyle at play.

"Quite an active man," Shane extolled.

"Yep, that's what life's all about," Bobby Doyle tittered in his hillbilly drawl.

"You're a religious man as well as a business man?" Shane remarked.

"That's right. I'm a trustee at the First United Methodist Church of Callaway. I own Hatfield's Fishing Tackle and Cold Storage in the town of Buin. And I'm a good friend and neighbor." With a boastful chuckle, he added, "And I like to fish and hunt."

"Just the kind of citizen we're proud of here in Potoama County," Shane Houston said appreciatively.

They walked outside and Shane exclaimed over the pristine property. "I don't think I've ever seen a property this well-kept," he said.

"I inherited this from my daddy," Bobby Doyle explained. "And he inherited it from his daddy, Jim Bob Hatfield."

As if trying to prove himself worthy of such a legacy, Bobby Doyle spoke proudly of his charitable works. He said, "I ring the bell for the Salvation Army at Christmastime. And very year, I let the little Nigra children hunt Easter eggs in the lower cow pasture over there." He pointed to a large pasture across the road. "They like that."

Shane flinched at his use of the racial slur but didn't comment. He followed him around the house to a budding vegetable garden and inspected the long rows of peas, tomatoes and cabbages. "I want a mess of everything," he kidded. Bobby Doyle grinned and gave pointers on planting and fertilizing at the right time of year.

As they rounded a corner, Mrs. Bobby Doyle waved from a large tractor where she appeared to be breaking ground for another crop.

The crew followed them to a white ornamented gazebo. As if on cue, his coffee colored maid brought out a tray with a pitcher of lemonade and ice-filled crystal glasses. The men chatted further about the good life. Bobby Doyle pointed to a pond beyond a medley of trees and said, "That's the first man-made catfish pond in Potoama County. Best catfish in the state," he declared.

A lively discussion as to whether salt water fish was better eating than fresh water fish began. The conclusion was that they liked most fish."

In this picturesque setting with two respectable White men talking about Bobby Doyle's idyllic life, the interview could well have been called "The Uncomplicated Life of a Southern Gentleman."

Towards the end, the reporter surprisingly challenged Bobby Doyle on his compassion. He asked, "As a responsible citizen of the community and a dedicated man of God, what do you think should happen to the accused robber of Prengle's?"

Without hesitation, Bobby Doyle said, "I feel like any lawbreaker should be prosecuted to the fullest extent of the law. Everybody knows the Prengles are some of the best businessmen in this county, heck this state. And they've been good to that Nigra, letting him work at the store all them years and taking care of him. For him to break in and take advantage of them like that is a disgrace. The law should have no mercy on him, 'cause I don't."

The reporter said, "Well, do you have any sympathy for his present situation?"

"I shore' don't," Bobby Doyle laughed as if that was out of the question. "I feel like he's faking. No doubt he's hoping folk'll feel sorry for him and let him off easy. But I don't agree with that. He's got to pay for what he done."

******

Sugarfoot walked into the lobby of Piedmont Hospital on his way to visit Ivan Goines. He recognized Aunt Ginny sitting on a bench looking lost. He went over to her. "Aunt Ginny, what're you doing here?"

She looked up at him through the perpetual tears stuck in the corners of her eyes. She said, "I'm here to see Batch. You know they brung him here about a week ago. They say he tried to kill his'self."

Sugarfoot felt sorry for her and regretted not to have checked on her. But things had kept happening. Ivan was stabbed by his wife and put in a coma for weeks. He'd been going back and forth to Atlanta to check on him. In addition, Abner was granted a contract to build houses in a subdivision in Columbus, Mississippi, and he was working longer hours. On top of that, he was doing part-time work of his own. So it was no exaggeration that he'd been busy. Still he was sorry he hadn't found time to check on the Blaine family.

Aunt Ginny looked out of place, and he wondered how she'd got to Lancaster. He sat down beside her and asked, "How'd you get here?"

"Miss Vanderway brung me," she answered.

"Miss Mary Ann?"

"No, sir, Miss Clarice. I'm waiting on her. She's going up in the elevator with me."

"Clarice Vanderway?" He repeated in astonishment.

"Yes, sir," she answered patiently. "She come and picked me up and brung me."

"I'm sorry to hear about Batch."

"Yes, sir, he stopped eating. He ain't never been a big eater. But since he been locked up, he don't eat nothing. He won't trying to kill his'self though. He just ain't got no stomach for food."

At that moment, Clarice Vanderway came through the revolving doors. She was simply dressed in a black pencil skirt, long sleeve white blouse with standup collar and fabric covered buttons. Black pumps showed off shapely legs.

Smiling, she walked over to them. "Hello, Deacon Collins," she said breezily. "What a pleasant surprise."

"Likewise," he answered, standing up.

Deacon Collins was a proud man with a fair understanding of himself. He knew that many women found him attractive. But he also knew his limitations. Clarice Vanderway, he felt, was a limitation. And though he wouldn't admit it to anybody, he'd been thinking about her ever since she'd ridden back to Sipsey with him that rainy night. Not in an intimate way, but in a surprising way. She'd been friendlier and more open than he'd expected her to be.

What had surprised him, though, was the reaction of the

crowd when they'd stopped by Nebb's Barbecue Pit. It was as if he'd walked through the door with a royal princess. No, it wasn't obvious applause, but subtle recognition. The joint was packed; people were laughing and talking, dancing, and eating. But when they walked in, for half a minute, everything stopped. The crowd stared with a precision that said they wanted to be sure their eyes weren't playing tricks on them.

Clarice Vanderway was heiress to the Vanderway fortune, (funeral homes, a thriving hotel in Atlanta, an insurance company, etc.), and it was assumed that she was off limits to the common men of Sipsey. Nobody had said it, it was just assumed. So to see her with a boy from the Quarter was staggering, even shocking.

Nevertheless, she'd been relaxed; laughing and talking with Lucy Dash and having a good time. The two of them displayed a casualness that gave no clue as to the nature of their relationship. The women played it off as "no big deal." But the men appreciated how challenging it was to be seen with Clarice Vanderway under any circumstance. So they thought Sugarfoot had pulled off something pretty spectacular.

He remembered a quick moment of intimacy between them from that night. Before going to the window to place her order, Clarice had stood on tippy toes to whisper something to him. He bent down to hear what she was saying. They both laughed as she walked to the window. It was a cute, if minor, gesture, but everybody noticed it.

Then, when they were leaving, he held the door for her. She handed him her largest bag and started out but ran back and said something to Lucy Dash. Returning, she flashed him a smile as they walked out.

Now, waiting for the elevator to take them upstairs, Sugarfoot listened to Clarice speak in soothing tones to Aunt Ginny. Out of the blue, he wondered if she'd thought about him since that night.

Immediately, he squashed the thought.

Returning to the present, he said, "What room is Batch in?"

"He's on the second floor in intensive care," Clarice answered. They've been tube-feeding him, but he's doing much better now. His doctor says he'll be put in a regular roomthis evening or tomorrow morning."

"That's good. So how long have you been bringing her here?"

"Ever since they transferred him," she replied. "Lucy and I are taking turns."

"Nice. Very nice."

They boarded the elevator, and when it stopped on the second floor, Clarice and Aunt Ginny stepped off. He called, "I'll stop by later to see Batch."

Clarice was a vision as she switched down the hall. He couldn't help noticing. He also couldn't deny her appeal; mellow yellow; slender, but with a nice figure. She had a few freckles and full lips.

"Nice," he whispered, "but not my type."

Suddenly she turned around and said, "Deacon Collins is your offer still good?"

"Excuse me?" She'd caught him looking her over. "Excuse me," he repeated, wondering what she meant.

She flashed a smile. "You said you'd take me to Sister Domaine's, whenever I wanted to go, remember? Well, I need to go down there."

He said, "Sure. When?"

"I'll let you know tomorrow at church."

"Good enough."

******

His visit with Ivan was interesting; Ivan said he'd slept so much during his coma that he wasn't sure he'd ever need to sleep again. He smirked suspiciously and said, "You go to sleep, my brother, and anything can happen."

"You still need to get your rest." Sugarfoot patiently advised.

He didn't visit long with Ivan and was happy to learn that he'd be dismissed by week's end.

On the way to Batch's room, he was again preoccupied with thoughts of Clarice. Like many in Sipsey, he wondered why she'd turned down so many men for marriage. "Could there be something wrong with her? It wasn't out of the question that men weren't her mate of choice. He knew women like that. Still, there was something womanly about Clarice Vanderway despite her upper class reserve. Perhaps it was as she'd told Deacon Whitehead; she just hadn't found the right man.

******

In fact, as he left the hospital, the only thing that surpassed his thoughts of Clarice was the story Batch Blaine had told. They'd put him in a regular room, and he'd had to ask at the information desk to find out where he was. Clarice and Aunt Ginny were with him.

Batch had raised up in the bed and cried, "Sugarfoot,

you came to see me."

He couldn't get over how frail and sad Batch looked. Calvin Goines's description of him had been accurate. Now it was even more pronounced. Batch Blaine was a tragic figure.

"How you doing, Batch?"

He shook his head and started crying. "I'm so worried about Mama," he said. "She ain't got nobody to look after her."

"Now, Mr. Blaine," said Clarice, "I told you not to worry about that. We're gonna take care of your mother."

Batch nodded in gratitude, but said, "Mama, would you and Miss Vanderway step outside for a minute? I need to talk to Sugarfoot."

When they were gone, Batch said, "Sugarfoot, I need to tell you something."

He listened as Batch revealed the shocker of what'd happened the night of the robbery. It was outrageous, but Sugarfoot thought back to that night. He remembered driving around observing the people and realized he could verify part of Batch's tale.

"Wow," was all he could say when Batch was finished. And he left the hospital knowing that he had to do something to help him.

******

But by the time he crossed the state line into Potoama County, his thoughts had reverted back to the night Clarice had ridden back to Sipsey with him. He remembered the songs that'd played on the radio, the elevated lilt of her voice as she complained about Maxine Jefferson, and the smell of her perfume.

He'd wanted it to remain an intimate affair between the two of them, but their appearance together became the talk of the town. Word got back to Manny who was excited by the thought. At Sunday dinner, as they sat on the back porch waiting for the women to put dinner on the table, Manny grabbed his head in shock. He said, "Cuz, I heard you were with Miss Vanderway last night."

Sugarfoot frowned. He didn't like the suggestion. Manny made it sound as if they were on a real date. That was the last thing he wanted out.

"And where did you hear that?" he asked.

"I heard about it before I left Maw's last night, and people were talking about it at church today too."

"Forget it," Sugarfoot advised.

"Why?" Manny cried.

"She's not my type."

"Man, if you got hooked up with her, you could. . ."

"Don't," he held up a restraining hand. "They're making a mountain out of a molehill. I brought her home from the hospital and she wanted to stop by Nebb's to get barbecue. End of story."

Manny sighed in disappointment. "Too bad. She's a mighty fine lady."

Chapter Twenty-Nine

Sugarfoot and Shetland Wayburn met up in the parking lot at the same time Sunday morning. Sugarfoot wanted to get the deacons involved in support of Batch. So he told Shetland what Batch had said. He listened with a sympathetic ear and said, "I believe it. Batch is foolish. But it's hard to believe he'd commit a robbery."

They planned a meeting with the deacons after church. Shetland had been dealing with the deacon board for a long time and knew their sensibilities. He said, "Don't be surprised if the brethren don't support this."

"I understand," Sugarfoot said, "but I have to give it a try."

Before Sunday school began, Clarice sashayed up to him looking chic in a knee length gray sheath dress. She smiled and informed him that she needed to visit Sister Domaine that afternoon.

"Make it around four-thirty," she said.

He gave her his undivided attention and assured her his afternoon was free.

Fourteen deacons showed up for the meeting. He shared Batch's version of what'd happened the night of the robbery. The deacons behaved as Shetland had predicted.

Deacon Warner said, "Batch is not a member of First Macedonia and his reputation is not good among our people. I don't think we should get involved."

Deacon Whitehead cautioned, "It's always dangerous to go against folks like the Prengles?"

"It is," said Deacon Porter. "Their influence reaches all

over this county. They done decided that Batch robbed them and they ain't gon back down. It's a shame, but a lot of it's his fault."

Sugarfoot realized he had to go it alone. It was the same frustration he'd felt when he decided to stand up to the Ku Klux Klan. Fortunately, the community had come through, but he would've done it by himself. Life had taught him that the man that wouldn't take a stand was more tortured than the one that did. And a real man couldn't sit back and watch injustice destroy another man's life.

He rushed home after church to eat dinner and visit with the family before leaving to pick up Clarice. For some reason he wanted to tell Manny about their date but he knew Manny would make too big of a deal of it.

Sunday dinner was the highlight of the week for the Carrie Mae Rudolph family. It was their chance to bond over a good meal and catch up on the week's events. Carrie Mae was at her best on Sundays and presided over the meal like a mother hen.

Today's gathering was boisterous as usual. All of the family was there except Bebe and Daisy Ruth's husband. The children taunted each other as the women worked in the kitchen putting the finishing touches on the meal.

Once the table was set, they assembled in the dining room. The space was comfortable and cozy. Everybody sat at the long, rectangular table especially designed by Sugarfoot for this purpose.

Jeannie was cross because her mother had told her that she had to help wash dishes after dinner. "Is Boot gon help too?" she cried.

"No," answered Rita Jo. "Boot is a boy and boys don't

do kitchen work."

Jeannie poked out her mouth and glared at Boot. She was several months older than he but they were in the same class at school. Jeannie had no respect for gender differences and thought they should be doing the same amount of work. To make matters worse, Boot laughed at her and stuck out his tongue.

"Did you see that, Big Mama?" she asked.

"Leave Jeannie alone, Boot," said Carrie Mae.

Jeannie kicked him under the table. The grownups started talking about the country preacher as they ate the sumptuous meal. Jeannie was still mad but left Boot alone.

Then he did the unforgivable. He reached for the last chicken wing leaving only drumsticks and short thighs on the platter. Jeannie cried, "Big Mama, I wanted that wing! Boot already ate three. Make him give it to me."

"Get a drumstick, Jeannie," she suggested.

Jeannie got mad all over again. "Boot gets all the wings every Sunday and you don't say nothing. You like him better than you do me."

Carrie Mae was caught off guard. "You ain't telling the truth on me, Jeannie" she said. "I ain't got no favorites. I love all of my grandchildren the same."

"Naw, you don't," she grumbled.

Jeannie pouted and mumbled under her breath until Rita Jo made her hush. Then, to everybody's surprise, timid Aunt Alma announced that she was going to babysit Bear and Boot so Daisy Ruth could go back to school. "She needs a chance to better herself," she said, speaking to Carrie Mae but not looking at her. "And I want to help her."

Everybody got quiet. Carrie Mae folded her arms across

her chest and poked out her mouth. The family waited, knowing she wanted to say something. But before she could speak, Sugarfoot interrupted. "That's good, Aunt Alma."

Manny looked from Carrie Mae to Sugarfoot waiting for a showdown. Her face showed blistering anger, but she held her tongue.

Jeannie couldn't believe it. She'd never known Big Mama to back down from a fight. But she also knew she didn't want to clash with Sugarfoot. So out of mischief, she said, "Big Mama, you gon let Aunt Alma do it?"

"Shut up, Jeannie," everybody shouted.

By ten past four, Sugarfoot was in his truck and on his way to Vanderway Circle. When Clarice climbed into the truck, his mind was preoccupied with thoughts of the robbery. But not so much that he wasn't aware of her presence; her smell, her voice, and her smile.

She looked pretty in a sleeveless pink dress and large sunglasses. He considered discussing Batch's situation with her, but she was still complaining about Maxine Jefferson. Specifically, she was upset that Maxine wouldn't let her missionary circle use the Banquet Hall for their scholarship gala. The Banquet Hall was a special addition to the Fellowship Hall and only used for special occasions.

"What happened?" he inquired.

She chewed us out," Clarice griped. "We've always had the scholarship gala in the Banquet Hall and she knows it."

"What reason did she give for turning you down?"

She mimicked Maxine saying, '*Last year y'all left the Banquet Hall in a mess and you left the stove on. It's a wonder you didn't burn this church down.*'"

He laughed. "Did you?"

She shrugged. "I don't remember. Lucy and Elvira said we didn't, but Maxine called them liars and said we did." She sighed restlessly. "I just don't get why she has all the say-so. We're tithing members of the church. Shouldn't we have some say?"

"Yes," he acknowledged.

"She's just nasty," Clarice said hotly. "And it never stops. Remember how she got smart with Deacon White-head at the hospital when he spoke to her? Well today, Sister Curry asked her how she was doing and blessed her out."

"What did she say?"

Frowning and puckering up her mouth, Clarice repeated her words. *'I'd be doing fine if y'all would stop talking about me and lying on me.'* "Then she stomped out of the powder room and slammed the door."

"Okay," he replied, chuckling quietly.

"Look at you," she said. "You're not taking this seriously. The women of the church are fed up with her and want something done about it. She's mad because people are still talking about her fake heart attack. She's taking it out on everybody. Maxine Jefferson is too mean to be over the Fellowship Hall, Deacon Collins."

"Well," he said provocatively, "Do *you* want the job?"

"*Me?*" She wailed. "I can't do it."

"What about your friend Lucy? You think she'd do it?"

"No! Lucy would be terrible."

"Elvira?"

"Absolutely not!"

"Mary Newlins?"

"You're getting worse."

"Well, baby, somebody's got to do it."

She blushed and smiled. "I'm just saying that Maxine needs to be nicer, not so quick to snap on people."

"That's a conversation that can be had," he said. "Maybe you could initiate it. She seems to like you."

Clarice stared at him. "*I* should initiate a conversation with her? Are you making fun of me?"

"No, I'm not. But there're layers to the problem that need to be considered. Maxine has," he hesitated and started over. "Maxine maybe grouchy, but she provides a service to the church that requires a skills-set that nobody else has brought forward. And," he continued cautiously, "she understands the job much better than she's given credit."

"And what's that supposed to mean?"

"It means that the manager of the Fellowship Hall has to be reliable and punctual; in the right place at the right time. Those two things alone would eliminate most members of First Macedonia. Then, she's got to manage a kitchen staff; take inventory to make sure there's enough food for special events; cook the food if necessary; serve the food; and clean-up the kitchen and Banquet Hall afterwards. And that's not all. She's got to be ready to do the same thing at the next event. Who do you know that would do that? Make a suggestion and I'll bring the name before the board."

Her mind raced as she tried to think of a better manager of the Fellowship Hall. Thinking of no one, she blew out loudly.

"Exactly," he said. "It's takes a lot of dedication *and* discipline to do that job. Not many people want it. Maxine has been doing it for years. I'll admit she rubs people the wrong way. But she takes the job seriously, and she does it well."

Clarice sulked, and he said, "Now you're mad."

"No," she disagreed. "I just thought you'd be more open-minded and try to see things from my point of view."

"I'm trying," he said. "But consider my position. If I make a big push to get rid of her, then, at the next repast when there's not enough chicken, green beans, and potato salad to feed the family, it's on me. And chances are you won't be anywhere to be found, Miss Vanderway."

She sighed. "Point taken."

"So can we agree not to be upset about it?"

She smiled. "I suppose so."

******

Sister Domaine's arthritis was still bothering her so she hadn't been back to church. Clarice had encouraged her missionary sisters to make care baskets for the sick and shut-in similar to the ones she'd seen at First Primitive. She was pleased with how nicely they'd turned out and was proudly delivering Sister Domaine's.

Her niece, Sasparilla, was visiting from Bruin. Sasparilla was a singer and a tap dancer that used to work on a cruise ship. When she was in the mood, she told interesting stories about famous people and exotic places.

Today, she didn't get a chance to tell a story because Sister Domaine wanted to go over the Sunday school lesson. Deacon Collins went to the truck and got his commentary and he and Clarice discussed it with her.

Afterwards, Deacon Collins asked if she'd heard the panther lately. She said, "I still hear it late at night, but it better not come close."

When they were preparing to leave, Sister Domaine pulled herself up with her walking stick and went into the kitchen. Moments later, she called Clarice."

"Here, I made these for you." She handed Clarice a brown paper bag. Inside was a tin of tea cakes and a pink and blue knitted scarf. "I have to give you something for all the nice things you do for me," she said.

"Thank you!" Clarice exclaimed. "You know I love tea cakes, and I really love this scarf. But you don't ever have to do anything for me, Sister Domaine. I love taking care of you."

Sister Domaine hugged her and said, "I hear your spirit's been low these last few months on account of your last engagement not working out. But I want to encourage you. Don't give up on marriage. A good man is hard to find, but they're out there. And when you find one, hold on and don't let him get away."

Clarice smiled. "Thanks, Sister Domaine, that's good advice. I'll keep it in mind."

The countryside was budding with signs of spring. Clarice was thankful for the deacon's presence. It helped put the landscape in proper perspective. Tall trees otherwise looking like raiding monsters stood studiously at attention. Far off mailboxes looked like what they were and not towering men with hatchets.

Suddenly, she cried, "Oh look!" Along the sloping hillsides, huge red plums hung heavily from the branches of tall bushes.

He stopped and said, "Let's pick a few."

They got out, scaled the shallow hill, and began picking the sun-sweetened fruit, eating some while putting more in the bag Sister Domaine had given her.

Trying to grab plums from a far-flung branch, she slipped

and fell. Struggling to get up, her feet slid on the damp grass and she went down again. Automatically, Sugarfoot extended a hand and pulled her up. She felt light-hearted and giddy, and he held her hand until she steadied herself. Back on solid ground, she chatted about her love of wild growing fruit, especially plums and blackberries.

The sun was just going down when he dropped her off. As she emerged from the truck,

she thanked him for his generosity. "It was a very pleasant visit wasn't it, Deacon Collins?"

"Yes," he said pleasantly.

"In that case, I'll let you know when I need to go again."

He nodded agreeably. Suddenly, without thinking, she leaned over the seat to peck him on the cheek. The move was unexpected, and as she got close to him, he turned his head and the kiss landed on his lips.

An electric current passed through them. She quickly pulled away and said, "I'm sorry. I didn't mean to shock you."

He was so stunned he couldn't reply. Then he felt a sudden annoyance at the thought that she was playing some kind of game. He just sat there staring at her.

"I truly apologize," she said sincerely. "I appreciate you taking up the time to take me down that scary road. It was only a gesture of gratitude."

He realized he was being silly. In what Universe did a man get angry when a beautiful woman showed her thanks by giving him a kiss? He smiled playfully and said, "Okay, I forgive you this time."

She sighed in relief. "Have a good evening, Deacon Collins."

As she opened the door and slid out, he said, "Have a good evening yourself, Miss Vanderway."

She felt light-hearted and gay as she strolled happily into the house.

Chapter Thirty

That evening, Sugarfoot called Calvin Goines and re-layed Batch's version of what'd happened the night of the robbery.

Calvin wasn't surprised. He said, "I never believed Batch robbed that store. I'm going to get Landon on the case. He thrives on this kind of thing." He sighed, "They set him up. A naïve man like Batch doesn't see the pitfalls. Those crooks have been doing things like that for a long time, and they're good at it." He sighed. "I've stopped being shocked by the nerve to these cowards. But Batch left himself open."

"Yes, he did."

"But do what you can to help him, Sugarfoot."

"Will do," he assured him.

So, Sugarfoot became a sleuth in search of the truth. He talked to everybody he recalled seeing the night of the rob-bery. He was surprised at how many people he'd seen and how much they remembered. He tried to fit what he knew and what they said into what Batch had said.

The news media didn't report the amount of money that'd been taken from Prengle's. They only said that their loss had been substantial. Rumor said power tools were missing. It was further reported that shelves were disheveled with merchandise flung over the floor as if the robber had been in a rage.

"Batch in a rage?" Sugarfoot laughed. When had any-body ever seen Batch in a rage? It didn't even sound right.

He suddenly felt the heaviness of living in a small south-ern town as a Black man. He sighed, "Would it be any different anywhere else?" Calvin Goines had called it right. It was so easy to end up on the wrong side of the law. All it took was for a White man to accuse you of doing something and you were suddenly a marked man.

"It's the fight that we have to fight," he said. "And the only way it'll change is if we change it."

******

He went to the home of Mary Newlins's half-sister, Drucilla Kilgore, to find out what he could. Drucilla was a dumpy, round-faced recluse with splotchy skin. She was nothing like her good-looking church going sister.

In fact, she was one of the strange characters of Sipsey. She'd joined the Navy after high school and claimed to have sailed the Seven Seas. Now, she called herself a private detective. She and her much older husband, whom she called Drummer Boy, rode around town late at night in a 1955 Ford with a hound dog they called Uncle Lester.

The Kilgores lived in a wooden cabin at the edge of town. On the outside, the house looked deserted. Stepping inside, it was disorganized and junky with newspapers and magazines strewn about.

She made room for him on the sofa besides a stack of books. Then she sat in a cushioned chair across from him. After a long stare down, she said, "You need help with something, Sugarfoot?"

He told her about his visit with Batch. "Batch admitted to being at the store that night, but he swears he didn't rob it. I saw you riding around doing your detective work. Did you notice anything unusual?"

She threw her head back and closed her eyes. Her cat-framed eyeglasses had

rhinestone trimmings with a chain that dangled on each side. The rhinestones glittered as her thoughts journeyed back to that night. She rolled her neck round and round. Finally, she said, "Could be that I did. Could be that I did."

She opened her eyes and looked at him. "Anytime I see something out of order, I writes it down. And I takes a picture. Uncle Lester knows when something ain't right too. We done learned him how to spot devilment. If Uncle Lester twitches his nose or turns his head a certain way, we takes notice. It's a lotta shady stuff going on in Sipsey after dark. You'd be surprise at who's doing what and with who."

"Well, think back to that night," Sugarfoot implored. "You might remember something that'll help Batch."

"I will," she said, "and I'll let you know what I have."

Sugarfoot left the house shaking his head.

******

Shane Houston gave his viewing audience a daily update on Batch's condition. He conveyed the doctor's prediction that Batch would soon be recovered and returned to jail.

"Batch Blaine is responding well to treatment," he informed them. "Doctors believe he'll be ready to stand trial in a few weeks."

Of course, Bobby Doyle Hatfield was happy to hear this news and said he was eager to testify.

Drucilla sent word by Mary that she had something important to tell Sugarfoot. He went to her house after work Thursday evening. Looking at the junky house, he couldn't help thinking that Drucilla's housekeeping skills were nothing like her sister's. Mary Newlins' house was so clean you could eat off her floors. Drucilla's you wouldn't want to.

She offered him a seat on the sofa surrounded by photographs. She said, "I wanted to see you because Uncle Lester remembered something strange from that night."

"And what did Uncle Lester remember?"

She threw back her head and rolled her neck. When she spoke, it was in a quiet, mysterious voice. She said, "Uncle Lester saw a white pickup truck speeding down Main Street just as the train's whistle blew. The truck rushed across the tracks and barely made it before the train came hurtling along. Uncle Lester thought that was mighty strange. That man risked his life trying to get across the tracks. Now what could be so important that he needed to get away so fast?"

"That's a good question. Did Uncle Lester see what the person looked like?"

"Yes. Uncle Lester saw his face and he's seen it before. The man don't live in Sipsey, but he comes here about once a month. He shows up in different kinds of vehicles. Uncle Lester also finds that suspicious." She handed him a photograph. "The man in the white truck meets with these two men behind Prengle's Hardware. They load something onto the truck. And that's every time he comes."

Sugarfoot looked at the pictures. He remembered seeing the white pickup truck parked near the gas station when he drove through town after dropping Manny off at Maw Shatling's. He looked closely at the two men in the picture and groaned. He couldn't figure out what they were up to, but it looked crooked.

"They can't be up to no good," Drucilla observed. "Drummer Boy calls them partners in crime."

Drummer Boy was sitting in front of the fireplace reading the newspaper. At the mention of his name, he looked at Sugarfoot. "According to the detective book, when folks meet late at night in dark alleys, they're usually up to no good. Them two got a racket going. I don't know what it is, but it's a racket."

"Thanks, Drummer Boy," he said. "I agree. And these pictures are very helpful."

He handed them back to Drucilla. She said, "Keep them. I have extra copies of everything."

Chapter Thirty-One

Sugarfoot discovered that the court had appointed a lawyer for Batch believing he had no legal representation of his own. Interestingly, the young man appointed was a recent law school graduate that the district attorney had selected. It appeared that the purpose of assigning him to Batch was not to help Batch. It was to give this young man courtroom experience and a sure win for the prosecution.

So, there was great surprise when Landon C. Pratt showed up in Sipsey; a tall, distinguished looking Colored lawyer wearing eyeglasses and a custom made suit. He came asking questions and demanding discovery materials.

He said, "I'm Batch Blaine's lawyer, and I'll be handling all legal documents pertinent to his defense. I need police records and transcripts of police interviews of witnesses, including Mr. Blaine. I'm also requesting photographs of the alleged crime scene, and any other evidentiary reports that you have."

Jennie, the secretary, was unnerved by him and said, "All of that's been sent to the courthouse at Creek."

"Thank you," he replied. "I'll contact them."

Furthermore, Landon's office informed the television station that their reporting was biased and slanted towards convicting his client before the trial. Sugarfoot turned over the pictures Drucilla had given him and identified the people in them.

After talking to Batch and Sugarfoot and checking out the pictures, Landon chuckled and said, "This trial is going to be interesting."

Landon and Sherri Lynn stayed at the Goines's farm as he prepared to defend Batch. Ivan was home and recovering nicely. Some nights he had trouble sleeping. On those nights, Deacon Goines sat with him and talked or read the bible until he dozed off.

The Saturday before Batch's trial began, the Goines's were gathered in their backyard for a family cookout. Calvin had driven down from Charlotte, and Earl and Karen were expected later in the day.

Ivan and Deacon Goines were in the pasture across the road attending to the livestock. And Sherri Lynn was on the telephone urging Lucy to bring her ground beef, tomato, and cheese dip. "And don't forget the chips," she said.

The backyard was a busy hub of activity. Sugarfoot pulled his truck under the large oak tree and began setting out chairs he'd brought from the church. Calvin was putting meat on the grill and debating with Sugarfoot whether their preferred professional basketball teams would make it to next year's play offs.

Clarice had arrived early and was hanging around the chicken coops talking to the hens and gathering eggs. Miss Liddy sat in a recliner peeling potatoes for her popular mustard and pimento potato salad.

Sherri Lynn came outside and yelled to Clarice, "What's the update on Stephanie Murray's wedding?"

"I don't know anything," she yelled back. "All of a sudden, Stephanie has gone silent. It's strange. Delphine got a note from her a few weeks ago. She was in the Caribbean, St. Thomas, I believe. All I can say is, my dress is ready."

"Very fishy," tsked Sherri Lynn. "We'll have to wait and see."

Deacons Shetland Wayburn and Milton Whitehead suddenly appeared with a cooler of fresh water fish. "Ivan says he's frying fish later," said Shetland. "Me and Milt gon get started cleaning this trout."

When she finished peeling potatoes, Liddy took them into the kitchen and put them on the stove to boil. When she came back outside, she saw Trapp vault from his lounging place under the tree. Barking madly, he rushed toward the barn where Clarice was fussing with the chickens. Seeing what had spurred him to action, Liddy cried, "Oh, my God, he's gon kill Trapp."

With horror, the family looked towards the barn and saw a terrifying sight. A large black panther was creeping slyly towards the barn. He was a beautiful specimen with a long graceful body and glossy black fur. His green eyes, piercingly ominous, cautiously surveyed the environment.

Suddenly, the backyard became a den of terror.

Somebody screamed.

Coolly, the panther leveled his glance and glared hungrily towards Clarice and the chickens. Clarice froze. The chickens, noting the danger, began clucking, and took flight into the barn. Barking wildly, Trapp burst on the scene and positioned himself between Clarice and the wildcat. The cat bared his teeth, and in cinematic slow motion, sped towards Trapp. Trapp soared into battle. And there began a deadly match between the two formidable creatures.

Clarice stood still with shock.

The yard became a frenzied camp of activity. Johnny Goines returned, shocked to see what was happening. Liddy cried, "Mr. Goines, get the rifle. He's gon kill Trapp."

Like a young man, Johnny Goines broke for the house.

Sherri Lynn stood on the porch with her mouth hanging open. Calvin started toward the animals with nothing but the long turning fork in his hand.

The moment was terrifying as the big cat jutted forward and went for Trapp's throat. Quickly darting away, Trapp bit into the panther's hide. The panther's fangs locked into his brisket causing Trapp to cry out.

Suddenly, Sugarfoot emerged from his truck with his .357 Magnum at his side. He moved rapidly but with caution towards the brawl. In a horrified daze, Clarice hurried towards him, and he quickly leapt between her and the animals. She grabbed him around the waist and wouldn't let go.

The panther's teeth hooked onto Trapp's coat, tearing it apart. Blood oozed out in ripples. But Trapp continued fighting with a savagery unseen before. Adrenaline rushed through Sugarfoot's veins as he realized he had to kill the animal to save Trapp. With Clarice squeezing his abdomen, his gaze locked on the panther. Sherri Lynn shouted, "Turn him loose, Clarice. He can't do anything with you holding onto him like that."

But she was afraid to let go.

So as not to hit Trapp, Sugarfoot's gaze locked on the panther's right flank. He took aim. In less than a flash, he pulled the trigger, striking the animal in the thigh. The panther howled but kept tearing into Trapp. There were gashes in his coat, but Trapp had a firm grip on the panther's jaw. Sugarfoot moved more aggressively and popped the animal twice more, hitting him in the neck and abdomen. He bawled, and this time quit the fight and ran howling back towards the woods.

Sugarfoot trotted after him, still firing while dragging

Clarice along.

As the animal went down, Trapp also collapsed. The panicked family came running. Johnny Goines's rifle had been trained on the panther in case Sugarfoot's shot missed. Now he threw down his weapon and ran to Trapp. He begged, "Come on Trapp. Come on, get up. You can do it."

Trapp tried to get up but each time he made the effort, he fell back down.

Ivan rounded the house and seeing Trapp down, rushed to the scene. He said, "Oh God! We've got to get him to the vet."

He and Calvin put Trapp on the bed of Sugarfoot's truck.

Clarice was crying uncontrollably. Sugarfoot put the safety on the gun and reached for her. She fell into him, shaking violently. He said, "It's alright. I got you."

But she wouldn't be consoled and held onto him. He said, "We've got to take Trapp to the vet. I'll be right back. Will you be okay til I get back?"

She nodded, unable to speak.

They left with the dog. Deacon Goines and Calvin followed them. The women were left to decide what to do about the cookout. Landon had been in the house looking over court documents. Sherri Lynn told him what'd happened. He said, "Bring the operation closer to the house. In the meantime, I'll call county officials and let them know they need to pick up a dead animal."

The women were still terrified and continued watching the woods for other signs of danger.

"I doubt if there's another one," said Liddy. "It's unusual for them to come this far south. He must be a stray. But we'll do well to be careful."

Clarice was so shaken up she couldn't be still. She couldn't stop thinking about what could've happened. After a while, she decided to go home. Sherri Lynn offered to drive her but she insisted she was alright.

When she got home, it was so quiet that she wished she'd stayed at the Goines's. Her father was working a funeral in Creek and her mother was in Atlanta helping to care for a great aunt that'd suddenly taken ill. So she sat alone trying to calm herself down.

Hours later, she was still smarting over the ordeal. Every time she closed her eyes, she saw the menacing animal coming towards her and then Trapp racing toward it. "I didn't know Trapp was that brave," she said, "He probably saved my life."

Later in the evening, Deacon Collins stopped by. He said, "I just came by to see how you were doing."

She invited him into the den and offered him a glass of fizzling cola. "It was so scary," she said. "If you hadn't had the gun both Trapp and I might've been killed."

"It would've been alright," he said reassuringly. "We wouldn't have let anything happen to you."

She was glad he'd come by. She said, "I've been sitting here reliving that scene all afternoon. Daddy's working a funeral in Creek and hasn't come home yet and Mother won't be back until tomorrow. I'm here by myself except for Bess who lives upstairs and doesn't like to be bothered on the weekends. So I'm thankful for your company. How's Trapp?"

He shook his head. "He's pretty bad. The vet patched him up and he's keeping him for a while. He says keeping him quiet and treating his wounds will help more than anything. If he survives, it's gonna be a long road back."

"I feel so guilty," she said. "He was trying to protect me."

"He was defending his territory," he corrected. "He would've done what he did even if you hadn't been there."

"I hope he'll be alright."

"So do I. Deacon Goines is very fond of that dog."

He stayed with her until Felix got home. He hadn't wanted to overstay his welcome, but she was so shaken up that he didn't want to leave her alone.

******

He assessed the day as he drove home. It had indeed been startling to see the wild animal stalking the Goines's farm. Poor Trapp. The fight had been so mismatched. Yet he'd fought gallantly. But if he hadn't shot the panther, Trapp most definitely would've been killed.

The gun had been a gift from an army friend, and he kept it in his truck, always hoping he wouldn't have to use it. But it sure had come in handy today.

Chapter Thirty-Two

Eddie Simpson got mad every time he saw Bobby Doyle Hatfield's face on the evening news. "I can't stand him," he said one evening after Bobby Doyle gave another lengthy version of what'd happened the night of the robbery. "He can't wait to see that Colored man on a chain gang. I'd like to put my fist between his eyes."

Jericho was sitting opposite him and was as annoyed by Bobby Doyle as Eddie. She said, "He hasn't always been a saint. There was a time when he was out in the world doing crooked things."

"He reminds me of why I left the south," said Eddie.

"You and a lot of others."

Outside of the Potoama County Courthouse, Shane Houston reported that Batch's trial had gotten underway. "It's in the very early stages right now; jury selection and various petitions, but the actual trial should get started in a day or two. They're not expecting a long trial, two or three days at the most. It's a pretty clear cut case."

"What about this new evidence we're hearing about?" asked the studio host.

"That's right," he said. "We're hearing that new evidence has emerged. It wasn't disclosed which side had this new evidence. But a civil rights lawyer, Landon C. Pratt, of Birmingham, has taken over the defense of the case. He's bold and has been very aggressive in his demands for discovery. We're unable to give details of the new evidence at this time. But as soon as we hear from Timothy Swain's office, *Straight on 8* will bring it to you. Shane Houston WBCC for

Straight on 8. Back to you, Martha."

"Good," cried Eddie. "Maybe that new evidence will be a help to the Colored boy."

Jericho grunted. "If you knew the Colored boy, you might not care so much. He ain't what you think. He's a Uncle Tom and a mess maker. Colored folks don't trust him, and some of us think he's getting what he deserves."

"Yeah, but his kind gets railroaded faster than anybody."

The relationship between Jericho and Eddie was still strained but she was tolerating him. For one thing, she realized that they weren't the young and foolish couple they'd been in New York City all those years ago. Time had mellowed both of them. She stopped finding fault with everything he did, and he avoided arguments with her.

She discovered that having somebody in the house all the time chased away the demons. Some nights there was no interference from them at all. Sleep was liberating. It brought peace and a break from the jitters. Even members at First Primitive noticed and commented that she was looking better.

They also took to Eddie. He and Revish Kane had hit it off from the start. "They're a mirror of each other," Viola had suggested. "And they've both raised their share of hell."

At Revish's urging, Eddie started singing in the choir, leading songs. The showmanship he'd displayed as a soul singer was still there. His voice was strong and generated the same excitement it'd done back then.

Jericho didn't want to judge the behavior of her members. But she found it annoying that with little or no preparation, Eddie enjoyed accolades just for singing old songs while it took her a week to prepare a sermon that brought only a few a-mens.

Rather than fight him, she used it to her advantage. She appointed him praise leader, and each Sunday, he opened the service with a soul stirring hymn. His contribution got the service off to a spirited start.

On one of those Sundays, after he "tore the church up" a young member caught up with her in the foyer. She said, "I'm glad Mr. Eddie came to our church, Sister Jericho. He adds a lot to the service, and he sounds like a real singer."

"You think so," she said and kept walking.

Eddie paid his tithes and offering and gave generously to special causes. The members were impressed. He was a big after service draw and a crowd flocked around him every Sunday, telling him what a good Christian he was.

"For somebody claiming he wanted to die a few months ago, he's done changed his tune," Jericho mumbled after watching him 'putting on airs' with a group of women.

He'd gotten so comfortable that he started making plans. One evening he said, "Me and Revish went to look at a car today, and I'm thinking about buying it. It's a 1962 Pontiac Grand Prix. It's a clean four door sedan with low mileage, and the price is right. I want you to take a look at it and tell me what you think."

She gawked at him, not knowing what to say. No man had ever asked her what she thought about anything. She felt he was trying to butter her up; laying on the charm so she'd ask him to stay in Sipsey.

She wasn't doing it. The only reason she hadn't kicked him out was Janelle. Her residency was ending at the end of summer and she still hadn't figured out what she was going to do. Janelle had been sad ever since she left and Eddie was worried about her. He'd had the telephone installed and called her every other day. They talked like old friends and Jericho heard him tell her he loved her and was proud of her. He also told funny stories about his life in and out of prison.

"I'm doing everything I can to cheer her up. I feel like it's my job to nurse her back to happiness."

It seemed to be doing some good. "The only bright spot in my life is knowing that the two of you are together and taking care of each other," Janelle had told Jericho.

Jericho didn't have the heart to tell her that she was ready for her to come and get Eddie.

In response to his question about the car, she said, "I don't know nothing about buying a car. I've been walking all my life, so I'm used to it. But it would be good for *you* to have a car since you have to pester somebody every time you get ready to go somewhere."

"So, you think I should buy it?"

"Suit yourself."

"I got something else cooking," he said. "I was looking at a house over in Ellington Square. There's a nice house for sale by some teacher that moved to California to be close to her daughter. I thought we could go look at it together."

"Why you wanna buy a house in Sipsey?" Jericho asked suspiciously.

He said, "When Temeka comes home, I don't want to put her out of her room. That house has got three or four bedrooms and some other rooms that we could use for whatever we wanted. I think it's even got a basement. It'll be enough room for everybody."

Jericho didn't believe what she was hearing. All her life she'd wanted a man to offer her these things, and she would've done anything to get them. As a matter of fact, she'd done some pretty terrible things trying to get what she wanted. Now he was handing them to her on a silver platter. And they didn't mean anything.

Eddie said, "Sugarfoot checked the house out and says it's in pretty good shape. I'm sure it'll need some upgrades; new cabinets and bathroom fixtures, things like that. He says he could make the repairs and have it ready in a month or two. It's a good deal. What do you think about that?"

"I think you're trying to push your way into my life," she answered. "You're still trying to set things up so you won't have to leave."

"That's right," he admitted without shame. "I like it here; it's a chance for me to start over. I've made a mess out of my life, but I want a second chance. If we could forgive each other for past mistakes, we could make something out of this."

"Forgive each other! What you got to forgive *me* for? I didn't do nothing to you."

Realizing he'd said the wrong thing, he moderated his tone. "You were a partner in everything I was doing."

"I was a *child*!" She admonished him.

"You were young, but you weren't no child."

"Well I'll be a monkey's uncle," she shouted. "You're trying to blame all of that mess you were doing on me?"

"I am not," he insisted. "But you joined in and you enjoyed the good life. And that made you a partner."

"You ain't changed," she hollered. "You ain't changed one bit. How you gon blame me for all that sh- - you were doing?"

He backed down. "I'm sorry," he said. "It's all on me.

So, if you can forgive *me,* we can move forward. The main thing is for us to support Janelle. She's going through a depression, and we need to be together in trying to help her."

She agreed but couldn't resist a swipe. She said, "It's good to know that you've finally figured out what being a parent is all about."

"Better late than never."

The issue of the house came up again. It was Mrs. Oleta Durning's house. She'd been a popular teacher at the high school for many years. She and her husband, a high ranking army officer, had built the house as a young couple. They'd raised their children there, and she'd lived there many years after his death. She'd announced in church that she didn't want to leave Sipsey. But as she approached old age, she said the house was too big and too much work to keep up. "My daughter wants me closer in case I need her," she said. First Macedonia was sorry to see her go and the announcement brought tears to many eyes.

Jericho was familiar with the house. It was a two story Southern Colonial with beige bricks, two or three chimneys and tall white columns. It was one of the prettiest houses in the neighborhood with *the* prettiest yard.

Making a decision about whether to move into a house with Eddie shouldn't have been hard, but it was. Janelle was her only consideration. Not getting the clinic had been a setback and she was still upset about it. If Jericho split with him, it would upset her even more.

This was one of the times Jericho realized she had to step back and take a look at herself. It wasn't right for her to blame everything that'd gone wrong in her life on Eddie. He hadn't caused her to have a longtime affair with Josiah Hess.

Neither had he murdered Luther McGill. She alone was responsible for those things. But he was trying to push his way into her life and this brought back memories of the things he *was* responsible for.

She said, "I've gotta pray about this."

He didn't press the issue. He said, "Mrs. Durning's daughter wants to sell as quick as she can. Revish says the bank is trying to buy it. They want to buy it at the low price and sell it at a profit. It won't be on the market long. I'll make the offer. If things don't work out," he shrugged, "it'll be an investment for Janelle."

She gave a grisly snort. "Of all the places you could go, this is the only place that you can set down roots and live a decent life?"

"It's not just that. I won't lie, I want my family. Family is the most important thing in the world. Our daughter taught me that. She came to me not knowing a thing about me, and she offered me love. That's what life's all about, Candy. As a young man, I didn't know that. And I didn't value my family. But I know it now, and I'll do whatever I have to do to bring us together."

Jericho grunted. Eddie had made up his mind to stay in Sipsey. She decided she wouldn't let it bother her. He was a grown man. He could live anywhere he wanted to.

Chapter Thirty-Three

Batch Blaine's trial began with only two people in the courtroom caring what happened to him. Landon cared about justice, and Aunt Jenny cared about Batch. The few Negroes that sat in were at the courthouse for other reasons. They heard about the trial and decided to peep in.

Sugarfoot had decided to attend the first day. But Abner Nichols was out of town negotiating a large project with a company from Lancaster. He'd asked Sugarfoot to lead the crew in Mississippi.

Right off the bat, the prosecutor, Timothy Swain, called Batch an opportunist and accused him of taking advantage of the good and righteous Prengle family.

He said, "You'll not find a better family anywhere than these people," and he pointed to the Prengles. "They're generous, God-fearing people, and this county wouldn't be the same without them."

After making his point, he lit into Batch, calling him sinister, a sneaky rogue, and one of the most deceitful men he'd ever known. He claimed to be saddened by the fact that the Prengles had trusted Batch so completely only to be victimized by him in a weekend robbery. "It's the saddest thing you could imagine," he declared.

Then he began calling witnesses. Several merchants from Sipsey spoke on behalf of James and Dave Prengle (present owners of the business). But they merely repeated what'd already been said, that the Prengles were so wonderful that the Earth couldn't spin on its axis without them. But when asked about Batch, their answers became vague. One witness said he looked sneaky and was a 'bad sort. Another said, "He's a Nigger with low character. Even the Colored people of Sipsey don't like him."

Most telling, when asked what they knew about the robbery, all shrugged and admitted they only knew what they'd read in the newspaper.

Landon determined to expose the prosecutor's witnesses as frauds. During cross examination of a recently employed clerk from the drugstore, Landon asked him to describe Batch, and he couldn't do it. This confirmed his belief that these testimonies were just window dressings to justify scapegoating Batch.

But the time finally came for Bobby Doyle Hatfield, star witness for the prosecution, to give his testimony. He strutted over to the witness box like a dressed up whore and threw his right hand in the air before being asked. Then he repeated what he'd been saying all the time, that he saw Batch Blaine running from Prengle's Hardware on the night of the robbery. But this time he added that dollar bills were falling from his pockets and he only slowed down long enough to pick them up.

Landon was amused by the picture he painted of Batch. Instead of the pathetic looking creature sitting next to him, Bobby Doyle created a crafty Batch Blaine clever enough to plan a robbery. According to him, Batch would've gotten away with the crime had he not been on the scene witnessing it.

The jury clearly believed Bobby Doyle.

But Landon found him incredible. He decided not to cross examine him right away but reserved the right to call him later.

When Bobby Doyle stepped down, he went over to the Prengles and shook their hands. He was heard mumbling, "This is gon soon be over."

All of the Prengles were there. Eighty-four year old Godfrey Prengle, patriarch of the clan, sat calmly in a wheelchair near his sons. He'd hired Batch some twenty-seven years earlier when he and Aunt Ginny first came to Sipsey. His youngest son, Steven, an insurance salesman, sat with James and Dave on the front row.

The two Prengle sisters, Peggy and Rebecca, sat behind them. Peggy's lips were painted a flaming shade of red and her auburn hair was teased so high that she looked silly. She even had the temerity to bring her poodle into the courtroom forcing the clerk (ever so gently) to tell her that dogs weren't allowed.

Other family members were present too, wives, children, uncles, aunts, cousins, and friends. All sat prepared to give testimony of how good they'd been to Batch. The whole county knew about their ordeal. But the family was said to be "holding up." Still, in their humiliated grief, they wanted the world to know that Batch Blaine had wronged them and they wanted something done about it.

Timothy Swain hadn't presented much of a case. He'd relied on what Bobby Doyle Hatfield claimed happened. Yet, there was no doubt that this jury would convict Batch on that flimsy evidence alone.

As Landon was called to argue his case, he winked at Drucilla Kilgore, his ace in the hole, and looked over the courtroom. Sitting there looking like model citizens of the county were the robbers of Prengle's Hardware.

Landon C. Pratt, son of a common laborer and his illiterate wife, was a graduate of the University of Pennsylvania Law School and staunch advocate for civil rights. His very presence was the opposite of what those observing him imagined a young Negro man to be. And that alone threw everybody off.

Even the few Negroes that'd drifted into the courtroom were stunned. Landon had to actually question witnesses before they believed he was really a lawyer.

Drucilla sat observantly on the last row looking like the cunning snoop she was. Dressed

in the fantasized garb of her trade, she wore a trench coat and dark sunglasses. Landon had thanked her for her assistance in cracking the case but said he'd only call her if it was absolutely necessary. "I don't want to blow your cover," he said. "I might need your help again."

The truth was, he didn't dare put Drucilla on the stand and risk having her talk about Uncle Lester like he was a person. Still, he thought she'd done some pretty good detective work.

And he would definitely use her again if the need arose.

Drucilla was satisfied that she'd done her part and was prepared to take the stand. As she'd told Uncle Lester, "If they call us, we'll have to testify."

Bobby Doyle Hatfied sat across from the Prengles. His smugness infuriated Landon. He swore under his breath. As Batch approached the witness box, he said, "Your honor, I beg your indulgence, but I'd like to request a change of witnesses. I do need to ask Mr. Hatfied a few questions."

The judge ordered Bobby Doyle back and told him he was still under oath. When he sat down, Landon said, "Mr. Hatfield, tell us again, to the best of your recollection, what happened the night of the robbery."

Bobby Doyle glared at Landon with the greatest contempt. His eyes said, "Nigger, how dare you question me?"

Sensing his anger, Landon said, "Whenever you're ready, Mr. Hatfield."

He said, "That Saturday night, I was riding down Main Street and I saw Batch go into Prengle's Hardware. He stayed in there for some time and then I saw him run out."

Landon said, "You know the defendant, don't you?"

"Yes, I do."

"And you know the Prengles, is that correct?"

"Yes, I know the Prengles; they're good friends of mine."

"And you were aware that they closed the store at six o'clock that Saturday evening, were you not?"

"Yes, I was."

"So, didn't you think it strange that Batch Blaine would be going into the store when it was closed?"

"Yes, I did."

"Was the door locked?"

"I don't know."

"But you know he went in the store?"

"Yes, I know that."

"Well, Mr. Hatfield, since you know Mr. Blaine, and since you're a friend of the Prengles, why didn't you go in the store and ask him what he was doing there?"

Laughter from the back of the room drew a stern look from the judge.

Bobby Doyle hadn't expected the questioning to turn on him, and he looked cornered. He stuttered, "Well, I was scared. I didn't know what he was up to. I didn't know if he might have a firearm. I just didn't know."

Landon smirked. "Have you ever known Batch Blaine to carry or use a firearm, Mr. Hatfield?"

Bobby Doyle responded, "I don't know what he carries, but no, I never heard of him using one."

"Had you been afraid of him before that night?"

"No, I hadn't."

"But on that particular night you were afraid of him?"

Bobby Doyle shifted. He said, "Like I said before, I didn't know what he was up to so I didn't intervene."

Landon paused. "Mr. Hatfield, you've known the Prengles and Batch Blaine a

long time, yes?"

"Yes. Yes, I have."

"And what is your opinion of their relationship?"

He gave a sarcastic snort. "I don't know anything about their relationship, but I know

they've let him work there at the store for a long time."

"And have you ever heard tell of him stealing anything from them or being accused of robbing them before now?"

"I don't know."

"Come on, Mr. Hatfield, Sipsey is a small town."

Bobby Doyle's hatred for Landon was visible. It showed in his body language as well as his speech. He said, "No, I never heard of it before."

"And you don't find this strange, that after twenty-seven years of loyal employment that Batch Blaine is all of a sudden a robber?"

"Yes, it's strange," he admitted.

"But there's no doubt in your mind that Batch Blaine is the robber."

"None whatsoever."

"So it is your testimony that you witnessed Batch Blaine going into Prengle's Hardware on the night of the robbery, and you saw him run out?"

"Yes, that's my testimony."

"Mr. Hatfield, did you see anybody else during the course of this robbery. Were there any passerby that you noticed?"

"None that I noticed," he answered.

"And is it your testimony that you also didn't see Jamie Prengle at any point during that day or night?"

"Yes, that's my testimony."

"You didn't see anybody but Batch Blaine that night?"

"That's right."

"And one last question. What were you doing at the hardware that night?"

"I wasn't at the hardware. I was getting gas at the filling station when I saw the robbery occur."

"Thank you, Mr. Hatfield."

Landon called Batch to the stand. He ambled across the room looking like an alien dropped in from outer space. He'd lost so much weight that he didn't look like himself. Dusty-skinned with a receding hairline, his thin body looked shorter than it was. Landon felt sorry for him. Not knowing his history in Sipsey, what he saw was a Negro man beat down by an oppressive system, a system he detested.

Batch raised his hand and promise to tell the truth. Landon said, "Mr. Blaine, did you rob Prengle's Hardware Store?"

"No, sir, I did not."

"Tell us about your history with the Prengle family."

He started crying. He said, "I went to work for Mr. Godfrey when me and Mama come up from Emelle. I been working at the store ever since."

"And how many years is that?"

He shook his head in confusion. "I don't know for sure, but they say it's 'bout twenty-seven years."

"How would you describe your feelings towards the Prengles?"

He looked confused. Landon said, "Do you like the Prengles, Mr. Blaine?"

"Yes sir," he said happily. "I do."

"And have they been good employers?"

"Yes, sir. They been real good to me and Mama. When we first come up to Sipsey, he give me this job, and Mr. Godfrey bought food for me and Mama. I been working for them all this time, and they been real good to me. I wouldn't take nothing from them." He looked at Dave Prengle. His eyes were misty, his demeanor dejected. He said, "Mr. Dave, I wouldn't do it. I wouldn't take nothing from you."

Dave Prengle looked hastily away.

But Landon had made his point. He'd given Batch a chance to look his accusers in the eyes, and he'd shown a sincerity that couldn't be faked. Under his breath, Landon whispered, "Only a bunch of fools would believe that this browbeaten man would rob and vandalize that store."

He said, "Mr. Blaine is there anything you'd like to tell this court?"

He shook his head. "No, sir."

"That's all, your honor."

The judge nodded to Timothy Swain.

He jumped up ready to tear Batch apart. But as he came towards him, Batch recoiled in fear. He looked pitiful, and his meekness wasn't lost on anybody in the courtroom.

It was a revealing moment. But for the expertise of Landon C. Pratt, Timothy Swain would've further humiliated Batch. But Timothy realized he was up against a formidable opponent in the Negro lawyer, and he didn't want to jeopardize the case. So he said, "No questions your honor."

The judge told Batch to step down. Not one of the Prengles looked at him as he went to his seat. Landon stood up and patted him on the shoulder. "Good job," he said. Batch looked back at Aunt Ginny and tried to smile.

At the end of the day, Landon felt good and decided that tomorrow the real perpetrator would be exposed and this sad chapter in Batch Blaine's life would be over.

Chapter Thirty-Four

The next day Landon called Batch back to the stand. He asked the same question. "Did you rob Prengle's Hardware?"

"No, sir, I did not."

"Do you know who did?"

"No, sir," he started crying and repeated what he'd said the day before. "They've been good to me, I wouldn't do that to them."

The Prengles sat like martyrs who'd been duped by this thankless Negro. Other businessmen from Sipsey watched curiously, no doubt, wondering whether the Colored men that worked for them were of the same caliber.

Landon said, "Mr. Blaine, you know who robbed that store, don't you?"

Holding his head down, Batch said he didn't. Landon looked at the robbers then said to Timothy Swain, "Your witness."

Timothy Swain stood and rested one hand on the table. He said to Batch, "Just to be clear, you did say you didn't know who robbed Prengle's Hardware, is that right?"

"No, I don't know who robbed the store."

Timothy Swain smiled triumphantly. "That's just what I thought you said." Looking at the jury, he scowled, "Ladies and gentlemen, we know who robbed and vandalized that store, don't we?"

He laughed and sat back down.

The judge told Batch to step down.

As Batch went to his seat, Landon said, "Your honor, I

call Jamie Prengle to the stand."

This was a surprise, and busy muttering filled the space. Batch had been employed by the family since Jamie was a boy. Spectators couldn't imagine why the defense was calling Jamie Prengle to testify.

Jamie wasn't the best representative of his family. Since his youth, he'd been at the center of family squabbles. He'd had fist fights with peers and had had a couple of brushes with the law. But the thing he was known for was his harsh treatment of Batch. Both Colored and White grumbled of his cruelty. He seemed to take pleasure in publicly humiliating Batch. This mostly happened when he felt Batch hadn't properly deferred to a White customer. Once when Batch dropped a stack of fertilizer Jamie had piled on his back, Jamie took off his cap and beat him all the way to the back of the store.

Now, being called to the witness stand, Jamie was confounded and looked questioningly to his father. He was used to James Prengle stepping in and getting him out of tough situations. Expecting him to do so now, Jamie waited. But his father shrugged and gestured towards the witness stand.

And to further dispel any notion that he had a choice, the judge said, "Jamie Prengle, "take the stand."

Jamie's eyes shifted crazily and he shot his father one last look for help. But when he stood up, he looked as if he owned the world. He was of average weight and height with bone straight light brown hair. He had a condescending manner and an air of superiority. At twenty-six years of age, he was married to Kathy Lynn Halson, the fastest baton twirling majorette Sipsey High School had ever seen. They were the proud parents of a three year old daughter and a seven month old son.

He placed his right hand on the bible and swore to tell the truth.

Landon smiled at him and said, "State you name for the court, please."

"James Edward Prengle," he said boldly.

"And do you know the defendant."

"Yes, his name is Batch Blaine. He works at my family's hardware store."

"How long have you known him?"

He shrugged. "All my life, probably."

"Do you see him often?"

"I see him two or three times a week."

"Where do you work, Mr. Prengle?"

"I run the gas station next to the hardware store."

"You own the station, do you not?"

"Yes, I do."

"And you say you see the defendant two or three times a week."

"Yes, whenever I go over to the hardware store."

"And did you see Batch Blaine the day of the robbery."

"No, I didn't. I'd gone to Jasper that morning and didn't get back 'til late. So, no, I didn't see him."

"Did you see him at any point during that night?"

"No, I didn't see him that night either."

"Did you see Bobby Doyle Hatfield at any time during that day or night?"

"No, I hadn't seen Bobby Doyle in a few weeks."

"Wow, you've got a good memory. You hadn't seen him in a few weeks?" he pondered. "He hadn't even dropped by the station to get a bag of potato chips?"

There was laughter as he answered, "No, not that I remember."

"So you're sure you didn't go back to the gas station that night?"

"Yes, I'm sure."

Landon was in a quandary at this moment. He wasn't sure that revealing everything in the courtroom was the best move. As angry as he was at what was being done to Batch Blaine, he knew he had to handle the situation delicately.

He decided to end his questioning.

Timothy Swain sprang up, but only to reinforce the fact that Jamie was the only son of the well-respected James Prengle and that the family had been defiled by Batch.

Landon said, "Your honor, I recall Bobby Doyle Hatfield to the stand."

Looking relieved, Jamie Prengle stepped down from the witness box. Bobby Doyle stepped uneasily in his place. The judge said, "May I remind you that you're still under oath."

Looking baffled, Bobby Doyle nodded.

"Mr. Hatfield, did you see Jamie Prengle at all the night of the robbery?"

"No," he answered too quickly.

"Are you sure?"

"Yes," he said indignantly.

Landon said, "Mr. Hatfield, this is a court of law. In order for us to get at the truth of what happened that night witnesses must tell the truth."

"*Whot?*" He asked.

Landon spoke more firmly, saying, "Did you see James Edward Prengle at any time on
the night of the robbery?"

"I just told you no," he snapped.

"Well, I have evidence that you did," Landon hit back.

Bobby Doyle's face shrank, and he looked foolish. He said, "I don't remember seeing Jamie that night."

Landon went to the defense table, grabbed a folder and took out a picture. He showed it to the judge, the prosecutor, and then to Bobby Doyle. Bobby Doyle's face turned an unnatural shade of red. He looked up at Landon. Landon said, "There're more, many more pictures with you in them from that night."

Timothy Swain cried, "Your honor, the defense is pulling a stunt straight out of a crime novel. We don't know whether these pictures paint a true picture of what happened that night or not."

The judge ordered them to the bench. He told Landon, "I don't appreciate theatrics in my courtroom. Evidence not handled property will not be admissible."

Landon said, "I apologize, your honor, but this evidence has been in the forensics lab being authenticated and was just released to me yesterday evening." He handed a stack to the judge. "I believe you'll find that these photographs offer proof that these two witnesses have perjured themselves."

The judge looked at the pictures. Various expressions of shock distorted his face. Franklin T. Reindale, peacemaker of the county and servant of the people, tried to live up to the title, honorable judge. Whether White or Colored, he weighed every man's deeds according to the law and judged them accordingly.

The pictures held him spellbound. Meticulously, he examined one, put it behind the other, and studied the next. What he was witnessing were felonies far greater than what

Batch Blaine was accused of. But the pressing issue was the case at hand. What was happening in the pictures would have to be dealt with later.

Judge Reindale looked with regret from Batch, to Bobby Doyle, to Jamie. It was times like these when decency called upon him to prove the measure of man he was. Handing the pictures back to Landon, he said, "I will allow this evidence to be entered, but due to the nature of it, I'm going to clear the courtroom of spectators."

He handed Landon four pictures. "These are adequate to show the jury what they need to see."

Furious, Timothy Swain snatched off his glasses and glowered at the judge. But he knew better than to dispute a Franklin T. Reindale ruling.

As the spectators filed out, Landon returned to the witness box and looked Bobby Doyle Hatfield in the eyes. Bobby Doyle realized he was busted and would have to answer the question. Landon asked, "Were you with Jamie Prengle at all on the night that Prengle's Hardware Store was robbed?"

Quietly, he answered, "Yes, I was."

"Why? Why were you with Jamie Prengle that night?"

"We had some business to take care of."

"What kind of business?"

He wouldn't answer.

The pictures circulated amongst the jurors. Landon said, "Mr. Hatfield, would you please tell the court what really happened that night?"

Bobby Doyle didn't move a muscle.

Landon handed him the four pictures. He said, "Those pictures are dated and timed, verified by the Alabama Forensic Science Laboratory in Auburn. They tell an interesting story, wouldn't you agree?"

Bobby Doyle scowled, and Landon could feel the hatred emanating from him. Unmoved by it, he sneered at Bobby Doyle then turned around to do the same at Jamie Prengle. He said, "According to these pictures, you two were at Prengle's Hardware the night of the robbery, and you weren't alone. You wanna tell us what you were doing there?"

He still wouldn't answer.

Landon said, "Mr. Hatfield, you've been on television ever since this robbery took place saying you saw Batch Blaine leaving Prengle's Hardware that night. Did he even go into the store that night, Mr. Hatfield?"

"Yes, he did," Bobby Doyle angrily stood by his claim. "He broke in that store and stole that money."

"How much money was taken, Mr. Hatfield?"

"The paper said it was a thousand dollars."

"And what paper was that?"

"The Potoama County Gazette."

"No, Mr. Hatfield," he shook his head. "The newspaper never mentioned an amount. It only stated that it was substantial. So how would you know what the amount was?" Bobby Doyle cocked his head and stared at Landon. His face was a study in hypocrisy. Here was a man used to lying and getting away with it. His demeanor suggested he had every expectation that he'd get away with it this time. So he did what he always did, he kept his mouth shut.

Landon said, "Mr. Hatfield, answer the question. How do you know how much money was stolen from Prengle's that night?"

His eyes fixated on an obscure object on the back wall. The judge said, "The witness will answer the question."

Bobby Doyle cleared his throat and whispered, "I heard somewhere that it was a thousand dollars. Maybe it wasn't the newspaper, maybe it was at church, or the rotary club, but that's what they're saying."

This was a plausible excuse, so Landon let it go. He said, "Mr. Hatfield, you and Mr. Prengle were seen at the store that night by one other person, and that person is here today." He looked at the judge and said, "Your honor, I call Syretta Attaway to the witness stand."

Chapter Thirty-Five

Just a minute," Timothy Swain jumped up. He said, "Mr. Hatfield, I apologize for the defense continuing to make this trial about something other than Batch Blaine robbing Prengle's Hardware. Do you stand by your testimony that you saw him leaving Prengle's on the night of the robbery?"

Sighing, Bobby Doyle breathed easier. "I absolutely do."

"That's all," Timothy stormed back to his table.

"Syretta Attaway, take the stand," the judge said.

There was loud, confused rumbling at this surprising turn. Everybody looked back to see the unassuming Colored woman stand up. What could she possibly know about Bobby Doyle Hatfield and Jamie Prengle being together on the night of the robbery?

Bobby Doyle began to wipe sweat.

Syretta came from the back of the courtroom. She was a bashful twenty something year old woman with an unsteady gait. Well-known in Sipsey for her unholy alliances with men, she had three out of wedlock children. Gossips said they were all by three different men. Petite with just enough meat on her bones to be called "fine," she had a warm brown complexion. Her clothes were starched and ironed to perfection, and her hair was shaped in a stylish bob.

She shook with nervousness as she was sworn in. Landon walked over and asked her to state her name, age, and place of residence. When she did, he asked, "Do you know Batch Blaine?"

"Yessir" she answered in a high-pitched voice.

"And do you know Bobby Doyle Hatfield and Jamie

Prengle?"

"Yessir," she said nervously.

"Tell the court how you know them."

"They live in Sipsey, and I do too."

"Have you ever had contact with either one of them?"

She hesitated. "Not Mr. Bobby Doyle or Mr. Jamie."

"What about Mr. Blaine, any contact with him?"

"Yessir

"And what is the nature of your contact with him?"

She shrugged and spoke indifferently. "We talk. He comes and tells me if somebody wants to see me."

"Excuse me?"

The discomfort in her voice was noticeable. "He tells me if somebody, a man, likes me and wants to be with me."

"Really? So, he's your pimp?"

Her lips tightened in a shamed pout. "I guess," she answered.

"You must know that what you're doing is against the law," he said.

She flinched uncertainly, but when she spoke, her voice was firm. She said, "I don't have much money, and I have a sick child. Twice a month, I have to take him to the doctor. It takes money to pay doctors and buy medicine. I need the money."

"So you earn this money by being with men?"

She nodded.

"And Batch Blaine tells you who'll pay to be with you?"

"Yessir."

"So, that brings us to the night of the robbery. Did Batch Blaine come to you and tell you somebody wanted to be with you?"

"Yes. He came and got me and we walked downtown. But when we got there, it was these two White men."

Landon looked vacant. "So?"

"I said no," she answered.

"Why?"

She squared her shoulders and looked at him. "I don't mess with White men," she said indignantly.

Low rumbling echoed throughout the courtroom.

"So, what happened after you turned them down?"

"I walked away."

"And where did this take place? Where were you?"

"We were in the alley behind Prengle's Hardware."

"Did Batch Blaine leave with you?"

"Yes, sir, he came right behind me."

"Did he say anything?"

"Only that the men were mad. He kept begging me, trying to get me to go back, but I wouldn't."

"Did Batch go inside Prengle's Hardware Store?"

"No, not while I was with him."

"And you're sure he left when you left?"

"Yes, sir, he was walking behind me trying to talk to me, but I wouldn't talk to him. I told him to leave me alone."

"And where were Bobby Doyle Hatfield and Jamie Prengle?"

"I guess they were still in the alley."

"Thank you, Miss Anderson."

Timothy Swain approached her with contempt. He said, "You don't expect the ladies and gentlemen of this jury to believe you turned these two men down when you've admitted what you do to earn money?"

"I told the truth."

Looking towards the jury, he said, "What I believe is that you and Batch Blaine tried to extort money from these men, and when they wouldn't go along, you cooked up this scheme. You two plotted to rob Prengle's Hardware."

She shook her head. "We didn't do that. I don't rob, and I don't steal. I take in washing and ironing, and I clean houses. I have a little money, but when my child gets sick, I need more. And that's why I go out with men."

"What's wrong with your child?"

"He was born with a heart condition," she answered. "He needs an operation, but I can't afford it. But the treatments help."

"Where's the child's father?"

"I don't know."

"So you use men to pay for these medical treatments?"

"I do."

With this answer, she showed audacity unheard of in Franklin Reindale's courtroom. She was a single mother with a sick child admitting to committing illegal and immoral acts to get money for his medical treatments.

Timothy Swain realized he had to discredit Syretta and was prepared to do it but feared the jury's reaction. She could pass for anybody's coveted maid, so he searched for the right angle.

Syretta read his mind and intercepted his plan. She said, "I know what I do is wrong. Every year at revival, I go back to the church and ask the Lord to forgive me for my sins and help me to take care of my children in the right way."

Timothy Swain sighed. He couldn't touch that. He feared that at least a few of the jurors might sympathize with her. Moreover, this jury would appreciate that, while she needed the money, she refused to do these immoral things with White men. That showed she understood the importance of not mixing the Colored race with the White.

He gave up. Continuing to question her was too much of a gamble.

Chapter Thirty-Six

Landon called Bobby Doyle back to the stand. By now Bobby Doyle knew that Landon meant business.

He said, "Mr. Hatfield, did you rob Prengle's Hardware?"

"No, I did not," he said.

"Do you know who did?"

"I saw Batch Blaine run out of there that night."

"That's your testimony?"

"Yes, that's my testimony."

"Thank you."

He said, "I call Jamie Prengle to the stand. Jamie Prengle came back looking frustrated and foolish.

Landon said, "Mr. Prengle, did you rob Prengle's Hardware?"

"I did not," he said.

"Did you witness Mr. Blaine running out of the store?"

"No, I didn't."

"Did you ask Batch Blaine to bring Syretta Attaway to the alley behind the hardware?"

His face turned red, but he denied it.

Landon addressed the judge. He said, "Your honor, I ask for leniency in the moment.

There're discrepancies in what these witnesses are saying and what the pictures show. I believe that continuing in this line of questioning will bring a satisfactory resolution. The judge nodded, and he called Bobby Doyle back to the stand.

He said, "Mr. Hatfield, did you tell Batch Blaine to bring

Syretta Attaway to the alley behind the hardware?"

"No, I didn't."

"Did you and Jamie Prengle meet a man driving a white pickup truck at Mr. Prengle's service station?"

"No, we did not."

Landon showed him pictures of himself and Jamie Prengle talking to a man in front of a white pickup truck. "So what do these pictures mean?"

"I don't know," he said.

He called Jamie Prengle back to the stand.

Landon looked at him. He said, "Mr. Prengle, your family is well respected in this county. The name means something here. You're a part of the family. So the name ought to mean something to you. You don't honor your family by continuing to do this. In fact, you diminish them. Tell the truth," he said firmly. "Not for me, not for Batch Blaine, not even for yourself. Do it for the honor of your family. Do it for your parents, your uncles, your children. Tell the truth, Mr. Prengle."

The courtroom was completely silent as they waited for his response. Arrogant as he was, nobody expected Jamie Prengle to cave. Quite possibly, he wouldn't have. But his family's reaction to the questioning was startling. James Prengle was wiping back tears, and Dave was looking like he was about to take flight. The other Prengles were sitting as if they'd been turned to pillars of salt.

His mother yelled, "Jamie Prengle, don't you lie in this courtroom. Tell the truth. Just tell the truth."

He hesitated and then obeyed her.

******

There hadn't been a robbery at Prengle's Hardware. Batch Blaine hadn't even been in the store that night.

Landon nailed him when he said, "So, when Batch Blaine wasn't able to convince Syretta Attaway to go along with your rendezvous, you became angry? Matter of fact, you got so angry that you vandalized your family's business, took a thousand dollars from the cash register, and blamed it on Batch Blaine. Isn't that right, Mr. Prengle?"

Jamie Prengle threw his head back as if wondering whether he should try and lie his way out of it. Landon shoved a provocative picture in his face. It was of him and Bobby Doyle with Syretta and Batch standing in the background. He said, "Take a good look at this picture. It might help you remember."

Jamie Prengle sighed as if he was tired. He said, "I borrowed money from the cash register that I intend to pay back."

"Have you informed your family and the police of this?"

"No, not yet."

"When had you planned to tell them."

"When I got the money," he said.

"Why would you do that, Mr. Prengle? Why would you willfully steal from your father and his brother and blame it on Batch Blaine?"

He sniffed. "Bobby Doyle wanted to get back at Batch 'cause he brought the wrong woman to the alley."

The courtroom gasped and Bobby Doyle turned red as a beet.

"So Batch Blaine didn't rob Prengle's Hardware?"

He stared coldly at Landon but answered, "No, he didn't."

Timothy Swain was presenting his closing argument. The fight had gone out of him as he realized his case had fallen apart. The trial had taken a crazy turn. He'd thought it was about a Saturday night robbery. He would've won that case. But it turned out to be about so much more.

"Pennsylvania Law School must work miracles," he thought. "How else could a Negro pull off what Landon C. Pratt had done?"

The pictures he'd presented had been the smoking gun that wasn't anticipated. Then he'd relentlessly cross-examined Bobby Doyle Hatfield and Jamie Prengle, calling them back to the witness stand again and again, bearing down on them, throwing out conjectures, and winding them up so tightly that they told lie after lie. Finally, at the outburst of his mother, Jamie Prengle broke down and told the truth about what'd happened that night.

As he tried to save face, his concern was only for James and Dave. He said to the jurors, "Ladies and gentlemen, remember the outstanding contributions the Prengle family has made to this county. They were instrumental in the formation of the Southern Heritage Festival; they launched the automobile museum with their own antique vehicles, and they lobbied for the statues of Confederate Soldiers to be put on the lawn in front of the courthouse. They're stalwarts of this county, and they've earned all the consideration we can offer them."

Still, he couldn't help but bemoan the turn the trial had taken. Jamie Prengle and Bobby Doyle Hatfield had to be the stupidest White men alive. To blame a staged robbery on dim-witted Batch Blaine was insane. It was a wonder the judge hadn't placed them in contempt for perjury.

"Oh well," he grunted in defeat, "You win some you lose some, *Que Sera Sera.*"

He rubbed the bald spot in the back of his head, pushed his glasses up on his nose, and went to his seat.

As soon as he sat down, Landon moved for judgment of acquittal. Citing perjury, a robbery that never was, and a malicious act of deceit by two witnesses, he said, "For spiteful reasons, Batch Blaine was accused of something he didn't do. His name has been slandered and dragged through the mud by Bobby Doyle Hatfield and James Edward Prengle. He didn't deserve this. He loves the Prengle family and has been their loyal employee for many years. This man has suffered enough, and I ask the court to show mercy on him and acquit him of these false charges."

Before the judge could respond, someone handed the bailiff a note. He read it, frowned and asked the judge for consent to approach. The judge granted permission, and the bailiff handed him the note. He read the note and beckoned for the lawyers. As they approached, the judge whispered something to them. Their startled looks suggested that the trial was about to take another turn.

Speaking to the courtroom, he said, "Court is in recess for forty minutes.

We'll continue on the hour."

The judge and the two lawyers went to his chambers. Sitting there in his wheelchair was Godfrey Prengle. And standing beside him was his son Steven. "Afternoon, Godfrey," the judge spoke cordially.

Godfrey Prengle was a pleasant looking man with a thin face and a head full of white hair. Wheelchair bound since his stroke, he left the running of the hardware store to his sons. Today, he seemed eager to have his say. He said, "Thank you for seeing me on such short notice, judge. I know you're busy so I won't take up much of your time. I've known Batch Blaine for twenty-seven years, ever since he came to this county. He's kind of slow, not learned in the ways of the world, but he's a hard worker. Now I don't know what happened the night of the robbery. But I can say with a straight face that Batch Blaine has never taken a dime from me. And I don't want folks in this county to remember the Prengle family for sending a man to prison for something he didn't do. I want the charges against Batch to be dropped."

Landon C. Pratt breathed a sigh of relief. *There was a God somewhere.* He fully understood that if he hadn't presented the evidence he had, Godfrey Prengle wouldn't be sitting here trying to save his family's name. Still, he could only conclude that Godfrey Prengle was a man with a conscience.

The judge showed no expression. He said, "Thank you, Godfrey. I'll take your statement into consideration as I prepare to rule."

At two o'clock, the trial was back in session. The judge thanked the jury for their patience and attention to the proceedings. He said, "After listening to all testimonies, perusing the evidence, and giving careful consideration to all aspects of this trial, I'm ready to rule." He clasped his hands together and looked at the people.

He said, "In a criminal case, such as we have here, a man's freedom is at stake. The trial is held to examine the facts. These facts allow a jury to make a determination as to whether the defendant is guilty or not. But the process is reliant upon those who testify telling the truth. Witnesses that don't tell the truth corrupt the system and make it impossible for facts to determine outcome."

He paused. "The defense has filed a motion to acquit. Acquittal means that the defendant may have actually committed a crime but the prosecution wasn't able to prove it beyond a reasonable doubt. In this case, it's been established that the defendant didn't commit this crime. The witnesses weren't truthful, therefore their testimonies are expunged. In light of this, my judgment is that all charges against Batch Blaine be dismissed." He sounded the gavel and said, "Case closed." And he left the courtroom.

There was a loud gasp as the spectators processed what the judge had said. Landon smiled and slapped Batch on the back. Batch didn't know what it meant and sat there looking dazed. "He dismissed the charges against you," Landon exclaimed.

Aunt Ginny stumbled over to Landon. "What do that mean?" she asked tearfully.

"It means you can take your son home."

Chapter Thirty-Seven

Lucy Dash had brought Aunt Ginny to court. She'd thought Batch would surely be convicted and was prepared to console Aunt Ginny afterwards. The last thing she expected was for the charges against him to be dropped.

Speaking frankly, she said, "Batch, my money was on you going to prison, but my cousin's husband has got you off."

"We got a lucky break," Landon said humbly. "The judge did the right thing."

Drucilla walked up looking mysterious in cat-eye sunglasses. "We did it," she spoke huskily. "I can't wait to tell Uncle Lester."

Landon smiled. "Yes, we did. And I need to talk to you. I've got another little job for you and Uncle Lester."

"We'll do what we can," she bobbed her head lightly.

Poor Batch was still sitting there looking lost. He still didn't understand that the trial was over and he was free to go.

Reverend Eugene Pugh appeared out of nowhere wearing his clergyman's collar, smiling, and nodding. They didn't see his brother, Hebron, but he was headed out the side door on the opposite end of the courthouse. They'd just paid off big fines for bootlegging and cock fighting in the county. Yet Reverend Eugene posed as a proper country preacher.

He said, "Brother Batch, it seems that the Lord has heard our prayers and pitied our every groan. You're free. Our brother here," he nodded towards Landon, "performed a wondrous act. So hold your head up, my brother. Give thanks unto the Lord for he is good and his mercies endureth forever. And now," he smiled impishly. 'Introduce me to these delightful people."

It was then that Batch stood up and looked at Landon as if for the first time. He said, "I don't know you, but the Lord sent you, and I thank you." He looked at Aunt Ginny. "Mama, he says I'm free; that I can go home?" He looked to Landon for confirmation.

"Yes, you can go home," Landon gave consent.

Reverend Eugene smiled flirtatiously at Lucy and said, "And what might your name be, pretty young lady?"

With a shrewd eye, Lucy looked him over. He was pure chocolate; well-built with a cocky swagger. This, plus an engaging smile, presented not a half bad specimen.

She said, "Don't flatter me. I know about you."

"And what do you know?" his playful eyes smiled.

"I know you're a jackleg preacher and a bootlegger that's always into something," she retorted. "I have friends in Creek and Myrna, you see."

"Well," he said matter-of-factly, "they would know. But let's not dwell on it. Let's talk about it over a dinner of pig feet and collard greens."

Lucy laughed, realizing she was in the company of a cunning if charming man. "How do you know Batch?" she asked.

Reverend Pugh pulled a small bible from his jacket pocket. "I'm the son of the Most High God. I believe in the birth, death, and resurrection of our Lord and Savior, Jesus Christ. And I minister to the poor in spirit at the Potoama County Jail."

"You are so fake," Lucy couldn't help laughing.

He didn't deny it and walked in step with her toward the exit. It seemed everybody they passed knew him and spoke. He tipped his hat and spoke back.

Lucy felt a kinship and decided to encourage him. He was witty, flamboyant, and reckless; just what she needed for her weekend parties.

******

The Sipsey community was shocked that Batch was set free. It was unusual for a Colored man to be charged with such a crime and not be found guilty.

Upon learning that there hadn't been a robbery and that Bobby Doyle Hatfield and Jamie Prengle had lied on Batch, many silently begged forgiveness. They were ashamed that they'd believed the worst about him. Others regretted that they hadn't been concerned by his lengthy imprisonment.

Current attention centered on Syretta Attaway. What she did was on everybody's mind. By admitting that Batch had followed her back home, she'd provided him with an alibi. And she was applauded for not 'lowering herself' with White men.

"What she's doing might be wrong," went the talk. "But at least she's got the decency to stay in her race."

She became the talk of the town. So she decided not to wait for revival but immediately went back to the church and confessed her sins. She swore she was gonna straight up her life and do better. The people forgave her and soon stopped talking about her.

******

But things weren't back to normal. A few weeks after the

trial ended, the community received another shock. *Straight on 8* reported that Bobby Doyle Hatfield and James Edward Prengle had been arrested.

Shane Houston clumsily reported, *"An early morning sting operation conducted by the Federal Bureau of Investigation, the Potoama County Sheriff's Department, and the Sipsey Valley Police, has resulted in the arrest of two prominent Sipsey men. Bobby Doyle Hatfield and James Edward Prengle have been charged with operating a racketeering ring right here in Potoama County."*

This information had been uncovered thanks to the investigative work of Drucilla and her team.

Landon C. Pratt had shown copies of her pictures to Timothy Swain. With haste, he passed them on to the sheriff who dispatched them to the FBI. An undercover agent showed up in Sipsey within the week. There was no hiding place for Bobby Doyle Hatfield and Jamie Prengle. And shortly thereafter, the raid was staged.

Details of their operation would be unraveled weeks later and serialized in the *Potoama County Gazette* as well as segments of *Straight on 8.*

Shane Houston was dumbfounded. In talking to his viewers, he confessed. "Occasionally, something happens that shocks us to our core. Well, this was it for me. This is the most shocking thing I've ever reported."

The upshot: two upstanding citizens were caught growing cannabis plants right under the noses of local police. In a backroom of Jamie Prengle's service station, they were processing the herb into the illegal substance, marijuana. A third unidentified man was picking it up from the hardware store late at night and distributing it to a network of buyers.

Drucilla was proud of her work. Her high definition camera had photographed the field with the distinguished crop a few months ago. She thought it strange that the two men would sometimes be working in the field late at night. One night she sent Uncle Lester to tear off part of a stalk. Drummer Boy examined the leaves under the magnifying glass and compared them to forbidden plants pictured in *Snoop Magazine*. He thought it might be a type of corn plant, but Uncle Lester had known better.

Shane informed the viewers, *"According to officials, this operation has been going on for many years. It was brought to the attention of court officials during the trial of Batch Blaine. You will recall that Bobby Doyle Hatfield incorrectly identified Batch Blaine as the robber of Prengle's Hardware Store which occurred earlier this year. It was revealed in court that the robbery was staged by the two men. It's not clear why they did it, but both men admitted there'd been no robbery; the charges against Batch Blaine have since been dropped. Bobby Doyle Hatfield and James Edward Prengle are free on bail, awaiting trial.*

The camera showed the field across the street from Bobby Doyle's house, the very one he claimed he let lil Nigra children hunt Easter eggs in.

******

Eddie Simpson, Jericho, and others in Sipsey were watching the evening news when the story broke. Eddie was delighted to see the cameras following Bobby Doyle leaving the courthouse after posting bail. Instead of the arrogant swagger he'd flaunted earlier, he walked in an angry stride. "Can you tell us about your homegrown drug operation, Mr.

Hatfield," Shane asked, following him as he left. Bobby Doyle looked straight ahead and wouldn't respond.

"Now what you got to say?" cried Eddie. "You scum, trying to send that man to jail for what you did." He glowered. "It never fails that these self-righteous people always turn out to be just as crooked as the rest of us."

******

Drucilla watched the coverage with Uncle Lester relaxing beside her. She'd figured that the white truck she'd seen racing with the train that night was the third man in their racketeering operation.

Drucilla told Uncle Lester, "The bearded man must've been rushing to get across the railroad tracks before the police answered the burglar alarm."

Uncle Lester howled in agreement.

She leaned back in her recliner with a mug of warm milk. "Clever, Uncle Lester. Very, very, clever."

Chapter Thirty-Eight

Eddie Simpson was making progress. He'd gotten his Alabama driver's license and bought the Grand Prix. Immediately, it became a temptation that turned into a problem. Specifically, the women at the church fell in love with the car and wanted a ride home every Sunday.

Jericho steered clear of it. Having declared she didn't need a car, she chose to continue walking everywhere. But that made her a minority of one. Sundays became hitch-a-ride day. Women all dressed up in suits and hats came flouncing up to Eddie after church. "Eddie, can you please give me a ride home?" they purred.

It was getting on Jericho's nerve, not because she was jealous but because they were making fools of themselves. They'd been walking before Eddie bought the car, now all of a sudden they needed a ride?

And Eddie was eating it up, packing as many into the car as he could.

One Sunday, she left church mumbling about the way the women were carrying on over him. As she approached the downtown district, rain poured down, drenching her. Then, like a bat out of hell, Eddie came flying by, driving so fast that she had to leap for the shoulder to keep from getting splashed.

And he had a car load of women.

It was all she could do not to throw a brick at the car.

Later, in defense of himself, he said, "I asked you if you wanted to ride and you said no. But you always get first shot at the front seat."

She didn't speak to him for days.

This was uncharted territory and half the time she didn't know what to do. Eddie had changed for the better, she had to admit. And this made her uncomfortable. She wished Temeka would come home just to have somebody else in the house. But Temeka was absorbed in college life and hadn't been home since Christmas. So, Jericho was stuck with him day after day, watching television, reading the bible, and waiting to talk to Janelle.

What made it worse was that people had started gossiping about them living together. By now, everybody knew he was Janelle's father. They remembered that she'd left Sipsey with him as a teenager. They were also aware that he'd been her pimp in New York City. Folks said they were common law married, shook their heads, and called her a hypocrite.

She knew something had to be done. She thought about announcing to the church that Eddie was handicapped *and* homeless and needed someone to take care of him. She'd make it clear that they were sleeping in separate bedrooms and had no interest in each other. "It ain't no romance between us," she'd tell them.

As she thought it through, Eddie brought it out in the open. He said, "Candy, me and you could help each other out if we wanted to."

"How?"

"Well, we could make this a legal arrangement. It wouldn't have to be a real marriage, but we could put a respectable face to it."

Jericho looked at him like he was crazy. "You must be outta your mind. You know I ain't gon marry you. I don't trust you no farther than I can see you."

"Think about it," he said. "I'm gonna close on the El-lington Square house as soon as the inspections are done. As I said before, it's a big house. We wouldn't have to get in each other's way. It could work."

The idea was absurd, and she mentioned it to Viola. "Now you know I ain't gon marry him," she said, expecting her to agree. "I realize it don't look good having him staying at my house. So when his house is ready, I'm putting him out."

Viola had stopped by the church to chat a minute and to tell her that Bobbie Sue was still in Cincinnati. "Cindy done had the baby so I don't see why Bobby Sue don't come home."

Jericho ignored the snip. She and Bobbie Sue had a strained relationship that went all the way back to high school. Neither one was interested in a peace treaty. Jericho loved both of them and wished they could get along. But since they couldn't, she stayed out of it.

Today, Viola sat on the sofa and, as usual, asked for a glass of tea. As soon as one of the church ladies brought it, she took a sip. Swallowing, she said, "Sweetberry, you know I don't bite my tongue, so I'll be straight. If you don't want Eddie, put him out. But if you have any thoughts of ever wanting him, don't do it."

Jericho hadn't expected this response. "Viola, I told you how he treated me when we lived together in New York. He was awful, and I ain't forgot it."

Viola was only mildly sympathetic. She'd put up with years of abuse from Revish Kane before he matured and found grace in the Body of Christ. She thanked God that they'd finally come to a place of peace. But she hadn't forgotten the cost.

She said, "You got to forgive him. I know he done you wrong, but he paid for it. You said yourself he's changed. And you need somebody. I commend you for the way you've turned your life around after all the hell you went through with Josiah and Luther. But time heals all wounds, and the Lord forgives us, so we must forgive each other."

Jericho sat quietly behind her desk, not at all receptive to this point of view.

"Well," Viola took another sip of tea. "Suit yourself, but ain't nobody perfect, and Eddie will do alright for his'self. These women like him. I hear it's more than a few of them that's trying to get next to him."

"Who?" Jericho cried. "What women?"

"More than you think."

Mortified, Jericho refused to think any more about it.

But Eddie didn't give up. He didn't say anything else about a "legal arrangement," but he tried to convince her of his sincerity. He allowed the women to continue riding in the car, but he wouldn't let anybody sit on the front seat beside him.

Jericho swore none of this mattered and still refused to see him as anything but an intrusion.

But everything changed the afternoon they received a hysterical telephone call from Janelle.

It was a Thursday evening and they were watching a game show on television when

Eddie answered the phone to Janelle's hysterical screaming. She was ranting about something horrible that had happened that afternoon. It was hard to make out what she was saying and Eddie kept saying, "Calm down, Janelle, calm down and tell me what happened."

"They shot him, daddy. They shot him!" she screamed.

"Who?" Eddie cried. "Who got shot?"

Janelle words were garbled. Jeremy took the phone and tried to explain what had happened. Jericho stood behind Eddie and listened to the conversation. He explained that some students from Janelle's college were visiting for the week. They were at the subway station waiting for the train. Some local gangsters came up and pulled a gun, attempting to rob them. One of the men fought back and was shot."

"Is he dead?"

Jeremy said he was. Eddie tried to console her, telling her to go to the emergency room and get something to calm her down. Jericho could tell from the shrill sound of her voice that she was too distraught to act on what he was saying. She paced as Eddie tried to get through to Janelle.

He said, "Janelle, have you talked to the police? Is the man in custody? Was anybody else hurt? Pull yourself together and tell me what's going on."

Eddie stayed on the phone, listening to her repeatedly tell what'd happened. Occasionally, Jeremy took the phone and tried to answer Eddie's questions, but Jeremy hadn't been there and wasn't sure about the details.

This was Jericho's worst nightmare. Every time her children left her, she was terrified of something happening to them. When they were small, she knew where they were every minute of the day. But with them being away, she felt out of control and helpless. Even with Temeka just a few miles away in Lancaster, she still worried.

At this moment, she was more worried than ever.

Eddie stayed on the phone until Janelle was composed.

She said she didn't want to go to the hospital but promised to take an aspirin and lay down. "If you need to talk again, call me back," he said. She promised she would. "And Janelle," Eddie's voice was filled with emotion. "When somebody pulls a gun, cooperate. You have to assume that if they pull it, they'll use it. And ain't nothing in your pocketbook more valuable than your life."

When Eddie hung up, Jericho fell apart. "That could've been my child," she screamed. "That could've been Janelle."

Eddie was shaking as he held onto the phone. The panicked look on his face said he was thinking the same thing.

Out of frustration, Jericho began pacing. She went back and forth from the sitting room to the kitchen. She tried to pray but the words wouldn't come. Not knowing anything else to do, she started crying. And once she started, she couldn't stop. She cried for all the years she'd wanted to cry but couldn't; for Janelle, Temeka, and herself; for the times she'd failed them through her own selfishness. She cried for the woman she'd been, the woman she was, and the woman she wanted to be. She cried for every mother that wanted to know what to do in times like these but didn't. Finally, she cried for the young people that'd come face to face with the devil; for the young man that was killed and the one that'd done the killing.

To end it all, she cried for the world and everybody in it.

Eddie said nothing, but the sad look on his face said he sympathized with her suffering. In doing so, he had to acknowledge some things. She'd done a lot of living since she left New York. And he knew now that much of it hadn't been good. And yes, he was responsible for some of it. She *had been* a child when he'd known her. She'd looked to him for guidance and support and he'd done to her what he did to everybody. He used her and left her. He could only imagine the crooks and turns life had thrown her. He wished he could take her in his arms and tell her everything would be alright.

Finally, spent, she went to the bathroom and washed her face. She began talking to the Lord and praying for strength. When she returned, she sat down in the rocker and begant-widdling her thumbs.

Eddie said, "I've been worried about Janelle ever since she left. She was depressed then and now this. She sounded like her whole world had come tumbling down. We can't let her go through this alone."

Jericho had no idea how they could help "What can we do?" she wept. "We're down here in Alabama, a thousand miles away, and she's way up there. What can we do?"

"Get some clothes together," he said suddenly. "I'll load the car. We're going to New York."

Part Five

Chapter Thirty-Nine

The town of Sipsey was that magical place that spawned ordinary wishes and wild extremes. Nothing was too great or small to envision. Thus, there was no such thing as a coincidence. Everything was possible, believable and expected. In a matter of seconds, a natural disaster could destroy the environment, or in less than a week, an unpopular Negro could be cleared of robbery.

No disaster had occurred lately. But Batch Blaine was that lucky Negro.

With the help of a number of people, not necessarily friends, and the ruling of a rankled judge, he walked out of the Potoama County Courthouse a free man. And because he'd beaten the odds, Negroes tipped their hats to him.

Another oddity occurred about the same time. Stephanie Murray's wedding came together at the last minute. She'd rushed into town two weeks before the big day and started ordering everybody around. Her bridesmaids were understandably frustrated, and all except Clarice Vanderway threatened to quit. But thanks to a special plea by her future husband's best man, they were persuaded to stay. And who was her future husband's best man? None other than Ivan Goines's surgeon from Georgia Medical Center, Dr. Chuck Okafor.

His appearance in Sipsey was about as likely as Mary Newlins or Lucy Dash being
transported to a remote village in Africa. But he was just what was needed to get the wedding party back on track.

A showdown had occurred at Stephanie's grandmother's

house when she complained that the bridesmaids' blush pink mermaid gowns weren't the ones she'd chosen. "I didn't pick a gown with a square neck and spaghetti straps," she argued. "I wouldn't have done that. The gown I picked had cap sleeves and a round neck."

"Well, mighty funny everybody got the same pattern," said an irate bridesmaid.

"That's right," said another.

The language between Stephanie and her bridesmaids became so severe that several grabbed their purses and headed for the door.

This was when Chuck Okafor, who was serving as Stephanie's chauffeur for the week, stepped in. Outside the formality of the hospital, he was relaxed and had a way with words. He pampered the disgruntled women, saying, "You're very important to this wedding. In her absence, you've worked hard to comply with Stephanie's wishes. You've shown yourselves to be good friends and generous persons. The wedding can't go on without you."

They listened and believed.

And they weren't his only fans. The Goines family was delighted when they heard he was in town. Ivan had been unconscious when he was brought to Piedmont Hospital and hadn't met the doctor. He was grateful for the opportunity to thank him in person. On Thursday afternoon, he cranked up his Poppa's truck and made the trip to Lancaster to the Sidney Duvall Guesthouse near Dubois campus. It was where the African delegation was staying.

Upon meeting the mild mannered doctor, Ivan said, "Thank you, thank you, thank you for your expertise and commitment to my recovery."

He told the doctor that his family would like to see him and invited him to the farm. Dr. Okafor was surprised that the Goines family lived in Sipsey and was delighted to see Ivan. He accepted his thanks and said it'd be a pleasure to see the family again. "I would like to accept your invitation," he said. "I have to go to California immediately after leaving here. But I will make a special trip to come and visit with you later. And I look forward to seeing you at the wedding."

Clarice's friend, Delphine, was staying with her for a few days. She'd passed the word that Stephanie wasn't marrying the man she was engaged to. "The other guy dumped her. That's why we didn't hear anything from her for a while."

Lucy Dash got wind of it and told Elvira. "Stephanie moves fast," she said. "She just met this African dude a month or two ago while she was on vacation in the West Indies. And now they're getting married. You have to give it to her, she moves fast. But from what I've seen of Stephanie, the other dude was smart to dip out."

"I never did like Stephanie," Elvira said, puffing on a cigarette.

Nevertheless, the Saturday of the wedding couldn't have been more perfect. The packed church was beautifully decorated with lush greenery and pink and white roses.

Stephanie was a vision of loveliness in a fitted organza gown that was almost too raunchy for the sanctuary. Her groom stood eagerly at the altar and admired the russet beauty as she strolled down the aisle.

The reception was held at the Southside Community Center. It was a gymnasium and reception hall recently built in honor of the late Josiah Hess. County officials wouldn't name it after him due to the fact that he'd committed murder and had died with blood on his hands.

It was a fine gala, but the setting was somewhat awkward. The Africans stood on one side of the room and the Negroes, whose ancestors descended from Africans, stood on the other. They looked each other over suspiciously, not realizing that they didn't look all that different from each other.

The couple seemed happy if bizarre. Stephanie was at least a foot taller than her slender husband and had a much more gregarious personality. Breaking from protocol, she toasted herself and then him, leaving her guests with the impression that they'd known each other for a long time.

When it was time for her to throw the bouquet, a crowd of young women huddled together in a pack. Lucy Dash goaded her way to the front, shoving several women out of her way. Then she pumped out her elbows, squatted to a tackler's position, and cupped her hands for the prize.

"Ready?" Stephanie called. She made sure all of the women were paying attention before she turned her back and threw the bouquet. Lucy leapt for it, but it was in Clarice's hands that it landed.

Lucy swore while others clapped with glee.

Still, the party was lively and Stephanie came down off her high horse long enough to thank everybody for attending the wedding and supporting her. Around midnight, the party began to break up. Clarice found herself stranded. She'd ridden to the wedding with Delphine but planned to return home with her parents. But when they were ready to leave, she'd wanted to stay longer. So she told them to go ahead and she'd catch a ride with a friend.

Now, leaving the center, she looked over the crowd to

see who she could ask. She spotted Ivan Goines talking to Deacon Collins and walked up to them. "Excuse me, gentlemen," she said, "but Ivan, could you give me a ride home?"

"Gee, I'd love to, Clarice," he said, "but I promised Stephanie I'd take a few more pictures. Can you wait?"

Clarice wiggled her nose. "How long will it take? You know Stephanie; she'll be here all night."

"I'll drop you off," Sugarfoot immediately offered.

This was music to her ears. "Thanks, Sugarfoot," she replied.

Shortly thereafter, they bid Ivan good night. Taking in the crisp evening air, she felt slightly tipsy from too much sparkling wine. She held onto his arm as they walked to the truck. Inside, she breathed easier. "I hope you don't mind me taking my shoes off, but my feet are killing me."

"Help yourself," he answered.

Having her in his truck again offered him the opportunity to make a request of her. He was concerned with how she'd take it but decided to ask anyway. He said, "I have a favor to ask, Miss Vanderway."

"Sure," she said, ready to oblige.

He anticipated her reaction, "Sugarfoot," he said, "is a nickname that I'm growing less and less fond of. So, I'd like for you to call me something else."

She was slightly offended. "So I don't get the pleasure of the nickname? Everybody calls you Sugarfoot. It's endearing."

"But you're not everybody, and I don't necessarily find it endearing."

"Well," she drawled, "what do you want me to call you?"

He said, "Call me Deacon Collins. Or," he paused,

"some in my family call me Bray. You can call me Bray."

"What's the difference?" She wanted to know.

"Just do it," he ordered.

He didn't understand it himself. He just knew that he didn't want classy, sophisticated

Clarice Vanderway calling him by a nickname. To him, it was childish and didn't represent the seriousness of character he wanted to project.

"Will do," she said trying not to take it personally.

Cruising down the road, they saw Aunt Ginny and Batch walking. He sighed. "Where, oh where, are they going this time of night?"

"Let's stop and ask," she said readily.

He stopped and said, "Where're y'all going, Batch?"

"We're going over to Mr. Clyde Anderson's place," he replied. "That's where we're staying now."

"Come on, I'll drop you off."

Clarice scooted over and Aunt Ginny and Batch climbed into the cab. As soon as he closed the door, Batch said, "Sugarfoot, I thank you again for what you done for me. If it hadn't been for you telling people about what was happening, I would've done serious time for robbing the hardware."

"I know," he answered. "Nobody wanted to see you take the rap for something you didn't do. I didn't make the trial, but I kept up with it."

"Yeah, I just 'preciate what you done. It's good peoples here in Sipsey."

Batch's head drooped and he drew himself up as if to hide. Calvin Goines had said he felt sorry for him and now Sugarfoot understood why.

He asked, "Why're you staying at Clyde Anderson's

place?"

"Mr. Peter put us out after Batch was let out of jail," Aunt Ginny said. "They still b'lieve he done the robbery."

"But Mr. Clyde offered me a job at the Seed and Feed," said Batch. "He said we could stay in the Moss-Moan shack long as we want to. So, with the help of God, me and Mama gon make it."

That Peter Emory would put them out of that awful shack angered Deacon Collins. He said, "Well, he did you a favor. The Moss-Moan house is a much better house than the one you were living in."

"Yes, it is," Aunt Ginny mumbled quietly.

Clarice brightened the conversation by telling about the wedding. Aunt Ginny found it fascinating. She said, "One day you're gon be the bride, Miss Clarice, and you gon be the prettiest bride it ever was."

"Thank you, Aunt Ginny. You're probably the only person in Sipsey that believes that."

After they were dropped off, Clarice said she'd talked to the housing authority about a unit in Homestead Housing Projects. "They were approved, but they prefer living in the house."

"It was nice of you to try," he said.

"Thanks. At least they're out of that horrendous shack they were living in."

She continued chatting about the wedding. "Why didn't I see you dancing at the reception?"

"I was D J-ing," he replied. "I took turns spinning records with Ivan. Stephanie's band didn't show up."

"Wow," Clarice groaned. "Somebody must've forgot to book it. I'm surprised heads didn't roll for that."

They laughed, both finding the new Stephanie Murray hard to take.

When they reached Vanderway Circle, he came around the truck, opened the door and helped her out. As they walked up the sidewalk, she felt comfortable enough to say, "Deacon, it seems you're always rescuing me."

"It's my pleasure," he said earnestly.

At the door, she lingered. As he anticipated her move, she smiled mischievously and said, "Don't worry, I'm not gonna kiss you." He faked relief and she quickly pecked him on the cheek. "Good night."

Shaking his head, he walked away. She started into the house but turned back around. "Deacon Collins, I have a favor."

He looked back. "Sure."

"I want to come to the block party."

"Come again."

The Sullivan Quarter Block Party was an annual event. It'd started out as a homecoming for past and present residents of that neighborhood but had grown into a city-wide affair. Now the entire Negro community got together for a day of fun and fellowship. There was music, food, games, and an afternoon baseball game. It was a much talked about event, but the Vanderways had never attended.

"What did you say?"

"I want to come to the block party," she repeated.

His brows creased in surprise. "Of course. Anybody can come."

"But I don't wanna feel out of place. Would you invite me?"

He relaxed. "Sure, you're welcome to come as my

guest."

He started off again, and she said, "Can Mother come too? She's always wanted to come."

He was truly baffled. "Sure she can. And I'll pick you up if you like."

"Yes, we'd like that."

He stepped towards her and said lightheartedly, "Now you realize this is not a pearls and high heels affair?"

His tone was playful, but there was a hint of seriousness to it.

"I know," she answered sweetly. "We know how to dress."

"Good."

She said, "Good night, Deacon," and strolled into the house. Once inside, she peeped out the window and watched him drive away. Beaming happily, she said, "I'm gonna have fun at that party."

Chapter Forty

The Sullivan Quarter Block Party was the official start of summer. On the third Saturday in June, grills were fired up before day with slabs of pork ribs, pounds of chicken, ground beef, sausages, and wieners being prepped for cooking.

Clarice and her mother were up early getting ready. It was exciting for them to be finally going to the event. Because of who they were, people assumed they weren't interested in community affairs.

Felix Vanderway didn't spend much time with his family. He was a busy man who spent most of his time managing his business affairs. But he was generous with his wife and indulgent of his daughter. Still, absent of his direction, they weren't sure what their role in the community should be. So they mostly stayed in their splendid mansion isolated from the rest of the town. Clarice, the more outgoing of the two, associated with the public more than her mother, but neither felt embraced.

But today was their coming out party and they were hoping to make a good impression. Clarice sprinted to her mother's bedroom before seven o'clock. Mary Ann was rummaging through her closet.

"Mother, what're you wearing?" she exclaimed. "Deacon Collins made it clear that it's not a fancy dress affair so we have to go casual."

"I know," Mary Ann giggled happily. She turned away from her closet with two outfits, a blue striped halter dress in one hand and a black and white capri set in the other. Which one?" she asked.

"The dress," Clarice spoke definitively. "It's cool and crisp, and it highlights the blueness of your eyes."

For herself, Clarice chose beige shorts with a three quarters length brown shirt. She pulled her hair back in a ponytail and clipped on gold hoop earrings. Fully dressed, they both looked casual and quite appropriate.

Deacon Collins picked them up at ten o'clock. They'd been sitting on ready for two hours. But they didn't want their eagerness to show. So they let him believe that they'd finished dressing just a few moments before he arrived.

When they got to the park, things were in full swing. So many people were there that they couldn't be counted. Groups were sectioned off by family, church, friendship, or whatever connection pleased them.

And there was food aplenty; pans of meat, salads of all kinds, vegetables, and different kinds of desserts. As rhythm and blues music played in the background, Quarter women made ice-cream in wooden freezers. Children played relays and ran around chasing each other while grownups played cards, dominoes, or sat on lawn chairs engaged in lively conversation.

Upon arrival, the Vanderways delivered their contribution which included a case of soft drinks, potato salad and an apple pie made by Telma. They were met with welcoming smiles as their rations were put with the others.

Batch and Aunt Ginny arrived shortly afterwards. The people weren't sure how to greet them. They hadn't forgotten what a sneaky Uncle Tom Batch had been and how much they'd despised him. Still, most were polite, and he was cordial. At Aunt Ginny's urging, he walked over to a group of men and said, "I want everybody to know how much I appreciate y'all praying for me while I was locked up. If it hadn't been for the Lord hearing y'all's prayers, I'd be doing time in Kilby Prison."

Nobody disagreed with that.

Drucilla and Drummer Boy drove by several times but didn't get out. No dogs were allowed, and they couldn't bear to leave Uncle Lester alone in the car.

Former citizens that never missed the event had come from near and far. Among them, the tall, good looking Goines brothers; brilliant, distinguished looking Calvin; Earl, the light skinned, curly-haired pretty boy, and Ivan, skinny, scholarly and almost as handsome as Earl. They lent a helping hand with the chores then took time to mingle with the crowd.

There were also Sipseyites that'd relocated to large cities They talked loud as they showed off their fancy cars.

Lucy Dash said, "When they leave here tomorrow, the trunks of them rented cars are gon be dragging the ground with our stuff."

Other snide remarks were made about northern folks coming back south acting rich. "They come here claiming they've got so much," sniffed Mary Newlins, "but they leave here loaded down with stuff they've begged or stole from us. They ain't doing no good in them big cities."

They would've continued bashing city folk except two things grabbed their attention. Sophie Grant, the pious usher from First Macedonia, showed up arm-in-arm with Jack Bynum's West Indian house guest, and Reverend Eugene Pugh stepped out of a 1962 baby blue Cadillac dressed to the nines in a matching tuxedo.

"Well, well, well," said Elvira. "The devil and all his kinfolks decided to come to the block party."

"Mind your business," advised Lucy.

Elvira was too busy staring to notice Lucy's tone. She said, "I ain't never seen Sophie Grant with a man. And I don't even know what to say about Reverend Eugene."

She needn't to have worried. Reverend Eugene knew how to work a crowd and before long, had women eating out of his hands.

The Goines brothers joined the Vanderways who'd found seats on a bench under a shade tree. A small child had crawled up Mary Ann's leg and climbed onto her lap. Calvin and Earl marveled that it'd been "quite a while" since they'd seen her.

She explained, "I've been spending a lot of time in Atlanta helping with my invalid great aunt. She doesn't have children so we all have to pitch in."

Sugarfoot soon joined them. The men greeted each other with handshakes and the bombastic joking of Black American men.

Earl, who couldn't help himself, began teasing Clarice about never finding a husband. "The men are scared of you," he said. "Nobody wants to meet you anymore."

"Good," she retorted. "I don't want to meet them either."

The remark was met with laughter.

Sugarfoot turned to Ivan. "How're you doing?"

He shrugged, "Physically, I'm great. But personally, things could be better. Landon served my estranged wife, but she's decided to be stubborn and contest it. So I've got to wait two years to get divorced."

In quiet tones, Sugarfoot said, "So she wants you back?"

Ivan frowned and pulled him aside. "You won't believe this, but I'm gonna tell you anyway." And he told Sugarfoot about the night Deanna sneaked into his hospital room dressed as a nurse.

Sugarfoot couldn't believe it. "You think she was really trying to kill you?"

He grunted. "Yes, she was. She's got guts if anything. Man," he laughed bitterly. "I could tell you some things that would blow your mind."

Sugarfoot believed him and whistled his shock. "I'm at a loss. All I can say is let your conscience be your guide."

"That's just what I intend to do."

The broader conversation tweaked their interest when Calvin announced that he and a group of friends had bought the notorious *Sable* Magazine.

Clarice frowned. "That's a surprise."

Sable was a monthly periodical known for showcasing voluptuous brown-skinned women in risqué outfits and telling graphic stories too vulgar for general audiences.

"Not your normal coffee table publication," Clarice mocked. "I'm surprised you'd even think about buying it."

"What do you mean?" cried Earl. "That's the greatest magazine that's even been published. Many men will mourn the death of it."

Clarice shot Earl a horrified look as the men snickered.

Calvin smiled. "We're changing directions; targeting the Black middle class and professional women like yourself. It'll be family oriented and therefore more marketable. And you'll be the first to know that we're officially changing our names from Colored/ Negroes to Black."

"Touche," said Earl.

Freddie Dee Varner, desperate to get back with Sugar-foot spent the day stalking him. She racked her brain trying to find a connection between him and the Vanderways. Her ambitious hope was that they were kin. She envisioned him bringing Clarice over and explaining that they were second cousins and that she had nothing to worry about. They'd laugh about it and he'd call her silly.

It was a comforting thought, but the exchanges between him and Clarice were intimate in a way that made her vision far-fetched and unbelievable.

After he finished chatting with Lucy Dash, she confronted Lucy. "What is the Vanderways doing here with Sugar-foot?" she asked.

Lucy had been on friendly terms with Freddie Dee before she attacked Annette. Now, she wasn't sure about her. Disliking her tone, she urged her to calm down. "They're just friends, Freddie Dee."

Freddie Dee looked doubtful and continued spying on them.

Every so often, Sugarfoot came back to check on the Vanderways. She was right behind him. Watching her, Lucy, said, "Some women just can't take no for an answer. I wouldn't want a man to know I wanted him that bad."

Elvira sighed. "A lot of us want him."

"But you keep yours under control."

"I try,"she said good-naturedly.

Without a hint of pity, they ridiculed Freddie Dee for being desperate. Then, putting her out of their minds, Elvira said, "Let's go over and talk to the Vanderways." Lucy agreed and they put on their cutest smiles and strutted across the field.

By now, Mary Newlins and Darlene Crawford had joined them. Present discussion centered on the huge turnout and how well everything was going. "But," Darlene observed, "some of the regulars are missing. Has anybody heard from Sweetberry?"

"Yes," said Lucy. "She's called Viola several times. Janelle had a friend to get killed and she was so upset about it that they went up to New York to see about her."

Clarice was distressed by this. "I hope she's alright. Janelle has worked so hard to get where she is. It'd be a shame for something to hinder her now. You know she's supposed to graduate from medical school this summer."

"She will," Lucy spoke with assurance. "They're leaving New York for Nashville then they're coming back here."

"What about her man," inquired Elvira? "Is Eddie coming back?"

"I'm sure he is," Mary supposed. "He just bought Miss Oleta's house, so it looks like he plans to stay in Sipsey."

"But is Sweetberry moving in with him?" Elvira's asked pointedly.

"I don't know. I just know he bought the house."

This was a subject to be continued.

There was much interest in the Vanderways. Just before lunch, Napoleon LaRue, an army veteran and tailor, came over and ever so meekly asked Sugarfoot if he could go over and speak to Miss Mary Anne. "I know her," he said. "I do all of her alterations, but I wouldn't want to be out of order."

Sugarfoot shrugged. "I guess it's alright. She'll let you know if she doesn't want to talk to you."

But Mary Ann Vanderway seemed delighted with all

the attention she was getting and welcomed everybody that came. The child had gone to sleep in her lap. When her grandmother realized this, she called to her teenage daughter who was enjoying the day with her friends. She yelled, "Tammy, come and get yo' baby. Miss Mary Ann didn't come here to babysit for you."

The girl looked embarrassed as she came to take the sleeping child away.

Lunchtime officially started at one o'clock. Tables were set up buffet style. Viola Kane

and some women from the Quarter stood behind the tables and served the food. Viola was delighted to see the Vanderways and said so. Clarice confessed that they'd wanted to come long before now.

"Well, you've been welcome every year," said Viola. "So I expect the two of you to be here from now on."

As the words left her mouth, Lucy was heard from some distance away screaming at

Reverend Eugene. "What're you trying to prove?" she shouted. "You're skinning and grinning with every woman out here. I thought you came here to see me!"

Mary Ann smiled. "Yes. We won't miss another one."

But Viola was distracted by Lucy's outburst. She felt obliged to intervene. "Pope," she yelled to their cousin, Calvin Goines, "go over there and tell Lucy to stop acting a fool or go home!"

Chapter Forty-One

Around four o'clock, the baseball game began between the Cougars and the Pelicans. Sugarfoot was the player/coach for the Cougars, and Ivan headed the Pelicans. Every man that wanted to play was promised a chance. But they started the game with the best players.

The Cougars were dressed in blue and the Pelicans in red. The Cougars got off to an early lead. Sugarfoot hit a home run his first time at bat. His family, including Big Mama, was in the stands cheering him on. Clarice and Mary Ann were cheering too.

Calvin Goines was playing on Sugarfoot's team, and Earl was playing on Ivan's. With two on base and two out, Calvin got a base hit and drew in a run. But the next player struck out. The Pelicans took the field. They didn't score a run. Ivan ran down high flys and ground balls proving his body had made a remarkable recovery.

The Cougars got two more runs and began bragging. They predicted a shutout. But the Pelicans came back and fought to a tie. For a couple of innings, nothing happened. Finally, at the bottom of the ninth, Ivan hit a home room and three runners scored, ending the game at 7- 4.

The Cougars couldn't believe they'd lost and began the after game joshing. They argued that the Pelican had cheated their way to victory. But it was all in good fun and they left the field laughing.

Late in the afternoon, the planning committee called for clean-up. Many participants stayed to help, but some snuck away, including Lucy Dash who left with Reverend Eugene.

Manny didn't show his face until then. Sugarfoot scolded him. "Where've you been? I've been looking for you."

"I was with Syretta," he answered, "we were over by the tower."

Sugarfoot flashed a smile and left it at that.

Clarice and Mary Ann pitched in and helped. Watching them, Freddie Dee's temper boiled. The suspicion she'd had all day was greater than ever. She told Elvira, "Something's going on between Sugarfoot and Clarice."

"Oh no," Elvira shooed her off. "They ain't each other's type. He ain't rich; ain't got no college education; don't put on no high class airs; and she ain't hot-bloodied enough for him." She shook her head. "Those two would never make a match."

Freddie Dee tried to be encouraged.

By sundown, the park was as they'd found it. Everybody said good-bye and hoped to see each other next year.

It'd been a glorious day for Clarice. She chatted happily as she and her mother walked with Sugarfoot to the truck. When they reached it, Freddie Dee was standing there. She said, "Sugarfoot, I need to talk to you?"

He looked surprised but excused himself. They walked a short distance away. "What're you trying to do?" she angrily demanded.

He frowned. "What do you mean?"

"That?" She pointed to Clarice and her mother. "What're you doing with them?"

"They're my guests," he said.

"So you're with her now?"

"Who?"

"Clarice."

"As I said, they're my guests."

"You think I believe that?"

He sighed impatiently. "It doesn't matter. Now, if you'll excuse me, I have to go."

He started to walk away. She stepped in front of him, blocking his path. "So just like that you gon walk away from me?" she scowled.

He shrugged. "I don't have anything else to say, Freddie."

"Well, I have something to say!" she yelled. "I have something to say."

She opened her mouth to settle things, but nothing came out. She wasn't sure what she wanted to say; she just knew what she was feeling. There was a fullness inside of her weighing her down. She wanted it to go away and wished for the lightness she'd felt when she thought he cared about her.

Looking into his eyes, she strained to see a sign that it'd been real. She didn't see it. What she saw was indifference. It was as if he'd never held her in his arms, kissed her, and laughed at her off-color jokes. It was as if he never knew her.

Suddenly, she wanted to hurt him, to make him feel as rejected as she did. She started to speak again, to tell him what was in her heart. She was prepared to beg and plead for another chance at the happiness she was convinced she could only find with him.

"Just give it a chance," she wanted to say. "What I feel for you is strong enough for both of us." With her mouth open and her heart throbbing, she tried to speak. But what sprang forth was anger; bubbling, boiling, anger. Instead of words, he got reflex as she hauled off and slapped him so hard he staggered.

Clarice and her mother heard the impact and gasped in shock. "Oh, my God," Clarice exclaimed, "she slapped him!"

Her mother sighed and shook her head.

Sugarfoot only stared at Freddie Dee. She stared back as if expecting him to return the blow. The moment was tough, and he was embarrassed. The day had been fun. Everything had gone well. And yes, he'd been proud to present Clarice and Mary Ann as his guests. It would take Freddie Dee to ruin the day. But he fell back on his military training and showed no reaction.

This infuriated her more. She wanted a response. How dare he act like her feelings didn't matter? He'd dismissed her, and it was the worst kind of rejection.

She raised her hand to slap him again but he grabbed it. He said, "It's been a long day. Go home and get some rest."

Clarice suddenly appeared. "Deacon Collins, is everything alright?" Her voice was wired with alarm.

Both he and Freddie Dee were surprised that she'd inserted herself into their dispute. But Clarice didn't back down. She and Freddie Dee locked eyes. Remembering how viciously she'd attacked Annette, Clarice wanted her to know that she wasn't afraid of her. Doggedly, she repeated, "Is everything alright, Deacon Collins?"

Looking at Freddie Dee, he said, "Yes, everything's fine." Fuming at the audacity of Freddie Dee, Clarice rejoined her mother.

Sugarfoot backed away, walked around the truck, and opened the door for the Vanderways. They climbed inside with Clarice claiming the seat next to him. He went to the driver's side, turned the ignition, and drove off. Freddie Dee was left standing there staring after them.

He apologized for the incident, but they dismissed it. "We really appreciate you taking

time with us today," said Mary Ann. "It was perfect."

Nevertheless, he was self-conscious. When they reached Vanderway Circle, he tried to be gracious. He parked the truck in their driveway and walked them to the front door. "Have a good rest of the evening, ladies," he tossed an affectionate smile.

"Thanks for everything," Clarice said gratefully. "It was as much fun as I thought it'd be."

Mary Ann smiled, "Next year, deacon."

He nodded and said good night, certain they'd never go anywhere with him again.

As he drove through town, his thoughts rambled. Passing Prengle's Hardware, he thought of Batch. Today, he'd been able to mingle in public without doing something to make everybody mad. And he'd seemed sincere in thanking people for lifting him up while he was in jail. But Sugarfoot had no doubt that in time, Batch would return to his old ways.

Reluctantly, he thought of Freddie Dee. His face still stung from her slap as did his pride. "At one time I actually liked her. I pity the man she marries," he said.

It was thoughts of Ivan that made him smile. He was a walking miracle. Those days at Georgia Medical had been terrifying. But he'd fought his way back. "His spirit may not be healed," he acknowledged, "but thank God his body is on the mend."

Unsurprisingly, his thoughts turned to Clarice. She'd changed. Or had he? Yes, his opinion of her had changed.

In her concern for others, she'd proven herself worthy of respect. And she was no shrinking violet. She'd stared Freddie Dee down without flinching. Maybe that's what being rich was about. Maybe common people didn't scare you. "Hats off, girl," he chuckled.

As soon as he got home, he went to bed. He anticipated the dream. And when she came to him, he was ready. The very scent of her aroused him and his body throbbed with desire as she whispered her edict of love.

He surrendered, wallowing in the pleasure of her passion as the taste of her sweetness lulled him to sleep.

Chapter Forty-Two

Sunday morning was the beginning of a new week and the chance for a new beginning.

At his farm, Deacon Johnny Goines woke his household for prayer before going about his farming duties. His sons were tired and a bit hung over from the block party, but they obeyed the rules of the house.

The deacon had never been to a block party fearing there'd be drinking, cussing, and other manners of nefarious behavior. But he looked forward to it every year. It brought his beloved sons home and afforded him the opportunity to show them off.

He thanked God every day that Ivan was comfortably settled at the farm. This morning, he got up early to help his father. Top of the list was checking the fencing in the backyard. He had to make sure there were no openings for predators to get through and attack Trapp. The panther had critically injured him, ripping his coat so badly that one hind quarter was permanently skinned. He was nearly blind in one eye, and his trot was unsteady. But he was in good spirits and wore his battle scars with pride.

At Sunday school, Deacon Collins greeted the teachers in brotherly love. And he boasted of the good job they were doing. "I didn't know what to expect when I accepted this job," he said. "But I can declare without a doubt that First Macedonia has the best teachers in town, and we're proud of you," he raved.

Mary Newlins led the congregation in applause.

******

Clarice and her Mother made their way to church in splendidly designed French frocks. They hoped to see Deacon Collins and thank him again for the wonderful time they'd had at the party. Clarice wanted to urge him not to be upset by Freddie Dee's behavior but realized she didn't know him well enough to advise him.

******

Three of Marcus Mixon's classmates waited at the door of the pastor's study to inform Pastor Brough of Marcus's latest mischiefs. The preacher invited them inside and offered them lollipops. Licking on the coveted confection, they voiced their complaints. And each boy verified his charge by looking to the others and saying, "Didn't he?"

When they were finished, the pastor praised them for their concern for Marcus and reminded them to be good little boys themselves.

During worship, he called the children to the altar and implored Marcus to pray for them.

Marcus was always eager to fulfill his duties as junior minister. He stood at the podium on his custom made steps, impressive in his purple and gold robe, and stretched his hand forward. He said:

"To the Father of Abraham, Issac and Jacob, the only true and living God, you are greater than anything I could imagine. And you are worthy of all of my praise.

This morning I bow humbly before you thanking you for being my God and for giving me everything I need. I pray for my friends and my enemies, especially the ones that's lost and hell bound. I pray for my teachers and the kids at the training school. Bless the ones that don't know how to share, that don't tell the truth, and that get mad because some people have more friends than they do. I pray for the people that lie on me and say mean things about me because I like girls. Well, my daddy says I'm supposed to like girls. And they like girls too, the girls just don't like them."

Knowing Marcus's rambunctious reputation, Clarice was amused by his prayer. Hoping no one could see her, she peeped out of one eye to check his expression. Satisfied that he was sincere, her eye flittered about and locked with Deacon Collins who was also peeping out of one eye. They smiled then closed their eyes and listened to the rest of the prayer.

He prayed: *Lord, I'm gon keep on doing what's right, cause I know you're gon keep on blessing me. And as I close this prayer, I ask you to bless me and my Mama and Daddy. Bless Pastor Brough and this church. And bless everybody under the sound of my voice. And one more thing, Lord, help me to be a better preacher and a better person. And I'll always give you the glory and the praise. In your son's Jesus's name, A-men."*

Though odd, the prayer was well received. Women in the powder room talked about it after church. "It was just cute," said Lucy Dash, unaware that her son, Theodore, was tattling on Marcus every Sunday.

Viola realized that they were concerned about Jericho. She said, "I'm gon read part of the letter I got from Sweetberry the other day. She knows everybody is concerned about her and want to know what's going on. She read, "We gon be out of town longer than we expected. Janelle has accepted a job in a town in Indiana. It's called Gary. We hope she's gon like it here. I have a lot more to tell you but it'll have to wait 'til we get back home. Please keep us in your prayers. We should be back about the middle of August."

"Well," said Mary Newlins, "I guess that settled the question whether Eddie is coming
back with her."

******

Clarice and her mother had been able to speak to Deacon Collins after church. She'd talked to him long enough to inform him that they'd be going to their summer home in Pensacola in a few days. "I don't plan to stay all summer as I usually do," she said. "But it's good to get away for a while." "Have fun," he said enviously.

It was on the tip of her tongue to invite him down for a weekend, but she hesitated. There was nothing in his demeanor that led her to believe that he wanted to come to Pensacola to see her. And just because she'd accidently kissed him on the mouth that one time didn't mean she had to keep thinking about it.

******

Sunday dinner at Carrie Mae's house was lively as usual. The family waited for Sugarfoot. And as soon as he walked in the door, the women began putting the food on the table. He was pleasantly surprised to see his mother, Bebe, helping with dinner.

He went over and kissed her on the cheek. She turned around and grabbed him in a tight embrace. "I saw you yesterday. You did good."

"I didn't see you. Where were you?"

She smiled. "I was around."

"Come on, Bebe, sit down," said Daisy Ruth. "I'm gon serve you today."

Bebe was the center of attention. Rita Jo sat next to her and said, "Sis, you look good. I see you're taking care of yourself."

Suddenly, Jeannie had an epiphany. She said, "Y'all look alike. Both of y'all are tall with good hair and big round eyes. But y'all ain't as dark as Big Mama."

Carrie Mae rolled her eyes at Jeannie. She said, "The blacker the berry the sweeter the juice."

Jeannie laughed. "I must be sweet 'cause I'm black like you."

Her younger sister, Victoria snarled, "You're black, but you ain't sweet."

"That's enough," Rita Jo warned her daughters. She smiled at Bebe and whispered, "We got so much catching up to do."

Carrie Mae didn't embrace her daughter's presence, but she didn't object to her being there either. This was a sign of progress and nobody commented for fear she'd start in on Bebe about all the mistakes she'd made. She said, "Bray, bless the food."

He said grace and they began passing dishes. Manny talked nonstop, full of details about the block party.

"Sugarfoot, y'all should've won that game," he said, making small talk so nobody would ask where he'd been all day.

"He did his part," said Daisy Ruth. "He scored all the points."

"Not all of them," rebutted Rita Jo. "Calvin Goines

scored some points too."

"*Runs*," said Bear impatiently. "In baseball they're called *runs.*"

"Well, he did good," said Carrie Mae, passing the macaroni and cheese and swelling up with pride that her grandson had played such an important role in organizing the party. "He sho' did."

"I like Sugarfoot," said Victoria.

"Everybody likes Sugarfoot," said Bear.

"That's 'cause he's nice," declared Carrie Mae. "You can get a lot farther in life by being nice. If you be nice to people, they'll be nice to you."

"Well, what about Syretta?" questioned Jeannie. "You gon be nice to her if she be nice to you?"

"Shut up, Jeannie," said Rita Jo.

It was known to everybody but Carrie Mae that Manny had spent the day sneaking around with Syretta.

******

New adventures were on the horizon. The little job Landon had for Drucilla and her crew was to investigate voter suppression in Potoama County. Landon said, "I believe people are being paid to discourage Negroes from registering and voting. I've got some leads, but I want to be sure I'm right. This could be tricky," he warned. "It'll almost definitely be somebody you know and possibly respect. So if you don't want to do it, I understand."

Drucilla asked Drummer Boy what he thought, and he said they had to do it. "If we don't
who will?" he asked.

Drucilla said, "If Uncle Lester agrees, we'll do it."

After a long talk, Uncle Lester nodded his head in agreement. So late Sunday evening, they rode around town with their camera, notebook, and binoculars. They cruised down dark alleys and along country roads.

"You never know where dirt is being done," said Drummer Boy.

No, you didn't, and you also didn't know when a surprise would turn up and take the town by storm.

The late bus arrived at the bus station about nine o'clock Sunday evening. It drew to a stop and only two passengers got off, a young woman of unclear racial origin and a boy about seven years of age. He held tightly onto her hand. They looked scared and lost. The cook on duty asked if she was visiting someone in Sipsey. Speaking in a foreign accent, she said, "I'm looking for my husband, Branhope Collins."

The cook's shocked look turned mischievous. He said, "Did you say you were his wife?"

"Yes," she answered. "And this is his son."

The cook looked to the woman sitting near the window. She'd come to see her mother off to Memphis. Hearing the woman's claim, she came forward.

"Hi," she said helpfully, "I'm Freddie Dee Varner. I know Branhope Collins, and I know where he lives. I'll be glad to take you to his house."

Discussion Questions

1. Did you sympathize with Freddie Dee Varner? Was it love for Deacon Collins that made her behave the way she did? Have you ever met a woman like her? How did you handle it?

2. Given that he is a young man with a reputation with women, was Deacon Collins's vow of celibacy realistic?

3. Were you surprised that Janelle Armstrong had gone to New York City and found her father? Was it fair to Jericho for her to bring him to Sipsey and expect Jericho to receive him? Do you see spiritual growth in Jericho's interactions with him as time progressed or is she justified in being stuck in bitterness?

4. In the year 2000, Alabama struck down its ban on interracial marriage. Did it surprise you that Janelle and Jeremy couldn't legally marry in 1965? In their future, should they marry and live in another state where it would be legal, or should she fight the miscegenation law in Alabama?

5. Jericho admitted that Jeremy was the kind of man she wanted for Janelle but opposed the marriage because he was White. Was she right to oppose the marriage? Have you faced this issue with a family

member? If so how did you respond? If not, how do you think you would respond?

6. Discuss reasons that marriage to Eddie Simpson might help Jericho? What might the drawbacks be?

7. Did it surprise you that the Prengles were willing to believe that Batch Blaine had robbed them. Why do you think they weren't willing to give him the benefit of the doubt?

8. Why, do you think, Calvin Goines was able to look beyond Batch's faults and see his suffering when other members of the community weren't?

9. Deacon Johnny Goines was very proud of his children and apparently thought he'd raised them to perfection. Were you surprised to find that his son, Ivan, was less than perfect and had married an imperfect woman?

10. Do you think Ivan Goines should forgive Deanna and give their marriage another chance or proceed with the divorce? Why? Why not?

11. Was Jericho's reluctance to forgive Eddie about her past with him or her guilt toward her own transgressions?

12. Deacon Branhope "Sugarfoot" Collins thinks that in time, Batch Blaine will return to his old self. Do you

think he's right? How might his experience with the criminal justice system motivate him to change his behavior?

13. Freddie Dee put risqué pictures in a letter to Sugar-foot, and he didn't destroy them. What are some possible outcomes of him not destroying the pictures?

14. What does Clarice Vanderway's scene with Freddie Dee Varner tell you about her?

15. Are the women likely to have future conflicts?

16. The end of the book suggests that Branhope "Sugar-foot" Collins hasn't been honest with the people in his life. Does this seem out of character for him? What explanations might he give for this discrepancy?

God's Sacred Feast is the second book in the series *Chronicles of the Hamlet of Sipsey*. The first book in the series is *The Burden of Sweetberry*.

Please visit Carol at https://www.amazon.com/Carol-Gosa-Summerville/e/

www.ingramcontent.com/pod-product-compliance
Lightning Source LLC
Chambersburg PA
CBHW070407260626
47161CB00001B/308